About the Author

Will Shindler has been a broadcast journalist for the BBC
for over twenty-five years, spending a decade working
in television drama as a scriptwriter on *Born and Bred*,
The Bill and *Doctors*. His time on these leading prime
time dramas has given him a rich grounding in authentic
police procedure, powerful character development and
gripping narratives. He currently combines reading the
news on BBC Radio London with writing crime novels
and has previously worked as a television presenter for
HTV, a sports reporter for BBC Radio Five Live, and
one of the stadium presenters at the London Olympics.

He is the writer of *The Burning Men*, *The Killing Choice*
and *The Hunting Ground*. The fourth book in the DI Alex
Finn series – *The Blood Line* – will publish in 2023.

WILL SHINDLER

The Hunting Ground

HODDER

First published in Great Britain in 2022 by Hodder & Stoughton
An Hachette UK company

This paperback edition published in 2022

1

A CIP catalogue record for this title is available from the British Library

Paperback ISBN 978 1 529 34086 0

Typeset in Plantin Light by Hewer Text UK Ltd, Edinburgh
Printed and bound in Great Britain by Clays Ltd, Elcograf S.p.A.

Hodder & Stoughton policy is to use papers that are natural, renewable
and recyclable products and made from wood grown in sustainable
forests. The logging and manufacturing processes are expected to
conform to the environmental regulations of the country of origin.

Hodder & Stoughton Ltd
Carmelite House
50 Victoria Embankment
London EC4Y 0DZ

www.hodder.co.uk

I

They were supposed to be the best of us. The great and the good of British business: politicians, financiers, oligarchs and the odd lord. Men. Three hundred and fifty of them gathered in a five-star West End hotel to raise money for worthy causes. For those whose lives had been devastated by the virus.

For people like me, thought Sadie Nicholls as she surveyed the room.

'Over here, darlin' . . .'

She looked across and saw a middle-aged man in a tuxedo snapping his fingers at her. He was paunchy with a sweep of yellow-blond hair sitting above flushed pink cheeks. His face was deadpan serious, but the schoolboy sniggering from the rest of the table told her what to expect. She walked over, forcing a professional smile.

'Can we have some more champagne? We're running a little dry – the Krug Grande Cuvée?' He leant in confidentially, whispered, 'It's the fizzy stuff in the dark green bottles . . .'

Sadie maintained her smile.

'I know which one it is, thank you.'

Her soft Geordie vowels made the words sound unintentionally prim. The man pulled an expression of exaggerated concern, held up a hand in mock apology. His friends sniggered.

'*Why aye love* – I'm sure you do,' he said, and they sniggered some more.

Sadie turned and braced herself, felt the palm of his hand connect firmly with her left buttock just a second before she heard the roar of the table's laughter. In any other situation, she was fairly sure she'd have taken his head off, but she'd been warned. When she accepted the job she'd been told what kind of evening to expect.

The Knights Association dinner was in its twenty-seventh year and held something of a reputation for its regular attendees. There was a reason the only women there were hostesses, why they were all wearing low-cut tops and short, tight dresses. She'd felt humiliated before the first guests had even arrived. But the money was good, and beggars couldn't be choosers.

The brief was simple: keep the clientele happy and fetch drinks when required. On stage, entertainers had come and gone, though it was hard to tell if anyone was even listening to them. Champagne, whisky and vodka were all on tap and it hadn't taken long for inhibitions to drop. It began with some hand-holding as she'd taken the first orders. From there it didn't take long before, emboldened, they began pulling some of the hostesses into their laps. About an hour in, an elderly man directly asked her whether she was a prostitute. He'd said it so sympathetically too, like a kindly uncle talking to a favoured niece.

Now as she crossed the room to fetch the champagne from one of the ice buckets at the back, Sadie felt dizzy and nauseous. She just needed to try and keep her cool, get through this and pick up the money at the end of the night. Composing herself, she thought of her three-year-old son, Liam, fighting the urge to whip out her phone and look at his picture for support. The only reason she hadn't smashed a champagne flute across the head of the man who'd just assaulted her was because of her boy.

She took a deep breath, picked up a bottle of Krug and placed it on a silver tray. Out of the corner of her eye, she could see the hyenas at the table watching her closely, anticipating her return. She took her time and glanced at some of the other hostesses, each engaged in their own private battles. A girl, surely not even out of her teens, struggling to keep the distress off her face on one side of the room, a woman in her thirties handling it like a pro on the other side. Sadie checked her watch and felt her heart sink – they weren't even halfway through this yet.

'Come on, sweetheart – there's *workin'* men getting thirsty over here.'

The twat with the blond hair laid on the cod Geordie accent again. She looked back over at her table of tormentors and produced another shit-eating smile. For Liam, she thought. For Liam.

It took another forty minutes before she reached the end of her tether. A man she vaguely recognised – a politician perhaps, from way back – slipped his hand up her dress without missing a beat of the conversation he was holding. He didn't even look at her. When she'd discreetly tried to remove it, he'd squeezed harder, holding it there and not letting her move. She'd stood frozen to the spot, unsure how to handle the situation until he'd finally released his grip. Not once did he make eye contact with her.

'Fuck this for a game of soldiers, Luce,' she said, kicking off her heels and rummaging in her bag for her trainers. She was now in one of the hotel's smaller conference rooms that'd been converted into a makeshift dressing room. 'I'm sorry I got you into this,' she said, as she fought to free the tongue from one of her battered orange sneakers.

Lucy Ahmed, like Sadie, was in her mid-twenties. They were old friends, and it'd been Sadie who'd helped get her the

3

job. They'd worked together once at a small coffee shop near Borough. Then the virus came and the cafe had closed its doors. They'd stayed in touch though, and Sadie had been glad to push some work her way.

'Just stick it out for another hour. They haven't even had the auction yet,' said Lucy.

'Fuck the auction,' said Sadie, unclipping her hairpiece and stuffing it in her bag. She ran her hand through her natural brown bob, glad to feel it free again. 'I don't care how good the money is – it's not worth it. If I stay here any longer I'm going to hurt someone. I don't want to end up on the front pages for smashing some MP's teeth in.'

'I know what you mean – I can't say I'm enjoying it either. I just think if you go, you'll regret it tomorrow.'

Sadie was slipping her jacket on now.

'I've got to be able to look myself in the mirror. No – fuck that – I've got to be able to look my boy in the eye.'

'He's three years old, he doesn't know.'

'It matters to me, Luce. I don't know how you're putting up with it, to be honest.'

Lucy shrugged.

'Because I need the cash. Apparently some of the others – they really *are* working girls. This is a regular gig for them. Half these guys have already got rooms booked.'

'You're not thinking of—'

'No – of course not. I'm just saying – the men in there . . . it's what they were expecting.'

Sadie shook her head.

'Well, not from me.' She zipped up her jacket and walked to the door. 'You take care of yourself. Don't let those fuckers take any more liberties with you. I hope their wives all cut their balls off . . .' She stood at the door to the corridor; when she opened it they could hear the hubbub echoing down from the main hall. '*Men!* Can't live with them . . .' She pretended to think about it for a second. 'Nope – still can't live with them.'

Lucy grinned.

'Text me when you get in – let me know you got home safe.'

Sadie nodded and, with a wave, headed out.

She hurried along, eyes fixed on the carpet, keen to slip away without being noticed.

'Sadie, wait . . .'

The voice was rich and moneyed and as she turned, she knew exactly who it belonged to. The man at the end of the corridor was in his mid-forties. Tall with perfectly groomed brown hair, he was immaculate in his tuxedo, wearing a burgundy-coloured bow tie and cummerbund combination. Another peacock in a whole flock of them, she thought.

'Where are you going?' he said, a look of concern on his face.

'Where do you think I'm going? Home.'

He looked chastened.

'I'm sorry – I've been looking out for you all night. But I'm with the rest of the trustees – I've got to keep them happy, you know?'

'Well, that's very nice for you. I hope you enjoyed your lobster risotto too . . .'

'Don't be like that. I told you what kind of night it was going to be.'

'You didn't say anything about getting sexually assaulted.' She pointed down towards the banqueting hall. 'There's about five men in there I could have nicked right now.'

He moved in close.

'I'm sorry. I'm your friend – you know that. I thought you could use the money. Please stay.'

She faltered, unsure for a moment.

'Why? Got a room booked, have you?'

He looked pained and took her wrist.

'That's a bit unnecessary, isn't it?'

'Get your hands off me – I've had enough men pawing at me tonight.'

He didn't release his grip but moved in even closer instead.

'It's *me* – I'd never hurt you.'

'Get off!'

She grabbed his hand, dug in her nails and he broke his hold, flinching in pain.

'What the fuck, Sadie?'

She turned and left, her patience exhausted.

It was on the train home it all caught up with her. She could smell someone eating a Big Mac a few seats behind, and her stomach cramped with hunger. The last thing she'd eaten was a Pot Noodle at around four o'clock. She'd been sorely tempted to buy herself something at Charing Cross, but couldn't justify the expense. Particularly now she'd probably blown her night's fee. Lucy's warning that tomorrow she might regret leaving was already out of date. She looked out of the window and saw her own pensive reflection staring back. Snapshots of the evening began coming back to her.

'Why aye love.'

Patronising bastard. She shuddered as she remembered the hand on her inner thigh. The calm, precise tones of the man it belonged to, as he carried on talking. You just knew he'd done it before – and probably worse. She sighed. It was times like this Sadie just about wished she still had a boyfriend. Someone to hold her when she came through the front door. Someone to get angry on her behalf. She felt her eyes sting, couldn't prevent the tears from coming a little. She was desperate for a cigarette but only had two left and wanted to make the packet last. Instead, she pulled out her phone, saw the wallpaper picture of Liam – that wide, toothy grin, the curly brown locks – and couldn't help feeling like she'd failed him.

She lived in a small, rented ground-floor flat in Lewisham. It was far from perfect, but the scuffed wooden front door felt welcoming as she slipped her key into the lock. She'd surrendered on the walk back from the station and stubbed out the remains of the cigarette she'd been smoking into a chunky glass ashtray by the entrance. The thought of that one last fag left in the packet depressed her.

'Hiya . . .' she called, stepping through into a compact but well-maintained living room. An acned sixteen-year-old girl was sitting on the sofa, watching TV with a cup of tea in her lap. Chloe was her babysitter and a godsend. She didn't really do it for the money – she was well aware Sadie couldn't afford to pay her much. She was there because she enjoyed the work, and it gave her a welcome night off from her parents into the bargain.

'How's he been?'

'A little bugger if you must know – spent most of the night using your kitchen table as a climbing frame.'

Sadie smiled.

'Nothing new there, then.'

Chloe glowered at the baby monitor; there was a slight rustling and they both waited for more, but nothing came.

'I *think* he's down.'

Sadie opened her purse and pulled out a note. Chloe shook her head.

'Pay me next time.'

'Don't be stupid.'

The girl got up, put on her coat.

'It's fine – honestly. I've eaten you out of biscuits tonight, so I reckon we're quits.'

'Thanks, love. I'll make it up to you, I promise.'

She meant it too. Chloe said her goodnights and left. Sadie went over to the small kitchen area and began scouring the cupboards for something to eat. She was sorely tempted by a slice of toast but wanted to make the loaf last for the week. There were more Pot Noodles, but tonight's snack was also tomorrow's lunch. She sighed, went over to the sink instead and poured out a large glass of water. She downed half of it in one go, felt it fill her belly, then crossed over to the sofa and collapsed into it. As she kicked back, a thought occurred to her. She grabbed her phone and tapped out a text.

Home safe. Hope ur okay x

She waited for a moment but there was no reply from Lucy. She could only imagine what was going on in that hotel right now. Sod the money – leaving had been the right decision.

'*Muuummmy!*'

The voice came from the baby monitor and she sighed.

'Oh pet, don't do this to me.'

With a sigh, she dragged herself to her feet and was about to head into the small double bedroom she shared with her son when the doorbell rang. Her immediate assumption was that Chloe must have forgotten something. She went over to open it and was thrown when she saw who was standing there. What did *he* want at this time? She greeted him but he didn't reply. Instead, he stepped forwards into her flat. She felt her heart sinking – all she wanted to do now was settle Liam down and try and get some sleep of her own.

'What can I—' she said. She didn't have time to finish the sentence. Almost casually he picked up the ashtray by the door and swung it round. The full weight of the glass crashed into the side of her head, shattering her skull instantly. The second blow caved in her forehead, while the third destroyed what was left of her face. She fell to the ground, blood, bone and brain matter spilling out around her. The figure watched her hand twitch briefly as if reaching for something, before finally going limp.

The intruder stood still, breathing heavily.

'Mummy?' said a voice.

A small boy was studying him uncertainly from the other side of the room. The man stared down at the ashtray, saw the blood dripping off it, and looked back at the boy.

2

Nancy Deen listened to the front door slam and lifted a spoonful of granola up to her lips. A crack squad of elite commandos appeared to be rushing up the stairs and she sighed as she ate. A front door key wasn't so much inserted as slammed into the lock of the flat, and she waited as her partner Mattie Paulsen swept into the room. Paulsen glared at her, sweat glistening on her forehead following her early morning run. Nancy wasn't too bothered – it was standard Paulsenese for 'the run was good, thanks for asking'.

'There's fresh coffee in the pot if you want some,' she said casually.

Paulsen ignored her, went straight over to the fridge, pulled out a bottle of mineral water and greedily gulped down several mouthfuls.

'Alternatively, there's water,' said Nancy. Paulsen went over to the coffee pot, plucked a cup from the dish drainer and poured out a dark brown stream. 'Or water and coffee if you prefer,' Nancy added. Paulsen took a hit of caffeine and gave her a thumbs-up.

In her mid-twenties, tall, slightly gangly and with a jet-black bob of hair, Paulsen cut a distinctive figure. Mixed race, she possessed the hint of a Scandinavian accent thanks to a Swedish father. She was a detective constable with a major investigations team in south London and was frequently misconstrued as a little insensitive by those who didn't know her. But Nancy knew her better than anyone and understood that like many brusque no-nonsense types, there was a rather sensitive soul buried not too far beneath the surface. She knew too that her partner had a lot on her mind at the moment. Paulsen's father had been diagnosed with Alzheimer's the previous year, and while it was still in its early stages, the disease was beginning to make itself felt. Her parents lived in Norfolk and though Mattie was making frequent trips, the after-effects of those visits often left her feeling preoccupied and restless.

A social worker by trade, Nancy's own people skills were none too shabby and she was trying her best to be as supportive as Mattie would allow. The pair shared a home in Tufnell Park, and though it drew a nice dividing line between their personal and professional lives, Paulsen's elongated journey home across the river meant she often worked a particularly long day.

'Will you be late tonight?' said Nancy. 'I thought we could eat out, maybe. That new Swiss place on Upper Street?'

Paulsen screwed up her face.

'*Swiss?* All melted cheese and grated potatoes? No, thanks . . .'

Nancy sighed.

'Alright – what about a curry then?'

Paulsen beamed unexpectedly, showing off a set of brilliant white teeth.

'Now you're talking.'

Before she could say more, Paulsen's phone began to ring loudly. She delved into the pocket of her tracksuit bottoms and took the call. Immediately her smile morphed back into a frown and Nancy already knew what was coming.

'Sorry, but I think we're going to have to postpone that curry,' said Paulsen a few moments later. 'There's been a murder – and a kid's gone missing.'

★　　★　　★

Detective Inspector Alex Finn parked his car, killed the engine and surveyed the scene in front of him. Pennington Road was an unremarkable backstreet lined with terraced houses on both sides and a pub that had seen better days at the far end. He guessed it was normally one of the area's quieter avenues. Not today. He could hear the roar of a police helicopter moving slowly overhead. The vast majority of the street was sealed off with parallel lines of police tape at each end, while uniformed officers were conducting house-to-house inquiries. Midway down he could see a group of blue-gowned SOCOs gathered in a huddle and began to walk towards them.

As he moved down the street, he was quickly aware of the faces watching from the windows. The elderly, the young, husbands and housewives, all trying to make sense of what was unfolding. By contrast, Finn was feeling a guilty surge of adrenaline. A tall, imposing figure in his mid-forties, his tightly shorn brown hair was beginning to fleck with grey these days. Carefully moisturised skin, horn-rimmed glasses and a pair of impressively sculpted cheekbones gave him a slightly bookish air. Dressed in a sharp tie-less suit, the whole ensemble suggested a misplaced advertising exec rather than a senior Metropolitan Police officer.

He'd expected to be discussing resourcing issues with his DCI right now in what was euphemistically described as a 'capacity' meeting. But his plans for the day – for much of the near future, most likely – had changed with a single phone call. That in itself wasn't unusual – as the DI of a major investigations team, he was used to working multiple murder inquiries simultaneously. What marked this one out as different was the missing child.

As he approached the small flat Sadie Nicholls once called home, Finn could see Paulsen in deep conversation with one of the SOCOs. The distress on the man's face was clearly visible. That was unusual in itself; they were all well used to dealing with gruesome crime scenes. He didn't judge the officer negatively for it, but it did tell him something about what they'd found inside.

As she saw Finn approaching, Paulsen broke off the conversation and headed over to join him. She was wearing full forensic apparel and greeted him with what might easily be misconstrued as a frown. But Finn was well versed in that particular expression, aware it was more an indicator of ferocious concentration than a measure of hostility.

'So, what do we know?' he said.

'The victim's name's Sadie Nicholls. She was twenty-four, unemployed, and lived here alone with her three-year-old son, Liam.' She motioned over at an area in front of the building. A second, smaller inner cordon had been established there in front of the property and a forensic tent was surrounding the entrance itself. The SOCO she'd been talking to was now kneeling in front of it next to a numbered cone. 'The dustman this morning saw a splash of blood, then noticed the door was open . . .'

'. . . and he went inside,' said Finn. 'Have you taken a look in there yourself yet?'

She flinched almost imperceptibly and from that, he took his answer. The slightly pained look which remained in her eyes was small, but there nevertheless. She nodded.

'There's no sign of a break-in or a struggle. Whoever it was, I think she let them in.'

Finn walked up to a white van parked a few feet away, emblazoned with the Met's familiar yellow and blue livery. 'Incident Unit' was written on the side. The back door was open, and he began helping himself to a gown, nitrile gloves and plastic overshoes from a crate.

'Do we have any idea when this might have happened?'

'Off the record, the pathologist reckons maybe about nine or ten hours ago.'

Finn checked his watch.

'So around ten or eleven o'clock last night. And no sign of a murder weapon, I take it?'

'There's a quantity of ash on the floor and some cigarette stubs as well – so we think it might have been an ashtray, but there's no sign of one anywhere.'

He nodded, stretching his hand inside a nitrile glove as he slipped it on.

'The question is – is this an abduction or did the boy wander off after seeing his mother getting her head smashed to a pulp?' he mused.

'If he wasn't taken, where would he have gone? If the pathologist's right about the time, then surely someone would have seen him by now?' said Paulsen. The gloominess of her tone managed just for once to dull the usual sing-song melody of her natural Swedish accent. Finn nodded grimly.

'I agree, and the blood outside's not a good sign – he could be hurt or hiding somewhere, particularly if he's traumatised. We've got a specialist search team working on it and I activated a Child Rescue Alert before I left base.'

The alert meant details were quickly being circulated to other forces and media outlets. They would be texted, emailed and posted to anyone and anywhere that might help. Their biggest assistance in finding the boy wouldn't be a uniformed police officer in the surrounding streets, but more likely a member of the public. There was another grim truth they were both well aware of too: in just over three quarters of cases when a child is abducted and killed, the murder takes place within three hours of their disappearance. Abducted or lost, if the pathologist's estimation of when

Sadie died was accurate, then they were already far too many hours behind.

Finn took a deep breath. He wasn't just bracing himself for the horror inside the flat, he was preparing his mind to do its job. They'd already received one significant steer – Sadie had opened the door to her killer. If she knew who attacked her, then the clues would be found in the details of her life. The quicker Finn could absorb who she was, the faster he could find her son and bring her killer to justice.

He and Paulsen walked gingerly through the forensic tent and up to the front door. Finn stepped inside and his first thought was that the living room smelt of flowers, the yellow of the foliage on the kitchen table catching his eye for a split second before the crimson horror on the floor. Usually, it took a corpse around twenty-four hours before it began to smell, though it was never a precise science. Sadie was lying face down, her arms prone by her sides. The blood had pooled on either side of the body and he could see a small portion of her brain peeking through the shattered eggshell of her skull. Spatter pattern spread across the carpet and on to the wall behind. Sunlight shone through the window, giving the scene a strange, quiet serenity.

He looked again, absorbing as much of the detail as he could.

'What do you make of the clothing?' he said to Paulsen.

'Not what you'd wear for an evening in front of the TV, that's for sure – and too formal for a night out with mates . . .'

'I agree. Looks like the sort of thing a cocktail waitress would wear. Do we know where she was last night?'

'No, but I'd definitely say she was out.'

She pointed at Sadie's bag, which was sitting on a side table. A long black hairpiece was next to it; a smart pair of heels lay scattered underneath the table.

Finn surveyed the room. It was cluttered, but not messy. There was an area packed full of toys, a child's top and trousers draped across a radiator, an ironing board and hoover stowed neatly together in another corner. This was someone making an effort, a sense of cheery optimism about the place. Bright posters adorned the walls, a big, framed red one proclaiming 'Keep Calm and Smile!' Blood had sprayed on to its frame and he could see the reflection of her broken body in its glass.

'Did she own this place?'

'No – rented, according to the neighbours. We've got the landlord's name; we're trying to get hold of him. He'd have had a key too.'

Finn nodded, looking around the room again trying to imagine the sequence of events. This woman's final thought would surely have been of her son. Terror at what her assailant might do to him once he'd finished with her. She'd died with that fear and the idea turned his stomach every bit as much as the visceral horror in front of him.

'Guv.'

The voice belonged to Detective Sergeant Jackie Ojo. In her mid-thirties, known universally to the rank and file at Cedar House as 'Jackie O', it took a lot to throw her. As she stepped into the room, he thought she took in the scene with as much concern as if Sadie Nicholls was sitting on her sofa sipping a freshly brewed cup of tea with them.

'The door-to-doors have turned up a few things. There's a girl at number twenty-six . . .' She referred down to her pocketbook. 'Chloe Ashton . . . says she was babysitting here last night. She told me Sadie was working as a hostess at some charity dinner in Mayfair. The Royal Grand Hotel? Left early I'm told . . . got back here at around 10.15.'

'Do we know why she left?' said Finn.

Ojo shook her head.

'It was hard work getting anything out of her – Chloe's in bits, sounds like she was very attached to both of them. She gave me the name of the father too – a guy called Harry – said Sadie split up from him about a year ago.' She paused. 'It was pretty ugly apparently.'

'This ugly?' said Paulsen, motioning at the body, but Ojo shrugged.

'She didn't know much more.'

Finn was listening, staring at the blood spray on the wall in front of him. Could this really just be a particularly horrific domestic? It would explain the fury of the attack, and also why the child was missing. But it didn't feel quite right either. He looked again at the body, the way it was positioned face down, with the arms straight by the sides – it looked unnatural, almost as if she was just resting. Given the nature of the impact, he would've expected her to have landed face up.

'Don't suppose Chloe knows Harry's surname or can give us any clue where we might find him?' he said.

'No, Sadie didn't talk about him too much apparently. Doesn't sound like he had a great deal of access to the kid either.'

'He's the boy's father – he needs to know what's happened, and there are questions he needs to answer too,' said Finn.

'It shouldn't be a problem finding him. His name will be on the birth certificate. We also picked up a laptop in the bedroom earlier. It's gone with Sadie's phone to digital forensics. His details must be in one of them,' said Paulsen.

'Tell them what we're looking for and that we need the information as a priority.'

Finn was aware a lot of the legwork was already underway. There were no CCTV cameras in the street – it was too small for that – but it joined a main road at the end. It was possible cameras and ANPR there might have picked up someone either coming or going in a hurry. There were at least some decent trails to start following up. It'd been a frenzied attack and frenzied didn't tend to equate to careful. With any luck, there was a fingerprint or a DNA sample somewhere here that would help shortcut them to a name.

'I want to build a timeline as fast as possible of Sadie's movements last night. Why she left that charity dinner early and what route she took home. It's quite possible someone might have followed her here as well.'

He took one last look at the room, the dead woman on the floor, and walked out.

3

'Don't tell me you went and had a look? Let the police go about their business. Nothing worse than rubberneckers,' said Tom Daws, not bothering to look up from his book as his daughter Abi crashed through into the living room. In his mid-sixties with a head of thinning white hair, he wore thick black-framed glasses which he absently pushed up his nose, before taking a sip of tea from the mug precariously balanced on the armrest of his chair. Classic FM was blaring from a radio and Abi casually turned it down as she dropped a bag of shopping on to the floor and began removing her coat.

'Of course not, Dad. I couldn't have got close even if I'd wanted to, there's all sorts going on out there,' she said. She looked at him curiously. 'Have you had any breakfast yet?'

He waved a hand.

'A slice of toast. I'm not that hungry, to be honest; I didn't sleep brilliantly.'

Abi's expression turned to one of concern. In her late thirties, she lived alone with her father in the same terraced house she'd grown up in. Since the collapse of her last relationship, she'd moved back into the family home in Pennington Road and it hadn't been quite the awful step back in time she'd feared.

There was something calming about the place, there always had been. Not just the warming memories of her childhood, but the building itself. It had always reminded her of Cornwall,

21

though she wasn't entirely sure why. There were plenty of rustic fixtures and fittings, wooden beams, framed pieces of art gathered over the decades and shelves packed with books from floor to ceiling. You felt as if the front door should open out on to a small fishing village rather than a backstreet of south London. The contrast was made all the more startling this morning given what was unfolding just a few hundred feet away.

For a moment the sound of the police helicopter above drowned out any further attempt at conversation, and Tom gave up on his book.

'It's impossible to concentrate with that racket. How long do you think it's going to go on for?' he said.

'They're looking for the little boy, Dad,' said Abi.

His face instantly transformed, the exasperation turning to genuine concern.

'What do you mean?' he said.

'There's been a murder. A young woman. And her son's gone missing. They think he's been abducted.'

There was a second as he digested the words.

'What happened?'

He looked haunted and Abi shrugged.

'I don't know the details. I was eavesdropping while I walked back. Half the street's watching from their doorsteps.'

Tom shook his head with disgust.

'There's something else.' She looked at him carefully. 'It happened at number eighteen . . .'

His eyes narrowed and instinctively he looked over at the bay window and out on to the street as the helicopter swept over again.

Patrick Clarke frowned up at the dark shape in the sky and watched as it hovered before moving on again. He became aware of some heads turning towards him. Neighbours, standing in their porches, watching with different degrees of fascination the police activity outside number eighteen. He ignored them and opened his front gate. Clarke himself was in his early thirties, tall, muscular and dressed in paint-flecked overalls. He walked over to a minivan parked a few yards away. The words 'Clarke Landscape Services' were written on the side. It was right in the middle of the no man's land between the two cordon lines. He sighed and looked around helplessly. A police constable was talking to a fat man with a bike on the other side of the street. He crossed over and interrupted them.

'Oi, mate – I need to go to work, can I move my van?'

'No chance – not until we're finished. It's a crime scene,' said the constable.

'So what am I supposed to do?'

'You'll have to wait until we get the all-clear, I'm afraid.'

'And how long's that going to be?' The policeman shrugged. 'Fuck's sake . . .' muttered Clarke.

'It's a murder investigation, sir. It could take some time.'

Patrick held his hands up.

'Fine, fine, fine . . .' he said under his breath and turned and went back to his van. He opened it up and began removing some bags and equipment. If he had to go on foot, then so be it. Out of the corner of his eye, he saw a familiar silhouette and felt a chill. Standing at the cordon tape by the pub was a large, heavily tattooed man with a shaven head, walking a bulldog on a lead. He was smirking at Patrick, having seen the exchange with the police officer. Making direct eye contact with him now, the man put a finger to his throat and slowly dragged it across. His smirk was turning into something uglier.

'What's going on, son? Have you found out?' came a voice from behind with a warm Caribbean accent.

'Someone's been murdered, Mum. At number eighteen.' There was a silence, and he could hear her breathing heavily – knew, too, what she was thinking.

'Are you okay?' she said.

'I'm fine. Go back inside – I'll put the kettle on.'

'Aren't you going to work?'

'Just go back inside, Mum.' He heard her grumbling, her slippers tip-tapping on the concrete. But he hadn't taken his eyes off the man at the end of the road. And the man hadn't taken his eyes off Clarke either.

David Hermitage stared down at the crispy bacon on his plate and cut into it. He was trying not to vomit. His wife Emily was at the window with their thirteen-year-old daughter Charlotte.

'I've never seen police vans like that before – not even on telly!' said the girl.

'Me neither – it must be for the CSI people or something,' said Emily.

'Is that a thing? *CSI: Lewisham*?' said Charlotte, laughing, but her mother wasn't smiling back.

'It's not funny, love – it's horrible.'

They hadn't needed to find the news – it had found them. A uniformed constable knocking on the door half an hour earlier, asking if they'd seen or heard anything suspicious the previous night.

'Come away from the window,' said David, still trying to force some food down. 'Someone's died – it's not something to gawp at.'

Emily turned in exasperation.

'Aren't you at least concerned? A woman's murdered literally yards away from where we live and all you're interested in is your breakfast?'

He pushed the plunger down on a cafetière and poured himself a coffee, taking a swift gulp in the hope it might just bind his stomach together.

'Of course I'm concerned, but I'm sure when the facts emerge it'll probably just be a jealous boyfriend or something.'

'Or some random nutter who could have picked on us.'

The thought clearly hadn't occurred to their daughter, who turned and looked at her mother with concern.

'Em, you're scaring Charlie,' said David.

Emily turned to her daughter.

'I'm sure your father's right – it'll be some domestic situation. And you're quite safe. No one can break in here – we always double-lock the doors at night.'

Emily motioned at her to come away from the window and the pair joined David at the table. He picked up the cafetière again and poured his wife a cup which she took gratefully.

'I used to see that girl around quite a bit, in the corner shop with her son. She seemed really nice – bubbly, you know? She absolutely doted on that kid,' said Emily.

David surrendered on his breakfast, threw his knife and fork into the centre of his plate and sat back.

'Aren't you hungry?' said Emily.

'I'm fine,' he lied.

'She was nice,' said Charlotte suddenly. The excitement of the activity outside had worn off, the reality of what was going on dawning on her now.

'I didn't know you knew her, sweetheart?' said her father.

'It's like Mum says – she always seemed to be out there, pushing her boy along in that buggy.'

'I'm sure the police are doing everything they can to catch whoever did this,' said her mother. 'Don't let it spoil your day. Go and get ready for school and try not to think too hard about it.'

The expression on her daughter's face suggested that might be easier said than done. Charlotte left them and headed towards the stairs that led up to her bedroom. Emily looked at the congealing remains of her husband's breakfast.

'Are you hungover – is that what it is?' she said.

'Of course not. Believe it or not, I didn't actually drink that much last night.'

Emily looked unconvinced.

'Didn't smell like that when you came in . . .'

'Thanks.'

'Want to tell me how it went? You haven't said a word about it yet.'

He shifted in his chair uncomfortably.

'Honestly there's not much to tell you. You know how much I hate these work dos. It's all glad-handing and networking – mainly with arseholes.'

He stood and grabbed his suit jacket from the back of the chair, ignoring his wife's continued scrutiny.

'How well did you know that woman?' she said, nodding at the window.

He didn't answer for a moment, swung on the jacket, and pulled the ends of his shirt out from the folds of his sleeve.

'A little – said hello once or twice in passing.' He went over to look for himself at the SOCOs painstakingly scraping and collecting outside. 'It's sad though, really sad.'

He pulled at the sleeve again, discreetly checking it was fully covering the semicircle of livid red marks on his wrist.

4

The possibility that a traumatised Liam Nicholls had simply wandered off into the night was feeling more and more remote to Finn by the minute. He gathered his team together in the incident room and was keen to make sure they were all focused on their next steps. In these situations, where time was everything, his main priority was to ensure the leadership from the top was clear and unambiguous. The senior officer in overall control of the major investigations team, DCI John Skegman, had ventured from his own office to join them.

A thin wiry figure with darting eyes, Skegman looked more like a shoplifter the custody sergeant had misplaced than the man in charge. But all that disguised a sharp mind and a forensically dispassionate attitude. Despite an occasionally bumpy relationship with Finn, the pair shared a mutual respect. It had certainly endured some peaks and troughs in the two years since Finn's wife Karin had died of a brain tumour.

Finn – a tightly controlled individual at the best of times – had slowly unravelled in the aftermath of her death. Everyone, it seemed, except the man himself could see he was struggling with his loss. There'd been a genuine fear he was heading for some sort of breakdown. But in recent weeks, he seemed to have finally turned the corner. Instead of working himself into the ground – arriving at the crack of dawn, leaving last thing at night – his working pattern had settled into something more reasonable. He wasn't trying to do everything himself either, delegating tasks a lot better than he had for months. He was still a moody bugger, of course, but to those who knew him well, that was more a reassurance than a cause for concern.

Just the faint doubt lingered in Skegman's mind that Finn was having them all on – putting on a performance at work to allay suspicion. But with each passing week, it became less of a worry. He watched as Finn chivvied the troops and gathered them together. This was the man he liked to see – focused and controlled, directing the traffic of the room with a calm authority. The overall respect of his team might never have gone, but it had certainly wobbled for a time and that had rectified itself too.

A board had been prepared with a picture of Sadie Nicholls' face culled from her Instagram pinned to it. Next to it was a blown-up portrait of her son, a round smiling face topped by ringlets of curly brown hair frozen in a moment. There was also an enlarged map of the area surrounding Pennington Road – a flag positioned carefully at the point approximating Sadie's address. Finn, satisfied everyone he needed in the room was there, strode forwards and waited for the final stragglers to settle down.

'For obvious reasons, I want to keep this brief. We've a missing child, and if this boy's still alive, then I want him found and in safe hands as quickly as possible.'

He looked around at the faces in front and was pleased to see he didn't need to labour the point. There was none of the usual banter, people conducting their own private conversations or more preoccupied with finding sugar sachets for their coffees. Everyone was alert and paying close attention.

'The victim's name is Sadie Nicholls; she was twenty-four years old and from Newcastle originally. She'd been living in London for six years according to her family.'

It hadn't taken long to retrieve some useful information

from Sadie's phone. Once they had the details, a local officer had been dispatched to give the death message to her mother. Finn himself had then rung her a short time later. She'd listened to his condolences and in soft, quiet tones filled in some of the missing details about her daughter. Sadie's father had died a few years earlier and her only living relations were her mum and younger sister, who both still lived in the north-east.

'The blood trail outside of the property stops at the street . . .' he continued.

'So the boy was taken to a vehicle?' said DC Sami Dattani. Sami was only a little older than Paulsen but seemed to have been part of the Cedar House furniture forever. There was something of the wide-eyed schoolboy about him which Finn rather liked. He saw enough jaded cynics in the service as it was.

'Possibly – we've conducted extensive searches of the surrounding area and there's no sign of Liam or any other blood spots, but that's not conclusive yet. We all know the stats – if he's still alive, the motive's more than likely sexual.'

It was a simple truth that unless it was a domestic matter, the vast majority of child abductions were committed by paedophiles. Known sex offenders in the area were already having their cards marked as a matter of course.

'I know what the stats say, guv, but paedophiles are predators. It's in their nature to operate in the shadows,' said Paulsen with a frown.

'What's your point?' said Finn.

'Just that violent attacks on adults are unusual in abduction cases – the whole objective is to fly under the radar. I can't think of too many child abductions where an adult has been attacked like this.'

'Then maybe it was something else,' said Jackie Ojo.

'Whatever happened could have just blown up out of nothing and a traumatised toddler walked out of that flat looking for help. Or he was taken away to keep quiet. Either way, we can't jump to any conclusions because we simply don't have enough information yet.'

'I'm not ruling anything out at this point, Jacks. What do we know about the landlord – have we managed to locate him yet?'

Ojo nodded.

'The place belongs to a retired couple who live out in Berkshire. They were having a meal with friends near Reading last night.' She stopped for a moment. 'One thing I noticed – the rent was very reasonable. Just eight hundred quid a month. Most one-bedders round there you'd expect to be paying another four hundred pounds or so for.'

'Any idea why?' said Finn. From memory, there hadn't been anything unusual about the place that had caught his eye.

Ojo shook her head and shrugged.

'They didn't really give a reason ... they were a bit shell-shocked, to be honest.'

'Do we know who the boy's father is, guv?' said Dattani.

Finn nodded.

'He's a builder from Eltham called Harry Boxall. We're still trying to track him down – we've been told he had an acrimonious split from Sadie, and there doesn't seem to be much evidence he was playing a significant part in their lives either.'

Paulsen held up some paperwork.

'I've been looking through some of Sadie's bank details. It looks like Boxall was making some small – and I mean small – maintenance payments. And pretty irregularly too,' she said. 'Whether that's because he couldn't be bothered or simply didn't have the money . . .' She left the question hanging.

Finn nodded.

'Either way, we're searching for him and the sooner we can talk to him and get some answers to these kinds of questions, the better. He's a potential suspect – until he isn't.'

He turned to a whiteboard behind him and picked up a marker pen. 'We're also beginning to build a rough timeline of Sadie's movements last night. We know she was at the Royal Grand Hotel in Mayfair where she was working as a hostess at the Knights Association dinner. According to the babysitter, Sadie left early and got home at around 10.15. We're still checking with TfL – but it looks like she probably took the tube to Charing Cross and caught the 9.47 train from there to Lewisham. So, assuming she didn't deviate, she probably left the hotel at around 9.30.' He marked up the whiteboard with the timings as he spoke.

'Have you heard what went on at that hotel last night?' said DC Dave McElligott suddenly. Finn turned and looked at him with a hint of mild irritation. McElligott had a tendency to hijack briefings, always enjoying an opportunity to show off in front of a captive audience. This wasn't the morning for it.

'No, Dave – but if you have something relevant you want to share?'

'It's probably nothing – but I've got a mate who works at Westminster nick – he says they've had some calls this morning. Sounds like things may have got a bit out of hand.'

At the back of the room, Finn could see Skegman shifting slightly uncomfortably on his feet, his beady eyes focused now on McElligott.

'Out of hand in what way, exactly?'

As ever McElligott was stretching things out, enjoying the attention.

'Nothing concrete, as far as I know. No arrests have been

made. But some of the girls who were working there have come forward – they're saying the men got a bit lively, if you know what I mean . . .'

'Which might explain why Sadie left early,' said Paulsen.

'I agree,' said Finn. 'There might be something – or *someone* – that specifically caused her to leave. Do you want to follow that up?' he said, directing the instruction to Paulsen. She nodded, enjoying McElligott's slightly crestfallen reaction at having his thunder stolen.

'We also know Sadie sent a text to someone at around 10.35,' continued Finn. 'Digital forensics have confirmed the number belongs to a woman called Lucy Ahmed. Sounds like she was a friend of some sort – give her a call as well, Mattie, and see what she can tell you.' Finn added the time of the text message to the rough timeline he was assembling on the whiteboard. He turned back to the group. The clock on the wall at the far end of the room was now nudging towards 10 a.m. and Finn was keen to wrap things up.

'Uniform are ploughing through the CCTV from the surrounding streets, but nothing's been flagged up yet. We know a little bit about Sadie and her world, but not nearly enough yet. It's coming on for twelve hours since Liam went missing and we're playing catch-up. Jacks, do you want to go back to uniform and see if the searches have turned up any new witnesses? Sami – liaise with digital forensics and see what else they've pulled from Sadie's phone and laptop. The rest of you – you know the drill. Let's interrogate every inch of this woman's life. She opened the door to this person late at night – so it's highly probable she knew who he was. We need to know who *she* was, where she went, who her friends were, who her enemies were. Somewhere in there is the clue to who's done this.'

Finn signalled that the meeting was over and watched

closely as his team dispersed. He'd been here before, of course – Liam Nicholls wasn't the first missing child he'd dealt with over the years. There'd been successes – children found and reunited with parents who'd privately given up hope. And there'd been failures, the ones who hadn't been so fortunate. People he still thought about randomly months, sometimes years, later. They were experiences that had taught him valuable lessons. Working at speed was important, but his job was also to stand back from the urgency and remain measured. While his people stepped up the pace, almost perversely his role was to slow down and keep an overview. Nobody, least of all Liam, would be helped if something critical was missed in the rush to find him.

As Skegman headed for the door, he motioned at Finn to join him. The pair began walking down one of Cedar House's long grey corridors towards his office.

'A word to the wise, Alex, if you're looking into the Knights Association dinner ... tread carefully. There's a lot of very well-connected people who were in that hotel last night. None of them will want to be connected – however peripherally – to an investigation like this.'

'And I'm supposed to care about that?'

'You might not have any choice in the matter. And I'd rather not have the chief super asking me awkward questions about you ...'

'God forbid,' said Finn as they reached the DCI's office. Skegman pushed the door open and slipped behind his desk. 'Don't suppose you've ever been to this thing yourself, have you?' said Finn, arching an eyebrow innocently. Skegman didn't see the funny side and he immediately realised why.

'Jesus, you don't think one of these guys killed her?'

Skegman smiled wearily.

'Let's bloody hope not. That's a whole shitstorm we don't

need. But you might want to give Paulsen a steer before she leaves. If anyone can start a major incident out of nothing . . .'

Finn smiled. He knew the dig was only semi-serious, but Mattie Paulsen wasn't always known for her diplomatic skills. Skegman glanced at his PC screen and frowned.

'The media requests are stacking up on this – I don't want it to get in your way though. I can front something up if you'd like.'

'It's okay, I don't mind – I was thinking of calling a press conference anyway,' said Finn.

There were two reasons he'd been mulling the idea. If Liam was lost on the streets of south London, then a renewed call to the public for information, in addition to the Child Rescue Alert, made sense. In his heart he was fairly sure someone would have spotted the child by now, but the appeal wouldn't hurt. Alternatively, if the boy had been taken, then there was no harm putting some early pressure on his abductor.

'What's happening with the girl's family?' said Skegman.

'Sadie's mother and sister are on a train to London as we speak. I've arranged for a car to pick them up from King's Cross later. I'll see what state they're in first, but if either of them feels up to it, then we could do a joint presser.'

'Okay – keep me in the loop. We're throwing everything we can at this in terms of manpower. My only concern is if something big happens elsewhere . . .' said Skegman.

Finn pulled a face.

'You had to go and say that out loud, didn't you?'

Skegman smiled grimly. He was actually enjoying the banter; it reminded him of how their relationship used to be – before Karin Finn had died.

'It's good to see you've found your sense of humour again, Alex,' he said.

'I've no idea what you mean,' said Finn, deadpan.

'Oh, I think you do,' said Skegman lightly.

For a second the two men exchanged a look, then Finn gave the smallest of nods, turned and left. He felt a pang of something as he walked back to the incident room, and tried to ignore it. It was good that his relationship with Skegman was back on a more even footing. That it was built entirely on a lie was, for the moment, completely irrelevant.

5

The Lamb's Head never did roaring business even before the pandemic turned the world upside down. Tucked away at the far end of Pennington Road, it was a pub that never really set out to welcome newcomers. The dusty lamps dotted around the walls kept the place gloomy, while the eighties décor had looked dated even in the eighties. The ever-present smell of sweat and ale and the brooding quiet of the lounge was usually enough to dissuade the odd accidental visitor. For its regulars, though, the Lamb was an institution. An old-fashioned London pub in the best traditions of another time, relatively untouched by the horrors of craft beer and cappuccino machines.

Ronnie Fordyce had been drinking there for as long as he could remember. A tall, well-built man in his late sixties, he could easily pass for at least ten years younger. His natural reaction to the police activity outside his house had been to head for the pub and he was pleased to see its doors on the right side of the taped cordon. He wasn't surprised to find it even quieter than normal as he entered. A large white English bulldog dozing in front of the bar looked up, recognised him, and immediately lowered its head again.

Behind the counter was a heavily tattooed, balding figure in his late fifties. Alan Baxter was the pub's landlord, and as he saw Ronnie enter, he automatically began drawing him a pint of bitter. The head was already settling as Ronnie climbed on to his regular perch.

'Well, this is some proper old shit, isn't it, Al?' he said, looking up at Baxter before lifting the glass to his mouth and taking an appreciative sip. The other man nodded before running a hand through his stubbly scalp.

'I don't like it, mate. Not one little bit. It's not the usual, is it?'

Both men were accustomed to violent crime in the area; that in itself wasn't the issue. There didn't seem to be a passing week where a teenager wasn't stabbed, shot or beaten within a reasonable radius of their homes. But the gangs of south London tended to keep their business in-house. A young mother killed in such violent fashion, her young son missing . . . this was something different. And all of it, literally on their doorstep.

'I know what you mean,' said Fordyce. 'What do you reckon happened?'

Baxter sucked his teeth.

'A pretty young thing like that? Some little bastard who couldn't keep it in his trousers probably. But taking the kid . . .' He shook his head in disgust. 'That's different gravy.'

'Bradley from number 68 reckons it's the boy's dad – says he used to knock her about as well,' said Fordyce. Baxter looked around the pub. It was nudging towards lunchtime now, and the only other clientele were a couple of road workers having an animated conversation in the far corner. Baxter leant in and spoke confidentially.

'You know who I saw out there taking a good look earlier? That black bastard from number thirty-nine . . .'

Fordyce gave him a sharp glare.

'Come on, Al – you know how I feel about that sort of talk. There's no need for it.'

Baxter immediately looked chastened and nodded apologetically.

'You know what I mean though – it's not like Patrick Clarke doesn't have some form. How long's he been out? Four months, five months? Leopards and spots, all I'm saying.'

Ronnie took another sip of his pint and sighed.

'That's the thing about London these days, it's not like it was when we were young. You knew everyone in the street back then. Who they were, what they did. Now you don't know what you've got living next door.'

'Do you think I should say something to the cops?' said Baxter.

'What – about Clarke?'

'They should know what he *did* . . .'

The two road workers in the corner got up from their seats and headed for the door. Fordyce waited for them to leave before answering.

'Keep your nose out of it, mate. Causing trouble just invites trouble in my experience.'

Baxter looked like he wanted to argue the point, before surrendering. He grabbed a blue cloth from the sink and began wiping the bar down.

'Funny it should happen there though – at number eighteen. After all this time . . .' he said. Fordyce frowned, but before he could respond, the saloon door swung open again and Abi Daws walked through with her father in tow. Ronnie greeted them both with a broad smile.

'Here he is . . . don't just stand there, Al – man needs a drink. You got time for one, Abs?'

'I wish, Ron – I've got to get to the office for a meeting.'

Abi worked part-time as a conveyancing solicitor at a firm in the nearby high street. Since the virus, she'd done the brunt of her work at home, but occasionally there was no avoiding a trip into the office.

'Shocking, what's happened, isn't it?' she said.

39

'Awful. Just like all those years ago. Sure you're not stopping? Not even a quick tomato juice?'

She checked a watch.

'Oh, go on then. Five minutes.'

Baxter turned, placed another pint glass under the taps and reached for a small bottle of juice while it filled. Tom Daws was already settling at a rickety wooden table in the centre of the room. Abi sat down next to him, and with a slight wheeze, Ronnie lifted himself from his stool to join them.

'Your hip giving you grief again?' said Tom.

'It's nothing. Just a slight twinge – not letting them cut me open just yet.'

Baxter brought the drinks over and for a moment they all watched through the windows as yet another police car pulled up and stopped outside. Baxter shook his head and went back to the bar.

'Have they knocked on your door yet, Ron?' said Abi.

'Yeah, first thing – some wooden top barely old enough to shave. Wasn't the brightest spark. You do wonder where they get them from. You?'

Abi nodded.

'Not the sort of conversation you ever expect to be having.'

Tom didn't seem to be listening to them. His beer was sitting untouched in front of him, his attention on two uniformed police officers wearing fluorescent jackets in deep conversation outside.

'Stop looking at it, Tommy Boy – it won't help,' said Fordyce. Daws nodded and took a tentative sip of his beer.

'Sorry, mate. Didn't sleep too well. All this nonsense woke me up.'

'I can't stop thinking about that little boy. Such a smiley little thing. God knows what's happening to him now,' said Abi.

'Al reckons the young man across the road was showing an indecent interest earlier – our gardener friend,' said Ronnie. Abi rolled her eyes.

'I think we all know what Al's got against him. It's not fair – Patrick's a decent guy when you get to know him. He fixed our fence when the storm knocked it down a couple of months back.'

'You know what he did though?' said Ronnie carefully.

'Yes,' said Abi. 'But I think he's just trying to rebuild his life – doesn't mean he killed Sadie Nicholls. And what about the kid? What's he supposed to have done with him then?'

Ronnie held his hands up in mock surrender.

'I never said he did anything . . .'

Abi took a thoughtful sip of her tomato juice.

'Do you know who I used to see talking to Sadie a fair bit? Always struck me as odd because they weren't a pair you'd put together . . . that posh bloke from number fifty-two. David wotsit . . .'

'Twat,' shouted Baxter from behind the bar, automatically. Abi smiled, despite herself.

'Yes, he is, Al, but his wife's actually quite nice when you speak to her.'

Baxter shrugged.

'I wouldn't know. Oddly enough they don't come in here very often. And he tends to cross the road when he sees me walking Samson.'

'Funny that . . .' said Tom with a smile. Baxter gave him a friendly two-fingered salute.

Pennington Road had changed over the years. Like so many parts of London, its working-class roots had diluted over time. Its proximity to a railway station and the relatively short commute into central London had helped push up property prices. What had once been a dilapidated part of south London was now an attractive and upcoming area. In this pub, which had proudly refused to move with the times, the change didn't always sit well.

Fordyce finished off the dregs of his pint and wiped the residue off the top of his lip with a look of confusion.

'What do you mean you saw them talking together?'

'It was a few weeks ago. They were by the swings in the park. He was sat on a bench with her. I only noticed because he usually looks like he doesn't want to know any of us. And then a few days later, I saw them again, coming out of the One Stop together.'

'You don't think . . .?'

'It's a bit unlikely, isn't it? She was young enough to be his daughter.'

Ronnie thought about it for a moment then shrugged.

'Not our job to speculate, is it? We all just need to stay calm, leave it to the Old Bill.'

Tom suddenly looked at him sharply.

'Your hip giving you grief again, Ron?'

Ronnie and Abi exchanged a look.

'No, mate, just a small twinge,' said Fordyce pleasantly, as if it were the first time the subject had come up. Abi took a deep breath and drained the last of her drink. She picked up her bag off the floor.

'I've got to get to work. I'll come and pick you up later, Dad. I've made a cottage pie for dinner.'

She kissed him on the forehead and turned to Fordyce. Out of her father's line of sight, she quietly mouthed 'don't let him drink too much'. Ronnie gave a subtle nod, and she left.

'You seen the back of the *Standard*, mate? They reckon Millwall are going to sack their manager,' he said.

But Tom Daws was staring out of the window again.

'Eyes on me, Tommy Boy, eh?' said Ronnie gently but firmly and the other man switched his attention back.

'About time,' said Tom. 'Should have got rid of him months ago . . .'

Patrick Clarke had done a lot with his morning in the end. He'd pretty much completed a whole job in Catford, despite having to get there by bus. An old dear who'd simply wanted a neglected square of grass tidied up and a few patches of colour planted ahead of the summer. As he turned back into Pennington Road, he felt his stomach rumbling with anticipation for the lunch spread he knew his mother would have waiting. As he passed the geriatrics' pub, he could see Alan Baxter's sweaty dome through the window, bobbing around behind the bar. Saw too the usual crowd of old men supping their beers, gossiping like housewives. It wasn't hard to imagine what Baxter was probably saying either. Who the first fingers of suspicion were being pointed at and why.

He stopped by his van and threw the toolbag he'd been carrying into the back. If anything, the police activity on the road seemed to have got busier since he'd left. The forensics officers were now dotted halfway up the street. Some were on their knees, scooping fragments of dirt carefully into evidence bags and containers, while others were scraping the nearby walls and fences. He saw too the uniformed PC he'd spoken to earlier, now manning one side of the cordon with a bored expression.

He opened the small wooden gate to the terraced house he shared with his mother and noticed a few weeds poking through the paving stones by the front door. Appearances were important and he never wanted his mum to look like a second-class citizen on this street. Not to any of them. He felt his stomach rumble and decided it could wait until after lunch.

Lynda Clarke was sitting in the living room waiting for him. A small, diminutive figure with a shock of white hair, she was eighty-three and time was beginning to catch up with her. Patrick's only objective these days was to try and protect her from any unnecessary aggravation. The virus had been harrowing for both of them. He hadn't been home then, and she hadn't been able to visit him, and all he'd been able to do was pray that God would show them both some mercy. That was the only time he'd regretted it – the choice he'd made and the logic behind it.

'There's some ham and cheese on the kitchen table, but you'll have to cut your own bread. I don't like that big knife – it's too blunt,' she said with a frown. He didn't offer to sharpen it for her – he'd seen how much her hands shook these days.

'Have you already eaten, Mum?'

'I'm not hungry. All this drama outside. It's heartbreaking – that poor young thing. Ayesha from number seventy-six says someone beat her to death.' She rocked on her chair, clearly distressed by the idea. He perched on the seat next to her, his face softening.

'Have you been nosing around out there? It's probably best just to try and ignore it all,' he said.

She turned her head towards him and he could see in her eyes what she was looking for.

'Doesn't this upset you too?' she said.

He'd been thinking about nothing else all morning but didn't tell her.

'It's very sad – but it's also none of my business.'

'Did you know the girl?'

'A little.'

'You never mentioned that.'

'Why would I? She was friendly. Saw her around to say hello to, that's all.'

Lynda nodded, ran her tongue around her gums.

'Should I be concerned about anything, Patrick? You know what some people round here will be saying . . .?'

'Who cares what they think? Just ignore them, Mum.'

He stood up and walked towards the kitchen.

'You think it's that easy?' she said.

He sighed and turned back to her.

'I've got another job this afternoon – out in Norbury. I'm going to grab a bite and then head off. Is there anything you need?'

She pulled the face he'd known all his life. A stare into the middle distance, the displeasure contained, the expression neutral, but her feelings more than clear.

'Don't you think you should keep your head down for a bit?' she said.

'And why would I want to do that?'

His rising anger immediately turned to guilt as he saw the distress spreading across her face.

'Because I don't want you to get hurt. Not again.'

Jackie Ojo was standing in the middle of the road in the expanse between the two cordon lines. She took in the scene and tried to pin down her emotions. She knew streets like this, had spent most of her career knocking on doors just like these. She understood the fine calibration between community spirit, petty disputes and guarded privacy that always existed in these neighbourhoods. The events of the previous night would have caused a shockwave. It might have prompted a burst of genuine neighbourly concern this morning, a little more respect than normal, perhaps, between the people who lived here. But not long after the forensic team packed up and the cordons came down, things would sag back like a memory foam mattress. The old pattern of relationships would resume.

That was London for you – it was a simple, dispassionate truth.

She turned to head back to her car. As per Finn's instructions, she'd been talking to the POLSA – the police search advisor who'd been overseeing the hunt for Liam. Nothing new had emerged, and though they were still hard at it, she was feeling a sense of inevitability now. How far could a toddler have got on his own without being spotted by someone? Liam Nicholls had been abducted – of that, she was personally quite sure.

'Sarge . . .'

She turned to see a uniformed officer walking at speed towards her, a look of urgency on her face.

'You got something, Kelly?' said Ojo. Despite herself, she could feel the blood suddenly pumping.

The young woman nodded.

'One of the local residents just grabbed me – she's lived here all her life . . .'

'And?'

'It's about that building . . .' She pointed over at Sadie's front door. 'Apparently, it's not the first time someone's been killed there.'

6

'There was a double murder in the same flat in 1993. A young woman called Vicki Stratford and her four-year-old son Ben,' said Ojo an hour later. She was back in the incident room and it hadn't taken her long to find the details of the previous investigation at number eighteen Pennington Road. 'Like Sadie, Vicki was a single mother bringing up a young boy on her own.' She waited to let the significance of her words land. Finn was frowning so hard, she thought he might pull some-thing, while Paulsen was also sporting a familiar scowl of concentration. Only Dattani looked slightly dubious about what he was hearing. Their reactions pretty much aligned with her own first take on it. This was either important new information or one hell of a coincidence.

'What exactly happened?' said Finn.

Ojo glanced down at the paperwork in her hand.

'Vicki was bludgeoned to death with a lamp, while Ben was found in the bedroom with stab wounds to the neck from a pair of scissors. A career burglar called Dean Rawton was convicted of both murders.'

As she spoke, she watched their different reactions; first, picturing the crime scene and trying to deduce the order of events. Second, attempting to understand how this incident – buried nearly three decades in the past – might potentially connect to the very urgent task at hand.

'Where's Rawton now?' asked Dattani.

'Still inside – he got a life sentence and has been refused parole twice. About the only thing we know for certain is that he didn't kill Sadie Nicholls,' said Ojo. 'I think it's also the reason why Sadie's rent was so low – the place must have a reputation.'

'And how did we find out about all this?' said Paulsen.

'From someone who was living in the street at the time – she said a few of Sadie's neighbours were around then too. I think it's worth a chat with them,' said Ojo.

'I agree,' said Finn, nodding.

'You think there's something in it, guv?' said Dattani, not hiding his scepticism.

'You don't, Sami?' said Ojo.

He shrugged.

'It's just a coincidence, isn't it? Has to be.'

They were all subtly watching Finn, waiting for him to pass some sort of judgement on it. His frown still looked like it could cut through butter.

'Maybe,' he said finally. 'But how many times have you encountered a coincidence like this? I can't remember one quite like it before. I think it needs properly looking into.'

'I haven't had time to fully go through the details of the original investigation. But there's quite a bit of information there if you want me to?' said Ojo.

'I do,' said Finn, grabbing his jacket from the back of his chair. 'In the meantime, let's speak to these very unlucky neighbours.'

Paulsen liked the house. It had character and smelt of wood and good cooking. Finn was sitting awkwardly on the sofa next to her. Even though they were here on police business, his uneasiness in these situations never failed to surprise her. The friendlier the environment, the more uncomfortable he seemed to be.

'I was just a child at the time, but I've never forgotten it. I can't believe it's happened there again,' said Abi Daws, putting a tray with a couple of mugs of tea on the coffee table. A half-opened packet of digestives was rolling around next to them. Paulsen, who hadn't found time for lunch yet, surreptitiously leant forwards and levered one out.

'Can you tell us a bit more about it?' said Finn as Abi settled into a chair by an old-fashioned desk bureau.

'Will it help find that poor boy?' she said.

'I've honestly no idea,' said Finn. 'But if you can tell us what you remember, that would certainly be helpful.' He smiled reassuringly. Abi crossed her legs, cleared her throat and gathered her thoughts.

'Her name was Vicki and her son was called Ben; he and my brother used to play together. It was just like this morning. Someone found the bodies, called the police, and it all looked very similar to what's going on out there now. It really does bring back some horrible memories.'

It struck Paulsen then how young Abi must have been at the time, perhaps only nine or ten.

'I'm sorry, it must have been terrifying for you.'

Abi nodded.

'I was thinking that, earlier – the kids in the street now, going through the same thing I did. What they'll remember about it in the years to come.' She screwed up her face as a thought struck her. 'But they caught the guy who did it – there was a big trial at the Old Bailey. You can't think there's a connection with what happened last night?' she said.

'Dean Rawton – that was his name,' said a dry voice with a slight London accent.

Finn and Paulsen turned and saw a thin white-haired man standing by the door to the hallway. He was holding a large mug of coffee in his hand and Paulsen saw a brief look of concern cross Abi's face.

'I thought you were having a nap, Dad.'

'Some chance with all that kerfuffle going on outside. I take it you're police.'

He introduced himself and settled into a well-worn armchair. Finn explained why they were there.

'My daughter's right – I can't see how what happened back then has any bearing on this,' said Tom, motioning at the window.

'Did you know Vicki Stratford, Mr Daws?' said Paulsen.

'Yes, I did. Vicki was an accountant – good with numbers. She helped a lot of people around here. It was an awful thing and we were all very relieved when they made an arrest.'

'What about Rawton – was he known around here too?'

Tom nodded.

'Vaguely – used to see him in the pub occasionally. I mean, we all knew he was a wrong'un even before he did what he did.'

'In what way?' said Finn.

Tom took a moment, staring into space as he rolled the years back.

'That he'd done time before for thieving. I don't think anyone thought he was violent though. It sounded like a break-in that went wrong – Vicki must have walked in on him and he . . .'

He left the sentence unfinished. Paulsen noticed that Abi was watching him closely as he spoke. She looked troubled by something.

'Dad, you hate black coffee . . .' Her father looked at his drink, momentarily confused. 'You've forgotten to put the milk in,' she said, standing and gently taking the cup from him. He gave a good-humoured shrug.

'Oh well, first time for everything.'

Finn frowned, keen to get the conversation back on topic.

'Did you have any reason to think he had any other motivation for killing them?'

'No,' said Tom. 'As I remember, the evidence against him was pretty clear-cut. His fingerprints were all over the flat, and some witnesses saw him running from the area covered in blood. But that's more your territory. Surely you've got all this on file somewhere?'

Finn nodded, and Paulsen could tell he was trying to compute what he'd been told. Sometimes conversations like this threw up little nuggets. Sometimes they only told you what you already knew and wasted your time in the process. This didn't feel like either – but if there was a link between the two sets of murders, it certainly wasn't jumping out at her. Finn rose to his feet.

'Thank you both for your time – we should be getting on. One last thing ... did either of you know Sadie Nicholls particularly well?'

Tom shrugged.

'It's like I told your colleague earlier, I used to see her out and about. Always had a smile on her face – but I don't think I ever had a proper conversation with her.'

Abi shook her head.

'Me too. I often saw her with her son heading off to the park, but that was all.'

Finn thanked them again and headed for the front door. Abi, still holding the coffee cup, accompanied them. But even as Finn left, Paulsen found herself still watching her. The woman's mood had subtly changed as if a cloud had passed overhead. Her father was now over by the window in the living room, observing the police activity outside. She looked across at him anxiously like a worried parent, then caught Paulsen's gaze and smiled awkwardly back at her. A moment seemed to pass between them before Paulsen followed Finn out.

'What do you make of it?' she said as she caught up with him in the street.

'It's intriguing. There are far too many similarities to just simply dismiss it. Equally, we could waste precious time looking into something that really is just a coincidence. Be interesting to know who else was living around here at the time. We should get back – there's plenty to do.'

Behind his desk, John Skegman rubbed his forehead with the tips of his fingers as Finn explained where they were.

'It doesn't sound to me like it could be connected. Don't waste too much time on it,' he advised finally.

Finn tried to formulate an answer and struggled, largely because he still hadn't settled on a clear view about it himself. In many ways, he and Skegman were similar characters: precise and logical men who preferred to work with hard facts and keep their speculative theories grounded in evidence-based argument. Finn famously poured scorn on the concept of copper's nose whenever an officer tried to use it. The fact he frequently followed his own hunches wasn't lost on his team, who were long used to his minor hypocrisy on the subject.

'You disagree?' said Skegman, picking up on his hesitation.

'Not necessarily. It's just too much of a coincidence for me – another young single mother with a boy of a similar age to Liam in the same flat. If it was just some old codger who'd been battered to death, I'd write it off happily.'

'The facts say otherwise. There's a man who's serving a life sentence with absolutely no suggestion it's an unsafe conviction. When was the last time he appealed it – back in the nineties? Looks pretty open and shut to me.'

Finn nodded, but still the uneasiness wouldn't leave him. If the area was a hunting ground for a killer who'd got away with it the first time around, he didn't fancy repeating the mistake.

'Indulge me. I won't overcommit resources on it, but I want to make sure everything is as watertight as it appears to be.'

Before Skegman could respond, there was a knock at the door and Dattani entered without waiting to be invited.

'Guv, sorry to interrupt, but I thought you'd want to know – we've tracked down Liam's father.'

7

Harry Boxall was telling a dirty joke when they arrived. A builder, he'd been out on a job in Kidbrooke for most of the morning. It was his girlfriend who'd told them where to find him. He always switched his mobile off while he was working, which in part explained why he'd been so difficult to locate. Finn and Dattani found themselves at a comfortable semi-detached in suburbia whose owners were in the midst of a kitchen renovation. They were led through by a young woman who seemed more disturbed that her refurb was being inter-rupted than by the fact they were police detectives.

She took them into a long, narrow kitchen where two men in overalls were sitting around a sheet-covered table appar-ently taking a tea break. A radio was blasting out loud dance music, or at least that's what Finn assumed it was. A man in his mid-twenties with a mop of unruly black hair was in the middle of a tale about a nun in a condom factory when they walked in.

'Harry Boxall?' said Finn.

The curly-haired man turned, the joke dying on his lips. Finn guessed that the second individual – a short, heavily muscled character with a ginger buzz cut – was his partner. He flashed his warrant card at him and asked if he could give them some privacy. There seemed to be a delay while the request made its way from his ears to his brain. He finally grunted something unintelligible, which might have been about waiting in a van, and left them alone. Boxall's expression was now turning to one of alarm.

'What is it – what's happened?' he said.

Finn leant forwards and turned the radio off.

He didn't waste any time and quietly explained why they were there. There was a silence as Boxall took in the implication of what he was being told. Disbelief was spreading across his face now.

'I don't understand – is Liam alive? Where is he – what are you saying to me?' The questions came tumbling out. Dattani discreetly crossed to the kitchen sink and poured him a glass of water which he ignored. Hating himself, Finn knew he'd have to bypass the sensitivities of the situation. He looked the younger man directly in the eye, and when he spoke, it was with a measured clarity.

'I'm really sorry, but I need to ask you some questions about Sadie. The more you can tell me, the quicker we might be able to find Liam. Do you understand?' Harry nodded and this time took a snatched swig of the water. They swiftly established he had an alibi for the previous night. A trip to the cinema with some friends that would need corroborating. It was when they got on to the subject of his relationship with Sadie that he began to lose it again.

'It's some perv, isn't it? They've taken him – that's what's happened. Jesus, this is unreal.' He rubbed his face with both hands. His eyes were red and wet now. Finn waited patiently and then resumed his questioning.

The break-up with Sadie had been ugly, the virus – like for so many things – the catalyst. Work had dried up for both of them, and trapped together with a young baby, the pressure had quickly become intolerable.

'We had no money and we couldn't stop rowing. I kept trying to tell her I couldn't just magic up work out of thin air.

When the government stopped bailing us out . . . that's when it became impossible.'

'Did the rows ever go beyond arguing?' asked Finn carefully. He was already pretty certain that Boxall wasn't the man they were looking for. You couldn't fake the reaction he was giving them. But it was still to be proven, and difficult though the questions were, they needed to be asked. He was mindful that Sadie's babysitter had suggested the relationship ended acrimoniously. Harry fixed him with a hard stare.

'What are you trying to say?'

'Did you ever raise your hand to her, for example?' said Finn.

'What's this got to do with finding Liam?'

'Please – just help us to help you.'

A whole multitude of emotions seemed to half form across his features before crumpling into pain again.

'Once,' he rasped. 'Just once. During the second lockdown, when I was going out of my mind. And I know that's no excuse.' He saw Finn make a note and looked at him with rising fury. 'You think I did this? You can't be fucking serious.'

Finn leant in, one of those rare moments when his own loss helped him empathise.

'I need to know everything about Sadie and her life. It doesn't mean you're a suspect. But the more I know about her, the better our chances of finding your son – do you understand?'

Harry was breathing heavily now and made a visible effort to rein himself in.

'She never forgave me and made it very difficult for me to see Liam after that. Things got a bit better, but she never forgot.'

'How often did you see him?' asked Dattani.

'Initially every weekend, but it quickly became a lot less. It became quite difficult to work out how I fitted into their lives after we split up. Neither of us wanted to involve lawyers, and we never really solved it.'

'You were making payments to her though?'

Harry nodded.

'It took me a long time to get the business going again. I didn't have a pot to piss in, and nor did she. I gave her what I could when I could.' He looked as if he was about to throw up. 'That one time I struck her. I wish I could change that more than anything else I've ever done. God spare my life, that's the truth.'

'Do you have any idea who might have done this?' said Finn.

Boxall shook his head.

'No one she knew – she was just sunshine. Honestly, she was.' He looked up, a lost little boy with the eyes of a raging demon. 'You have to find my son. Because I'm telling you now, if anything happens to him, I . . .'

He never finished the threat; instead, he dropped his head into his hands and held it tightly.

At Cedar House, Mattie Paulsen was struggling to find her focus. While the room swirled with activity around her, thoughts of her father kept intruding – worries about her mother's ability to cope with him, and concern at exactly what point that situation was going to get *really* ugly. She didn't like admitting it to anyone – even Nancy – but deep down she was scared, and it was a feeling which always produced a measure of self-loathing. And, she thought with a degree of wry dispassion, she truly hated herself for all the self-loathing.

Distractions aside, it had been a mixed day so far. She'd contacted the uniformed constable at Westminster Police

Station McElligott had mentioned earlier. It turned out that Dave's 'mate' was nothing of the sort.

'Irritating bugger. I met him once, out on a shout – the bloke's never stopped texting me since, just in case any decent jobs come up here,' the PC had explained. But Paulsen's amusement had quickly evaporated. As they talked, it became clear that what had gone on at the Royal Grand Hotel the previous evening was becoming something much bigger. A hostess had now made an allegation of rape against one of the guests, and more stories were starting to emerge.

'We're still trying to get a sense of what actually went on – but the more we're hearing, the uglier it sounds,' the constable had said. In her mind's eye, Paulsen was picturing a pack of pissed-up middle-aged men treating the female staff as their sexual playthings. The idea that this was how Sadie had spent her final hours was sickening.

Her next call had been to Lucy Ahmed, the last person – as far as they knew – Sadie had communicated with before her death. At first, they'd both been at cross purposes, and it had taken Paulsen a few moments to realise that Lucy had also been at the Royal Grand Hotel the previous night. She'd then explained that wasn't the reason for the call and broke the news of what had actually happened to Sadie and her son. It wasn't the first death message Paulsen had given and she knew from experience the different ways the human brain was capable of processing it. In this case, there was a stunned bemusement.

'How can she be dead? It's impossible – she told me she got home okay . . .'

That was just under an hour ago. Paulsen was now sitting in a coffee shop in Hackney. Despite the ticking clock she'd thought it wise to give Lucy a short window of time to gather herself. It wasn't simply a matter of sensitivity – the woman was in shock. The more composed she was, the more likely she might remember something useful. The cafe was close to where Lucy lived, and was classic east London hipsterville. All rustic wooden tables, glasses for cups, and overpriced sandwiches the size of matchboxes.

In person, Lucy was a tall, striking woman with long black hair. She was wearing sunglasses, even though the spring skies outside were grey and overcast. As she entered, Paulsen saw the bearded barista behind the counter sneak an admiring glance – and kept her eye on him just long enough to let him know she'd clocked it. He glowered with embarrassment and began polishing the saucer in his hand with a renewed intensity. In the context of what had happened to Sadie, these small moments were almost as offensive to Paulsen as the kind of stuff that had gone on at the gala dinner. Since she'd got out of bed that morning, it'd felt like she'd travelled through the full spectrum of it. A discreet glance in a coffee shop, groping men at a banquet – someone's brains pebble-dashed across a carpet.

Paulsen gave her a small wave and Lucy came over and sat down, removing the sunglasses to reveal a set of expressive mahogany eyes.

'I'm sorry for your loss,' said Paulsen automatically, but Lucy didn't seem to hear.

'Before we begin, you didn't tell me exactly how Sadie died. It's been bothering me. Do you mind me asking?'

Paulsen understood the impulse. Without all the information, how could she begin to make sense of the incomprehensible? And so she told her – a sanitised, precised version of the horror she'd seen earlier.

'*Fuck . . .*' said Lucy, her eyes reddening as her hand moved to cover her mouth. The bearded barista was approaching their table, and Paulsen tried to warn him away with a glare, but it didn't work. He ignored her and smiled pleasantly at Lucy instead. Could he not see the state she was in? She requested a glass of tap water and then ignored his attempts to charm her into something that actually cost money. Paulsen waited for him to go before resuming and began by asking about the previous night, explaining that one of the hostesses had now made an allegation of rape.

'I can't say I'm surprised. Everyone was getting groped – but we were warned what to expect,' said Lucy.

'Who warned you?'

'The woman at the agency who hired us. Sadie got me the job – they were looking for people and we both needed the cash.'

Paulsen nodded, remembering what she'd seen at the small flat in Lewisham. The essentials-range biscuit wrapper on the kitchen counter. The cupboards of dried pasta and tinned soups, the near-empty fridge.

'How badly did Sadie need the money?'

'Desperately. You know how it's been – there's just no work any more. It's slightly different for me, I don't have a kid to raise . . .' She faltered suddenly as she realised what she'd said. 'Oh God, Liam . . .'

'We're doing everything we can to find him,' said Paulsen, keen to keep Lucy focused. 'Why did Sadie leave the dinner early last night if she needed the money so much?'

Lucy looked slightly shamefaced.

'For her self-respect. She made that very clear. But that's what she was like – once she made up her mind, you couldn't stop her.'

Paulsen nodded and jotted in her pocketbook.

'You didn't see anything specific happen then?'

'No, not a thing. She just said she'd had enough, left, and sent me that text to say she'd got home okay.'

'Do you know if she had any enemies?'

'No. I mean, she didn't really have many friends either. She didn't have the time – her whole world was Liam. But there was . . .' She stopped as if trying to identify a memory.

'Go on . . .' said Paulsen.

'I think she was borrowing money off someone. Someone she probably shouldn't have.'

'A loan shark, you mean?'

'Yes – it was the only way she could pay some of her bills.'

'Did she mention a name?'

'No – just that it was someone local.'

Lucy shook her head slowly.

'Sadie was a right laugh . . . I mean really funny – especially on a night out. But the world just didn't stop grinding her down. It was relentless. One thing after another until it finally got her.' She looked up at Paulsen. 'That's how it feels – that it doesn't matter who actually killed her, because *everyone* did. The whole fucking world.'

8

It'd been several months now since Finn had last heard his wife's voice. He and the late Karin Finn used to talk a lot after her death. She'd accompanied him everywhere – offering the same acerbic, editorial view of his world she'd had when she was alive. It wasn't some voice from the grave of course, but he knew her well enough and understood their relationship so perfectly that he could recreate her almost effortlessly. The way she used to hold him to account – the way, daily, she made him a better person. A virtual Karin who spoke to him when he most needed to hear from her.

'*Come on, get up off your arse,*' she'd chide when he lay in bed on a Saturday morning, wondering what to do with his weekend. But that voice had gradually faded to silence and he didn't know why. The same part of his subconscious which had resurrected her had killed her all over again. Worse still, it felt as if it signified something important, a sea change that he didn't quite understand.

The loss coincided with a slow slide into something darker. The black dog of depression was a constant companion now, his job merely the hours of the day when he wasn't alone with it. The only positive was that he'd learnt how to disguise it from his colleagues. He'd become a lot more streetwise in that respect – understood what they looked for, what they noticed, and found ways to disguise it. At Cedar House, he was the quiet, cerebral man he'd always been. At home, there was nothing. Not even the echo of Karin's voice now, just the yawning void she'd left behind and increasingly the bottom of a whisky glass.

As he watched his team working with a controlled intensity around him, not for the first time he felt like an imposter hiding amongst them – a fraud taking everyone for a ride. He'd done everything right with this investigation so far. All by the book, even earning a patronising compliment from Skegman. And yet, his thoughts kept drifting back to his own problems as they always did, like the swirling water of a draining sink. And he didn't have time for that – not today.

He took some large discreet breaths and tried to focus his mind. Digital forensics had made a clone of the hard drive of Sadie's laptop. It was a treasure trove of pictures, emails and video clips that would help build a more complete picture of her world. Finn had tasked Dattani to go through it earlier, but on a whim decided to take the job on himself. A life condensed into a series of digitised pictures, sounds and words was as close as you could get to actually stepping into someone's head. And if anyone could resurrect a dead woman, he could. At least he used to be able to, anyway.

He plugged the hard drive's cable into the USB socket of his PC and an array of folders immediately opened on the screen in front of him. Each had its own title – separated for simplicity by the digital forensics team. *Pictures, Emails, WhatsApp, Video* and *Documents*. He clicked on the one marked *Pictures* and a series of thumbnails appeared. His eyes were immediately drawn to one in the middle, a stamp-sized portrait of Sadie. He double-clicked on it and waited as the image expanded.

It showed her face in far more detail than the single photo pinned up on the board at the end of the incident room. The grin was warm and friendly, but you could see the weariness behind it too. There were lines on a face that shouldn't be lined yet, and they also told a story, of a life spent in daily combat with the world. There was fragility as well, as if the smile was only being held up by the slenderest of scaffolds, which could collapse at any moment. The slight hint of worry and concern in her expression would never be assuaged either, he thought. There would be no happy resolution for this woman, no chance to see her son grow up, no chance to grow old herself. And Finn didn't need a therapist to understand why *that* resonated with him.

Next, he opened a portrait of Liam. It almost looked like a professional shot, clearly taken in a park on a summer's day. The close-up of his face had caught a smile of pure pleasure. He had his mother's eyes, and there were traces of his father's boyish good looks too – the same unruly mop of curly hair. One day he would have broken hearts, thought Finn. *Might* still break a few hearts, he reminded himself sharply.

He then opened the folder labelled *Video* and double-clicked on another thumbnail. The first thing he heard was laughter, an infectious giggle as the camera settled on its subject. It was the same living room he'd been standing in earlier. Liam was sitting roughly where his mother's brains would later spill. He was methodically tearing up a piece of paper, placing a single small scrap of it on the head of a toy bear.

'What are you doing, love?'

The voice was out of view, warm and distinct, and Finn felt goosebumps at the sound of it. A dead woman talking, but the Geordie accent helped him get a sense of her. He could already see her in his mind's eye, but now he could hear her too. On the screen, Liam looked embarrassed, turned his back on the camera and placed another square of paper on the top of a large purple dinosaur.

'Hats,' he said simply.

'That's very kind of you, Liam. Is it going to rain then? I'd better get me umbrella, hadn't I?'

The camera pulled back to show a circle of soft toys all similarly covered with little paper scraps. Liam peeked around bashfully, pleased with his efforts, and his mother laughed again.

'You've missed one ...' she said. The boy looked confused and checked back over his handiwork.

'Haven't,' he said uncertainly.

'Have ...'

A hand snaked out from under the camera, picked up a stray square of paper and placed it on the boy's own head. He immediately shook it off in a fit of giggles and squealed with pleasure. The clip ended there, frozen on his delighted expression.

Finn stared blankly at the child for a second, before focusing again. He ran his mind through the permutations. Everything that should and could be done was being done. All he could do was wait until something came back, something he could work with. Soon, Sadie's family would be here, and when they asked him where Liam was, he'd have to look them in the eye and tell them he didn't know. He hugged himself discreetly, wishing more than ever that his wife might talk to him again.

David Hermitage had been sitting at his desk for two hours now, and still he couldn't concentrate properly. The deputy chief executive of the Fight Hunger Foundation, he was trying to read a five-page proposal outlining the charity's plans for expansion in Central America. The trouble he was having was that in his current state of mind, the document was just a huge word salad. Every time he tried, he couldn't seem to make it to the second page. Absently he looked down at the marks on his wrist, the small red cuts left by a dead woman. He hadn't covered them with anything for fear of provoking unwanted attention. The feeling of biliousness he'd been carrying all morning wasn't going away either.

He attempted again to digest the information in front of him and didn't even make it to the second paragraph this time. Surrendering for the moment, he peered through his office window to check no one was approaching and opened the internet browser on his PC. He flicked through a few news pages and read some of the headlines. The *Mirror* had been the first to put something up.

'*Child missing after mother slain in horror attack*'.

A picture of a very familiar street was below the words, culled from Google Maps by the looks of it. He flicked through a few more sites, all carrying much the same. It was when he reached the *MailOnline* he felt his nausea rise again.

'*Police probe complaint after charity dinner*'.

The details were mercifully scant, but the fact it was there in the first place was worrying enough. In the finest traditions of 'what happens in Vegas, stays in Vegas', there'd be more than a few people from last night who'd want that story closed down. People with better connections than him, who'd doubtless already be working to ensure it happened. Neither Emily nor Charlotte were exactly newshounds, so there was a fair chance they wouldn't see it. With luck, whatever the police were investigating wasn't too serious and the story would disappear on its own.

His office door suddenly opened and he made a decent fist of containing his reaction, smiling at the visitor while simultaneously closing his browser.

'How was last night, David? We haven't had a chance to catch up,' said the convivial man in front of him.

'Oh, you know me, Gordon, I can make one glass of champagne last a very long time.' He forced a chuckle. 'It was the usual – showed my face, made sure the trustees enjoyed themselves, left in time for the last train. All very painless.'

He spoke briskly and efficiently, hoping to close the subject down. Trusting, too, that the CEO had been too busy to peruse the same web pages he'd just been looking at. Or worse – talking to someone else who'd been there last night.

'Was there something you needed?' said David.

'I wondered if you'd had a chance to read the Guatemala proposal yet?'

'Just flicking through it now actually – some very innovative ideas there, I think. Give me half an hour to gather my thoughts and I'll ping something over to you.'

'Good man, David, look forward to reading it.'

His boss smiled, flashing some artificially white teeth, and was already halfway out of the door before he'd finished speaking. Hermitage breathed out. Half an hour, he thought – why did he say that? He could have said an hour, two hours – or by the end of the sodding day.

He opened his office window and watched some boats wending their way down the Thames, saw the reflection of the huge Pacific Square building opposite rippling in the water. He pushed the window further open and inhaled some much-needed air. On his desk, his phone started to vibrate with an incoming call. He turned and saw a withheld number on the display. It was probably a nuisance call from some marketing company. The last thing he needed right now. He was about to ignore it when a doubt crept in and he answered it anyway. The voice on the other end was female – deep, strong and unfamiliar.

'I know where you were last night and how you got that scratch on your wrist. Talk to the police and I'll tell them about it too. Sadie sends her love, Dave . . .'

★   ★   ★

68

Finn was disappointed to find the investigation remained frustratingly static. It was over fifteen hours since they estimated the boy had gone missing. The expanded door-to-doors hadn't flagged up anything new, and a trawl of the CCTV footage from the surrounding streets showed nothing suspicious either. Most importantly, none of the search teams out looking for Liam Nicholls had found a trace of him. There hadn't been a single sighting anywhere of a lost young toddler. Finn was now as certain as he could be that the boy had been taken. CID and uniform had helped with the sweep of local paedophiles and sex offenders. All of them, it seemed, had alibis for the previous evening. Sadie had opened the door to her killer, and the connection still felt personal to Finn. It didn't rule out the possibility of a sexual motive, but the cocktail of ingredients gave this a slightly different feel.

Looking across the incident room, he saw Paulsen standing by her desk, swinging on her coat. Realising they hadn't caught up since the briefing, he rose quickly to intercept her before she left.

'What did Dave's mate at Westminster have to say?'

'Mainly that they're not mates,' said Paulsen. She relayed the conversations she'd had with both the uniformed PC and Lucy Ahmed.

'So Sadie left the hotel early on principle?' said Finn.

Paulsen nodded.

'According to Lucy, the agency who hired them wasn't too bothered at the end of the night. Sounds like they'd been expecting one or two of the girls to drop out. Happens every year apparently. I honestly don't know what fucks me off the most.' She shook her head with disgust. 'The men or these agencies taking advantage of women like Sadie, desperate for the money.'

'Do we know if any of the guests also left early?' said Finn.

'I can't say a hundred per cent yet, but I've spoken to the hotel and they say the guys on the door didn't see anyone else leaving at the same time.'

'So where are you off to now?' said Finn.

'Back to Pennington Road. I think we've underestimated how badly Sadie was struggling for cash. I've just been going through more of her banking details. You add together all her credit cards and loans and she was nearly thirty grand in debt.'

Finn raised an eyebrow.

'So maybe that's what this is all about?'

'Possibly – Lucy told me she'd been borrowing from a loan shark – someone local. I'm going to see if I can find a name.'

'Why would a loan shark take the boy though?'

Paulsen shrugged.

'Because he was a witness? I don't know – but I think it's worth looking into.'

Finn nodded, snatching a glance at the clock on the wall which was now nudging accusingly towards half past one.

'This isn't looking too brilliant, is it?' said Paulsen quietly.

His jaw tightened.

'Then it's down to us to change that, isn't it?' he said.

She didn't bother replying and headed for the door.

9

A long stream of piss was pooling along the pavement. Alan Baxter waited patiently while his dog multitasked urinating against a lamp post while absently sniffing a discarded chocolate wrapper. It could have been worse, Baxter thought. He loved Samson but was less keen on picking up his turds, cheerfully ignoring the requirement to do so. It wouldn't be long before the bleeding-heart liberals wanted you to wipe the animal's arse as well.

He saw Patrick Clarke emerging from his front door on the other side of the street and watched as he knelt and pulled up some weeds by the doorstep. Unable to resist, Baxter heaved at the dog lead and they crossed the road. It was like low-hanging fruit, he thought, and waited for Clarke to look up and notice him.

'All this bringing back some memories, is it, son?' he said, gesturing at the still-intense police presence further up. Clarke raised himself warily to his feet, holding the weeds in a gloved hand.

'How many times do you need to walk that dog a day, anyway?' he replied.

'They must have knocked on your door by now, surely? I mean, you lot can't keep yourselves out of trouble, can you?'

Their eyes locked.

'*Us* lot?' said Patrick.

There was a movement at the window, and Lynda Clarke peered at them through the net curtains.

'Yeah . . . the criminal fraternity. What else would I mean?' replied Baxter with a smirk. Patrick ignored him, started walking towards his van. 'I imagine the boys in blue would be very keen to know where you were last night. I know I am.'

Patrick opened up the back door of the vehicle, pulled out a rubbish bag and disposed of the weeds.

'Nothing to say? Anyone would think you had something to hide . . .' said Baxter.

Patrick spun around angrily.

'Look, mate, I don't want any trouble. You want to do this stupid shit every time you see me, then knock yourself out. I can't be arsed with it.'

Baxter's leer widened at getting the reaction he'd been chasing.

'And what will you do if I don't?'

Clarke looked him straight in the eye.

'Absolutely nothing. Nothing at all.'

Somehow he managed to make the words sound both reasonable and threatening. Baxter's sneer melted into something a little less certain. He yanked at the dog lead.

'Come on, boy, shift yourself . . .' he said, moving on, adding under his breath, 'fucking prick.'

Patrick let him go then turned to see his mother still watching through the window, her face impassive.

In the end, it hadn't taken Paulsen long to identify the loan shark who'd lent Sadie money and where she might be able to find him. Her first port of call had been to Chloe Ashton, the babysitter who'd been looking after Liam the previous night. She confirmed that Sadie had indeed borrowed some cash and knew too the identity of the person who'd lent it. Getting a name from the teenager hadn't been easy though, and it only came after Paulsen agreed not to divulge to anyone how she'd come by the information. A few follow-up questions provided all she needed to know about the individual concerned. And as she walked the few hundred yards up the street, Paulsen could already feel her bile rising.

She entered the lounge of the Lamb's Head, looked around and tried to contain her distaste. Paulsen enjoyed a good pub as much as the next person, but this she could tell straight away wasn't a good pub. She'd known places like this when she was growing up – all chunky men with signet rings sitting in silence opposite women with dyed hair and baleful stares. This one could almost be a museum recreation.

She was surprised to see Tom Daws there, engrossed in a game of cards with another man of a similar age, surrounded by an array of empty pint glasses. She saw him as soon as she entered but he didn't seem to show any recognition back. Deciding to test a theory, she walked over and smiled warmly at him.

'Nice to see you again, Mr Daws,' she said, deliberately refraining from adding 'we met earlier, remember?' There was some hesitation while the dots joined and then she saw the lights come on.

'Where are my manners . . .' he muttered, standing and proffering a hand. 'Nice to see you again too.' He turned to his drinking companion. 'Ron . . . this is Detective Sergeant Poulton. She came round our place earlier about this business at number eighteen.'

'It's Paulsen actually . . . and I'm only a detective constable.'

'Nothing "only" about it, I'm sure,' said Fordyce, before introducing himself. 'Are you any nearer to finding that poor lad?'

'Not yet, but we're throwing everything we can at it. It's why I'm here, actually. I'm looking for Alan Baxter – I was told he's the landlord. Is that him?'

She nodded at the man behind the bar. Baxter's place there had been taken by his son, a thirty-something clone of his father complete with fading tattoos and shaved scalp.

'No – that's his boy. Alan's out walking his dog,' said Tom. 'He won't be long though. His bladder's not so good these days.' He realised what he'd said and laughed. 'Samson, that is, not Al.'

'What do you need to talk to him about?' said Fordyce. 'If you don't mind me asking.'

'We're speaking to everyone we can on the street,' she said, not wanting to develop the point. Quickly, she added: 'So how long have you two lived here?'

'Oh, since time began,' said Fordyce grandly. 'I used to run a building business back in the day. I've probably done up most of the gaffs in these parts at some point. And Tommy Boy here . . .' For a second it looked as if Fordyce was going to speak for him, but then deferred.

'I worked for British Rail back when there *was* a British Rail . . .' he said. Ronnie chuckled.

'He's being bashful, don't let him fool you – that was only part of it. Tom was a union man.'

'National,' said Tom. 'National . . .' He faltered, stumped momentarily.

'. . . Union of Railwaymen,' completed Ronnie gently. Even then it seemed to take a second or two before Daws smiled and nodded.

'That's the one – back when there *was* a National Union of Railwaymen.'

'Right old firebrand, weren't you,' said Ronnie.

'It was a long time ago,' said Daws, getting to his feet. 'Feels like the Stone Age. I'm going to take a leak – can I get you a drink on my way back?' he said to Paulsen. She shook her head.

'I can't, I'm afraid.'

'I'll have another if you're passing that way,' said Ronnie.

Tom nodded and they both watched him slowly amble towards a brown wooden door at the side of the bar. There was a pregnant pause, then Ronnie answered her question before she asked it.

'You'll have to forgive him a few things. So you know – Tom's got dementia. It's not too serious yet, but it is starting to become more noticeable.'

Paulsen nodded.

'I thought so, I recognised the signs. My dad's got it too – they must be about the same age.'

'I'm so sorry,' said Ronnie. 'You'll know all about it then. Abi leaves him here with me quite often. We go back years and he's drunk in this boozer all his life.'

Paulsen was ahead of him.

'So it's a kind of safe place for him?'

'Exactly that. You should compare notes with her some time – I bet you two have got a lot in common.'

Paulsen wasn't so sure about that. Her family life was something she kept close, and certainly didn't offer up to strangers easily. But Abi's reactions earlier now made much more sense to her. It was exactly the same way she was with her father. The same bittersweet mix of concern and sadness.

'Does she have any help with him – is there no other family? I thought she mentioned a brother earlier?'

'Yes, Luke – but he lives in Australia these days so she pretty much has to do it all by herself. We do try and help her with Tom though. I mean, that's what neighbours are for, aren't they?'

He broke off as a white English bulldog padded into the

75

room followed by the squat form of Alan Baxter. Paulsen, who didn't like dogs, watched the animal saunter up to the bar before chasing its tail briefly and collapsing in a heap. She rose to her feet, mindful of why she was there.

'Alan Baxter?'

'Who wants to know?' he said.

She produced her warrant card and asked if they could talk privately. He led her over to a table in the corner, which, given the lack of punters, was as private as anywhere. The expression on his face was one of barely disguised suspicion.

'I'm investigating the murder of a young woman at an address in this street, and the disappearance of her three-year-old son,' said Paulsen formally. Her voice carried its usual slight sing-song Scandinavian inflection and she could see he was listening *at* her as much as to her.

'No shit,' he replied. 'What's that accent of yours then? Danish?'

Paulsen already had a good idea why there may be some reserve – she'd been forewarned about Baxter's world view by Chloe Ashton earlier.

'I'm half Swedish,' she said.

'You don't look it.'

And there it was, she thought. If Finn had been there with them, he'd be shooting her warning looks now. But he wasn't there.

'My mother's family are from Jamaica.' She was now matching the look of cool distaste on Baxter's face with one of her own.

'Quite the mix then, aren't you?' he said, and she decided she'd had enough of this already.

'It's been alleged you lent Sadie Nicholls some money. That you're a moneylender. Is that true?'

If he was thrown by the question he didn't let it show.

'Yes, it is. I lent her three hundred quid about a month ago.'

'So she owed you then?'

Paulsen could see Ronnie and Tom in the centre of the room frowning into their beers, listening closely to every word. She kicked herself for not taking the conversation out of the lounge. They seemed like decent people and she wondered what they privately thought of the man in front of her.

'She came to me and I felt sorry for her,' said Baxter. 'Sadie was a good kid and I put no pressure on her to pay me back.'

'Really?' said Paulsen sceptically.

'Really,' he replied.

'Can I ask where you were last night?'

'Course you can. I was here, behind the bar.' He nodded at Ronnie and Tom. 'Same as those two if you want to check.' He smiled confidently at her. 'I helped Sadie out because she was in trouble, and I'm devastated by what's happened to her. But I suppose because I'm a white, working-class Englishman, you'll automatically think I must have had something to do with it. You people always do.'

She wasn't entirely sure whether 'you people' meant the police, others her age and class, or people of colour, but before she could answer, the pub door swung open. The bulldog by the bar rose, its tail wagging as it went over to greet the newcomer. Paulsen looked up to see Abi Daws entering. They caught each other's eye and exchanged a brief nod before Abi came over to join her father. Paulsen refocused on Baxter.

'We're talking to everyone we can. We just want to find Sadie's son. I'm sure you'd want to help us with that. Did you see or hear anything unusual last night?'

If anything, the derision on Baxter's face seemed to increase.

'As I told one of your colleagues this morning – no. Maybe if your left arm talked a bit more to your right arm you'd already know that. You might also know there's a guy who lives across the road who's done time for GBH. Attacked a young woman in the street and left her for dead.' Baxter stood, looked at Paulsen with open contempt. 'Try knocking on number thirty-nine – or look up the name Patrick Clarke on your computer. And then you can come back and thank me for doing your job for you.'

IO

Monday March 14, 15.13
From: sadie@diamondmail.com
To: lilypink@ymail.co.uk

Hey gorgeous – thanks for your email. Sorry it's taken me so long to reply, but guess what? I've been working!!! Don't get too excited, it's just a little bit of waitressing at a local cafe. Only one day a week right now and some cover work, but it's better than a kick in the teeth. My friend Chloe looks after Liam while I'm there so he's happy because she lets him run riot! He misses you and sends his love btw ☺

The good thing is it's distracted me from worrying about everything else. To be honest Lil, I don't know how long I can carry on living here. I reckon I can only afford to stay here for another couple of months and then I don't know what I'm going to do. I don't want to have to come home – there just isn't the space for all of us. I'm taking things day by day right now because you never know what's going to happen, do you? Investigating a couple of leads on potential work . . . I'll let you know how it goes.

So cafe job + Universal Credit is getting me by right now but it's hard. Two thirds of what I earn goes on rent – after that, I've just got seventeen quid a day left over. Seventeen fucking quid! Don't tell Mum, but I've been going to a food bank to get by. Been a few times now – it's keeping us fed, and that's what matters.

Never mind all that – you don't want to hear me moaning, you want the goss, don't you? Sorry to disappoint but there's nothing to report. After Harry I'm off men – unless they're filthy rich and hung like beasts ☺ ☺ ☺ That fella I told you about before – that's dead as a doornail. If I could take Liam with me, I'd go be a nun I swear! (how much do nuns get paid, anyway? ☺)

Give us a call when you've got time – I've attached some recent pictures of Liam being a little monkey. He gets cuter every day. Honestly without him . . .

Anyways – love ya

S xxx

Finn re-read the email a second time. Lily was Sadie's sister – he knew that from his phone conversation with her mother earlier. The message was the most interesting thing he'd found since he'd started rooting through her hard drive. Paulsen hadn't mentioned any kind of income in her bank details – so had this cafe paid her in cash? And could she have met her killer there? It easily might have been someone random she'd only crossed paths with briefly. Perhaps most important was that small hint of a recent romance. Whatever it was, it had clearly been brief and doomed. But anyone who'd been part of Sadie Nicholls' world was of interest.

He did feel like he was getting to know her better now. This was someone just about holding the threads of her life together. And yet she'd walked out on a job only twenty-four hours earlier that would have brought in some much-needed funds. It was now clear how important every penny had been to her. She'd left the hotel on a point of principle and that was interesting. She hadn't been too proud to use a food bank but drew the line at whatever had gone on at the charity gala. It felt important to him, a clue to her character and her decision-making processes. But before he could develop the thought, he was interrupted by Jackie Ojo.

'Guv – Sadie's family are at the front desk. They're asking for you . . .'

Paulsen had left the pub following Alan Baxter's revelation and walked straight up to number thirty-nine and rang the bell. She wasn't taking Baxter's word for anything, but the simplest way to find something out was, as ever, to go and ask some questions of her own. When she saw the colour of Lynda Clarke's skin, her scepticism about Baxter's motivations felt justified.

A few minutes later, she felt like she'd started a very slow-moving train that couldn't be stopped. Lynda was in the kitchen making them both a pot of tea that Paulsen hadn't asked for. Not just any pot of tea either – leaves were being chosen while the best china was laid out alongside an assortment of home-made cakes and slices. Paulsen had initially waited in the living room, but aware she didn't have time for this, she'd now joined Lynda in the kitchen. The old woman was standing impatiently by her kettle, and Paulsen avoided the obvious gag about a watched pot.

'I just want to say how very sad I am about what happened to that young woman. I used to see her around with her little boy. She seemed such a pleasant young thing,' said Lynda.

The kettle finally finished boiling and Paulsen watched with mounting concern as the old lady lifted it with shaky hands and filled a teapot to the brim. She popped a lid on it and pointed sternly at an ornate wall clock.

'Brewing time is four minutes exactly,' she said. 'Now, how can I help you? As I told one of your colleagues earlier, I was in bed and out for the count by nine o'clock last night. You could have had a marching band parade down the street and I wouldn't have heard a thing.'

She produced a wide, unexpected smile.

'It's actually your son I wanted to ask about,' said Paulsen.

'Then talk to him for yourself. He's out working right now but he'll be back later this afternoon.' Lynda's eyes were suddenly bright and wary, the earlier friendly warmth dissipating. 'You should know first that there are people on this street who have an agenda against my boy. What he did is a matter of record. You can find out about it easily enough, I'm sure. But he's served his time and that should be the end of it.'

'I'd prefer to hear it from you? Get the truth of things . . .' Paulsen smiled reassuringly, but it cut no ice.

'And I'd prefer not to talk about it. It's in the past and that's where it should stay,' said Lynda, crossing her arms. Paulsen nodded but there was simply no time to dance around anything.

'I have to ask you – for the record . . . where was Patrick last night?'

'Out.'

'Out where?'

'I don't know.'

There was a sharpness to the tone now, a firmness in her expression too. The tea leaves hadn't steeped for the full four minutes yet, but Paulsen was already pretty certain she'd outstayed her welcome.

It was interesting how much a face told you, thought Finn. Jill Nicholls hadn't been crying for her daughter on the journey down from Newcastle. But as he knew only too well himself, sometimes the tears don't actually come until much later. A lightly built woman in her late fifties with dark greying hair, she showed no emotion at all as he introduced himself. He briefly remembered the call he'd received telling him of Karin's death, his own polite thanks to the doctor on the end of the phone for informing him. He could still hear the unnatural calm of his own voice, understood exactly the nature of the dignified façade this woman was projecting.

Lily Nicholls was a whole different story. Unlike her mother, she'd clearly done nothing but cry for the entire journey down. She couldn't have been much younger than Sadie, perhaps in her early twenties. She had long, bleached blonde hair, but the same slightly feline quality around her eyes that he recognised from Sadie's pictures. There was a softer quality about her too. Sadie had been older and was a mother, fighting every day to keep her head above water. Life hadn't done anything to Lily yet, at least not until this morning.

Finn led them through to Cedar House's specialist victim interview suite. As its name suggested, it was a softer, quieter space than one of the building's standard interview rooms.

'Just be honest with us – how likely is it that Liam is still alive?' said Lily before they'd even sat down.

'We're very much working on the premise that he is,' said Finn genuinely. His answer didn't bring her any comfort and he knew why. Both the options confronting them were grim – if Liam was still alive, then you didn't want to think too hard about what was happening to him right now.

'Do you have anything – anything at all?' said Jill bluntly. Finn met the question head-on.

'No. That's why it's good that you're here. I've got a lot of questions about Sadie, if that's okay? The more you can tell me, the more it will help us.'

Jill nodded briskly. She filled him in on the basics – Sadie had wanted to be a dancer originally. A passion from childhood that she'd hoped to make a career out of. For a time, while she'd worked at a coffee shop in Borough, she'd been genuinely happy. There were just enough introductions and auditions happening to keep the dream alive, until Harry came along, followed by Liam and the virus. The three nails in the coffin lid of her ambitions. Finn wondered how long it had actually been since Sadie last danced. A while, he guessed.

'Do you know if she'd been seeing anyone?' he asked.

Jill instinctively looked at Lily, who shrugged helplessly.

'There was somebody recently. But she told me nothing about him – not even a name. It didn't last very long. I'm not sure they even . . .'

'Did she tell you what he did? Where he lived? Any detail at all?' said Finn.

Lily shook her head.

'I'm sorry. She was very cagey about it.'

'Did she have any enemies you were aware of?'

'No,' said Lily. 'She never really fell out with people.'

Harry Boxall's words came back to Finn. '*She was just sunshine.*'

'Can you think of anything out of the ordinary or unusual she mentioned recently? Someone bothering her, perhaps, or maybe hanging around outside?'

Lily looked like she was carrying the weight of the world, while Jill simply shook her head.

'No, her world was pretty small – it was just Liam. It was always just Liam,' said Lily.

And that's when Jill Nicholls finally lost control. She let out a small cry and put her hand to her mouth. As Finn struggled to find the words, Lily leant across and held her mother in a silent embrace. The detective glanced at his watch. It was now almost 4.30 p.m.

'There's something else I need to ask you both . . .' he said.

★　　★　　★

Paulsen was walking back to her car when she saw Abigail and Tom Daws walking up the street with Ronnie Fordyce. Even the trio's silhouette made her catch her breath. It was too close to home; the subtle concerned body language two of them were showing for the third.

'I'm sorry about Al earlier,' said Ronnie as they approached. 'He's a bit of a dinosaur. He means well but some of his views are a bit . . .'

He seemed to be struggling to find the right adjective and Paulsen was in no mood to help him. Watching white people defend racism wasn't one of her favourite pastimes. Abi seemed to read her expression.

'Ron . . . you're very welcome to stay for a brew if you fancy one,' she said. He didn't seem to catch on.

'She wants to chat to the policewoman alone, you daft twat,' said Tom. Understanding spread across Fordyce's face.

'Sure, of course. Come on then, Tommy Boy – let's get back and put the kettle on, mate.' Abi waited as the two men ambled up the street together.

'Sometimes I wonder which one of them has actually got the illness,' she said. 'I hope you don't mind me mentioning it – but Ronnie told me about your dad earlier. I'm so sorry. How far advanced is it?'

Paulsen frowned instinctively.

'I'm sorry,' said Abi immediately. 'I didn't mean to pry.'

Paulsen checked herself. For all her natural defensiveness, there was something undeniably reassuring about meeting someone in the same predicament.

'It's okay,' she said brusquely. 'About the same stage as your dad, I'd say. It's tiring, isn't it? The worry . . .'

'Yeah. I don't have any kids, but I guess this is what it must be like. I can't take my eyes off him.'

'I know what you mean,' said Paulsen, slowly nodding.

They were both watching as Ronnie stood patiently outside Abi's front door, while Tom fumbled for his door keys.

'I don't know how you do it alone. You've got no one to help you with him. That must be hard?'

Abi gave a resigned nod.

'I can't pretend it isn't. But my brother's coming over to visit in a few weeks – he lives in Australia. I'm hoping I might talk him into coming back permanently once he sees what Dad's like. That would really make a difference.'

'Having good neighbours must help though?' said Paulsen.

Abi smiled.

'Definitely. Ron's a good friend. He gets Dad out of the house too. I don't drive, so he's a godsend in that sense.' Up the street, the two men were finally shuffling into the house. 'Look – what I wanted to say is you're very welcome to come round for a cup of tea sometime. If you just want to chat about things.'

There was a hopeful look on her face as if she was apprehensive about asking.

'I don't really have time at the moment,' Paulsen said immediately, then felt bad as she saw the hurt in the other woman's eyes. 'But maybe later, when the investigation's calmed down a bit,' she added clumsily. She fumbled in her bag for her card. 'If you need to call me though – this is my number.'

Abi brightened and took the card. As she handed it over, out of the corner of her eye Paulsen saw a brief flicker of movement at a window on one of the houses opposite. She could see a wiry middle-aged man peering down at them.

'Who's that?' she said, and Abi wheeled around to look.

'I don't really know him – he's new,' she said. 'Only moved in recently. His name's Nathan, I think. Lives there on his own.'

'When did he move in?'

'A couple of months ago, maybe? We've barely seen him – he doesn't seem to like mixing.'

The man's expression was unreadable and he quickly disappeared back behind his curtains as he saw them both looking up. Mentally, Paulsen made a note – number sixty-four. And it was only as she was driving away and sneaked another glance that she saw he was back, and briefly they caught each other's gaze again.

II

'It's not too late to stop this. It's never too late to do the right thing. Please – if you've got my grandson, let him go – we love him very much and we just want to take him home.'

Jill Nicholls looked around the Cedar House press room slowly and deliberately as the cameras trained on her. Finn was sitting between her and Lily, the blue branding of the Metropolitan Police emblazoned on large boards behind them.

Around twenty rapidly mobilised journalists were there. Television cameramen were standing at the back and sides, and a clutch of recording devices was scattered on the table in front. Finn couldn't remember too many people handling this situation as coolly as Jill was. She'd understood the importance of using the media and had been firm, clear and concise with her language – not for her the role of teary-eyed victim.

The story was quickly gaining traction – already the reporting was referring to Sadie and Liam by their first names as if everyone was automatically familiar with who they were. Jill and Lily had jointly selected the photograph that had been provided to the various outlets. Mother and son together, beaming in the sunshine, the slight hint of a shared secret in their smiles. It was the image that would appear countless times on screens and pages in the months ahead. To the day when hopefully a judge would deliver a verdict and all of this would become past tense.

The queries when they came were brief. With such a paucity of information, there was little that could be asked. The purpose of this press conference wasn't to answer questions but to ask them instead. To appeal for information and potential witnesses, to plant that photograph in the public consciousness, and hopefully put pressure on one very specific individual.

Lily remained largely wan and silent, speaking only to briefly describe what kind of person her sister had been. It was when Jill spoke that Finn felt a genuine energy spreading around the room. As if by injecting force into each syllable, she could exert an actual physical pressure on her daughter's killer.

'Are you certain Liam's been abducted?' someone asked.

'I can't say anything definitively at this point,' Finn replied. He stared up at yet another accusing wall clock. 'But it's been roughly eighteen hours since we believe he went missing and there's been no sign of him since. In our judgement, if he wasn't taken, then it's highly likely he'd have been found by now. Either way, we're making this appeal in the hope someone might have seen something.'

Finn talked through what they thought Liam might be wearing, thanks to a description the babysitter Chloe Ashton had given them. He made short work of the follow-up questions before bringing things to a halt. There was no need to sustain this any longer than necessary. Jill and Lily watched, almost forgotten, as the cameramen packed their equipment away and the room dispersed. Jill suddenly turned to Finn – the same clarity in her voice as when she'd been speaking to the cameras a few minutes earlier.

'I need to go there. I want to see for myself where my daughter died.'

Finn gathered his team together in the incident room afterwards. Jill and Lily were being checked into a local hotel – he'd agreed to Jill's request, but for the moment, the task of finding Liam remained the immediate priority. Paulsen had now returned and was sharing what she'd discovered.

'How come we didn't know a violent ex-con was living five minutes away? Surely someone knocked on this guy's door earlier?' said Sami Dattani. Paulsen stared daggers at him.

'What – you thought he'd just volunteer that up?'

'What are the details, Mattie?' said Ojo. Paulsen looked down at a sheaf of paperwork she was holding.

'A woman called Cassie Wilcox was attacked in the street as she was walking home . . .' she frowned at the document for a moment, 'on the night of April 9th 2014. She was badly beaten and suffered a serious head injury. It was Clarke who called the police and LAS. When they got there, Wilcox was conscious and accused him of attacking her.'

'Why?' said Finn.

'He never said under interview, though he accepted responsibility for the attack. Wilcox made a full recovery but then refused to make a formal allegation against him. The CPS decided they had enough to go with and that it was in the public interest. In court, Clarke pleaded guilty to GBH.'

'What did they think was the motive?'

'Never established, though it looks like the investigating officers thought it was a robbery.'

Finn and Ojo exchanged a glance.

'An attempted robbery – and yet the suspect called the emergency services and the victim didn't want to push it? Something already smells off,' said Ojo.

'How long did he get?' said Finn.

'Seven years – he was only released just before Christmas. And for what it's worth, he was out last night, but his mother doesn't know where.'

'He hasn't come up as a match with any of the fingerprints we've found in Sadie's flat,' said Finn. 'But that doesn't mean anything. Let's pull him in for a chat – find out where he was yesterday evening.'

Paulsen nodded.

'Did you find anything on Sadie's hard drive, guv?' asked Ojo and Finn ran through some of the scraps he'd picked up from the email he'd read.

'The family don't know anything about this mystery man she was seeing – but I'd like to find him. Let's get uniform to talk to some of her neighbours again – see if they saw her with anyone, and better still if they can give us a description of him.' He gathered his thoughts for a moment. 'The biggest picture that's building for me is of Sadie's financial problems – she told her sister she reckoned she only had enough money for two more months of rent, and bearing in mind how low her rent was—'

Paulsen cut in.

'She was definitely struggling. I found the loan shark she borrowed from. His name's Alan Baxter; he's the landlord of that shitty pub at the end of the road. He's low life – trust me, I saw that for myself first-hand. He claims he was fond of Sadie and lent her three hundred quid as a favour.'

'*Fond* – is that a euphemism for something?' said Dattani.

'I doubt it,' said Paulsen darkly. 'Unless her taste in men was for bald old racists.'

'It wasn't,' said Finn, remembering Harry Boxall's chiselled good looks.

'Does Baxter have an alibi?' said Ojo.

Paulsen nodded.

'He was in the pub all night – corroborated by some of the regulars.'

'Doesn't mean someone didn't act on his behalf,' said Ojo. 'Wouldn't be a loan shark without some muscle.'

Finn nodded in agreement.

'Maybe it was a bit more than three hundred quid he lent her too. There's still quite a bit we don't know about her finances – it looks like she was getting some cash-in-hand work at a local cafe. Dave's trying to find out which one it was.'

'Is the Knights Association dinner still something we're looking at?' said Sami. 'I've just seen something about it online – there have been more allegations.'

Finn hadn't been asked about it at the press conference and assumed the media had yet to make the connection with the other big news story of the day.

'Any of those reports you've been reading mention Sadie?' he said.

Dattani shook his head.

'Good,' replied Finn. 'At the moment it looks like there isn't a link – Mattie, have you got any more on that?'

'Yes – we've got the cell site analysis back on Sadie's phone from last night. She came straight home without any deviation. It pretty much fits the timeline we mapped out . . .' She stopped, troubled for a moment. 'There is just one thing from the hotel – I got an email a few minutes ago from the PC I spoke to before – Dave's *mate*.' She said the word 'mate' as if it smelt. Ojo arched an eyebrow. 'Don't go there,' said Paulsen. 'Anyway – one of the chefs thought he saw her arguing with someone just before she left.'

'One of the chefs?' said Ojo.

'Yes – he'd gone to take a leak, and reckoned he saw her in the corridor with a guest.'

'Did he give a description of this guy?' said Finn.

'No, only saw him from behind so didn't see the face. He wasn't even sure it was a row – just said Sadie looked upset.'

'Maybe this bloke just wanted another drink while she was on her way out?' said Dattani.

Paulsen shrugged and Finn weighed it up for a second.

'I asked Nishat to go through the call list on her phone.' He motioned at a female DC sitting on the other side of the office. 'Sami – why don't you see how far she's got with that – I'd like to know who Sadie's been talking to over the last few weeks. Maybe she knew one of the guests from elsewhere? There might also be something to help us identify this man she was seeing.'

Dattani nodded. Paulsen looked hesitant for a moment, as if she wanted to add something.

'Something else?' said Finn.

'Yes. There's a guy at number sixty-four – apparently, he's just moved in. Abi said no one seems to know much about him. Middle-aged, lives on his own, doesn't like to mix.'

Finn bristled slightly.

'So? There's nothing wrong with that.'

There was the briefest of awkward silences before Paulsen continued.

'His name's Nathan Roach. He was watching out of his window when I left. I know half the street's been doing that, but there was something a bit furtive about it. I checked with uniform – they spoke to him earlier when they were doing the door-to-doors and he told them he was in watching TV last night, which is obviously uncorroborated.'

'Any particular reason you're singling him out?' said Finn.

'Nothing specific, and uniform saw nothing suspicious, but I think he's worth a look into. He seemed quite jittery when he saw me.'

Finn nodded, looked around the room briskly.

'I'm formally calling this an abduction now. Forensics say the blood smear patterns inside the flat suggest someone moving. As they're certain Sadie fell where she died, that's either the child or the killer. So, given the time that's elapsed,

I think it's safe to assume Liam didn't wander off, and it also suggests he may well have been hurt.'

There was a sober silence in the room. They had plenty of leads, but nothing that was promising an imminent break-through. 'Let's use that to focus our minds,' said Finn. 'Any more for any more?' he said, looking around the room.

'What about the historical murder, guv?' said Ojo. 'Are we still interested in that?'

Finn nodded.

'Definitely. But I want something more substantial to work with before we start trying to make a connection. Have you found anything useful?'

Ojo looked non-committal.

'I've been looking at the guy who got convicted for it – Dean Rawton. He pleaded not guilty at the time and was adamant they'd got the wrong man. He launched an appeal, lost it, then went very quiet. He's never tried to appeal it again.'

'You think it was potentially an unsafe conviction?' said Finn.

Ojo spread her hands.

'I don't know – maybe he simply accepted things once he was inside because he knew he was guilty. But if there's any chance it *was* unsafe . . .'

One of the desk phones rang and Paulsen turned to grab it.

'Go through it with a fine-tooth comb,' said Finn. 'It was almost thirty years ago—'

Before he could continue, Paulsen interrupted.

'That was the front desk – it's Patrick Clarke. He's down-stairs – says he wants to talk to whoever's leading the investigation . . .'

12

'I haven't killed anyone. Not back then. And not last night.'

In his early thirties and wearing a smart blue checked shirt and chinos, Patrick Clarke looked more like a lawyer or a teacher than a gardener, Paulsen thought. When he spoke, it was softly but with a definite authority too, and above all, there was a stillness to him. There was something strangely compelling about the whole package that drew your attention.

They were sitting in one of the station's interview rooms, and he'd made a point of giving his attention to both Finn and Paulsen while they talked, as if trying to build a rapport at a job interview.

'No one's saying you've killed anyone,' said Finn.

'No – but I know one or two people have been airing their views.' He looked at Paulsen meaningfully. 'In the circumstances, I don't blame you for having a few questions. I just don't want my mum troubled. As you saw for yourself, she's old and quite frail. I thought it might be easier for me to come here and talk to you in person.'

His directness seemed to take them both by surprise and he smiled politely.

'So, in that spirit – what would you like to know?'

'If you'd like to tell us where you were last night – that would be a good start,' said Finn.

'Sure. Someone I know was struggling with a personal issue. He needed a friend, so we went for a quiet chat.'

'Where did you go?' said Paulsen.

'Somewhere private.'

Finn and Paulsen exchanged a glance.

'Does this friend have a name?' said Finn.

'Yes, but I'm not going to give it to you. Like I said – it was a personal matter.'

'It's a bit strange to come in and say you want to answer our questions and then withhold information. It's also not much of an alibi if it can't be stood up,' said Finn. He said the words without exasperation, matching Clarke's own even and courteous tone.

'It's also the truth. And I'm not a suspect, am I? So that's as good as I can give you, I'm afraid.'

He sat back and crossed his arms. There was nothing confrontational about his body language – if anything, it seemed scrupulously mannered, like a waiter apologetic that the dish of the day was off.

'Okay,' said Paulsen. 'Do you mind if we ask about your previous conviction?'

'You can ask . . .'

'Do you want to tell us what happened – in your words?'

'I assume you've looked it up on your computer?'

Finn nodded.

'That's the point – no one really knows what took place that night other than you pleaded guilty.'

'I've never talked about the details of it. And out of respect to the victim, I'm not going to start now. But I'll say this – I attacked her and I meant to hurt her badly. I pleaded guilty because I *am* guilty.'

Paulsen was starting to get vaguely irritated now. A slight sense he was taking the piss rather than cooperating with them.

'When you say "out of respect to the victim" – what does

that actually *mean*? This conversation is completely off the record. You're not under arrest,' she said.

He looked her bolt in the eye.

'It means exactly what it means. Out of *respect*. I have never talked about it, and I never will. But please understand, justice was done.'

'I looked through your prison record earlier – you were a model inmate by all accounts,' she said. Something flickered behind his eyes, but she couldn't work out what. She could see by the look on Finn's face that he was as fascinated as she was.

'That's right. I've done my time, and now I just want to rebuild my life, look after my mum and earn a living. That's it.'

Finn smiled pleasantly at him.

'Did you know Sadie Nicholls?' he said.

'Yes,' said Patrick. 'I mended her gate a few weeks back. She was friendly. Seemed genuine too. When you've been inside . . .' He faltered for a moment. 'Well, it's nice when you meet someone like that, isn't it? And afterwards, she always made a point of saying hello when she saw me in the street.'

'That was the extent of it though? We won't find phone calls or texts and emails – anything like that?'

Paulsen was pretty sure Finn was now trying to provoke a reaction. To see if he *could* provoke a reaction.

'No, and that's the truth. If you don't believe me, I'd understand, given my past. You're very welcome to search my home if that's what you need to do – I've nothing to hide.'

He settled back into his seat and Paulsen briefly saw something in his expression that just might have been sadness.

'That was plain weird,' she said to Finn as they walked back up to the incident room afterwards. 'He's lying about something. I don't know what – but my every instinct says he is.'

'I don't know about lying,' said Finn. 'But he's certainly holding something back. If he killed Sadie and abducted Liam, why come in and give us that performance?'

'A double bluff maybe? To put us off the scent?'

'Possibly, but I think he was just trying to make sure we didn't fold him into this because of his past – which is understandable. Let's get a warrant to search his address though. We'd look pretty stupid if he did turn out to be the killer and we hadn't investigated him thoroughly.'

Paulsen nodded and pushed open the doors to the incident room. Sami Dattani was on his feet before they were halfway through.

'Guv – I think I've got something. I've been going through Sadie's call list. There was one number that kept recurring over the last few weeks. I found a name easily enough – a guy called David Hermitage.'

Finn frowned. He'd seen or heard that name somewhere else today.

'If it seems familiar it's because he lives several doors up from Sadie – at number fifty-two. I did a bit of digging into him – turns out he's the deputy chief executive of the Fight Hunger Foundation.'

Finn made the connection immediately.

'That's a charity – is it part of the Knights Association?'

'Yes, and I cross-checked him with the list of guests Mattie was sent – he was at the Royal Grand last night.'

Suddenly it felt like a jigsaw piece falling into place. Nothing to help illustrate the wider picture perhaps, but significant all the same. Was this the mystery man Sadie had been seeing?

'Do we know where he is right now?'

'At his office. I've already put a call in – he's expecting a visit . . .'

The Fight Hunger Foundation occupied the fourth floor of a tower block close to Millbank. By the time Finn arrived, most of Hermitage's colleagues had already left for the day. Driving through the evening rush hour, it wasn't hard to see that the events at the gala dinner were starting to take on a wider prominence. Finn's day had been so completely occupied by Sadie and Liam Nicholls that everything else had become extraneous noise. But now he was beginning to get a sense of it for himself. Radio news bulletins were reporting on it and the late edition of the *London Evening Standard* had splashed its lead with *'Police investigate scandal-hit charity dinner'*.

Finn could guess well enough what sort of night it had been. He'd investigated a few black-tie occasions over the years that had got out of hand – nothing quite like this by all accounts, but enough to know how it might have played out. For some men, a tuxedo was a form of fancy dress, nothing more than an excuse to behave in a way they'd never dream of doing in any other context. It confirmed a deeply held suspicion of his that the more important the man, the bigger the child within. After all, just look at Donald Trump. It was also a truth he'd observed that you generally never saw the same issue with high-profile women.

Hermitage met him by the lift, and it was clear he wasn't having the best of days. He was jittery and his voice hollow as he tried to force some pleasantries. Sensibly Dattani had only mentioned the charity dinner as the reason for the police interest, and that gave Finn a chance to read the man's reactions before they even began talking. He looked pale, with bloodshot eyes, and his smile as they shook hands was disingenuous. Finn didn't return it, and let Hermitage make some awkward small talk as they walked to his office.

'Can I get you a tea or coffee – there's quite a decent machine in the main office?' he said and Finn declined. Hermitage sat down and smiled uncomfortably.

'I just want to say from the off that the Fight Hunger Foundation utterly deplores what took place last night. I was sat with a group of our trustees and I can tell you we were all appalled at what we were seeing.'

'I'll come on to that – I'd actually like to ask you about Sadie Nicholls first,' said Finn. Hermitage's eyes didn't quite widen into saucers – though figuratively speaking they might as well have done. Bingo, thought Finn.

'I see,' said Hermitage, at least not pretending not to know who she was or why Finn might be asking about her. 'It's terrible what's happened. Just awful.'

For all Finn knew, this man was a kind, principled individual, who'd played no part in what happened either to Sadie or the sordid nonsense at the hotel, but for whatever reason he felt no great urge to make the man feel comfortable.

'I know one of my uniformed colleagues spoke to you this morning. Can I ask why you didn't mention to her that you were at the same event as Sadie last night?'

Again, the same startled rabbit expression. Hermitage wiped a stray strand of hair from above his eyebrow.

'I simply didn't think it was relevant. I mean, whatever happened to Sadie clearly occurred after she got home, didn't it?'

'It's a murder inquiry, Mr Hermitage. Every piece of information, every connection matters.'

Hermitage nodded and swallowed.

'Can you tell me exactly what your relationship with Sadie was?' said Finn.

'Obviously, I knew her. You'll know how close she lived to me. I overheard her talking to someone in the street a few weeks ago, and got a sense that she could use some extra money. I happen to know the agency who recruits for the gala dinner every year, so I put her in touch with them. A good deed, that's all.'

A bead of sweat was forming on his forehead. Good deed, my arse, thought Finn, again perhaps rather unfairly.

'We've been through her phone records – your number's come up a lot.'

'Well, it would – we went back and forth a bit about the job. She had questions about it, that sort of thing.'

'Which she asked you, not the agency who hired her?'

'Yes . . . I mean, because she knew me, I suppose.' He sighed, and when he spoke next, there was a genuine sadness in his voice. 'I'm devastated by what's happened. She was a bubbly, sweet thing, she really was.'

Thing, Finn noted.

'And there was nothing more between you?'

Hermitage looked shocked – or at least, did a decent job of affecting it.

'God, no. I've a wife and daughter who I love very much. I would never . . . I mean . . .'

Finn nodded politely.

'Did you have any idea what was going to happen at the dinner last night?'

'No – as I say, it was disgraceful.'

'But you've been to this event before. You're saying this was the first time you've seen it get out of hand?'

Hermitage floundered, and at that point, Finn knew he was lying, knew this *had* happened before. Effectively, he'd procured a job for Sadie knowing full well what kind of night it was going to be.

'No,' he replied weakly.

'We have a witness who says they saw Sadie arguing with someone before she left. Do you know what that was about?'

Hermitage fidgeted, tugged nervously at his sleeve.

'I wouldn't call it an argument. It wasn't serious. She was upset by what was going on and I didn't want her to go – I knew how much she needed the money. I was just trying to persuade her to see it out.'

'So it was you she was talking to?'

His face fell and he nodded in confirmation.

'And what time did you leave?'

'Around eleven.' There was a delayed reaction as the implication of the question sank in. 'You don't think I had something to do with her death? That's insane . . .'

'Can you tell me where you've been today?'

There was genuine outrage on his face now.

'At home this morning – then I caught the train to work. And I've been here all day, so I hope—'

Finn stood abruptly, cutting him off, not interested in hearing it. He'd got as much as he needed, and smiled curtly.

'Thank you, you've been very helpful.'

Hermitage waited for Finn to clear the building before pulling on his coat. He looked at the cuts on his wrist, still sore and contributing to the general feeling of nausea that just wouldn't leave him. He'd handled the conversation well enough, he thought, even if he'd been economical with the truth. The woman who'd rung earlier threatening him hadn't been in touch again, and strangely enough, that was one problem he was less concerned about now. He'd explained his relationship with Sadie to the police – so whoever she was, what could she do? It had to be one of the other hostesses chancing their arm, surely?

He started walking to the lift, his thoughts turning to the evening ahead. He'd need to find a way to calm himself down before he got home. There'd undoubtedly be more questions about the previous night from Emily later. He flashed back to his conversation with Sadie in the hotel corridor. The fury in her voice, the sharp pain of her nails digging into his flesh. The contents of his stomach suddenly began to rise and he just about made it to the nearest wastepaper bin in time as it surged up and out. He knelt, staring at the vomit dripping off his chin on to the carpet, and realised he was kidding himself. This wasn't over – not by a long chalk.

Finn felt guilty as he drove back to Cedar House. Hermitage was probably exactly who he appeared to be: a decent man who worked for a charitable organisation who'd tried to help a neighbour. Finn would get someone to cross-check what time the man left the hotel last night, but the likelihood was that he was telling the truth. He sighed and looked at the dashboard clock – it was now almost 7 p.m. Twenty-one hours or so since Sadie was killed and Liam went missing. It was weird, he thought – but it was in these moments he missed Karin the most. Strange, too, how his bereavement sapped gently at his self-confidence.

'*My boy's still out there . . .*' he heard an unfamiliar voice say. It took him by surprise and a brief moment to place it. '*. . . and all you can do is feel sorry for yourself,*' said Sadie.

13

Roughly twenty-four hours after the murder, DC Dave McElligott walked into the incident room carrying a tower of pizza boxes. Just about everyone was still there and no one was in a rush to leave. The fate of Liam Nicholls made it difficult. It would be hard to switch off when they eventually did head for their homes. Finn knew the emotions all too well. Psychologically they needed a breakthrough, however small.

'What do you want, guv? There's a couple of meat feasts, two Hawaiians, and some margheritas . . .' said McElligott.

Finn flipped open the lid of the nearest box, peered at the congealing mass inside and closed it again. Paulsen came over to join them. McElligott thought about offering her a pizza, saw her expression, decided against the idea and left them to it.

'You got something, Mattie?' said Finn.

'Not really. But I thought you'd want to know – we've obtained a warrant to search Patrick Clarke's house tomorrow morning. I've just rung to let him know.'

'How did he take it?'

'Politely.'

Finn couldn't help a wry smile. Clarke had stayed with him since their conversation earlier. It was hard to identify what, but something wasn't quite right. There was a story there for sure, but whether it was pertinent to this investigation was a moot point.

'How was the guy you went to see – Hermitage?' asked Paulsen.

'Sweaty little sod. He was bricking himself about the gala dinner. Claimed to be horrified and disgusted by it all.'

Paulsen scowled.

'Yes – I bet there's a few who've been saying that today,' she said.

'I don't think he's our killer – his movements since the murder make it unlikely, though not impossible.' Finn took a moment to focus his tired brain. 'My biggest fear right now is that this is a stranger attack. We've all been assuming Sadie knew this man.'

'Or woman,' said Paulsen, and Finn took her point. He'd made that mistake before and it didn't hurt to interrogate your own assumptions. But if this was a stranger, he didn't want to think what their chances of finding Liam would realistically be.

'So what do you want to do?' said Paulsen.

Finn looked around the room. Sami Dattani was talking to Dave McElligott, both of them wolfing down slices of tepid pizza. Jackie Ojo was at her desk, studying the crime scene photographs intently. The rest of the team, going through the minutiae of one young woman's life. They all looked dog-tired, and he was tempted to send them home but resisted the urge.

'Come on – let's see where we're at before we call it a night.'

He stood in the middle of the room and gathered them together. One by one they went through what they'd been doing – McElligott had identified the cafe where Sadie had been working and spoken to its owner. She'd more or less confirmed the details in the email Finn had read earlier. Cash-in-hand work, no questions asked – but no customers who'd shown an obvious and unhealthy interest in her.

In the wake of the conversation with Clarke, Dattani had done some more detailed background checks on the other residents of Pennington Road.

'Patrick's not the only one with a colourful history. Ronnie Fordyce has got some form as well. He was done twice for assault in the late 1970s. From what I can tell, he wasn't the nicest guy in the world back then. "A poor man's Ronnie Kray", the judge called him.'

'Anything since?' said Finn.

'No – he must have mellowed with age.'

'And he's got an alibi,' said Paulsen. 'He was in the Lamb's Head all evening with Tom Daws.'

Dattani glanced down at some paperwork.

'I also looked at that guy at number sixty-four you mentioned, Mattie. Nathan Roach. He sold a property in Bromsgrove a couple of months ago to move down here. According to the electoral register, he shared it with a wife and two kids. Looks like his marriage must have gone tits up. No previous convictions though.'

'That probably explains why he's a bit of a recluse then,' said Paulsen.

'Nothing else flagged up close by,' said Dattani.

Finn saw Ojo frowning at something she was looking at. He knew that look.

'What is it, Jacks? Found anything more in those historical murders?'

She shook her head with tired frustration.

'I don't know – maybe it's just me, but I want you guys to have a look at something.'

She opened up a brown file, pulled out an A4-sized print and held it up.

'This is the crime scene from 1993 – and that's the body of the victim, Vicki Stratford.'

A woman in a white top with long black hair was lying on the floor, dark patches of blood pooled on either side of her. Her forehead was split open, and an eyeball jutted out of its socket as if barely held in place. Ojo produced another photograph, this time a print of the current crime scene. For an instant Finn felt a stab of something as he saw Sadie's broken skull again, the bone poking through bloodied dark hair.

'What are we supposed to be looking at, sarge?' said McElligott. 'It's two dead bodies on the floor, isn't it?'

'Look at Vicki – the way she's lying, her arms straight by her side,' said Ojo.

Finn recalled his initial reaction when he'd seen Sadie in the flat that morning. That slight suspicion that it didn't look quite natural.

'You think Sadie was posed the same way?' he said.

Ojo looked defeated.

'I don't know – that's what I'm not sure of. I've been looking at these two pictures for the last half hour and I still can't make up my mind.'

'I'm with Dave,' said Sami. 'It's just how they've fallen. It's not like they're identical – it just looks a bit similar.'

'Maybe,' said Finn. He looked again and shook his head. 'Or maybe not . . .'

'If we're going to compare . . .' said Paulsen, 'and the inference is this is a copycat – why would the same person kill Vicki Stratford's son, but abduct Sadie's?'

Ojo shrugged helplessly.

'I didn't say I had all the answers . . .'

'But if you're suggesting it's the same killer following a pattern – then they're not, are they?' said Paulsen.

'What do you reckon then, Mattie? You tell me what you see,' said Ojo, holding up the photos again. Paulsen stared closely at them for a moment, then shook her head, unsure.

'It could be deliberate – it could also be pure coincidence.'

The room fell silent. Their brains had reached saturation point, thought Finn, and so had his.

'We're all too tired to see the wood for the trees. Get some rest and we'll come back at this fresh again tomorrow,' he said.

There were some tired nods of resignation, and Finn felt his stomach rumble as his nostrils picked up the scent of cold pizza. As his team drifted back to their desks, he returned to his own and gathered up the scattered mess of paperwork into a sheaf. The external drive was still attached to his PC and on a whim, he unplugged it and stuffed it into his backpack.

14

Mattie Paulsen walked through her front door, kicked off her shoes and headed straight for the fridge.

'Please tell me there's beer,' she said, without looking at Nancy, who was sitting on the sofa watching TV. Paulsen opened the fridge door, looked at the selection of colourful tins at the back and randomly selected one. She examined it suspiciously.

'What the fuck is mango-flavoured beer?'

'It's the one I told you about on Sunday. The one from the microbrewery who won all the awards? You said it sounded nice . . .'

Paulsen could barely remember what she'd had for breakfast, let alone a conversation from the weekend. She shrugged, opened the can and took some deep swigs. It was cold, fruity and hit the right notes.

'Long day?' said Nancy, as Mattie came over to join her.

'I've had better.'

She explained how it had unfolded, and Nancy turned the TV off.

'It sounds horrible. That poor little boy.'

'He's not dead yet,' said Paulsen with a conviction she didn't feel. She felt like talking though, which was unusual for her. Normally at this point, she was keener on having a hot shower, cleaning the day away, and getting in as much sleep as she could. But tonight felt different.

'It's more than just the victims, Nance.'

She told her about the connection to the Knights Association dinner, and that Sadie had left in disgust before the end.

'I read about it in the *Standard* on my way home from work. Honestly, one day I'd like to go to an event like that, I really would,' said Nancy.

'You would?'

'Yeah – because I'd fork in the balls the first fat fuck who tried that shit on me and then we'd see how brave *he* was feeling.'

Something about Nancy's deadpan contempt combined with the alliteration made Paulsen laugh out loud.

'Thanks – I needed that,' she said, and meant it. Then her smile began to fade and she told her about Tom Daws.

By the time he arrived at his small one-bedroom flat near Wandsworth Common, Finn knew there'd be little point going straight to bed. His brain was still overheated and ticking, like a car engine after a long journey. He made himself a bacon sandwich and ate it with an accompanying glass of single malt before collapsing in a heap on his sofa. Instinctively he looked straight up at the framed photograph of Karin on the mantelpiece. He deliberately confined himself to just the one picture of her on display in his home. He didn't want a shrine there, preferring instead a single image which he would refresh every few weeks or so.

This one was from a holiday in Tuscany. Her face was healthy and brown, a million miles away from the ghastly white pallor of her final days in a hospice. It contained just a hint of that knowing smile he'd found reassuring, and simultaneously so sexy as well.

'Miss you,' he said out loud, waiting for an answer that didn't come. He took another sip of whisky and looked around the room restlessly. The way Sadie had spoken to him as he'd driven back from the Fight Hunger Foundation had unsettled him. He hadn't had time to really process it until now and he wasn't sure what he made of it. The central heating was starting to warm the place up but he felt cold and shivered. What was his tortured psyche doing to him now? He should go to bed, he thought. *Should.*

Heaving himself to his feet, he picked up his backpack from where he'd slung it and walked over to a large rustic oak desk in the corner of the room. He fished inside the bag, pulled out the hard drive and plugged it into a battered laptop. Powering the machine up, he waited as the folders displaying Sadie's collated electronic life displayed on the screen.

For the next hour, he took a deep dive into it, watching video after video, clicking through hundreds of photos. He read her emails and listened to her voice, playing the same clips back over and over. He'd have liked her in life, he thought. There'd been a spark to this woman, a zest for life that single motherhood, global pandemics and increasing poverty had failed to extinguish. Just about – God knows it was clear those combined pressures had taken their toll on her too. But somehow she'd found a way to ring-fence her essential self and survive. He could see the same quality in Liam too – the same glint in his eye, the same infectious laugh. It was also present in their relationship, like a secret unspoken language between them.

He clicked on a folder marked *WhatsApp*. There was a selection of screenshots, which the digital forensics team had pulled from her phone's SIM card. Most of the conversations were with her sister, general chit-chat mainly, but one exchange in particular caught his eye.

Sadie

I can't come home, Lil. It's not fair on Mam.
Liam's such a handful . . . she couldn't cope
with him. U don't know what it's like. I love
him, but he's almost too much for me
sometimes.   15:26

Lily

I'm worried about you, Sades. You sounded really
bad on the phone the other day. R u ok?   15:27

Sadie

I don't know. It's like the walls are closing in.
Feels like my head's going to explode. I don't
even know how I'm going from breakfast to
lunch sometimes . . .   15:28

Maybe it had got to her in the end, reflected Finn, finally
ground her down. That last sentence hit a nerve with him
because he knew what she was saying only too well. He and
Sadie may have been very different people, but alone in their
flats, that sense of claustrophobia and fear was something they
very much had in common. He slumped back into his chair
and exhaled. He was feeling particularly small and empty. This
wasn't police work he was conducting, no serious attempt to
truly find a clue to this woman's murder. It was simple morbid
curiosity, a fascination directly tied to his own feelings of loss
– and that realisation made him feel even worse.

'Jesus, I'm a mess,' he said softly to himself.

'*Yes, you are,*' came a voice that might have been Sadie's.

'Other people do get Alzheimer's, Mat,' said Nancy carefully.
'You're going to encounter it as you go about your work. I do
all the time.'

Paulsen had no reason to disbelieve her – as a social worker in east London, it was inevitable that Nancy's days were probably filled up with as much sadness as her own frequently was. She felt a sudden flash of guilt that she didn't show anything like the same interest in Nancy's work as her partner showed in hers.

'It's not that, Nance. It was more his daughter – I could see so much of myself in her and it made me feel uncomfortable.'

'Why?'

Mattie Paulsen didn't often talk like this and the room suddenly felt quiet.

'You could see . . .' Paulsen struggled to find the right description. 'Not just sadness . . . but *neediness* there.' She remembered the look on Abi's face as she'd suggested they meet for a cup of tea, how her first instinct had been to reject it.

'You're not needy, Mattie. It's the last thing in the world you ever are.'

'I'm scared about what's coming though,' she said, and for a moment Nancy kept her own counsel.

'Maybe you should talk to this woman. Perhaps it would help? Just saying . . .'

Paulsen thought about it for a moment and suddenly felt very tired.

Finn was now back on the sofa, staring gloomily into space. He wanted to go to bed, but didn't trust himself to fall asleep – there was too much rattling around his head. He looked up again at Karin's photograph for the umpteenth time. Tentatively he picked up his phone and scrolled through some old text messages. He found the one he was looking for and stared at it for a moment.

Call if you're in trouble.

He wasn't a man who by nature found it easy to ask for help. The strong desire to simply sweep his feelings under the carpet bed was there too. He'd be up early tomorrow, booted and suited, ready to go once more. Rinsing and repeating the cycle all over again. It was more his deep-set reluctance to go to bed which finally pushed him into tapping out the message.

Are you up?

For a few seconds – and with some relief – he thought the person he was trying to contact had gone to bed themselves, but then his phone began to ring. He glared at the handset accusingly and immediately got cold feet on the idea. Had he wanted an actual conversation? What *did* he want? His finger decided for him, jabbing out and answering the call.

'Hello, Alex,' said a warm male voice with a Scottish burr.

Murray Saunders was a man Finn had met almost accidentally. An AA counsellor working at a meeting group close to Cedar House, a chance meeting the previous year had developed into a proper friendship. It was an odd one though, given that Finn wasn't an alcoholic. They didn't socialise and rarely met in person, but he was the one person Finn found he could genuinely open up to. He trusted Murray in a way he trusted few others and even he wasn't quite sure how that had come about.

It was as if there needed to be someone in his life he wasn't lying to, someone he was accountable to. It took the edge off his guilt. But even then, there was some hypocrisy to it – Murray listened and offered good, pragmatic advice but Finn rarely took it, which is precisely why he was where he was.

'You don't usually call this late,' said Murray. 'I'd ask what the problem is, but I already know, don't I?' he continued pleasantly. 'Are you in trouble?'

Finn said nothing. And that also was a familiar problem – he had nothing new to say on the subject. Murray picked up on his hesitation.

'I was just about to have a shower and I'm standing stark bollock-naked, so if this is going to be a long one . . .'

'I'm struggling a bit tonight. A new murder investigation started today – there's a missing child too. It's stirred a few things up.'

'Right. I'm gonna need a towel, aren't I?' There was some brief rustling and he returned. Finn talked through his day, what had happened to Sadie, the search for Liam, and the contents of her laptop.

'Aye, well . . . I'm not entirely sure it's a surprise it's affecting you the way it is.'

'It shouldn't. Do you know how many murder investigations I've led?' said Finn.

'Oh, plenty, I'm sure. But that was before you developed a mental health disorder . . .'

'A *what*?' said Finn.

'Okay – I've been talking to a few people about you. Don't worry, no names mentioned. The general consensus is that you're suffering from something called complicated grief. And before you say, "no shit, Sherlock," complicated grief is the name of an actual *thing* – a syndrome. You can Google it when you get off the phone. But here are the bullet points . . .'

Finn sandwiched the phone between his ear and shoulder and went over to pour himself another drink.

'. . . you need to watch your drinking, by the way. It's part of it – and that *is* my field of expertise,' said Murray.

'Bullet points, you said?' said Finn.

'Basically, it's bereavement as addiction. When healing doesn't happen and you become locked in an open state of mourning. Ring any bells?'

'Do you do this piss-taking at AA meetings?' said Finn. 'I'm amazed you've never got hurt.'

'No, oddly. Perhaps because folk there actually listen to me?'

Despite the banter, Finn enjoyed Murray's gentle sarcasm and the honest way he shared the truth. It had created a mutual respect between them, a suspicion too that the dry humour masked a pain of his own.

'Sorry,' said Finn guiltily. 'Go on.'

'Anyhoo – the gist of it is that it's the same area of the brain that affects addicts. But instead of a longing for, say, drink or drugs, in your case, it's for *memories*. You keep going back to the well but with diminishing returns each time you do.'

This was just a bit too close to the bone for Finn. He could feel the room starting to spin.

'Are you okay, Alex?' said Murray, his tone more sympathetic now.

'Yeah. No . . .' said Finn finally. 'So the way I'm feeling is – as you put it – some sort of actual condition?'

'Exactly that. Your intellect and emotions are in conflict. Or put another way – your head knows Karin's gone, but your heart still hasn't caught up with the news. It's that mismatch which is doing the damage.' There was another long silence. 'Self-blame and shame are common symptoms too. Do you ever feel any of those things?'

Finn laughed unexpectedly.

'Where do you want me to begin?' he replied.

Sometime later, when Finn had finally crawled into bed, he lay on his back staring up at the ceiling as the implications of the conversation began to resonate. What Murray had told him was nothing in his heart he didn't already know, but hearing his pain diagnosed and named was still a shock. In the dark, his face creased in pain. He had a mental health condition; he could say that definitively now. If it was a physical problem, he'd go straight to the doctor – so why, to his very core, did he still feel reluctant to act? He turned on his side and surrendered to his fatigue.

15

The old man hated joggers with a passion. It was like they thought they owned the pavement. God forbid they should have to break their stride for any reason. He watched the young woman in the grey training top pound towards him, lost in whatever music she was listening to through her over-sized headphones. He tried to make eye contact, but she resolutely looked away as if he were invisible. There was a brush of air as she passed him, a faint whiff of perfume that might have been deodorant. He watched her go with a slight shake of the head. Part disapproval, part bemusement.

He enjoyed his morning walk – he'd got into the routine during one of the lockdowns and had maintained it as the world slowly returned to some form of normality. It felt good to get up for something, to see the day before it started properly – to have the anticipation of some breakfast when he got home. Sometimes, like today, he'd vary the route. He liked to walk past the new shopping centre under construction. He was old enough to remember the grocer's shop that had been there when he was little, the Woolworths that had replaced it. He marvelled at how quickly it was progressing too, like they were building a spaceship in the middle of south London. And it was then he spotted the dark red puddle next to the skip.

At first, he thought it was ketchup from an old fried chicken box, but as he got nearer, he could see it was unmistakably blood. His eyes followed the sticky trail that led away from it. With a wheeze, he bent over and saw the tear-shaped droplets staining the side of the yellow skip. Peering up, he saw something poking out from under the dark tarpaulin that might have been a foot. He glanced around, unsure, as if worried about being seen, and peeled the covering away.

'Oh Lord, I'm sorry . . .' he said, the words tumbling out instinctively. He looked around again, this time urgently in search of someone, anyone. But he was alone – even the jogger had disappeared from sight. Slowly he forced himself to look again.

The child's head rested on some crumbling bricks. Lifeless eyes stared up at the grey sky as if searching out something behind the clouds. A pale hand was stretched out in supplication. The old man stepped closer, appalled and hypnotised in equal measure. And it was only as he leant in that he could see the flies beading through matted curly hair, congregating around the crater where the back of the infant's head used to be.

16

Wednesday March 23, 10.43
From: sadie@diamondmail.com
To: lilypink@ymail.co.uk

Hey gorgeous . . .

Thanks for the parcel which I received in the post today. Giant Cadbury's Whole Nut! Body lotion! And vodka! What more could a girl want! All my favourite things. Going to make them last as long as possible – almost cried when I opened it. Liam's already got his eyes on the chocky. You shouldn't have spent so much on us though.

Good news – got some serious money coming in soon! A big gig working at some fancy charity do. It's just one night but the cash will really help. Liam badly needs some new clothes and every penny goes on feeding him. The flat's freezing and I can't afford to turn the heating on, so I wrap him up – but his clothes are falling apart. Isn't it supposed to be summer soon?

He's such a good kid though – he doesn't complain (well, not much) – reckon I moan more than he does. Having said that, last night he had this EPIC tantrum in the bath. I've never seen him do that before. Honestly Lil, it wasn't normal and I didn't know where it came from or what to do about it. Sometimes doing this on my own is sooo hard.

I do wonder what's going to become of him though. I hope he's like one of those film stars or footballers who remembers how tough things were when they were growing up but got to the top anyway. He's got film-star looks – I think he's gonna be a hunk. I've just got this feeling he'll do alright – better than I ever did, you watch.

Love you, sis. And thanks for the parcel again, it's the best surprise I've had in ages.

See you soon.

S xxx

17

News of the discovery of Liam Nicholls' body in New Cross, just a couple of miles away from his home in Lewisham, didn't take long to filter through to Cedar House. Finn had been at his desk early when it came – predictably he hadn't slept properly following his late finish the previous night. He'd woken hot and bothered at around four in the morning and knew instantly there was little chance of dropping off again. So he'd spent another couple of hours going through the hard drive, this time forcing himself to look more forensically at its contents. He couldn't magic up a breakthrough, but he could at least try – just for once – to park his emotions for the sake of a missing child.

But with one phone call, his best intentions had gone up in smoke. It had been Jackie Ojo who'd taken it just before eight. His heart had sunk like a stone as the details of the grim find in New Cross were relayed to him. He couldn't help but think of all the effort Sadie had put in just trying to stay afloat. All for nothing, as it now turned out. Around him, the room was sombre and quiet, the scudding dark clouds outside matching everyone's mood.

Finn hadn't been the only person in early. Ojo had already been at her desk when he arrived, while Dattani hadn't been far behind. Others had joined them, without the usual morning pleasantries. Jackets had come straight off, work from the previous evening resumed immediately. But for all their efforts the nature of the investigation had now changed. There was still a killer to find, but they'd lost their battle with the ticking clock – if it had ever been a fair fight in the first place. There wouldn't be a pay-off to satisfy anyone from this – no beers in the pub afterwards celebrating a good result. Now it was just about being professional, getting the job done and finding the bastard that had done this.

For Jill and Lily Nicholls, there would be no happy reunion with Liam, and even if they were braced for the bad news, its reality would still come as a devastating blow. That was Finn's next phone call – the first had just been to Paulsen, diverting her journey in from Tufnell Park to the crime scene in New Cross.

'Feels like we've failed, doesn't it?' said Ojo.

Finn turned to see her standing almost apologetically in front of him. She pulled up a chair and sat down. It didn't look as if her night's sleep had been much better than his.

'Feels like it, but we haven't,' he said. 'From the little I've just been told, it sounds like the body's probably been there since Monday night.'

Ojo exhaled and shook her head sadly.

'It's a crazy, isn't it? It's got to be a crazy. Someone sane doesn't smash a three-year-old's head in and dump them in a skip.'

'No. They don't,' said Finn. On the other side of the room, he could see one of the younger DCs sitting at her desk, staring absently through her computer screen. Liam's death was like a punch to the solar plexus for all of them.

'But we've got a match now, haven't we?' said Ojo, looking at him. 'A dead single mother and her son – just like thirty years ago.'

*　　*　　*

Mattie Paulsen hated football, she decided. Never more so than at this particular moment. She was watching some construction workers chatting loudly about it on the other side of the road. They clearly didn't have a clue or simply weren't interested in the crime scene opposite. The spot where Liam Nicholls had been left felt like the most desolate place in the world right now. The weather couldn't make up its mind whether to spit or pour but Paulsen hardly noticed. Her over-riding emotion was one of huge deflation. Up until Finn's call, she'd kept the faith that Liam was still alive and could be found. Now the search operation was over, and a murder investigation had become a double homicide.

She watched as a familiar car pulled up just beyond the cordon and saw Finn step out and take in the scene. A forensic tent now surrounded the skip with a second outer cordon protecting them both. He stopped briefly to talk to the scene guard before coming over to join her. He was at his most impassive, which Paulsen knew meant nothing. The more Finn tried to convey neutrality, the less he was feeling it – she knew that much about him. Knew too that it would be foolish to vocalise that thought.

'Early indication from the forensic pathologist is that Liam died at around the same time as his mother,' she said. 'There's no sign of any clothing here either.'

'So we're back to thinking it's a sex crime?' said Finn.

Paulsen shrugged.

'Who knows? We'll have to wait for the autopsy on that. But if it isn't – then why move the body?'

Finn had clearly been thinking about this.

'To destroy evidence? Maybe there's DNA on the boy or his clothing and the killer didn't want to risk leaving any trace of it inside the flat? And that suggests he was worried we might find a match . . .'

One of the construction workers opposite let out a loud booming laugh. It seemed to echo around the whole street and Finn scowled at them, even though they couldn't see him.

'Does the skip belong to them?' he said.

'No.' She pointed at a building adjacent to the construction site. 'One of the residential flats over there is having some work done. The builders weren't around yesterday, so that's why the body wasn't found sooner.'

Paulsen watched a forensic officer emerge from the tent carefully holding an evidence bag with what looked like some fragments of bloodstained rubble inside.

'I don't understand why they'd leave Liam *here*?' she said. 'We're only a couple of miles from Sadie's flat – and this is hardly a proper attempt to hide the body, is it?'

Finn looked up and down the street.

'I don't know. It's as good as you're going to find at short notice – there's not much by way of street lighting and there's no camera coverage either. It would have been pretty dark at night. It was probably opportunistic when he saw the skip. Let's see what the door-to-doors give us.'

Paulsen tried to put herself in the killer's shoes. There were several large country parks in the area. If you really wanted to hide a body, there was plenty of woodland within a short drive, even some lakes. In all likelihood, it would have delayed the discovery for a bit longer at least.

'Maybe the killer was in a rush for another reason,' she said. 'Perhaps they needed to get *back* somewhere fast. Somewhere close by?'

'Which brings us again to the why? If the motive wasn't sexual, then what was it?'

Paulsen had no answer for him. The two construction workers had finished their conversation now and one of them was whistling loudly.

'How are the family?' she asked.

Finn pulled a face.

'How do you think? I'm just on my way to see them,' he said.

And by his expression, she didn't envy him the task.

'At least we have some closure,' said Jill Nicholls. She seemed determined to maintain a stiff upper lip, to the point where Finn found her intensity unnerving. 'Overnight . . . I couldn't stop thinking about those people who never find out,' she continued. 'I couldn't have taken that.'

Finn was now standing with Jill and Lily Nicholls inside Sadie's flat. The forensic work there was far from complete and they were all wearing the necessary apparel to protect the scene from contamination. Jill had been adamant she wanted to see where her daughter died – even more so now.

She'd been here before when Sadie was alive, but Finn understood why she needed to revisit it one more time. It existed now as the final freeze-frame of her daughter's life, a place where a little piece of her still lived on. As he watched the Nichollses trying to make sense of their pain, Murray's words the previous evening came back to him. *Complicated grief.*

For obvious reasons, he found other people's experience of loss fascinating. Jill would be just like him, he thought – it takes one to know one. She wouldn't be sharing her feelings with a counsellor any time soon, though Lily probably would. No, Sadie's mother would contain it, learn to live side by side with the emotion, while projecting an entirely different face to the world – that of the stoic survivor. The irony was he could see dispassionately that it was a weakness and he wanted to tell her so. But he knew too that he couldn't.

'I'm so sorry. Both the autopsies are scheduled for tomorrow. We don't want this to drag on for you both,' he said.

Lily launched into a stream of questions Finn couldn't answer. Had Liam died quickly? Had he been sexually assaulted? Had Sadie been sexually assaulted? Did he have any clue who'd done this? And if not, what exactly *had* they been doing for the past twenty-four hours? Finn answered each one as honestly as he could. He noticed as they talked that Lily was standing stock-still, her round, reddened eyes centred on him throughout. He suspected she couldn't allow herself to look at the pile of toys in the corner, the child-size clothing on the radiator, or she'd lose it altogether. He held her gaze like a lifeline.

Jill was only half listening to their conversation, her mind elsewhere as she imbibed the room. There was a palpable sense of growing anger inside her. He knew that emotion too.

'Sadie just tried to do things the right way,' she said finally. 'That's how I brought her up and that's how she lived. Being strong, trying to solve her own problems without making herself a burden to anyone. And this is how the world repaid her. She should never have come to this city. Where were her neighbours? Leaving a young lass to drown in plain sight like this. You people down here – you've lost your souls.'

The words and the venom with which they were expressed would stay with Finn later.

'Fuck me sideways ...' said David Hermitage under his breath. He was at his desk watching live news coverage on the television in the corner of his office. A reporter was standing in a street doing a piece to a camera with a white forensic tent in the background. The rolling strapline across the bottom of the screen said, *'Missing toddler found dead in south London'*.

His mobile buzzed with an incoming text, making him jump. He snatched it up and saw it was from Emily.

Are you watching this? It's awful.

He ignored her and turned up the volume on the TV.

'*Police are now trying to trace Sadie's last movements on the night of her death. They say they're following up on a number of leads but as yet have no idea what the motive for these murders might have been. Sky News has been talking to local residents who say they're shocked ...*'

An image appeared of an old woman Hermitage recognised. A miserable old battleaxe who lived up at the far end with a battalion of cats.

'*It's awful. None of us can believe it. She was such a sweet—*'

He muted the sound and put his head into his hands. His phone buzzed again.

'Fuck off, Em,' he muttered under his breath, before picking up the handset again. This time the message wasn't from his wife.

Meet me – unless you want your wife to know the truth.

'I'm sorry, Alex,' said John Skegman as Finn caught up with him at Cedar House later. 'It's not the outcome any of us wanted.'

'We all knew the longer it went on, this was how it was probably going to pan out. At least it didn't drag,' said Finn. The words sounded harsher than he'd intended but Skegman didn't seem to notice. Finn suspected he was making a slightly less sympathetic calculation. Now that this wasn't a search operation any more, the amount of available manpower would increase. Murder was an awful lot more economical than abduction.

'What are you telling the media?' said Skegman.

'An appeal for information has already been sent out. It's a second crime scene, not too far from the first. Someone must have seen something.'

'Did you get anything useful out of yesterday's press conference?'

'A lot of calls – most of them nothing but we're still sifting through. We now know broadly the journey the killer took, and what time it probably took place. I've widened the trawl of CCTV coverage between the two locations to see if we can pinpoint a vehicle. But there are quite a few routes between Lewisham and New Cross that they could have taken. We've a lot of footage to get through.'

'So is this a random attack, or are we still working on the assumption that Sadie knew who killed her?' said Skegman. Finn blew through his cheeks.

'It's not Liam's father, I can tell you that – we've checked out his alibi and it stands up.'

'How is he?'

'Destroyed. I've assigned Nishat Adams as FLO but he's in pieces as you might expect.'

'Did he know of anybody new in her life?'

Finn shook his head.

'Harry wasn't really in touch with Sadie, so doesn't know much about her recent relationships. There's nothing in her world we've found so far that's flagged up anyone suspicious.' He checked himself. 'Except for one guy she seemed to have had a brief . . .' he struggled to find the right word for a moment, '*something* with.'

Skegman's beady little eyes darted as he tried to make sense of this.

'Who is he, do we know yet?'

'No, not a clue. We're still looking into it. So no – I can't tell you either way whether this is random or not.'

'And this guy, Patrick Clarke . . .' Skegman sifted through some paperwork on his desk. 'You know the press are on to him?' He passed over a print-out from the

MailOnline. Finn skimmed through the first couple of sentences.

'*The Mail has learnt a man with a previous conviction for GBH lives just yards from the property where tragic Sadie Nicholls was murdered on Monday evening. Locals have described the individual, who was only released from prison months ago, as "withdrawn and private".*' The inverted commas on the last three words might as well have said 'a dangerous psychopath', Finn thought.

'This doesn't help,' he said. He explained the conversation they'd had with Clarke the previous day and the impression he'd formed of the man. 'We've got a warrant to search his home. Jackie and Mattie are overseeing that later. At the moment I think his presence is just coincidental. There's no hard evidence he ever set foot in Sadie's flat.'

Skegman nodded, but there was also concern on his face.

'Then make sure this doesn't become a witch hunt – now the media has got a sniff, they'll be digging into him . . .'

'What about the historical murders – Vicki and Ben Stratford?' said Finn. 'I know you weren't convinced earlier – but I think it's a viable line of inquiry. Especially now Liam's dead. There are definite parallels.'

Skegman pursed his lips while he considered it, then shrugged.

'If you think it's worth looking into – then by all means dig. At this point, I don't think you can ignore anything. But if you're trying to tell me it is the same killer – then who the hell's been banged up in prison for the past thirty years?'

18

Hermitage recognised the woman immediately. She'd texted him instructions where to meet – a bench overlooking the Thames close to Embankment station. The last time he'd seen her she'd been pouring his drink at the Royal Grand Hotel. She was Sadie's friend; he remembered briefly being introduced to her on the night. Ruby? No, Lucy . . . that was it.

The fact he now knew who his would-be blackmailer was gave him a welcome sense of control. He'd been giving this meeting plenty of thought since they'd exchanged texts earlier. He'd decided a charm offensive was the right strategy. The most pressing priority was to establish just exactly what this woman knew and how much damage she could do. As he approached the bench, he greeted her like an old business acquaintance, smiling agreeably as he extended his hand.

'It's Lucy, isn't it?' She neither rose to greet him nor took his hand. He continued unabated and sat down next to her at a respectful distance. 'I'm so sorry about Sadie – you two were close, I'm guessing?'

She turned to look at him properly and he saw nothing in her eyes he liked the look of. If she was thrown by the fact he knew her name, she wasn't showing it.

'You've got some fucking nerve,' she said.

He injected his voice with as much measured integrity as he could muster.

'I was Sadie's friend and neighbour. That's all. I looked out for her and I'm *devastated* by what's happened.'

'Nice try, Dave . . .' she said.

Her hand shot out, grabbed his wrist and pulled his sleeve down. He yelped with surprise. The speed of the movement had caught him out and the red crescent of cuts he'd been concealing was now exposed. She held his arm up as if disciplining an errant toddler.

'I know how you got this – I was heading back to the banqueting hall and *saw* what happened between you two. Don't try and tell me you were her friend.' She released her grip and let his hand fall limply back down.

Keep calm, he thought.

'You've honestly got the wrong end of the stick. I know it was a horrible night – but I really was looking out for her. She needed the money, as I'm sure you know.'

Very briefly he thought he might be getting through.

'You're a liar,' she said, dampening that hope straight away. 'Because I know men like you – if you were helping her, it was because you wanted something in return.'

'That's just nonsense—'

'Shut up,' she said and he did. They were out in public and he didn't want to attract attention.

'What do you want?' he asked.

She stood.

'Justice for my friend. Because you owe her that much and I haven't even begun with you yet – I'll be in touch.'

She strode away; Hermitage could feel the panic rising in his chest and beat the feeling down. In business when you hit the brick wall of a problem, you reasoned your way out of it. You analysed the difficulty, identified a solution and applied it. And that's exactly what he needed to do here. But as he watched her go, there was suspicion too. If this woman wanted 'justice' for Sadie – why hadn't she gone to the police?

Paulsen and Ojo smelt it the moment they arrived. They'd come to search Patrick Clarke's house with two uniformed PCs and thought initially the manure out the front was something to do with his gardening business. Most of it had been tidied into a row of green sacks, but there was still enough scattered and smeared across the front patio to give away its true purpose. Scrawled in spray paint across the front door were the words: 'Pigs live in shit'. Clarke was trying to scrub the graffiti off. He turned and smiled at them as if welcoming guests to a dinner party.

'Sorry about the smell. This is actually quite good quality stuff, believe it or not – I'll be able to put it to good use later.'

Paulsen looked down the street – the crime scene outside Sadie's flat aside, things were as quiet as she'd seen it here. The camera crews, for the moment, seemed to have migrated to the new feeding ground in New Cross.

'When did it happen?' said Ojo. 'The area's been crawling with police.'

'Must have been overnight. I found it first thing. I've spent most of the morning cleaning it up.'

'You don't seem too bothered about it?' said Paulsen.

Clarke laughed. It was a warm sonorous sound accompanied by an easy smile that took her by surprise.

'Why would it? Someone's gone to a garden centre, literally bought a load of shit and dumped it here. And they've sprayed a few words on a door which could use a fresh coat of paint anyway. Seriously – why let yourself get wound up? It's their money and time.'

He made it sound so simple and Paulsen found it hard not to smile back. A definite first, she thought, when you're there

to execute a search warrant. Again, she felt the slight discon-
nect between the man she was looking at and the context of
the reason she was talking to him. She found him increasingly fascinating. Reminded herself too what he'd served
time for.

'I hope this hasn't upset your mother,' she said.

His smile faded.

'She's okay – she's been through a lot worse than this over
the years.'

'It's totally unacceptable. We'll look into it for you,' said Ojo.

Clarke shrugged.

'Aren't you interested in who might have done this?' said
Paulsen.

'I've got a broad idea. Think if you put your minds to it, you
might be able to guess too . . .'

Clarke opened out his palms as if it were obvious. Before
Paulsen could develop the point, she saw a middle-aged man
with thinning hair scooting quickly up the street. She knew
now this was Nathan Roach, and while he might not know her
name, the speed with which he was moving suggested he
wasn't keen on finding out either. He was carrying a bag of
shopping and swiftly opened his front door and scuttled
inside. Paulsen noticed Clarke watching him with almost as
much interest as she was.

'Do you know that man?' she said.

He shook his head.

'Not really – kind of keeps himself to himself,' he replied.

A few moments later Paulsen was standing outside Roach's
front door while Ojo got the search of Clarke's house underway with the two uniformed PCs. She'd rung the bell but
there'd been no answer. She rang it again and jammed her
finger on it this time for a few extra seconds. Finally, the door

narrowly opened. Roach looked out nervously through the gap and Paulsen held up her warrant card.

'DC Paulsen, Metropolitan Police—'

'I've already spoken to the police. I've told you everything I know,' he said, interrupting her, the words tumbling out in a gabble. Paulsen responded by smiling warmly. He was lucky, she thought – not many people were treated to that.

'I know, Mr Roach, but if you have a few minutes, I do have some more questions for you. It won't take long.'

For a moment she thought he was actually going to refuse, but with obvious reluctance, he opened the door and nodded her in.

The house was what an estate agent might describe as 'in need of some modernisation'. It was also noticeably empty – of furnishings, possessions, any kind of personality at all. It gave no clue as to who this man was, and there was little to indicate it was even someone's home. The living room lacked furniture, apart from a battered-looking leather sofa opposite an incongruously new-looking television. There were no pictures on the walls, no books on the shelves. A terraced house, it had the same layout as the rest of the properties on the street, and Paulsen immediately felt the contrast with the warm, welcoming feel of the Daws' residence. Even Sadie's place had possessed more charm. Roach ushered her towards a simple wooden table that looked in desperate need of a good scrub and the pair sat down. There was something worn down about this man, Paulsen thought, just like his home. Lifeless and without colour.

'So what do you need to know?' he said.

'A bit more about you would help?'

For a moment he looked frantic.

'Me? Why?'

She smiled pleasantly again.

'Let me tell you something about my job. A lot of it comes from keeping your eyes and ears open. So when you see someone obviously trying to avoid the police at all costs, in a street where a murder investigation's underway, you go and knock on their door.'

Roach swallowed.

'I'm not trying to avoid you. As I said, I spoke to your colleague earlier and I'm talking to you now.'

'And you're not in any trouble,' she reassured him.

He digested this, gave a small nod of acknowledgement.

'So are you just renting here?' she asked.

He nodded, without offering up any more. She motioned at the empty room.

'Are you here on business?'

'I'm a surveyor,' he replied.

It was like getting blood out of a stone. He was absently rubbing a wedding ring on his left hand and seemed unable to look her in the eye. Something was off about him, the house, all of it. Usually, when people acted like that around a police officer, they had something to hide, but it wasn't that kind of fear either, she sensed. He was too fragile – it was something else she couldn't quite pin down.

'I assume, as you're a married man,' she pointed at the ring, 'that this isn't the family home?'

She knew of course from Dattani's digging earlier that Roach had a wife in the Midlands, and hoped the question sounded a reasonable deduction.

'It's complicated,' he said.

'In what way?'

'I had to leave for a bit. For personal reasons. We're just having a trial separation.'

Paulsen studied him closely and chided herself a little. You got so used to looking for ulterior motives that sometimes you were in danger of missing the obvious. A middle-aged man whose marriage had broken down. Mix a loss of confidence with the resulting low self-esteem, add a terrifying act of violence in the house opposite, and this is probably what you ended up with.

'Do you have a car?' she said.

'Yes. It's at the garage having an MOT at the moment.' He shifted on his seat uncomfortably. 'Why do you ask?'

'Which garage?' she said.

He gave her the details and she jotted them down in her pocketbook. There was an awkward silence while she considered her next move. It was down to her judgement now how much this man was further investigated, on her shoulders if she got that calculation wrong.

'Thank you – you've been very helpful,' she said.

Even though Paulsen was only in the house for ten minutes or so, it felt a relief when she left. She took a deep lungful of fresh air, got the mustiness of the place out of her system and began heading back up the street to re-join Ojo.

'Is everything alright?' said a familiar voice. She turned and saw Ronnie Fordyce walking towards her. He'd clearly seen which door she'd just come out of and the question felt like a thin excuse to try and get some gossip.

'All good, thanks,' she said briskly, maintaining her stride.

'I saw the news about that young lad. It's appalling – we're a community here, it's going to really knock a few people for six. If there's anything I can do to help . . .' He said the words with an avuncular smile, which irritated Paulsen for some reason. Reluctantly she stopped.

'Not everyone seems to be embracing the community spirit,' she said, nodding at the graffiti on the Clarkes' door. He turned to follow her gaze, saw the still visible words, the bags of manure and dark residue still coating the patio.

'For Christ's sake,' he muttered. 'Do you want me to have a word with a few people? I know most of the folk round here. If there's one or two getting a bit silly, I can try and calm things down a bit for you?'

Paulsen was still trying to get the measure of Fordyce. He was very smooth for sure, but the previous convictions Dattani had uncovered about him had shaded him in a subtly different way now. And those two words 'for you' just tipped his offer into something which sounded vaguely patronising.

Before she could respond, he glanced sharply across the road. On the opposite side, Tom Daws was emerging from his front door. Fordyce gave his friend a wave which Daws hesitantly returned.

'It's up to you – only if you think it'll help,' he said, turning back to her. 'I might be able to see if anyone's heard anything.'

'That's really helpful, thank you,' replied Paulsen, keeping it courteous.

Tom was now closing his front gate. Seeing an oncoming car in the middle distance he jogged surprisingly smartly across the road towards them. Paulsen couldn't help but be impressed; her own father was already slowing down physically.

'We were just going to take a walk – there's a small park not too far away,' said Fordyce. He broke off because, almost in slow motion, Tom seemed to catch his foot on the kerb. He stumbled and fell forwards on to the ground. Fordyce and Paulsen immediately ran over to help him. Tom groaned in pain.

'You didn't tell me the pavement was so close, Ron,' he muttered. Paulsen was already checking him over with concern.

'Don't try to stand. Just take it easy for a moment,' she said. Daws rolled around and winced. He rubbed at his knee gingerly and pulled up the trouser leg. Underneath was an ugly red scrape and he looked at it with a mixture of confusion and fear.

'Are you alright?' said Paulsen.

'I don't think anything's broken if that's what you mean,' he said.

'*Dad!*'

Paulsen looked around to see Abi Daws running across to join them.

'What have you done?' she said.

'Just taken a bit of a tumble, Abs. He's okay though,' said Fordyce.

'I saw the butterfly, Ron,' said Tom suddenly.

Abi shook her head.

'Not this nonsense again, not now. Come on – let's get you home,' she said.

They helped him to his feet. Paulsen looked across at Clarke's house, where she could see some flickers of movement behind the net curtains. Ojo would be fine without her for the moment.

'Let me help you with him,' she said to Abi.

And as they slowly walked him back across the road, Daws said it again.

'I saw it . . . the butterfly. I *know* I did.'

He seemed to be directing it at Paulsen now, and she didn't know what to say. She was well used to these non sequiturs though, from home – it was all rather too familiar. She was about to humour him when her phone rang.

When she saw it was Finn calling, she apologised and took the call. His voice sounded urgent.

'We've had a breakthrough. Forensics found a set of fingerprints in Sadie's flat a short while ago and got an instant match when they ran them through the system. It's Hermitage – the guy she was with at the Knights Association dinner . . .'

19

Finn made the arrest himself. He agreed to Hermitage's request not to handcuff him, and they left his office as if he and Dattani were two old friends taking him to the pub. His fingerprints were only in the system because of a minor driving offence a couple of years before, but he travelled back to Cedar House like a man being led to his execution. There was a delay getting him into an interview room while they waited for his expensively appointed solicitor, but Finn wasn't overly bothered. Leaving men like this to wait in a custody cell was his profession's equivalent of marinating a piece of chicken before you stuck it under the grill.

'That's the first time someone's laid on a tea party while I've searched their house,' said Jackie Ojo as she and Paulsen swept back into the incident room. The search of the Clarkes' house hadn't uncovered anything, unless you counted yet more of Lynda's home-made cakes. 'It was worth doing though, guv – there were press back in the street when we left. We're definitely going to get asked more questions about Patrick.'

Finn leant back in his chair.

'He doesn't have a concrete alibi for the night Sadie was murdered. Do we have a *reason* to push him harder on that?'

Ojo and Paulsen exchanged a look.

'There's no sign of his van on any of the CCTV we looked through. His neighbours also reckon it was left there all night.

He might have another vehicle, but I think it's unlikely,' said Paulsen.

'Did you look inside the van?'

'Of course – but there was nothing that made me think we need to get it checked out forensically,' said Ojo.

'So what do you make of him?' said Finn.

Ojo ran a hand through her hair.

'I think he's telling the truth, and if anything, we need to look out for him. I know why he came forward and I can understand why he's concerned. Add a few more sly newspaper stories into the mix and he might have good cause to be worried.'

She explained to Finn about the manure and the graffiti they'd seen.

'Okay – I'll have a word with the DCI, make sure we keep an enhanced uniform presence in the street over the next few days,' he said.

'So what about this guy downstairs – Hermitage. What's the deal with him?' said Paulsen.

'His fingerprints are on one of the bedside tables in Sadie's bedroom. There's more in the kitchen area. That said, there's none with her blood on them and they didn't find any on or around her body. Nor on Liam's at the crime scene in New Cross, for that matter. However, when I spoke to him yesterday he denied having any kind of relationship with her,' said Finn.

'Right . . .' said Ojo with a face that suggested some cynicism.

'We've run a cell site analysis on his phone but didn't get very far because he turned it off shortly after Sadie left the hotel on Monday night,' said Finn. 'But CCTV from the foyer shows him leaving pretty much when he said he did at eleven.'

Ojo frowned as she tried to make sense of it.

'Surely the phone's irrelevant if he's inside the hotel – he still doesn't get home until well after when we think Sadie was killed. The timing doesn't tally.'

'Come on, Jacks, we both know the science of these things isn't precise. The murders could have happened at any point up until midnight and even beyond,' said Finn.

'So how does he get Liam's body from Lewisham over to New Cross?' said Paulsen.

'He and his wife both have cars – I've asked forensics to give them each a thorough sweep. But let's see what he has to say for himself first . . .'

'I only went inside Sadie's flat the once. She wanted to ask me a bit more about the gala dinner. That's all there is to it,' said Hermitage.

They'd been able to proceed after his solicitor had finally arrived. She was a hawkish woman who seemed to have a lofty contempt for just about everyone in the room, her client included. Finn already knew where this conversation was going though. Hermitage had never found himself in a police interview room before. He was visibly terrified and would either lie badly or simply spill everything from the start. The early indications were the former, though the latter would probably follow anyway. The solicitor knew it too, which is why she was sitting there with a face like thunder. Finn decided to play along for now.

'We found your fingerprints on the bedside table in her bedroom. So to clarify – that's where you had this conversation about the charity dinner?' he said, letting his face show the cynicism he was keeping from his voice.

The solicitor looked sharply at Hermitage and shook her head.

'No comment,' he said.

'We know Sadie had been seeing someone recently. She's mentioned it in emails we found to her sister. Was that you?'

Hermitage's eyes widened into something resembling two large dinner plates. Paulsen hadn't said a word yet but was applying perfect pressure of her own with an undisguised look of disgust.

'No comment,' he repeated, with a slight stammer this time.

Finn gave Paulsen a nod of invitation and she leant in.

'As you know, we took a sample of your DNA when you were processed. We're now taking further samples from Sadie's flat. From her furniture, her clothing, her *bedding* . . .'

Hermitage blanched and Finn almost felt some sympathy. Almost. In his mind's eye, he could still see Sadie's brain matter spilt on her carpet, the sightless eyes of the little boy in the skip.

'Okay, okay . . .' Hermitage said, holding up a hand in panicked surrender. 'I'll tell you exactly what happened – but I didn't kill her. It's absurd to even suggest it.' His solicitor looked alarmed and tried to whisper a few words in his ear, but he brushed her aside.

'Sadie and I had a brief . . .' he shrugged helplessly, '*thing*.'

The solicitor was now looking like one of those doctors that tell you to eat, smoke and drink less, knowing you won't listen and you'll probably kill yourself anyway. Finn was beginning to warm to her.

'What happened?' said Paulsen.

'We got talking at the train station one morning. We'd seen each other around and were on nodding terms. I felt sorry for her – you could see she was really bright, just in need of a break.'

'So you took advantage of her and then got her a job as a hostess where half the room thought she was a prostitute?' said Paulsen. There were times her bluntness was rather magnificent, Finn thought. Hermitage swallowed.

'I should never have got involved with her. It was . . . ill-judged. A mistake.'

'Why *did* you get involved with her?' said Paulsen. The solicitor was now listening with one hand on her forehead, shielding her eyes as if in some pain. A hint of sadness crept across Hermitage's face.

'I really don't know. We just struck up a rapport. She was very easy to talk to. One day I finished work early and was on my way home. She saw me and invited me in for a coffee. I swear, that's all either of us thought it was going to be.' He looked down guiltily as he remembered. 'It was a rare afternoon when she was alone. Liam was with his father, I think. And it just *happened* . . . only the once. It could never go anywhere. I got her work at the dinner because I wanted to make amends. Yes, I knew what kind of event it was – I warned her beforehand and thought I could look out for her on the night.'

'So why did she attack you before she left?' said Finn.

Again Hermitage produced his rabbit-in-the-headlights face but Finn felt no sympathy. It was often the weakest of men who wrought the worst violence.

'Attack's a bit of a strong word, isn't it?'

'One of the chefs saw you both arguing and said she grabbed you. And the custody sergeant saw the marks on your wrist when you were being booked in earlier,' said Paulsen. 'So don't bother lying about how you got them.'

Hermitage sighed.

'She was upset by what happened on the night and I don't blame her in hindsight. I don't think she meant to hurt me – it was just a silly incident in the heat of the moment.'

Finn left a deliberate pause before resuming.

'One more thing – just after Sadie left the hotel, you turned your phone off. Why?' he said.

Hermitage ran his tongue over dry lips.

'Does it matter?'

'Maybe, maybe not,' said Finn. 'It just seems an odd thing to have done.'

'I went for a walk just to clear my head after the row with Sadie. It had been a *really* horrible night. I wanted to get some air. I turned my phone off in case anyone from my table rang and queried where I'd gone.'

'Where did you go?' said Finn.

'Around the block, some backstreets close to the hotel. It was only for about twenty minutes and then I went back to the dinner, mainly to say my goodbyes.'

'Why didn't you turn your phone back on?'

Hermitage shrugged.

'I forgot. It happens.'

'You do realise we'll check the local CCTV?' said Paulsen.

'Do whatever you need to do – but please, don't tell my wife about Sadie. That's all I'm asking. I've got a daughter. You don't need to and I deeply regret what I did.'

He looked at them imploringly. Finn and the solicitor kept their expressions impassive, even as Paulsen doubled down on her own glare of revulsion.

'What a piece of shit,' Paulsen said afterwards, before taking a sip from a large soya latte.

'He's a piece of shit we'll have to kick loose unless forensics give us something to charge him with,' said Finn.

He, Paulsen and Ojo were holding a debrief in YoYo's Cafe, a much-loved institution for officers of all ranks at Cedar House. The small coffee shop situated on the opposite side of the road to the station offered a quiet space to escape for five minutes. The days of a bustling in-house canteen were long gone. The facilities at the station offered a fridge, a self-service machine, a small sink and a few tables. Not surprisingly YoYo's had never suffered for trade.

'He's petrified of his wife finding out about the affair – that makes him the first suspect we've identified with a nailed-on motive. And there's enough shades of grey about the timings for him to have done it,' Paulsen said.

'So let's do this the right way – and see how much of what he told us stands up,' said Finn. 'Talk to Westminster and get the CCTV for the streets around the Royal Grand.' He frowned for a moment. 'No one flagged up anything from the hotel's security cameras – but he might have left by a different exit. Give his wife a call too – ask her exactly what time he came home. And Mattie, try not to accidentally mention the affair, eh?'

Paulsen pulled a mock face of disappointment. Ojo had been listening to them with an ever-increasing frown. She stirred her peppermint tea thoughtfully for a moment.

'Just playing devil's advocate – yes, this guy's a good fit . . . but if he's as twitchy as you say he is, he'd have made a mistake. To commit two murders, then move a body without leaving *any* trace of evidence, takes a clear head. Beyond the fingerprints, forensics have found nothing that directly implicates him – not at either crime scene. What if he's exactly what he says he is? A decent, if rather spineless, bloke who tried to help someone?'

For a moment the only noise was the sound of the espresso machine gurgling and whooshing in the background as both Finn and Paulsen tried to fashion a counterargument.

'All I'm saying is let's not get too hung up on him yet,' said Ojo.

Paulsen shook her head.

'Don't underestimate him,' she said. 'He's the deputy chief executive of the Fight Hunger Foundation. He's no idiot. I see a manipulative man who took advantage of a vulnerable young woman. I can absolutely buy he had a clear enough mind to have killed Sadie and Liam. The nature of the killings was frenzied and that fits as well . . .'

'How do you mean?' said Ojo.

Paulsen thought it through for a moment.

'He and Sadie have a row before she leaves the hotel. He's admitted that. It gets physical and she attacks him – he's admitted that too. Say she threatened to tell his wife about the affair. He panics, leaves the dinner early and goes to confront her about it when he gets home. She repeats the threat to tell his wife and *boom* . . .' Paulsen clapped her hands together to make the point. 'And that's why he turned his phone off – because he's savvy enough to know his movements might be traced later.'

Ojo nodded slowly as she followed her logic. They both looked over at Finn.

'Jacks is right,' he said. 'This guy may be smart, but I don't buy he could kill two people without leaving *something* behind at one of the crime scenes. Let's wait and see what the forensics give us. It's still early days – with all of this.'

Finn's phone buzzed, interrupting them, and he put down the empty espresso cup he'd been rolling between his fingers to read an incoming email. He shook his head as he read it.

'That's the forensic pathologist – we won't get confirmation until the autopsy, but he says it doesn't look like Liam Nicholls suffered a sexual assault. And he's reasonably confident the boy died roughly at the same time as his mother.'

'So why move the body? Why take his clothes? None of it makes sense,' said Paulsen.

Finn shook his head.

'It makes sense to whoever did it. It's rare for a child to be murdered and treated this way if there isn't a sexual component. That makes me think again that this is personal. It's someone who knew Sadie, and the answer lies in her background. I'm sure of it – we just haven't found enough of the dots to join together yet.'

'It's someone who *hated* her,' said Ojo. 'Mattie's right – this was frenzied. They smashed her head to a pulp and then did the same to her little boy.'

Finn nodded in agreement.

'And that's what worries me the most. Whoever did this is clearly exceptionally dangerous. And until we know *why*, we can't rule out the possibility of another attack.'

20

Patrick Clarke had spent the morning tidying up the house after the police search earlier. They hadn't made too much of a mess – it was his mother, not the property, he'd been primarily concerned for. She'd been stoic throughout, had even taken something of a liking to the rather brusque detective sergeant running things. But it didn't stop him from feeling guilty. The stress of the last few years was surely taking an invisible toll on her. When she eventually did pass on, he'd never know how many days he'd robbed her of with all this. They'd lost his dad to a heart attack while he'd been in prison and he felt a huge responsibility for that too. He was trying to remember a time when he *didn't* feel guilty. The emotion wasn't just a constant companion; it was part of him now, like a persistent light headache. Sometimes you forgot about it, but it was always beating away in the background – just sharp enough to remind you.

He didn't have much work scheduled for the day, but there was still plenty to be getting on with. Finding something useful to do with several bags of manure, for a start. It wouldn't hurt to give Mum some space either – she knew exactly why he fussed around her and didn't always appreciate it. The guilt, again. As he walked out of the front door, he saw an edgy-looking figure hurrying along the pavement outside.

'Nathan . . .' he called out.

The man almost jumped out of his skin, then relaxed when he saw who it was.

'Where've you been? I've been trying to get hold of you,' said Patrick. 'How did it go with that cop earlier?'

Nathan shook his head.

'I didn't need that. I *really* didn't need it,' he said.

'Are you okay? Where are you going?'

Nathan didn't answer – he'd just noticed the washed-out graffiti on Patrick's front door, the line of green bags and the accompanying smell. He began to look alarmed again.

'What's that? What's happened?'

'Some shit. Literally . . .'

Nathan didn't smile.

'So it's begun then – the finger-pointing? I should have guessed.'

'Never mind that,' said Patrick. 'You should have called me – I've been worried about you.'

'What did the police want with you?'

'They know about my conviction, so we've been having a few conversations. You can't blame them. Everything's cool, though.'

Nathan's eyes widened.

'What did you tell them? Did you say where you were on the night Sadie died? Oh, Jesus . . .'

He put his hand over his mouth, and for a moment Patrick thought he was genuinely about to vomit.

'I told them the truth – that I was helping a friend with a problem. Because that's what happened. But I didn't mention your name . . .'

Nathan was now taking some deep breaths.

'Nathe, are you okay?' said Patrick with genuine concern. 'We've got to stick together – now more than ever. There's been journalists trying to get hold of me as well . . .'

'What?'

'It's not just the police who know about my history.' He looked grimly in the direction of the pub and shrugged.

158

'They've been tipped off, clearly. Don't worry, your name hasn't come up. Why would it?'

Roach shook his head, looked down at the ground and dragged his shoe for a moment on the concrete surface.

'I'm struggling with this, Pat. I don't mind admitting it. I'm thinking I may need to disappear for a while – until all this nonsense goes away.'

Clarke nodded understandingly.

'Do what you have to do. Have you got somewhere you can go?'

'Yeah. My sister – she lives in Ealing.'

Patrick recognised the emotions he was seeing all too well. This particular strain of fear had a very distinctive flavour. Once tasted, you never forgot it.

'I've lived with the way you're feeling right now for a long time, mate. I'm always here if you want to talk again.'

He gave him a firm pat on the shoulder and smiled reassuringly.

'Why did the police need to search my car?' said Emily Hermitage. David had eventually been released under investigation. The police hadn't sought an extension to detain him, and he'd taken that as a positive sign. In the circumstances, he'd decided to take the rest of the day off. But he was beginning to think that might have been the wrong choice now. His presence didn't seem to be helping his wife.

'I told you – they only questioned me because Sadie was working at the gala dinner. Of course they'd want to check everything out with both of us. But you'd expect that – there's really nothing to be worried about,' he said.

Emily was pacing around the living room, while David stretched out on the sofa. With Charlotte at school, they had the place to themselves. He was trying to project a sense of relaxed calm, the concerned husband who'd taken time off to be with his wife.

The fact was, he was terrified that the police would find something new in Sadie's flat to incriminate him. The place was tiny and probably covered with fibres, fingerprints and God knows what else. There was also the small matter that he *hadn't* told them the entire truth. He was walking a tightrope and just needed to get through the next few days. For now, getting things under control at home was the priority.

Emily had lost her job as an office manager during the pandemic and two years on, there was no doubt she was finding the lack of direction in her life increasingly difficult. She had too much time to think about things, and this situation wasn't helping.

'Why didn't you tell me before you'd got Sadie a job at the gala dinner? You never said a word about it – I had no idea you even knew her that well,' she said.

He laughed and it came out more forced than he would have liked.

'Why would I have said anything? I was just doing her a favour. I didn't think it was worth mentioning.'

He was about to launch into his 'decent neighbour' speech again when he noticed the faint look of distrust in his wife's eyes. To see her looking at him like that was about as distressing as anything he'd experienced in the last two days.

'The papers are saying this dinner – the Knights Association – that it's sleazy like that *every* year. You've been to at least the last three of them and have never said anything about it . . .' she said.

He shook his head.

'They're exaggerating. Look at some of the people who attend – there's former cabinet ministers, television personalities – CEOs, for God's sake. What do you think goes on? If anything really awful had happened before, the whole world would know.'

She looked conflicted now.

'So, why did the police want to know what time you got back? They think you killed Sadie and her little boy, don't they? Christ almighty . . .'

He rose from the sofa and went over to her.

'No, they don't. They're just dotting i's and crossing t's. I've done nothing wrong. What happened to Sadie and her son was awful and I was *happy* to help them with their inquiries.'

This seemed to mollify her. His phone interrupted them and when he checked the display, he saw it was Lucy who was calling. He felt his stomach begin to knot again.

'It's work – I have to take this. We'll talk more, later – maybe go for a walk? It's beautiful out there . . .' He smiled reassuringly at her, and strode out of the living room. Once out of sight he hared up the stairs, ran into his daughter's bedroom and closed the door. It smelt sickly sweet in there, of strawberry flavouring. He looked at the array of potions and lotions on her make-up table and swallowed. It briefly reminded him of Sadie's bedroom.

'Hello . . .' he said quietly into the phone. 'What do you want?' He listened carefully – not just for Lucy's reply, but for any indication that Emily might be following him up the stairs.

'I told you before – we've got unfinished business—' said Lucy.

'Except maybe it *is* finished,' he said, interrupting. 'I've spoken to the police myself since we met. There's nothing you can tell them they don't already know. I imagine this is all some sort of preamble because you want to get money out of me.'

This was good, he thought. He was in control – he'd planned what he was going to say since he'd met Lucy by the Thames, and was executing it perfectly. For the first time since that wretched dinner, he was finally feeling and behaving like something resembling himself.

'You're not going to get a penny from me,' he continued. 'If anything, I can't see any reason why I shouldn't tell them that someone's trying to blackmail me about Sadie. I'd imagine they'd take a very dim view of that. As would a court.'

There was silence on the other end. He looked around his daughter's room, not a clue who some of the people on the posters on the walls were. There was a pause.

'Hello?' he said, unsure if she'd actually hung up on him.

'I'm not bothered about the police,' said Lucy. 'I know you slept with Sadie. Yes, I want money, you're right about that. Because men like you think you can't be hurt by people like me, that we're too small to do you any damage. But if you don't do precisely as I instruct, I'll tell your wife what you did. I'll destroy your marriage and I'll destroy your relationship with your daughter. And then – just for shits and giggles – I'll tell the press about it and destroy your career too.'

The line went dead.

21

Never go back – that's what they say, thought Luke Daws as he turned into Pennington Road. He brought his suitcase to a halt with some relief. Its wonky wheels had been pulling in different directions ever since he'd left Cootamundra. That had been nearly twenty-four hours ago. Now standing opposite the Lamb's Head, he fought the urge to turn around and head straight back to the airport. He was a tall, tanned man in his mid-thirties with a mane of brown hair and a carefully trimmed beard. It didn't matter how many times he came back, the pub never seemed to change. It still looked like a dive even after all these years. He was half tempted to stick his head around the door just to see if it still *smelt* the same. That sour stink of piss and beer he remembered from the days his father used to drag them in there for a fish supper way back when. Through the windows, he could see a familiar shaven head bobbing around behind the bar. That told him all he needed to know.

With a tug, he pulled his errant case and headed on. He could see the crime scene outside number eighteen more clearly now. The memories were flooding back. Like the pub, the look of the street was the same as it ever was. The occupants of most of these properties had probably changed several times over – one or two must have even died off by now. He shivered – coming home really did feel like time travelling and he didn't like it one little bit. The past was welcome to stay buried.

He walked up to the familiar navy blue door of number thirty and rang the bell. Some cracked clay pots still full of bougainvillaea plants were sitting in the bay beneath the living room window. His mother loved those flowers – had the same outside her home in New South Wales and it made for a comforting symmetry. The front door opened to reveal his sister Abi and he greeted her with a broad grin.

'I suppose if I said "g'day" it'd be too much of a cliché,' he said in his smoky Aussie tones. He'd been rehearsing the line pretty much since he'd got off the plane and was pleased to see it have the desired effect.

'Luke!' She looked nonplussed for a moment. 'I thought you weren't coming until next month? That's what you said on the phone the other night . . .'

'Saw a cheaper flight come up so I swapped them. Thought I'd surprise you – hope that's okay?'

'Course it is, you daft twat,' she said, delight replacing the surprise on her face. He let go of his case, and it careered gently into one of the plant pots. She threw her arms around him and held him in a bear hug.

'Jeez. Are things *that* bad?' he said.

She slowly disengaged and looked up wearily.

'There's quite a lot I need to tell you about . . .'

If Finn prided himself on anything, it was understanding the tempo of a murder investigation. Those moments when things were alive and unfolding, and those other times when it was like wading through treacle. His job was to be metronomic throughout and right now he could sense things beginning to subtly flag. A day on, the cloud that had descended over his team since the discovery of Liam Nicholls' body hadn't lifted. He'd gathered them together again in light of the news from the forensic pathologist. If there wasn't a sexual element to these murders, then it reshaped and refocused what they were doing. They needed leadership, were looking to him for it, and somehow he needed to eek some out of himself. What used to come so naturally once was these days an effort of will. That too, he realised almost in passing, was a problem which had crept up on him.

'You know my views on motives . . .' he said, looking around the room. 'In some form or another, it always comes back to the four Ls . . . love, lust, loot or loathing. The question is – how do *these* two murders fit into that?'

'We can surely rule out money for a start. Sadie didn't have any,' said Dattani.

'Which might be the point . . .' said Paulsen. 'She'd borrowed from a loan shark, and was desperate. Personally, I think her financial problems could be key. I still think there's a lot we don't know about them.'

'What did the cafe where she was working tell you, Dave?' asked Finn.

McElligott checked his pocketbook.

'They admitted paying her cash in hand – said she was bright and bubbly, turned up on time and did the job well enough. The owner was just sorry she couldn't throw her more work.'

Finn turned back to Dattani.

'Sami – did you find any other sources of income?'

'Not really. Harry Boxall, as we know, was paying her some relatively low sums, as and when. She was claiming Universal Credit, and her mum was helping her out when she could. But that's it – her expenditure was next to nothing: just rent, bills and food. She never defaulted on anything though – somehow she found a way to keep herself going. I'm not sure how long she could have gone on like that; it was just starting to get out of control.'

Finn digested this and considered it.

'Mattie makes a good point – those are her finances as far as we know them. Was she getting cash in hand from any other sources we *don't* know about? Let's make sure we have the complete picture,' he said. 'When it comes to her relationships, we now know she had a brief fling with one of her neighbours.'

He pointed at a picture of David Hermitage pinned to one of the whiteboards. Taken from the Fight Hunger Foundation website, it showed him in a sharp suit smiling with a band of pearly white teeth. It was a far cry from the unctuous little man Finn had seen in the interview room the previous day.

'We've nothing to tie this guy in directly, aside from the fingerprints we've found in her flat. His account of what took place with Sadie more or less tallies with what she was telling her sister. The autopsy today may also reveal traces of his DNA under her fingernails. He had an altercation with her before she left which was witnessed and he hasn't denied.'

'Could he have paid her for sex?' said Dattani suddenly. 'They're a pretty unlikely couple and given her need for money . . .'

Finn considered it.

'I wouldn't rule it out, but my instinct is that it's unlikely. Sadie walked out of that hotel on a point of principle, remember? I can't see the same woman selling sex to a neighbour, however much she needed the cash.' He looked over at Paulsen. 'Mattie, have you managed to get hold of the CCTV from the streets outside the Royal Grand for this walk he says he took?'

She nodded.

'There's no sign of him – and there's nothing on the hotel's own cameras either. I think he's lying about that walk – I just don't know why.'

'Perhaps because he went home and killed Sadie Nicholls?' said McElligott.

Paulsen was looking unsure now.

'The hotel's cameras do confirm Hermitage left when he said he did – just after 11 p.m. – and his wife's now confirmed what time he got home. I don't think there's a window in there for him to have killed Sadie and Liam and then driven to New Cross and back.'

'Unless the wife's lying or complicit,' persisted McElligott.

'Forensics found nothing in either his or his wife's cars,' said Finn. 'Whatever his reasons for lying about that time, I'm not particularly interested. If he's not our man, then it's his own business.'

Paulsen was still not looking completely comfortable.

'I don't know, guv. Something about him wasn't right. You saw how concerned he was about his wife finding out about the affair. He's also a pretty well-connected guy. Is it that improbable he could have had Sadie killed to keep her quiet? That might be why he turned off his phone – so nothing could be traced back to him. And if all that sounds fanciful, remember there were some *very* powerful people at that dinner . . .'

'Possibly,' said Finn, nodding. 'It's a loose end from someone who's clearly comfortable with telling the odd lie. Dave, why don't you look into who his circle is, who he knows, who his contacts are – just in case there's someone who fits the bill lurking in there.'

He turned back to the whiteboards and saw the image of Sadie smiling out at them. For a second it felt like she was looking him directly in the eye.

'I've seen no evidence she had any significant enemies or had fallen out with anyone recently. Even her ex-boyfriend described her as "sunshine" – and critically, her world also seems to have been pretty small.'

'*Speak for yourself, mate . . .*' said Sadie.

He faltered, thrown by the unexpected intrusion. The way Sadie seemed to be supplanting Karin in his subconscious was beginning to disturb him. He knew it was a sign of something important, even a deterioration of sorts, and was reluctant to think too hard about its implication. The door at the far end of the room opened and John Skegman breezed in.

'Sorry to interrupt, Alex – the press have been all over me since we announced the discovery of the boy's body. They want to know more about the arrest we made as well.'

Finn used Skegman's interruption as an excuse to gather himself and brought the DCI up to speed.

'So where does this leave us?' said Skegman.

'With three areas of interest. We're looking extensively into Sadie's world as you'd expect – but also the gala dinner and the historical murder in the same property thirty years ago,' said Finn.

'And what do we know about Sadie's world?'

Finn shrugged.

'That's just it – she wasn't some businesswoman with a network of professional contacts. Or someone with a huge social circle and a complex love life. She was a lonely single mother who didn't have time for anything other than trying to provide for her son. You'd expect, given those limitations, an obvious suspect to present themselves. But we're struggling, to be honest.'

'What if this one doesn't fit your four Ls, guv?' said Ojo. 'We all know what the exception usually is in those circumstances . . .'

'Someone *without* a defined motive,' said Finn, nodding. 'A random psycho – which brings us back to the historical murders.'

The discovery of Liam's body had rightly taken their attention for the past twenty-four hours, but the deaths of Vicki and Ben Stratford in 1993 had been nagging at the back of his mind. The possibility the same killer had struck again looked impossible on the surface, which is precisely why it was bothering him. Skegman looked over at Finn searchingly.

'Is there anything concrete, however small – beyond the shared location – which ties them together?'

Ojo pulled out the photographs of the two crime scenes she'd shown them before and passed them to Skegman, who held them up, fascinated.

'There *is* a close similarity there,' he said.

'Possibly,' said Finn. 'But we've spoken to all the local residents and there's no one flagging up as suspicious.'

'Who have you come across who would have been living there back then?' said Skegman.

'There's a few . . .' said Paulsen. 'In the same street – Tom Daws, retired now, but some big union guy back in the day. Alan Baxter – a racist cock who runs the local pub.' She made little attempt to hide her contempt. 'And Ronnie Fordyce – an ex-builder, with some previous for GBH on his record.'

'None of them strike me as potential child killers,' said Ojo.

'Do they all have alibis?' said Skegman.

'Yes – they were all checked out during the initial round of door-to-doors,' Paulsen replied. 'All three were in the pub until closing and then went home. Fordyce is the only one who lives alone – he's a widower.'

'So he's a reasonable fit then?' said Skegman. 'If the time of death is potentially after the pub closed.'

Finn nodded.

'There's certainly enough wiggle room over the time of death to make that possible – but there's no motive or forensic evidence we've established to tie him in,' he said.

'And what about Daws?' said Skegman.

'Didn't you say he was suffering from Alzheimer's?' said Finn, directing the question at Paulsen.

'Yes, he also doesn't have a car either. And as we've discussed before – the killer was careful not to leave any evidence behind. From what I've seen of Tom, I don't think he's got the presence of mind to do that,' she said.

'Are we looking further afield? We seem very focused on that one street,' said Skegman.

'We can certainly widen the scope – see who else in the area might have been around in 1993,' agreed Finn.

'And is there any suggestion the original conviction might have been unsafe?' said Skegman.

Ojo shook her head.

'It all looked pretty solid to me when I looked through the details earlier.' She went back to her desk and rummaged in a pile of paperwork until she found what she was looking for. 'One thing did stand out though. The SIO was a DI Peter Tolson. Reading through this, he was initially pretty sceptical about the guy they nicked – Dean Rawton.'

'Why?' said Skegman.

'Rawton was a career criminal with a long history of house burglaries. But he had no previous for violence. His fingerprints were all over the flat though. Vicki was bludgeoned to death with a table lamp, her son stabbed through the neck. Also, separate witnesses saw Rawton near the property at the time of the killings. Another says she saw him sprinting away covered in blood.'

'What motive for the murders was offered up in court?' said Skegman.

'That he was an opportunistic thief who broke into the flat on a weekday afternoon. At his trial the prosecution claimed he panicked when Vicki and Ben walked in on him.'

'What did Rawton say to that?' said Paulsen.

'Denied it throughout and pleaded not guilty,' said Ojo.

'But didn't you say before that he appealed it?' said Finn.

'Yes, soon after he was convicted. But for whatever reason, he's never contested it again.'

'He wouldn't be the first person to simply give up,' said Dattani. 'When you think you haven't got a chance against the system . . .'

'Given what we now know I think it's worth taking a deep dive into,' said Skegman. 'What have you got to lose? Treat it like a cold case. See if you can find Tolson and go and have a chat with Rawton as well. I'd be interested to know what both of them think about your current investigation. And let's keep this from the press for the time being – they're already complicating things enough without this being chucked into the pot.'

Finn rolled the permutations around in his mind for a second, trying to analyse what he *did* think. Something had bothered him while Ojo had been talking through the details of Rawton's conviction.

'If this is the same killer, then what are the chances they've done nothing since killing the Stratfords thirty years ago? Have they really just been sat on their hands? Or have there been more deaths since that we don't know about?' He looked around the room. 'And if not – why now?'

22

The last time Mattie Paulsen visited HMP Brazely had been during her first week working at Cedar House, two years earlier. Tucked away on the London–Surrey borders, it was a sprawl of grey rectangular blocks behind a high perimeter fence. If you didn't know better, you might think it was an old-fashioned factory hidden away in the English countryside. But she shivered as she pulled up at the security gate and flashed her warrant card. She could remember only too well the prisoner she'd visited back then. Few people genuinely got under her skin, but the memory of this man was still embedded there.

One person she was pleased to see again was the prison's governor, Jane Prentice. An easy-going, pragmatic woman, Paulsen had been impressed by her when they'd first met. She'd kept an eye out afterwards on the annual prison inspector's reports and noticed that Brazely was one of the few in the country to regularly avoid significant criticism. 'If you want something done properly, put a woman in charge' was a view frequently espoused by Paulsen's partner Nancy.

Prentice's office was the same as she recalled it – all modern greys and minimalist furniture. Some well-chosen abstract art on the walls gave it a welcome splash of colour.

'It's nice to see you again, DC Paulsen,' said Prentice as she handed her a cup of frothy coffee drawn from an expensive-looking machine in the corner of the room. Paulsen found herself pleased that she'd been remembered. She explained her reasons for coming and why she wanted to talk to Dean Rawton.

'Out of curiosity – why hasn't he been granted parole? It's been almost thirty years . . .' she said.

'For the most part, Rawton's been a model prisoner, but there was an episode with him a couple of years ago. He attacked another inmate with a brick. It had come loose from a wall and he used it to fracture the guy's skull.'

'Any particular reason?' said Paulsen.

'Yes – he'd been bullied by this man for quite some time. The frustration must have boiled over. We all missed the signs, I'm afraid.'

'Was that frustration *all* to do with this guy – or was there anything else to it?'

'How do you mean?' asked Prentice.

'Rawton's been here for a long time – it must get to you . . .' Prentice took a sip of her coffee.

'I don't recall anything like that coming up in the psych report. Is it relevant to why you're here?'

'Possibly,' said Paulsen.

Ten minutes later, Prentice was leading her through the long cream-bricked corridors of the main complex.

'By the way, do you remember the man you came to see the last time you were here?' she said.

The person she was referring to was called Kenny Fuller, but his prison nickname had been 'Smiler'. Not because of his cheerful demeanour, but because of the large scar on the back of his head. He'd been attacked with a machete in his youth and it had left behind a long cavernous dent resembling a grotesque smile. That was the external damage; it'd also left a legacy of blackouts and psychosis. Paulsen could still vividly see the jagged indentation in her mind's eye.

'I thought you'd be interested to know he's just been released,' continued Prentice.

'*What?*' said Paulsen, astonished.

The reason she'd interviewed him was over his association with a particularly dangerous organised crime boss known as the Handyman. Fuller was also widely believed to have been behind the murder of a corrupt policeman who'd been imprisoned at Brazely as part of the same investigation.

'You're kidding?'

'I'm afraid not – nothing was ever proven with regard to the death of DS Mike Godden. He served his time and was released on schedule a couple of months back.'

The idea of Kenny Fuller out there in the world stopped Paulsen in her tracks. She looked at Prentice and held her hands out. The governor shrugged.

'You and me both,' she said.

Prentice left Paulsen in a small sparse room with a table and a couple of chairs. After a short wait, a prison officer brought in Rawton. He was a slight man in his early sixties, with the air of a beaten dog about him. When he saw Paulsen waiting for him, he seemed awkward and uncomfortable. The officer motioned at him to take a seat and he hesitantly pulled back the chair and sat down. As she watched him, Paulsen instinctively thought he didn't look like a man comfortable with violence, but she also knew that meant absolutely nothing. Recalled too Prentice's story about the inmate he'd attacked.

She introduced herself and went through the necessary formalities, quickly adjusting to a slightly warmer tone than she'd originally intended. She'd surmised in the few moments they'd been together that he'd clam up if she didn't handle this with care. She explained carefully about the murders at number eighteen Pennington Road earlier that week. There was a definite flicker of *something* in his eyes.

'What makes you think I know anything that can help you,' said Rawton. He had a surprisingly gentle voice, like a reassuring old grandfather.

Paulsen searched him out, looking for the man the courts said had callously battered a woman to death, stabbed a young child in the neck. She could see nothing other than weariness and scepticism.

'At your trial, you pleaded not guilty. You told the police that you were innocent.'

'That's right,' he said with a nod, as if all she was seeking was confirmation of the point.

'You appealed against your sentence at the time – and yet you've never done so again. Why not?'

He smiled unexpectedly.

'You've clearly done your homework, DC Paulsen. You'll have seen the forensic evidence against me, the witness statements. It's hard to fight stuff like that.'

'Interesting choice of words – do you think there is something there to fight, then?'

'It was all a long time ago. What does it matter now?'

'I'm just asking – do you still believe you're innocent?'

Rawton smiled.

'You want to know if they got the wrong man? Is that it?' he said. There was steel now in his voice and it struck Paulsen how many different emotions she'd seen from this man already in a relatively short conversation.

'Did they?' she said.

He smiled.

'What you have to try and understand is why I might *not* want to answer that,' he said.

'I don't understand. Are you telling me you're afraid of something? Of someone?'

Rawton took a moment to consider his response.

'I have a daughter and two grandchildren. I still have ambitions of spending at least *part* of my life with my family.' He paused. 'Now do you understand what I'm saying?'

Paulsen was beginning to. If Rawton was hoping to get parole at some stage, then telling a police officer he still didn't think he'd done anything wrong after all these years wasn't going to help his cause. The lack of perceived responsibility and remorse after all this time would more than likely count significantly against him.

'This conversation is entirely confidential and it isn't being recorded. There's nothing you can say to me here which will be used against you,' she said.

He slowly shook his head.

'I'm not risking it. There's too much at stake.'

Paulsen decided to try another tack.

'I see from your file that you used to live in Monteith Grove – that's the parallel street to Pennington Road. Most of the burglaries you committed were in other parts of London, which makes sense.'

Rawton nodded.

'Yeah, you don't shit where you eat, as we used to say back in the day.'

'Exactly – so it might be construed a bit off that you chose to burgle Vicki Stratford's flat on a Wednesday afternoon in broad daylight. Especially when nearly every other burglary you were convicted for was during the night.'

Rawton sighed.

'You have to understand what this is like for me. I'm sitting opposite a policewoman . . .'

'Police officer is the correct term these days,' corrected Paulsen.

'Whatever – a police officer who's telling me stuff I was telling the police *myself* thirty years ago. Can you understand how that makes me feel? I just want to laugh – nothing personal,' he said.

'Why's that, Dean?'

He shook his head and again chose to keep his own counsel. He knew *something*, she thought, but it felt like her chances of getting it out of him were receding by the second.

'Alright, let's try this another way,' she said. 'I'm going to throw some names out, tell me if any of them mean anything to you.'

He looked at her warily and she could feel he was very close to walking away from this if she wasn't careful.

'Tom Daws . . .'

His face softened.

'I remember Tom. Decent bloke – used to see him in the pub a lot. Bit of a lefty, if you know what I mean. What's he got to do with any of this?'

'Nothing at all, probably. You used to drink in the Lamb's Head then?'

'Yeah. It was a proper boozer back then. Still there, is it?' Paulsen nodded. 'And is Alan Baxter still the gaffer?'

'Yes – he was the next person I was going to ask you about.'

'I liked the pub. I didn't like him though. But then I've never liked macho men. He was one of those who was always pumping iron. Like the size of his muscles correlated to the size of something else, if you know what I mean.'

Paulsen could well imagine what a thirty-something Baxter might have been like and it wasn't pleasant.

'Did he strike you as a dangerous man?'

'He certainly had a temper – and if he took against someone, he'd hold a grudge. I saw him chuck some teenagers out once. They'd been a bit rowdy but that was all. They hadn't caused any trouble, but he proper lost it with them. I didn't

178

see what happened outside, but I heard it – we all did, and saw the blood on his T-shirt when he came back in.'

Paulsen was jotting every word down in her pocketbook as he spoke.

'Do you think he's capable of killing someone?'

Rawton gave her a sideways look.

'Let me get this straight – you're asking me about these guys because you think one of *them* might have committed these murders, this week?' Now it was Paulsen's turn to be silent. 'And by association, you think the same person might have killed Vicki Stratford and her boy too? That's your chain of logic, or am I missing something here?'

'We're exploring every avenue, Dean.'

'Is that what they call it?'

It felt like they'd reached some sort of impasse.

'You tell me,' said Paulsen. 'Is it that crazy a suggestion?'

Rawton leant back in his chair.

'To answer your original question . . . I've been banged up in here since 1993. So I've no idea how dangerous someone like Alan Baxter is these days.'

'But he was back then?'

'As I said – he could be a pretty nasty piece of work – especially towards women. His lady friends always seemed to have unexpected bruises or black eyes.'

'And was Vicki Stratford one of them?'

'Not as far as I know.'

There was an extreme weariness now to both his expression and tone.

'How well did you know Vicki?'

'I didn't. As I said at the time.'

'Do you want to tell me what happened the day she died? From your perspective?'

'Not really. Are we done yet?'

He turned to look at the prison officer at the door and Paulsen realised she might have pushed it too far.

'Almost. Just one more name for you – Ronnie Fordyce?'

Rawton sighed.

'Christ, he's not still knocking around, is he?'

'Still lives at number forty-five,' said Paulsen.

He seemed lost in the memories again.

'Another one I used to see in the pub. He and Daws were good mates. Baxter as well – which surprised me, because I thought Tom was one of the good guys.'

'And Fordyce wasn't?'

'I didn't say that. I just tried to keep a distance. Ronnie used to be quite well connected back then, if you know what I mean.'

He turned again to the prison officer at the door, who herself gave Paulsen a sharp look.

'And I think that's all I really want to say to you about any of this.'

'Why are you so reticent to give anyone your version of what happened in 1993?' she said. 'I promise you the conversation's totally confidential.'

Rawton seemed to genuinely think about the question.

'I'm sorry more people have died. But I'm a ghost from a long time ago and I don't see any good coming from this conversation. Not for me, anyway.'

'Did you kill Vicki Stratford and her son?' said Paulsen, deciding to go for broke.

'Just a ghost . . .' he repeated.

This time he rose to his feet and walked to the door.

23

The rain was crashing down on the M3 but Finn barely noticed. Retired Detective Inspector Peter Tolson lived in Winchester and he'd decided to visit him in person. If there was any doubt in the man's mind about the investigation into Vicki and Ben Stratford's deaths, it would be much easier to gauge face to face.

The rain was subsiding by the time he arrived in Hampshire. He parked and grabbed a sandwich in a cafe close to the large statue of King Alfred that dominated the city centre's Broadway. He watched as a couple of floppy-haired teenagers – Winchester College boys, judging by their uniforms – chatted quietly at the next table. There was certainly a different vibe to the place than you found in south London, though he was aware that, like all cities, it contained an underbelly. A few miles out from the affluent centre was the same poverty and inequality you found anywhere. But he could see the pull of retiring somewhere like this and briefly found himself wondering what Karin would have thought about it. German-born, she'd fallen in love with London and had made it her home. They'd never got as far as discussing what their post-retirement life might have looked like.

Tolson had certainly done well for himself. He lived with his wife in a semi-detached house on a leafy hill which gave a perfect view down on to the city's huge Gothic cathedral. Finn would have recognised him as ex-job even if he'd been in a crowd. A burly Yorkshireman with a lived-in face, he carried a quiet gravity about him. You wouldn't want to be the burglar who broke into this house – even in his early seventies, he looked like someone who could still handle himself. While Finn sized him up, he was also conscious Tolson was doing exactly the same thing in return, clearly curious to see what the new breed looked like. His wife was Thai and the interior of their home reflected her background. Ornate framed artwork lined the walls, and a large gold Buddha took pride of place on the mantelpiece in the living room.

Tolson didn't even bother offering him tea or coffee. Once Finn had set admiring eyes on the vintage bottle of Speyside sitting on his sideboard, the host had seen a kindred spirit. Clutching a small measure each, they spent a few minutes comparing then and now. Pipsqueak constables Tolson remembered bawling out back in the day were now borough commanders. Procedures Finn followed as second nature had the older man shaking his head in disbelief.

'I know what I miss the most about it all – having a pint with your mates afterwards in the bar. These days I suppose that's frowned upon? "Drinking cultures" and all that.' He said the words with clear disdain.

'Not really,' said Finn. 'It's just that nobody has the time any more. Most of us are too knackered to head to the pub after work.'

The tradition of celebrating a good result with a beer still went on, but Finn imagined the quiet, tired affairs with which his team marked their successes were a far cry from the more raucous occasions of Tolson's day. He explained the shift patterns at Cedar House and the former detective rolled his eyes.

'Typical – sounds like you've got a fraction of the numbers I used to have, doing three times the work. No wonder you haven't got time for a drink. I'm glad I'm out of it, to be honest.'

It was when the conversation turned to the subject of the Stratfords that Finn sensed a definite change in tone.

'I'm absolutely sure we got the right man, so while I'm happy to help you, I don't really know what it is you're looking to get from me,' he said to a question Finn hadn't yet asked.

'Given it's the same property, and the similarity between the victims' profiles, it's just a courtesy call really – to check there isn't something we're missing,' Finn replied, aware of how woolly that sounded.

'You drove down from London for a courtesy call?' said Tolson, not fooled. He leant forwards. 'It's pure coincidence, that's all. There's no way it can be the same killer. Dean Rawton killed Vicki and Ben Stratford – no ifs, no buts – and I'm quite comfortable with that.' He leant back again and crossed his arms.

Finn had wondered how Tolson might react to his visit. There wasn't a single one of them – past or present – who liked having their work questioned. Finn himself knew how much he bristled under the same scrutiny – not that it happened too often. But he'd been involved in a few investigations where this kind of follow-up had occurred. There were some events that you could never truly know the truth about. All you could do was try and narrow down the possibilities until you had something which, by common consent, was the likeliest scenario and then let a jury decide. These were of course the jobs that haunted you in case you *had* missed something crucial. Finn had been through a few of those and Tolson's defensiveness was telling.

He went through the details of the Nicholls murders before presenting the two photographs of the different crime scenes. Tolson spread them out on the coffee table in front of them and studied each one carefully. If the sight of Vicki Stratford's corpse after all these years bothered him, he didn't let it show.

'Is this all you've got – two dead bodies lying on a floor?' he said. 'Come on – copper to copper, what do you think?'

'I think there's a vague similarity to it. I accept there's a lack of hard evidence to connect them – and yes, it could well be coincidental – but ...' Finn spread out his hands, 'it's been nagging at me.'

'And you wanted to look me in the eye and decide for yourself whether I'd fucked something up?' said Tolson. Finn kept his own counsel. The mood in the room had become decidedly chilly. The older man looked away and considered the argument. Finn could guess the trajectory of his thinking. Once you got past your own ego, professionalism kicked in. Tolson had been in the job long enough to know Finn was within his rights to ask the question. It wasn't necessarily that some glaring error had been made all those years ago, but was there a seed of doubt over something? Some small detail he knew of that might now be coming back to bite him on the arse?

'I read the file before I came down,' said Finn. 'You had some reservations about Rawton when he emerged as a suspect, didn't you?'

And that's when he saw it – the first brief flicker of uncertainty in Tolson's eyes.

'Initially, there were a few things which didn't seem to add up. He didn't have any history of violence, for a start, and he also had an alibi.'

'Which was?'

Finn already knew from the file but was interested in seeing Tolson talk it through. Stress-testing his own investigation thirty years on.

'His wife said they'd been out shopping together that

afternoon. Nowadays with the number of cameras there are, it would be a fairly easy thing to prove. But back then CCTV coverage was much more limited. You're right – for a while I wasn't convinced, but that changed once the witnesses who saw him at the crime scene began coming forward. And of course, we found his fingerprints inside the property.'

'The witnesses didn't come forward for nearly ten days. Didn't you find that odd?'

Tolson huffed impatiently.

'Of course not. There's nothing unusual about that – happens all the time. Or used to – don't tell me that's changed as well.'

Finn nodded. Tolson was right, but what was bugging him was you'd expect a DI to be questioning *everything* dispassionately. Because that's what you did – asked yourselves those awkward questions to make sure you'd analysed it all from every possible angle.

'And what did you make of Rawton when you interviewed him?'

Tolson took a sip of his whisky, rolled it around his mouth for a moment.

'He was a deer in the headlights. You'll know yourself – with those sorts, that can mean anything.'

Finn briefly recalled David Hermitage shifting nervously on his seat and nodded.

'From my perspective, I was looking at a man I believed had panicked and killed a mother and child in a flat he'd simply intended to burgle. For me, his reaction was entirely consistent with that.' He drained the last of his drink and cupped the empty glass in his hand thoughtfully. 'There was something haunted about him too – and that sold it as much as anything. He wasn't angry or defiant at being accused. You could see he was deeply affected and that's something you can't hide.'

'Sometimes they're like that because they *know* they're innocent and they're staring down the barrel of a life sentence,' said Finn.

Tolson nodded.

'True – and we considered that. But when you took the evidence, an alibi that couldn't be stood up, and his demeanour under interview, I was comfortable we had the right man. And I would remind you the jury agreed – it was a unanimous verdict.'

'So tell me about Vicki Stratford – what kind of person was she?'

Tolson was now visibly looking irritated.

'How does that information help your investigation?'

'I can't rule out a connection between the two sets of murders at this stage – because I simply don't know enough. For all I know I'm dealing with a copycat. The more you can tell me about what happened back then, the more I can form a dispassionate view.'

Again, it was the common language of police work that he'd expect Tolson to understand. The man nodded gruffly.

'She was a bright girl as I recall. An accountant, I think – but one thing I do remember is she didn't have many enemies. Until Rawton presented himself, we were having a hell of a job finding a motive for what happened. If you've read the file, you'll know she wasn't sexually assaulted.' Tolson could see immediately that the answer was resonating with Finn. 'Which goes for a hell of a lot of murders, as you'll know,' he added.

Finn nodded, acknowledging the point.

'Out of curiosity – was there anyone else who came into the frame before Rawton?'

'From memory, we talked to a lot of the local residents. There was a nasty piece of work who ran the pub at the end of the street. We looked hard at him for a while because Vicki had turned him down at one point, I think.'

'Alan Baxter?' said Finn.

'That's the fella. He was behind the bar at the time of the murders, so we ruled him out. Unpleasant little shithole of a place it was.'

'Exactly the same alibi this time round,' said Finn, almost to himself.

Tolson didn't seem to hear him.

'And there was another man – Fordwych? Fordyce? Presented himself as some sort of pillar of the community, but had some nasty priors. He was painting a kitchen in Croydon at the time, so we ruled him out too.'

'What about Tom Daws?'

'I remember that name. Union guy, worked on the railways – kept asking me questions about the Police Federation.'

'Did you interview him?'

Tolson shook his head.

'Not as a suspect, no. His family knew the Stratfords though. I think their kids went to the same school. He was pretty cut up about the whole thing.'

Finn remembered Abi Daws mentioning her little brother had been a friend of Ben Stratford.

'Was he ever in the frame?'

'No – another one who had an alibi. I think he was working on the day.' He shrugged. 'It was all irrelevant in the end anyway because we caught the killer. There was simply no one else it could have been.'

Despite the emphasis of his words, there was nothing Tolson had said that was shifting Finn's unease. If anything, the parallels between the two sets of murders felt that bit stronger.

187

Once the conversation moved off the subject of the Stratfords, the retired detective seemed to relax again. They talked about a few high-profile court cases that had been in the news lately, and some of the more notorious Met Police investigations which had made the headlines in recent years. Tolson listened rapt, as Finn shared a few morsels of insider knowledge about them. And as they spoke, Finn sensed a restless spirit, making him wonder whether he was looking at his own future. Without his job, who exactly would he be? Just a man sitting at home, drinking vintage whisky, reading impotently about things he was no longer party to. The frightening thing was, Tolson wasn't fighting bereavement either.

'I retired at just the right moment,' he said as he walked Finn through the hallway to the front door. 'I was a heart attack waiting to happen back then, to be honest. The doctors said my cholesterol was off the charts and I had the blood pressure of a deep-sea diver. It was my wife who talked sense into me in the end.' He looked up sharply at Finn. 'Are you a married man?'

The question took Finn by surprise. It always did.

'No. I'm single,' he said quickly. 'Separated . . .' he lied, feeling like he needed to explain it. The other man nodded awkwardly.

'None of my business. But try and get yourself sorted out. Sometimes you need someone in your life to tell you what you don't want to hear.'

'*Ain't that the truth,*' said Sadie.

24

Finn drove out of Winchester thinking through the various questions the conversation with Tolson had thrown up. He stopped on the way back at a motorway service station near Basingstoke simply to give his head a break. Sitting in the corner of a deserted cafe, he tried putting himself into the other man's shoes. Looking at the evidence and the way the investigation had unfolded, he decided he probably would have come to much the same conclusion about Dean Rawton. But he'd heard enough – seen enough in Tolson's reactions – to know something wasn't quite right. He was also acutely aware Rawton had served a near thirty-year term for the offences. If Tolson had got it wrong, the price would be high.

Sipping at an overpriced can of Coke, he casually watched a young woman walk past his table hand in hand with a little girl, no more than around four years of age. The child nagged at her mother and the woman stopped wearily, took off the backpack she was carrying and produced a tissue from one of its pouches. She held it out for her daughter to blow her nose into, checked she was okay and smiled reassuringly at her. Reaching into the bag again, she pulled out a tangerine, which produced a broad beam of pleasure from the little girl.

Finn watched the whole process, entranced. It was a world he didn't know; one he probably wouldn't ever know now. Karin had pleaded with him before her death to find someone to have children with after she was gone. She'd thought it would be good for him. On reflection, he now understood why – she must have believed a new relationship, a family, would give him a fresh point of focus, something to move him past her. She'd foreseen all of this – the mess he now found himself in – and had tried her best to prevent it. He realised with a jolt of surprise that he couldn't remember the last time he'd thought about having children. Somewhere along the line, it had ceased to be important to him and he hadn't even noticed. He wondered if that was why the fate of Sadie and Liam Nicholls had so got under his skin, what demons beneath the surface they'd stirred.

He looked around the empty cafe, aware he was dallying when he should be hurrying, his heart dragging when it ought to be pumping with urgency. None of his emotional reactions to anything were quite what they should be, and he knew it. Finn picked up his phone, thought about what he was going to do and on an impulse speed-dialled Murray. The signal was poor and there was a silence as the device tried to connect. He looked down at the display as it offered its usual split-second choice: abort the call now and its recipient would never know it had ever been made. Instinctively his finger jabbed out and he killed it before it could connect. The woman and the little girl were now passing through the sliding doors of the exit and Finn suddenly felt like the loneliest man in the world.

'It's as if Rawton's given up,' said Mattie Paulsen as they regrouped in the incident room later. 'Not on getting out of prison, but on clearing his name.'

'And yet he still didn't want to tell you anything,' said Ojo. 'You'd think if he was the victim of a miscarriage of justice that all he'd want to do is talk about it.'

'To be honest, I couldn't work him out. I couldn't tell whether he thought he was innocent, or whether he'd simply accepted his own guilt after all these years. But I'm certain he was holding something back.'

Finn had been listening to Paulsen's account of her meeting with Rawton in fascination, given the context of what he'd been told in Hampshire. The strange ambiguity around both the man who was convicted and the man who'd put him away was striking. There was a waft of something smelly around the whole thing.

'Tolson was certainly defensive, but I didn't get the sense he was sitting on some huge fuck-up,' he mused.

'So what was he hiding?' said Ojo.

Finn ran his tongue around his teeth as he tried to nail it.

'I think . . . a general unease that *something* wasn't right back then. But before we all get excited – another thought's occurred to me . . .'

The photographs of the two crime scenes were now pinned to one of the whiteboards at the end of the room. Finn got up and went over to them.

'I can buy that there's a chance Rawton didn't kill Vicki and Ben Stratford. There's still plenty of compelling evidence that he did, by the way . . . but, I can accept that as a possibility.' He looked around the room to check he was taking them with him. 'If that's the case, then the implication is their killer is still free. But that doesn't necessarily mean the *same* person killed Sadie and Liam. The two things aren't necessarily mutually exclusive. We could still be looking at two separate killers.'

He let that sink in. Sami Dattani had joined the meeting late and was wolfing down a sandwich. He swallowed a mouthful quickly and held up a finger.

'Doesn't mean they're not either . . . all due respect, guv.'

Finn nodded in agreement.

'No, it doesn't, and there's also the possibility the killer – past, present or both – is someone local we haven't identified yet.'

Ojo glanced down at her notebook.

'I've been looking at some of the other homicides in the area over the past thirty years. There's not many unsolved and there's very few that fit the particular MO we're looking at,' she said.

'Is there even one on paper that looks like it might have been committed by the same person who killed either the Nichollses or the Stratfords?' said Paulsen.

Ojo shook her head.

'Not really. There's a lot of gang crime, plenty of drug-related stuff, domestics . . . but nothing like this.'

'So where does that leave us?' said Dattani, wiping the crumbs of his sandwich off his fingers.

'In pretty much the same position we were before, surely,' growled Paulsen.

'Is there anything other than the flat they lived in that links Sadie and Vicki Stratford together?' said Finn, ignoring her.

Ojo shook her head.

'It was one of the first things I checked after I compared the two crime scenes. Apart from dying before Sadie was even born, Vicki came from Islington originally. From what I can tell, her family lived their whole lives in north London. She bought the flat in 1991 as a first-time buyer. Nothing in her education or career connects in any way with the Nicholls family in Newcastle.'

Finn decided to gauge the temperature of the room.

'So how do we all feel about Vicki?' He pointed at the picture of her dead body pinned up behind him. 'Is this a relevant line of inquiry or a distraction that's eating up time and energy we should be devoting somewhere else?'

Dattani was the first to bite.

'I was sceptical at first – when we were just going by the two photos. But having heard what you've both said about

Tolson and Rawton, personally I think it's worth persisting with.'

'I agree,' said Paulsen. 'And there is one thing that links both Vicki and Sadie. Tolson told you he was struggling to find a motive until Rawton came along, that Vicki didn't have any enemies. It's almost an identical description of where we are with Sadie . . .'

Finn nodded, remembering how the same thought had struck him in Tolson's living room. There was an abstract symmetry to the four murders.

'As the DCI said before – let's treat this like a cold case,' he said. 'Jacks – do you want to see if you can find some of the witnesses who came forward at Rawton's trial? I'll get the evidence used against him dug out and sent for DNA testing.'

'There's someone else we should speak to, guv. Luke Daws – Abi's little brother. He was also around at the time,' said Paulsen.

'I thought he lived in Australia now,' said Finn.

'He does, but he's back in London. He flew in yesterday. Abi wasn't expecting him for a few more weeks so he's about if we want to talk to him.'

Finn looked at her curiously.

'When did you discover that?'

Paulsen looked awkward.

'Abi called me earlier,' she said.

Finn nodded.

'Tolson mentioned Tom's kids. He'd have been pretty small – but there might be something important he can remember.'

'And how do we feel about some of the other people, guv?' said Ojo. 'The ones who were there thirty years ago – Daws, Baxter, Fordyce . . .?'

'We keep an open mind and let the evidence lead us. Right now, that's what we're short of – something substantive we can work with. On that note – forensics are almost done, both at Sadie's flat and the crime scene in New Cross and the autopsies are complete. They've found nothing new that can help us. So we need to look harder – we know Liam was taken nearly two miles from his home before being dumped. There isn't CCTV in either street, but there must be some coverage on the routes between the two locations. There's also a murder weapon and Liam's clothing out there somewhere – I've asked uniform to widen their search. Let's shake the tree and see if we can't make something fall out for us.'

'*Bravo!*' said Sadie in Finn's ear. He did his best to ignore her.

The others got to their feet and began to disperse.

'Boss . . .' said a voice, and he turned to see Paulsen standing behind him. He briefly worried if she'd caught his slight moment of distraction.

'Yes, Mattie?'

'I meant to bring this up before, but I forgot. I spoke to Nathan Roach yesterday.'

'And?'

Paulsen looked unsure.

'At first, I thought he was just a guy having a mid-life crisis. But having slept on it, something about him was still bothering me. So I gave his old office a call earlier just to double-check I hadn't missed something. They said he quit very suddenly. Walked out on his job, walked out on his marriage, with virtually no warning. They still have no idea why. He told me he and his wife were having a trial separation.'

'Which might well be the truth,' said Finn.

'So why leave your job as well? Why leave the area? Why move away from your kids – especially if it's only a trial thing? It doesn't make sense.'

'Sometimes when people say trial . . . it can be a euphemism for something more permanent,' said Finn.

'I'm just saying – he's in his fifties now. He would have been in his early twenties when Vicki Stratford and her son were murdered. According to his birth certificate, he was born in Streatham. So what if he lived down here originally then moved away? And if so, *why* did he move away?'

Finn was now nodding as he followed her argument.

'It's certainly worth another conversation with him . . .'

He was about to add more when his desk phone rang. He checked the number, held up a hand by way of apology and took it. He listened for a few moments, then swore under his breath as he replaced the receiver.

'Guv?' said Paulsen.

'That was the media office. They've just been contacted by a journalist from the *Sunday Express* who was after a quote. They reckon they've got an exclusive interview with a woman who says Patrick Clarke killed her son.'

25

They found him knee-deep in weeds. Clarke was in the back garden of a small ground-floor flat in Blackheath. The estate agent sign with 'Sold' emblazoned across it was still standing outside the front. Earlier when Paulsen called to say why they'd wanted to speak with him again, there'd been no great reaction. Just as he'd been at Cedar House before, he was both polite and courteous. Clarke explained he was renovating the garden for a couple who'd just bought the property. He said he'd be happy to answer their questions but they'd have to come out to him. Having promised to start work on the place today, it was clear he intended to keep his word.

The garden certainly looked like it needed some help – a patio of broken paving stones stretched out on to a small jungle of wildflowers and overgrown grass. They were sitting around a plastic green table that looked like it had been there for some time. It was liberally smeared in bird shit, with a dusting of mouldy leaves. They'd barely taken their seats when Clarke began to speak. It came fast and fluently without any apparent discomfort or reticence, and he made sure to look them both in the eyes periodically too, just as he had in the interview room. If men were her thing, Paulsen thought, then Patrick Clarke might have stood a chance. Dispassionately she could see he was attractive, but it went deeper than simply his physical appearance. There was something undeniably hypnotic about the man.

'I was a teaching assistant once. A long time ago now. Teaching's what I really wanted to do, way back . . .' He took a melancholic look around the tangled garden. 'We were on a trip to the Lake District.'

'Sorry . . .' said Finn, interrupting. 'When was this, which school, and what age group are we talking about?'

Clarke gave a brief nod of apology.

'It was 2013. St Julian's Academy in East Ham. And they were thirteen- to fourteen-year-olds. So Year 9s.'

Paulsen jotted the information down and Clarke's gaze settled on her spidery writing as she wrote.

'One of the kids drowned.' He said the words matter-of-factly. 'He asked me for permission to go swimming in the lake and I said yes. I thought he meant generally – as part of the group – supervised, somewhere safe later on. But he slipped away when he should have been at the hotel. We found out afterwards. He'd been drinking alcohol as well. There was another kid with him who survived. He told everyone I'd given them the go-ahead to do it.'

'Did it go to court? That's a manslaughter charge, if you were the responsible adult,' said Finn.

For the first time, the calm flow of words stopped. Clarke was staring into space now, his voice audibly quieter when he next spoke.

'It should have done. I was lucky. I suppose that's what people would say. The view taken was that I'd been deceived. But his parents blamed me, so I'm not surprised they've given an interview to the papers now. They know where I live and spoke to the press when I was convicted the following year. It wouldn't have taken any journalist long to dig all this up. I was half expecting it, to be honest.'

Finn and Paulsen exchanged a glance.

'So this very tragic incident happens, then one year later

you attack and nearly kill a woman in south London,' said Finn. Clarke nodded calmly. 'I can't help but ask – is there a connection between these two events, Patrick?'

'Of course not,' he said.

'What I mean is – were you struggling with the boy's death emotionally? Did you get help in the aftermath or did you bottle it up?'

Paulsen was watching Finn carefully as he spoke. If you didn't know him, you wouldn't hear the slight hint of emotion in his voice. The tiny crack of it.

'What are you trying to say?' said Clarke.

'In your opinion, did the tragedy at the lake contribute to what happened later?'

Clarke smiled unexpectedly. There was something unnerving about it, Paulsen thought. She'd been finding him a fascinating, charismatic figure just minutes before, now suddenly he'd become something else. Something dangerous, even.

'If you like,' he said.

There was a silence, broken only by the distant squawk of a crow.

'Hypothetically, what if I *do* like,' said Finn. 'I mean, if I take that view – that you were someone deeply affected by a traumatic experience, which later led to a catastrophic loss of control – well, you can see where I'm going with that, can't you? Given the events of this week?'

Clarke nodded.

'It's a reasonable question to ask in the circumstances, yes. So let me be quite clear – I haven't lifted a finger in anger since I was released from prison – and that's the truth.'

'Where were you on the night Sadie Nicholls was killed?' said Paulsen.

'I've already told you – I was with a friend.'

'We're going to need something a bit more concrete from you now,' said Finn. 'Who were you with? Where did you meet? What time did you meet? When did you leave?'

'I can't tell you any of those things. I gave my word to someone – and as I've already explained, I like to think I'm a man of my word.'

'It's an alibi, Patrick,' said Finn. 'Do yourself a favour: rule yourself out of this investigation, get the press off your back, and most of all, spare your mother any further aggravation. You don't have to tell us who it was – but at least tell us where you were and when you were there?'

This seemed to penetrate and for a moment Paulsen thought he might crack, but he shook his head again.

'I'm sorry – I just can't. You've already searched my home and looked inside my van, and you can't have found anything inside Sadie's flat, because I was never in it. So you know what? I don't need to tell you a thing, do I? If you think I'm guilty of something – then prove it.'

'He's right,' said Finn later as they drove back across south London. 'Patrick's history is all very interesting and it explains a lot about him, but it doesn't mean he killed Sadie and Liam.'

'But does it explain everything about him?' said Paulsen. 'He was struggling to deal with this kid's death – so a year on, he attacks some random stranger in the street? I don't buy that.'

Finn focused on the road for a moment, thinking about it.

'I'm genuinely getting a sense of a man trying to rebuild his life. He had no criminal record prior to his conviction – so how else do you motivate what he did? Where did that violence come from?'

Paulsen thought about it for a moment.

'I can see that bottling up strong emotions over a period of time would have an effect on you. That's human nature, isn't it?' she said. 'I should know . . .'

Finn knew exactly what she was referring to. When he'd first met Paulsen, she'd been keeping a secret of her own, one that had very nearly consumed her. She'd blamed herself for the death of a paedophile she'd been investigating just prior to her transfer to Cedar House. The terse, take-no-prisoners woman she was today was a *lot* more relaxed than the person he'd first encountered. She'd been angrier then, more impulsive, and Finn liked to think, somewhat vainly, that his influence had helped calm some of her demons.

'You found a way to control your feelings, or at least get past them,' he replied. 'That's what I see when I look at Clarke – the same sort of self-control.'

Paulsen shook her head.

'I don't. I feel like I haven't got a proper sense of this guy at all. Who he really is or what he might be capable of.'

Finn thought about the two occasions he'd spoken to Patrick Clarke, the quiet stillness the man carried, and realised Paulsen was a hundred per cent right.

A short time later, the pair found themselves back in the warmth of the Daws' living room in Pennington Road. Paulsen had rung Abi just before they'd left Clarke in Blackheath, asking if they could speak to her brother. It was just the four of them – Tom was out taking a walk with Ronnie. It was clear to see that Abi was delighted to have her little brother back. Born in south London, Luke Daws looked and sounded like a guy who spent most of the year surfing and eating oversized langoustines from the barbie. All he needed was the hat with the corks, Paulsen thought.

'Why did you and your mother go to Australia in the first place, if you don't mind me asking?' said Finn.

'Jeez,' said Luke, almost under his breath, and Paulsen made a bet with herself that before the conversation ended, he'd call one of them 'mate'.

'Mum met a guy from Melbourne in London not long after she and Dad split up. She wanted to make a fresh start with him. I was very attached to my mother as a child, while Abi and Dad were always super close, so it seemed to make sense for me to go with her,' he said.

'It must have been a pretty amicable divorce then?' said Finn and Luke nodded.

'Their marriage sort of fizzled out – Mum never really had much interest in all the union stuff Dad was involved with,' said Abi. She looked across at her brother. 'And you're still a mummy's boy now, aren't you?'

Luke grinned infectiously.

'This is why I stay down under most of the time.'

'Do you see much of one another?' asked Paulsen.

Luke and Abi exchanged a look.

'It's difficult,' said Abi. 'The cost and then the pandemic has made visiting quite tricky.' She turned to look at her brother. 'But I speak to you and Mum . . . once every couple of weeks, I suppose?'

Luke nodded in affirmation.

'So what brought you back this week?' said Finn.

'A new job,' said Luke with a broad smile. 'I work in IT – I've had a rough couple of years what with everything – but now there's some money coming in, I thought I'd hop on a plane.'

'Out of curiosity what brought you back this week – I thought you weren't due for a while?' said Paulsen.

Luke grinned.

'Saw a cheap flight and grabbed it – reckoned I'd give them both a surprise.'

'You've picked quite a week to come,' said Paulsen. 'You've heard about what's happened at number eighteen?'

Luke's expression turned serious.

'It's incredible. The same house where the Stratfords used to live – what are the odds on that?'

'That's why we're here,' said Finn. 'We're looking at any potential links between the two sets of murders.'

Luke looked genuinely dumbfounded.

'But they caught the guy who did it . . .'

Finn was already nodding before he could complete the sentence.

'There may well be no connection, but there's a few things that are making us look again. You were friends with Ben Stratford, weren't you?'

'Yeah – he was my first best mate. I remember that flat very well.'

'What do you recall about what happened back then?'

Luke looked through the living room window and out on to the street.

'I remember that his mum was a nice woman. And that there were always Jaffa Cakes,' he said. 'China plates with Jaffa Cakes on – I've got a strong memory of that. The day they were killed I'd been playing with Ben just hours before—' He broke off suddenly and looked over at Abi. 'Wasn't Ronnie Fordyce having a thing with Vicki? I remember Mum saying years later she thought there was something funny going on there.'

Abi shook her head.

'Ron's always denied it.'

'You actually asked him?' said Luke.

'Of course – he didn't mind.'

Paulsen looked across at Finn as they listened. He gave a slight non-committal shrug in response to the information.

'It must have been a pretty traumatic event for you?' said Paulsen. 'Not many kids go through an experience like that.'

Immediately Luke looked upset. He was one of those people, she thought, who couldn't hide their emotions. They were written across his face and seemed to change according to each question. It was a fascinating, immediate contrast to the puzzle box that was Patrick Clarke.

'I suppose not. But in some ways my age protected me, you know? I was too young to know what was going on. Mum and Dad kept it from me at the time; I only found out what really happened years later.'

'Is there anything at all you can remember about the Stratfords or that period that you think we should know about?' said Finn.

'No, why would there be? The bloke that did it should stay in the slammer for the rest of his days – I know that much. I may not have understood what was going on but I saw the effect it had on people.'

'Specifically?' said Finn.

'Mum and Dad, Uncle Ron.' He saw their bemused expression and smiled. 'He's not really my uncle, but that's what I always called him. In hindsight, I can see that they were all pretty freaked out. I think it could even have played a part in my parents' break-up if I'm honest.' Abi glanced over at Luke and he held his hands out. 'Can't tell you exactly what I mean by that – but it just cast a shadow, you know?'

There was a silence and Finn looked over at Paulsen to see if she had any further questions but she shook her head and Luke shrugged.

'Sorry, mate. I don't know what it is you're looking for – but I don't think I've got your answer.'

'So Fordyce and Vicki Stratford were potentially in a relationship,' said Paulsen as they walked back out on to the street afterwards.

'What's interesting is Tolson told me the pub landlord, Baxter, was also interested in Vicki.'

'A love triangle, maybe? But how would that relate to Sadie's death?'

'It doesn't,' said Sadie.

Finn shook his head.

'It doesn't,' he said softly.

They walked a little further, crossed the road and rang on Nathan Roach's bell – the third person on their shopping list for the afternoon. There was no reply and as they looked the place over, they could see curtains drawn and shutters closed on both levels of the building. When they tried the next-door neighbour, she told them she'd seen Roach heading for the station with heavy-looking bags the previous night.

'Where's he run off to again and why?' said Paulsen as they headed back to Finn's car.

He was about to answer when something caught his eye, and she turned to see what he was looking at. A poster had been stuck on to the back of a lamp post. For a moment Paulsen thought it was an appeal for a missing pet. But the centrepiece was a crudely photocopied picture of Patrick Clarke, clearly taken from a distance. Above the image were two words in bold capitals.

CHILD KILLER

26

'The moment we start to bake these five core strategies in to our everyday processes . . .' David Hermitage drummed his fingers against the flip chart mounted on the easel next to him and produced a sharp smile, 'we can start to expect a ten to fifteen per cent better yield across the business as a whole. It's a win-win however you look at it.'

He looked around the meeting room, pleased to see the admiring nods of his three colleagues.

Things were back on an even keel and he was sick of feeling sick. He hadn't heard another word from Lucy since her threat to blackmail him. She was making him sweat – he knew that – but he was also holding out the slim hope that she was having second thoughts about the whole idea. As he'd travelled into work preparing his presentation, he'd even managed to convince himself that her silence meant she'd simply decided to fade away. Actual blackmail was something people did in those godawful soaps Emily and Charlotte were addicted to. It didn't happen in real life to people like him. That's what he'd told himself, anyway.

The presentation had gone well, with the added benefit that it had given him something to focus on too. At the moment it felt a little like he was playing the part of David Hermitage rather than being himself, but that didn't matter. After the week he'd had, it was hardly surprising if he felt a bit hollow. The fact he'd been arrested – and released – in connection to a high-profile murder investigation was something he'd managed to contain. Life went on, or at least an approximation of normality did.

'Thanks for coming in, guys – let's have a catch-up on Zoom next week and see how you're finding things.'

He maintained the slick smile as the three twenty-somethings picked up their belongings and said their goodbyes. He watched them go with no little envy. He remembered being that age – full of vim and vigour. The world hadn't done anything awful to them personally yet, but it would – as it did to everyone sooner or later. His smile faded and he gathered together his own scattered papers. He looked up and saw through the glass wall one of the marketing execs talking animatedly to an immaculately dressed woman with her back to him. They seemed to be getting on famously, laughing as they were walking. It was when he looked the second time he felt his stomach drop like he'd just driven over a hill at speed. The woman had turned slightly and now he could see the side of her face. It couldn't be, he thought, it just couldn't be. He was frantic to see her features properly. But if it was who he thought it was, he was equally desperate not to be spotted. He stood stock-still, caught in a corridor of uncertainty, and watched in horror as the woman reached out and shook the man's hand. She turned and headed towards the lift and now he could see quite clearly it was Lucy. She looked at him straight in the eye, winked, then followed the three twenty-somethings into the lift.

'Shit,' said David out loud to himself. He walked out of the meeting room, his mind playing catch-up with what he'd just seen. He briefly thought about chasing after the man she'd been talking to and stopped himself. He didn't want *anyone* knowing that he knew Lucy – God knows how that could come back and bite him on the arse later. Instead, he jammed his finger into the call lift button.

'Looking for someone?' said Lucy, as he finally emerged at the bottom of the building. She was standing patiently like a dog owner waiting for an errant pet to catch up.

'What are you doing here?' he hissed, aware the security officer manning the front desk had seen him sprinting from the lift doors.

'I set up a meeting with your marketing people. A really helpful guy called Greg. Nice to see you're not all pervs . . .'

'What do you mean, you set up a meeting?' he said, ignoring the dig.

She smiled, sharp as a blade.

'It's not hard. I phoned pretending to be from a digital advertising start-up. I've got a friend who's done some of that sort of stuff, so I know all the jargon. It was just a preliminary conversation about a potential deal that will never happen, so relax. I just wanted you to see how easy it is to walk straight into the centre of your world and create havoc.' The smile disappeared. 'Did you think I would just disappear?' she said.

'And if I do give you some money – will you go away for good?'

'Probably.'

The word hung there for a moment. He swallowed.

'You've got me wrong,' he said. 'I was Sadie's friend – and I really did just try and help her.'

Her expression didn't change. He held his hands up in surrender. 'How much do you want?'

'Thirty grand,' she said.

'*What?*' he shouted. The security guard at the desk looked up sharply. 'I haven't got that kind of money,' he said, lowering his voice.

'You'd better find it then. Or you know what will happen.'

The knifepoint smile returned before she turned and left.

★   ★   ★

'Have you seen this?'

Ronnie Fordyce stared with distaste at the flyer that had just been slapped down next to his plate of fish and chips. The blurred face of Patrick Clarke was looking back up at him.

'You know there's an actual fishmonger in Catford, Al? You don't have to keep serving up Captain Birdseye . . .'

Alan Baxter scowled and sat down next to him.

'Never mind the fucking food, Ron.'

Fordyce looked around the pub. It was nearly half past seven in the evening, and the place, as usual, was quiet as the grave.

'Perhaps if you made a little more of an effort to improve the culinary standard here, you might get a bit more business?'

Baxter stabbed at the poster with his finger.

'Doesn't this bother you?'

Fordyce looked slowly up at him.

'Your work, I take it?'

Baxter pursed his lips.

'I'm not talking about the bloody poster – I'm talking about what it *says*. The man killed a kid.'

Fordyce put his knife and fork down and sighed.

'Fuck's sake, Al, what *is* your problem with this guy? We all know your views on people of colour . . .' Fordyce gestured at the empty lounge. 'And that also might explain why this place isn't exactly the most popular. But this kind of bollocks . . .' he pointed at the poster, 'it's a bit school playground, isn't it, mate?'

'Clarke killed a child, then attacked a young woman and nearly killed her. In case you hadn't noticed, another young woman and her son were murdered this week – *in our street*, yards from where he lives. And all that doesn't bother you?'

Fordyce ignored him, forked some mushy peas into his mouth and washed it down with a swig of ale.

'Your fish may be frozen, but I can't knock your peas, mate. You do good peas, Al.'

Baxter looked ready to blow.

'Let the police do their jobs and keep your nose out of it,' said Fordyce, turning serious.

'I don't get you sometimes, Ron, I really don't. You put yourself out there as someone who cares about the local community. You and Tom bang on about the old days all the time. And yet when the time actually comes to *do* something . . . you don't want to know.'

'That's enough,' said Fordyce, with enough chill to turn Baxter's head. 'You're obsessed with this guy, have been ever since he came out of prison – why? What's he ever done to you?'

Before Baxter could respond, the door opened and Tom Daws walked in. Ronnie was about to greet him when he saw the man accompanying him. They eyeballed each other for a moment.

'Fuck me – it's Crocodile Dundee,' said Fordyce.

Finn was at the South Bank sitting on a bench overlooking the Thames. It was a favourite evening haunt of his when he needed to clear his head or the flat felt too small. The place didn't have quite the buzz it used to before the pandemic but he didn't mind that. Quiet was good as far as he was concerned. His laptop was flipped open and balanced on his knee. He was going through some more of Sadie's emails, further back than just the immediate few weeks before her death. He reached one she'd sent her sister, clearly fresh after her split from Harry Boxall.

Sunday July 18, 22.37
From: sadie@diamondmail.com
To: lilypink@ymail.co.uk

My heart is breaking, Lil. Liam doesn't understand what's
going on either. His little face used to light up when he
saw his dad – you've never seen such a smile. Last night
he was just sobbing and sobbing and wouldn't calm
down. He's too young to understand what's happened,
and now I'm thinking I've done the wrong thing. Maybe I
should have stayed with Harry after all. I was so sure
about going it alone, but now I don't know. I just feel so
lonely, I can't describe it to you. Once Liam's down and
there's just me – I feel tiny, like the smallest little pebble on a
beach. I know you and Mam are always on the end of a
phone but I can't keep doing that to you. It's hard to
describe, but I feel like I don't know who I am any more. Does
that make sense? All I do is live to keep that little boy fed and
safe.

Finn broke off, a sudden flash in his mind again of the weary
woman he'd seen in the motorway service station with her
young daughter. The weird thing was he knew exactly what
Sadie was describing, that feeling of *smallness*. Alone in their
own flats late at night, even hardened murder detectives could
query themselves – ask difficult questions about who they
were and what place in the world they occupied. When Karin
was alive, he'd never seen himself as one of those people
defined by their relationship – but it was shocking to him the
emptiness he'd felt since she'd gone. He suddenly felt a very
powerful urge to have a drink, and flipped the laptop shut.

He walked further up the river towards Borough and found
what he was looking for, a nondescript bar out of the way of

the more obvious drinking holes. He ordered a double scotch, downed it and immediately ordered another one. He could feel himself getting angry now, an almost white-hot fury from out of nowhere, and as the barman brought over his second drink, he began to understand who the rage was for.

'*Self-blame and shame are common symptoms too,*' Murray had told him. It was like an equation, Finn thought. What do you get when you take self-blame and add a healthy dose of shame? Self-loathing in spades, of course. His phone rang, and he saw the call was from Skegman. At this time of the evening, it was probably important. He ignored it and let it go to answerphone. He was in no mood for him, for work, or for other people, and he felt no great urge to go back home either. He took another big swig of scotch, enjoyed the burn and settled back.

Patrick Clarke walked past the Lamb's Head and resisted the urge to peer through the windows. He and Alan Baxter had made catching each other's eye something of an art form. He'd spent the evening at the gym and felt better for the work-out. His conversation with the police in Blackheath had stirred up memories he'd spent years keeping locked away, out of sight and mind. Pumping some iron and working up a sweat had helped him find his equilibrium again. He noticed a large white van parked not far from the pub. A man was sitting in the darkness behind the wheel but didn't seem to notice him. Patrick walked on – he could see the lights on in the living room of his mother's house. Mum would be reading one of her cookery magazines, peering over her glasses occasionally at the documentary she'd be half watching at the same time.

Behind him, he heard the van's engine start and it suddenly accelerated forwards, coming to a sharp halt just in front of him. For a moment he stood, caught in its headlights, unsure what the driver's intentions were. The back of the vehicle flapped open and several dark figures piled out. Now Patrick knew exactly what this was. He began to sprint, his most immediate thought to lead these people as far away from his home as possible.

'*Get him,*' barked a voice and he heard the pounding of footsteps from behind. The van was on the move again too. It shot past and stopped again around fifty meters ahead now. The driver jumped out and Patrick immediately saw the baseball bat he was swinging with intent.

'What do you want?' he screamed as the men behind swarmed on to their target.

'What the fuck do you think?' one of them shouted back. Two of them grabbed him on either side, restraining him, while a third held up something that looked like a sack. Patrick squirmed to free himself but he was held tight. They placed what he now realised was a bin liner over his head and everything went dark. There was a blow straight to his solar plexus and he gasped in agony.

'What was that?' said one of the men. 'Cunt said something. Didn't quite hear it?'

A second punch followed in the same place and a surge of vomit rose in his throat, not quite escaping. The men on either side lifted him and began to carry him. He could hear the van's engine still running as they got closer, but was in too much pain to even attempt token resistance now. They hauled him inside and he heard the doors slamming shut as the vehicle skidded off.

'What do you want?' he tried to say, the words only coming out as a hoarse whisper.

A fist immediately connected with his face, jerking his head back. He could feel warm liquid pouring down his nose on to his chin.

'I'll tell you what we want,' said the same voice as before. 'To take turns, old son. And then we're going to come back here and do the same to your mum.'

The next blow came before he could even scream.

27

Mattie Paulsen was pacing around the car park of Lewisham Hospital swearing loudly to herself. It was just gone 10 p.m. and she wasn't having the best of nights. She'd been in a restaurant with Nancy when she'd taken the call about Clarke. He'd been found dumped in a side street close to Pennington Road by a late-night dog walker who'd alerted the emergency services. A uniformed officer at Cedar House had recognised Clarke's name from the Nicholls murder investigation and immediately informed the major investigations team. It'd been John Skegman – working late – who'd then phoned her with the news. Of Finn, there'd been no word, to Skegman's clear irritation. She'd made her excuses to Nancy, her heart slightly breaking at the sight of her barely touched biriyani. Clarke was still being worked on by the doctors when she arrived and the severity of his injuries wasn't yet clear.

Now as she tried to contact Finn for the third time, she was becoming genuinely concerned. He always responded to a call. In over two years working with him, she couldn't remember when he hadn't. He was famously a man who didn't switch off, so this was significantly strange.

'Fuck's sake . . .' she muttered under her breath as his answerphone kicked in again. She'd already sent several messages, so killed the call and headed back into the hospital.

As she walked through to the waiting area outside A&E, she found Lynda Clarke talking to a doctor who looked young enough to be her grandson. He was smiling reassuringly while she nodded like a woman carrying the weight of the world. Paulsen held back, waited for the doctor to leave, then joined her.

'Has there been any news?' she asked.

It seemed to take Lynda a moment to connect the maelstrom of thoughts in her head with the question she was being asked.

'Patrick's going to be okay. They're checking him for concussion but it just seems to be cuts and bruises.' She swallowed. 'Very bad cuts and bruises.'

'Good – it sounds like he was lucky,' said Paulsen, and then immediately regretted her choice of words.

'Yes. He could have a broken back. Or I could have a funeral to arrange. So yes, praise the Lord for the mercy He's shown my boy tonight.' The dripping acid in her tone left no ambiguity and Paulsen guiltily looked down at her feet. 'I'll remember to be grateful too for the racist thugs who attacked him, and to have the wonderful Metropolitan Police on the case investigating it. Because you know, you have *such* a good record with these things.'

This jabbed at Paulsen.

'That's not fair. Shit like this matters to me,' she said, with enough edge to surprise even Lynda.

'I'm sorry. I didn't mean to be uncharitable. Your job can't be easy.'

Paulsen knew immediately what she was referring to – being a woman of colour within the police service, rather than the difficulties of the job itself.

'Besides – this wasn't a racist attack, was it?' said Paulsen. Now it was Lynda's turn to look away. 'Can I buy you a cup of tea?' she added, with a small smile.

A few minutes later they were sitting in the corner of the waiting area, nursing paper cups of watery brown liquid.

'The last few years must have been very stressful for you,' said Paulsen.

'Yes. But I believe – I *know* my son has a good heart. You'll think that's just the bias of a protective mother, but I've never doubted it. Still don't.'

'Whatever you might think, we're not going to let something like this just happen. We'll find the people responsible.'

'You *know* who was responsible,' said Lynda. 'We both do.'

'Alan Baxter?'

Lynda shrugged.

'One way or another – I'm sure he was behind those disgusting posters too. It's not like he hides how he feels about Patrick. And if it wasn't him, then it was someone he put up to it.'

Paulsen realised she was right – it was also entirely possible the message being sent by those flyers had been received by someone who'd decided to take their own retribution. Whether it was Baxter himself who'd attacked Patrick or not, his fingerprints felt like they were all over it.

'Do you mind if I ask you about the incident in the Lake District?'

The combative, tough woman she'd been speaking to suddenly looked all her years, a deep well of sadness expressing itself slowly across her lined features.

'Nobody's life should be bent out of shape like that. It wasn't fair – he did nothing wrong,' said Lynda.

'Patrick wasn't blamed for that boy's death; I mean not officially. No charges were ever brought against him.'

'Yes, but sometimes judgement comes in many different forms.' She took a deep breath, regained some control and gave her a curious look. Paulsen couldn't quite read its meaning, but later she would remember it.

* * *

When he walked into the incident room the following morning, Finn didn't seem to notice his team's concern. The fact he was running late just added insult to injury. Jackie Ojo didn't waste any time diving straight in and asking him where he'd been the previous night.

'I'm sorry – to be honest, I was working late and dozed off on the sofa last night. Doesn't happen often. When I woke, I went through the various messages and it sounded like there was nothing much I could do by that point.'

'You fell asleep?' said Ojo as if she'd misheard him. Her barely disguised incredulity was in part fuelled by the fact Finn's eyes were bloodshot while his voice sounded like he'd been gargling rusty razor blades. Superficially he looked his usual immaculate self – but the strength of Ojo's tone provoked an instant sheepishness.

'Sorry. Must be getting old. So how is Patrick this morning?' he said.

'The hospital kept him in overnight as a precaution, but he's expected to make a full recovery. I think whoever did this was trying to give him a scare rather than do some serious damage,' said Paulsen coolly. She hadn't bought Finn's explanation of his radio silence any more than Ojo. The sense that alcohol had played a major part in this was hard to shake. Had he been out on the lash? That was very un-Finn-like. The idea of him sitting at home, drinking alone though . . .

'Have we spoken to Alan Baxter yet? Sounds like he's the obvious candidate for both this and those posters we found,' said Finn.

'Of course,' said Ojo. 'He said he was behind the bar at the pub all night, right up until closing. There are witnesses who can corroborate that as well.'

'It's proving a handy alibi, that. What about his son?' said

Finn, sitting down at his desk with something of a heave. He coughed throatily and covered his mouth with a hand apologetically.

'Says he was in the West End last night but we're still checking that out. And whether Baxter might have put someone up to this,' said Paulsen. She looked across at Ojo and could see the detective sergeant was watching Finn closely. Hungover police officers, both uniformed and plain-clothed, were ten a penny in the building – it was the fact that it was Finn behaving like this during a major investigation that made it extraordinary.

'What time's Clarke expected out of hospital?' he said.

'Lynda said she'd text me,' replied Paulsen.

'All due respect – as nasty as this attack was, it's just a distraction. One we can leave to uniform to investigate. We've got two homicides to focus on,' said Ojo with emphasis.

Finn shook his head.

'I'm not so sure. I don't like coincidences. There seems to be a determined effort from someone to make the world think Patrick was responsible for Sadie and Liam's deaths.'

'What are you getting at?' said Ojo.

'Doesn't it remind you of something, Jacks? The way Dean Rawton conveniently came into the frame thirty years ago?'

He looked around the room, and for the first time since he'd walked in, his eyes seemed alive.

'Dozed off, my arse. He's lying,' said Ojo.

She and Paulsen had let things settle down, then slipped away for a quick walk around the hinterland of streets that surrounded Cedar House. They'd both needed a debrief after what had just happened but taking the conversation into YoYo's felt slightly risky. They'd staggered their departures and met outside so as not to arouse Finn's suspicion. As she'd left, Paulsen saw him working diligently at his desk and as ever it was so hard to read him. Now she felt guilty and wondered aloud if they weren't both over-reacting a bit.

'Are you taking the piss, Mattie? *Overreacting?* Did you see the state of him? It must have been one hell of a bender he was on last night.'

Paulsen knew things were serious – Ojo was puffing at an e-cig, leaving a cloud of menthol flavouring in her slipstream. Up until three minutes ago, she hadn't a clue the detective sergeant even used them.

'So what if he was? Who doesn't do that once in a while?'

'Me, for a fucking start,' said Ojo.

'That's because you've got a boy to look after.'

'Bollocks – it's because I'm a detective sergeant working a double murder investigation. It's about professionalism, Mattie. That's the point.'

'You want to query his professionalism?' said Paulsen. 'Finn? He can probably quote you the rule book in three different languages then recite it backwards for an encore.'

Ojo scowled at the gag and took another long drag on her vape.

'We both know what this is about, don't we? *Who* this is about.'

Paulsen nodded – it had been her first thought too, the moment he'd offered his flimsy excuse.

'In which case, aren't we being a bit hard on him?' she said. 'His bereavement's always going to be with him. Maybe we need to get used to that idea too? That things like this may occur once in a while.'

Before Ojo could reply, Paulsen's phone interrupted them. She glanced down at it.

'Sorry, Jacks, it's Abi Daws – I ought to take this.'

Ojo nodded and returned the vape to her mouth as Paulsen put the handset to her ear.

'Mattie – thank God. You've got to help us, I'm worried sick. It's my dad – he's disappeared . . .'

28

The whole street had mobilised to search for Tom Daws. Finn, to Paulsen's irritation, hadn't been particularly interested in the development. The police dealt with situations like this every day, and though he'd recognised the extra resonance it held for her, his first instinct had been to let uniform deal with it. She'd then made it clear that she intended to go and help Abi and Luke if she could, almost daring him to try and stop her. She understood his point – they were stretched as it was, and yes, it wasn't a job for the MIT – but the idea of that old man wandering alone was simply too close to home for her. She'd muttered something about exploring any potential loose connection to their investigation and he'd consented without arguing.

As she parked at the top of Pennington Road, it was hard to keep thoughts of Christer Paulsen from her mind. She was well aware difficult times were just around the corner for her family, and this felt like an early taster. She quickly spotted some of the Daws' neighbours out looking for Tom and they told her Abi was searching in nearby Manor Park. After a quick call, the pair rendezvoused by the River Quaggy – a narrow mud-coloured stretch of water that ran along the park's perimeter. Calling it a river was almost a breach of the Trade Descriptions Act, thought Paulsen. The Danube it was not.

'I thought he might have come here,' said Abi as they met. 'Ron's got an allotment nearby. They sometimes walk along the river when the weather's good.'

'We'll find him,' said Paulsen, with as much reassurance as she could manage. 'We've officers in the area out looking for him. Tell me what happened?'

Abi ran her hands through her hair and tried to gather herself.

'I just don't know. He got out of bed at the usual time, had breakfast and was sitting in his armchair with the paper. He was quiet and seemed happy. I nipped out to run some errands and when I got back, he was gone. I rang around but no one knew where he was – and that's when I started to panic.'

'Has he done anything like this before?'

Abi nodded.

'A couple of times. But he's never strayed too far – and we've been lucky, he's either been spotted or bumped into someone.'

Paulsen was struggling to compute what she was being told. Tom, she'd assumed, was still at a fairly early stage of his Alzheimer's. Those moments of confusion she'd witnessed had been relatively small, the fall in the road notwithstanding. It closely paralleled the same stage of her own father's illness and he wasn't pulling these sorts of antics. It was hard not to wonder if there was something else going on which might have triggered this. And if you wanted a recent traumatic event to point to – there was one very obvious candidate.

'Let's try the allotment – it's the same route along the river-bank Dad takes with Ron,' said Abi. 'He might have headed this way out of muscle memory.'

'I didn't realise things were this bad with him?' said Paulsen as they began walking. Abi's head was turning mechanically every few seconds, looking behind and around for any sign of her father.

'They're not usually. You've talked to him, most of the time he's okay. A little confused, perhaps, but he can hold down a conversation – sits happily chatting away in the pub – and gets me to make his dinner in time for Channel 4 News every night. This isn't a man losing himself, at least not yet.'

'Could Sadie and Liam's deaths have upset him more than you thought?' said Paulsen.

Abi shook her head.

'I don't know why they would – he barely knew them.' Paulsen was keen to push the point but knew this wasn't the right moment. 'I don't know – it's been a difficult week for all of us,' continued Abi. 'Maybe the emotion of it upset him more than I realised.'

She shrugged helplessly, her eyes beginning to redden. Paulsen could see she was embarrassed, trying to hold back the tears.

'It's okay . . .' she said, as she thought of another man, sitting quietly in another armchair.

'Come on, Tommy Boy, don't do this to me,' said Ronnie Fordyce under his breath as he walked up Lee High Road. He'd looked everywhere he could think of for his old friend, but to no avail. There were all sorts of scenarios running through his mind about what might have happened, might *be* happening, and he didn't like any of them. He'd seen a few familiar faces while he'd been out – neighbours helping with the search. Uniformed police were there too, stopping people in the street and asking if they'd seen anyone who matched Daws' description.

He and Tom went back a long way. They'd been in the army together, served in the Falklands. A lifelong friendship forged on the other side of the world. When they'd come out, they'd settled down in the same area – gone in different directions professionally, but always remained close. He thought of that brave soldier he'd first met in Port Stanley. The good-looking bastard who'd had women eating out of the palm of his hand, the guy stood on the picket lines of the eighties and nineties because he couldn't bear an injustice to stand. He was a better man than himself, thought Fordyce. But then that wasn't difficult.

He turned into Pennington Road expecting to see a hive of activity but found it deserted. The search was elsewhere of course, and as he passed the pub he half wondered if his old mate wasn't just sitting in his usual chair, wondering where everyone was.

'Is there anything I can do to help?' said a strong, rich voice behind him.

He turned and saw with some shock Patrick Clarke slowly walking towards him. For an instant, Fordyce was lost for words. Clarke's right eye was half closed and badly swollen; a long strip of stitches ran above his left eye. Smaller scabs and cuts were dotted around his face. He looked like he'd been in a high-speed smash. He was hobbling slowly too, clearly in some pain.

'I'm sorry . . .' said Fordyce instinctively. The sound of the words surprised him, coming out as an unintentional whisper.

'What for? Your racist mate?' said Clarke.

'Did *he* do that to you?'

'No – there was a vanload of guys waiting for me when I got home last night. But someone clearly told them where to find me . . .'

Again Fordyce struggled as he processed the information.

'You look pretty messed up. Shouldn't you be in hospital?'

'Discharged myself,' said Clarke with a growl. 'You have to show these people you aren't going to be intimidated . . .'

Fordyce shook his head, thinking about his recent conversations with Baxter. It was hard to disagree with Clarke's assessment of who might be behind it.

'I don't hold the same views as Alan. I don't like any of that stuff. I'm not a racist . . .'

Clarke gave him a weary look.

'No – but you drink in his pub, sit at his table, laugh at his jokes . . . and what do you do about it? Just shut your brain off at the bits you don't like?'

Fordyce was trying to find an answer but Clarke closed him down.

'Save it – I really couldn't care less. But I meant what I said – if I can help find your friend, I will.'

'Thank you,' said Fordyce genuinely. 'But maybe you should just go home and rest. We—' He broke off as he saw Luke Daws emerge from the house opposite.

'Any news on your dad?' Fordyce shouted.

Luke crossed over to join them, the worry in his eyes becoming clearer as he got closer.

'I reckoned he might have come home. Thought it was worth double-checking – just in case he'd got us all running about for nothing,' he said, the Australian twang in his voice sounding particularly pronounced.

'Sorry, son,' said Fordyce. 'We'll find him, I promise. He can't have just disappeared.'

'You spend a lot of time with him, Ron – do you have any bright ideas?' said Luke.

The pair regarded each other uncertainly for a moment and Fordyce shook his head.

'No, but if anything comes to mind, I'll let you know.'

Luke nodded.

'I'm going to try the Lidls on the high street – Abi says he likes going in there.'

Fordyce nodded, and Luke jogged away. Patrick was watching the whole exchange with some bemusement.

'Who's that?' he said.

'A stranger,' said Fordyce, almost under his breath.

David Hermitage was working from home. Not that much work was being done; he was too busy grappling with the idea of how he was going to find thirty thousand pounds. His options were limited. Either his efforts went into finding the money, or they went into making Lucy back off. It was one or the other. But he was aware there was one simple solution to all of this and hated himself for considering it.

'Fuck it,' he said. He rose from his desk and slowly descended the stairs, thinking through how best to do this. He found Emily peering through the curtains in the living room out on to the street.

'Have you heard? Tom Daws has gone missing. His daughter must be in bits . . .'

'I'm sorry,' said David, barely taking the information in, and not particularly caring either. Emily could immediately tell something was wrong and turned to face him.

'What is it?'

'There's something I need to tell you, Em . . .'

And he did. He told her about Lucy and about the blackmail. Of the thirty thousand pounds that had been demanded. But not of his affair with Sadie Nicholls. Instead, he lied, claiming Lucy was an opportunist taking advantage of the fact he was the common denominator in two national news stories. In his mind, it was simply a white lie – to protect his family and to help make this go away. As in business, the only thing that mattered was the outcome. He wondered at first if he'd thrown too much at her in one go. She was standing frozen to the spot with a look of horror mixed with bewilderment.

'Why don't you just go to the police? Tell them the truth – that this woman's taking the piss,' said Emily.

'Because she could tell them anything and then it would be my word against hers.'

'And? You'd rather give her thirty thousand pounds? It's a huge amount of money – you can't just let her walk all over you. Over *us*.'

Money had been a sore point for Emily ever since she'd lost her job. Even though David was well paid, they'd had to temporarily abandon their plans to move out of the area for somewhere more salubrious as a result. It had created a slight tension between them, because quite wrongly she thought he blamed her for that.

'You're not thinking this through,' he said. 'If she does go to the press, we could lose everything. Think about it – the gala dinner's all over the news. So's the murder. We'll forever be linked to the death of a woman and child. We'll never shake the stink of that off. It doesn't matter that I had nothing to do with it. I'd be finished – *we'd* be finished.'

Emily's bewilderment was now turning to anger.

'Who is this little bitch? How could you be so fucking stupid?'

Now the conversation was starting to go more or less as he'd expected. Whenever something awful happened, his wife's default reaction was to try and identify an error he'd made that had brought the whole problem down on them. Fortunately, he'd been here before.

'I'm sorry, Em, I've been really naïve. I was just trying to help someone out, someone who looked like they could use a hand.'

She was looking at him with suspicion now.

'Are you sure that's all this is about? Is there something you're not telling me – about the dinner the other night?'

He swallowed – this was always going to be the hardest bit.

'Of course not.' He looked her bolt in the eye. 'I've done nothing wrong. I swear to you on my child's life.'

They stood, eyes locked, and he held his ground. And as she always did, Emily broke first.

'Thirty grand, David! Where are we going to find that from?'

He had an idea, of course, but this needed careful shepherding.

'I don't know, I really don't,' he said.

'You have to go to the police – you've done nothing wrong. Apart from being fucking stupid . . .'

He patiently went through the reasons why he couldn't again.

'I'll ring the bank, take out a loan,' he said. He was close now, he sensed – but he didn't want to over-egg it. 'Perhaps if we remortgaged or something?'

Emily looked horrified.

'Oh, for God's sake!'

She turned and stared out of the window again.

'I could ask Mum,' she said finally. 'Tell her we need the money for a loft conversion.'

And there we are, thought David. Emily's elderly mother lived in Cornwall and was too frail to travel any more – it would be a simple deception to carry off. She was a wealthy woman with plenty of savings, who frankly wasn't going to need them for much longer.

'That's genius,' he said and meant it.

He felt like a huge burden had been lifted from his shoulders and the relief was real. His wife turned back to look at him, and he could see the relief in her eyes too. Forgiveness would surely follow in time for dinner. He wasn't proud and didn't like what he'd just done, but it was all about the outcome, he said to himself, as he met her gaze again.

*　　*　　*

It turned out Tom Daws was at Catford Police Station. He'd been picked up by a worried pair of constables who'd found him sitting on the ground, crying in the road. When they'd asked him what the problem was, he hadn't known and wasn't carrying any ID. They'd taken him back to the station, given him a bacon sandwich and some hot tea. They were about to try and talk to him again when word came through about the missing pensioner in Lewisham. Paulsen drove Abi straight over to pick him up. When they arrived, he was sitting in the reception area reading the back page of the *Mirror* as if in the dentist's waiting room.

'Dad – what were you thinking? We've all been so worried about you,' said Abi.

'Just glad there's been a quick resolution to this one,' said the genial custody sergeant who'd come out to greet them. But Paulsen didn't return his smile. Tom had been missing for not much more than an hour, but she still felt Catford had been too slow to get their act together.

'I'm sorry, love,' said Tom to his daughter. 'I just wanted to get a bit of air, that's all. I don't know what happened – I really don't. Everything suddenly seemed to get on top of me.'

Paulsen was watching him carefully. He appeared fine – a far cry from the man so upset he'd initially been unable to speak to the PCs who'd found him.

'I thought I saw the butterfly again, Abs . . .' he said suddenly.

Abi shook her head wearily.

'Course you did, Dad.'

Paulsen looked at her quizzically but Abi could only respond with a dismissive shrug.

'What butterfly, Mr Daws?' said Paulsen.

He focused hard, but couldn't quite pin down the thought and shook his head. And then something strange happened

233

– like a flash of a Rorschach print, Paulsen had the sense of an image too. Something she'd seen recently but couldn't quite place. Tom smiled at her, and instinctively she smiled back.

29

Finn felt like the day hadn't started properly yet. The thumping hangover he was carrying was probably something to do with that. He'd purposely steered clear of John Skegman for most of the morning. Having seen the scepticism with which Ojo had taken his explanation for the previous night, he didn't fancy trying it out again on the DCI.

His evening had been wretched. He'd drunk himself into oblivion and there was a vague memory of an argument with a barman who'd refused to serve him any more. He'd somehow managed to summon an Uber and get himself home. He could remember the walls of his flat spinning, and kneeling over the toilet retching, but not vomiting. And there'd been some crying too – proper full-on sobbing – but he was damned if he could recall where that had come in the sequence of events. He reached into his pocket and pulled out a crumpled box of ibuprofen. He shook out one of the foil packets and began popping a couple of pills on to his desk.

'Guv.'

He spun around like a teenager caught shoplifting and saw Dattani standing behind him, trying to disguise his own discomfort.

'You got something, Sami?' said Finn, subtly palming the pills.

'Yes – Nathan Roach used his bank card at an ATM in Ealing this morning. Looks like he's got relations that way

– we've pinned down a Colette Roach who lives close by. Possibly his sister, judging by her age.'

'Interesting. His neighbour said yesterday she saw him leaving with some bags – I wonder why he's decided to move out this particular week?'

'Do you want me to go and find out?'

Finn needed to get away and this felt like the perfect excuse.

'No, it's alright, I'll go and ask him myself – thanks, Sami.'

He waited for Dattani to leave, grabbed his water bottle and discreetly downed the pills with a grateful gulp.

Colette Roach lived in a boxy two-bedroom flat just behind Ealing Common. Finn had called on spec, wary of frightening Nathan away if he was indeed staying there. A no-nonsense woman in her early forties, she only confirmed her brother's presence when Finn assured her he wasn't in any trouble. As he followed her inside, a greying middle-aged man sprang up from the sofa as if he'd been jabbed with a cattle prod. There was immediate recognition in his eyes too – he'd clearly seen Finn before in Pennington Road and knew who he was. Colette intervened before either of them could speak.

'Just talk to the man, Nathe. Please – do it for me. And take as long as you need,' she said to her brother, before grabbing her coat and leaving them to it. Nathan waited for the door to shut behind her and the two men stood awkwardly eyeing each other.

'Mind if I get something to drink?' said Roach. Finn nodded and a few moments later he re-emerged carrying a pint glass of water. The pair sat down and faced each other on opposite sofas.

'You must have gone to some trouble to find me,' said Roach. 'I just don't understand why. I've already spoken to two of your colleagues. What is it you want from me?'

His thinning hair looked greasy and unwashed. The messy stubble on his face didn't look like an affectation either. Finn was starting to see what it was about this man that had piqued Paulsen's interest. He looked petrified.

'I apologise if it feels like we're picking on you, but we're not. It's a murder investigation – a woman and a three-year-old child have both been killed and we have to be thorough. You're just one of many people in the area we're currently talking to.'

The words seemed to only faintly pacify him, but he gave Finn a small nod of assent.

'Can you tell me why you've moved out, Nathan? Why come here?'

The look of alarm returned.

'Why does that matter – it's not a crime, is it?'

'Your alibi for the night of the murders remains uncorroborated and you clearly seem to find talking to the police . . . a difficult thing.' Roach looked up at him, as if there suddenly wasn't enough oxygen in the room. 'So what aren't you telling us?' said Finn, a little more gently. 'And why did your sister want you to talk to me?'

Now the man looked haunted. Finn opened his palms but said nothing. There was a long silence, which he felt no inclination to fill. Finally, Roach looked back up at him.

'I *have* lied to you. I'm sorry,' he said, his voice tremulous. 'The night that young woman died, I was with a friend – Patrick, from number thirty-nine. He was at my house. He can corroborate where I was.'

Finn took a moment to digest the information. Two points of the investigation had just been joined together by a line he hadn't seen coming. He was instantly mindful of his earlier thought too, that they could be looking for two separate killers. There'd be plenty of time to unsift all this later; right now he needed to refocus.

'What was Patrick Clarke doing at your house?'

'We were just talking – that's all.'

'And what time would that have been?'

'He arrived just after five in the afternoon and left at around midnight.'

Finn continued to turn the information over. Paulsen's comment the day before, about not knowing exactly who Clarke was, also came back to him.

'Patrick's been very reluctant to tell us where he was that evening, and what he was doing. Can you tell me why it's been such a secret, if all you were doing was talking? What were you talking about?'

'I'd rather not say. He hasn't told you anything because I asked him not to. He's been protecting me.'

'Protecting you from what?'

Roach wiped his brow with his hand, said nothing. There was a tension about him that Finn could feel. He was used to the rhythms of a secret. There was an art to teasing them out and instinctively he felt it was better to let this man get there himself, rather than to press too hard.

'We can come back to that,' he said. 'Why don't you tell me how you know Patrick then – you've only just moved in to the area, haven't you?'

Nathan nodded.

'A few weeks back, I had a panic attack in the supermarket. Patrick was in there as well and helped me to get home. We talked afterwards and got to know each other a bit then.'

'Why were you having a panic attack, if you don't mind me asking?'

Roach shook his head dismissively. A bony hand was gripping his knee so hard his fingernails dug into it, but Finn persisted.

'There must be a bit more to it than that for Patrick to go out on such a limb for you? Please, you really need to give me something.'

Finn sensed the dam was close to breaking, but as if reading his mind, Roach held his hands up.

'I'm sorry. I can't do this. I just can't.'

Was it a gay thing? thought Finn. He couldn't recall Patrick mentioning a partner or girlfriend, and Roach wouldn't be the first middle-aged man who'd come out following an unhappy marriage.

'If it's a personal matter, I promise you, it will stay between us,' he said. 'The sooner you can give me some clarity on all this, the sooner I can be on my way and leave you be.' Again, Finn left a deliberate pause.

'I can't, I'm sorry,' Roach repeated. It came out almost as a whisper.

He looked away and Finn got the sense he was reliving something now. The feel of Sadie Nicholls' skull as it shattered? He'd already admitted to lying about that. If this went on much longer, the conversation would have to become more formal. He hoped, for the other man's sake, things wouldn't need to go that far.

'What I'm about to tell you – it isn't easy for me. Do you understand?' said Roach, as if reading his mind.

Finn nodded.

'I'm only telling you this so you understand why Patrick was in my house and why he's been helping me. Ignore the bullshit in the papers – he didn't kill that woman or her son.'

Roach took a deep breath and steadied himself.

'I was a married man. I *am* a married man, I should say. I have two children and a wife I love very much. I'm a surveyor by trade, and a good one too.'

He broke off, his eyes focusing on the wall opposite, as if images of something were being projected on to it. 'I was out on a job. Broad daylight, mid-afternoon. I was walking across a small heath back to my car. Wasn't really concentrating – I was half writing in my head the survey on the flat I'd just seen.'

He stopped, took some more deep breaths.

'This guy began walking behind me really slowly, and it began to bug me; I could hear his footsteps so I slowed down to let him go past.' He faltered, his fingernails digging ever deeper into the denim of his trousers. 'He walks by and he's big. Really big – thick neck like a rugby player. And then he stops. Turns and stares at me. This dead, fish-eyed look . . .' He broke off again, his eyes still on the wall as if something terrible now was playing out on its blank canvas.

'Out of nowhere he punches me in the face and I go down. The next thing I know, I'm in the mud and he's on me. I think I'm being robbed or something.' He swallowed, and Finn could see real terror in his eyes now. 'But then he's pulling at my trousers, hauling them down . . .' He pulled up a hand, stretched it tautly over his chin and stopped again. For a second Finn thought the man might be about to throw up, but Roach held up a hand to indicate he was okay. Slowly he brought the hand back down and resumed. 'At that point I knew what was happening. I started to scream but there was literally no one else around to hear. He grabs my head by the hair and tells me to shut up. And then . . .'

He stopped again.

'. . . he raped you?' said Finn, cutting in. He'd heard enough – there was no need to make the man relive any more of this. Roach nodded silently, staring down at the floor now. Defeated by the telling of it.

'Did you report it to the police?'

'No. You're only the third person I've told – after Patrick and my sister.'

'You didn't tell your wife?'

Roach closed his eyes and shook his head, slowly opened them again.

'I couldn't. That day ... I went home and put on an act, pretended like nothing had happened. I thought I could contain it – but I was wrong. Do you know what it's like concealing something like that from the people around you? At home? At work? Putting up a front to the world, when all you want to do is throw yourself in front of a bus? It's like living your life in a permanent, silent scream.'

Finn tried to speak, but the words died in his mouth. Now it was his turn to gulp for air.

'Must be hard,' he rasped.

'My wife could see there was a problem, knew I was holding something back from her. But I couldn't say anything. I told her I needed some space, time apart to get my head together. I put it down to the pandemic, the stress of everything. It was better to leave them, better for them to hate me and be confused than to know the truth. That's how I reasoned it,' he said.

Finn shook his head.

'No,' he said instinctively, but Roach didn't even seem to notice.

'I came back to London because it's a place where you can be anonymous. Just fit in, and no one will ask you anything about who you are or where you're from.'

Finn remembered Jill Nicholls' words, that coruscating tone in her voice.

'*You people down here – you've lost your souls,*' she'd told him.

'You're right. It is a city where you can hide and not be noticed,' Finn replied. 'But that's not necessarily a good thing. Why did you choose to open up to Patrick?'

'Because he *knew*. Straight away in that supermarket – he looked me in the eye and saw something he recognised. And that's because he knows all about living with guilt. He told me his story – about the boy in the lake. So I told him what happened to me – and it helped. Both of us, I think. He's been a good friend to me.'

'Okay. So why did you come here – why move out of Pennington Road this week?'

'Because those two murders stirred it all up for me – the violence of it. I began to feel overwhelmed again, like I was drowning in it. I couldn't be on my own – I knew that much.' Roach drained the last of his water, gripped the pint glass like hot soup on a cold day. 'So now you know,' he said.

Finn considered it. There was nothing to corroborate what he'd just been told but he was absolutely certain it was the truth, that Clarke would confirm every word too.

'It's not too late to catch this guy,' he said. 'It's never too late – I can help you with that if you'd like.'

'I'm sorry, but it's the last thing I want. I know that's wrong, that it's putting other people at risk, but . . .' He shook his head. The tears were starting to come now. '. . . I just can't.'

Finn thought about all the times Murray had exhorted the benefits of therapy. Told him it wasn't just something he might find helpful, but that he needed it urgently – that it might save his life one day. And he thought too about his own deep-set resistance to taking that good advice. A resistance he could neither reason or articulate, but which had never left him.

'It's okay – I understand,' he said.

Afterwards he sat in his car for a while, the conversation still reverberating around his head. There were a million things to do, but he felt no urge to do them. He checked his phone and saw missed calls from Ojo and Skegman. There was also an answerphone message from Paulsen confirming that Tom Daws had been found. He knew he should go back to the incident room, but the afternoon felt like a mountain he had no inclination to climb. He started the engine and moved off, with absolutely no idea of his direction of travel.

30

Paulsen parked her car outside Cedar House, grabbed her bag, then stopped. She frowned, unsure why she wasn't already striding across the forecourt and back into the building. It wasn't as if she didn't have plenty to do, but something had been nagging at her since she'd left Tom and Abi Daws in Catford. She rummaged in her bag, pulled out her phone and tapped out a one-word message.

MP
Hey . . .   14:16

She waited, looked up briefly at the windows of the incident room. Her phone vibrated with a near-instant reply.

Dad
Hey yourself . . .   14:17

She smiled.

MP
How's things?   14:17

Dad
'Fine. Are you checking up on me now?'   14:18

245

The message was followed by an unexpectedly large emoji of a unicorn. Paulsen laughed out loud. This happened frequently. Another message followed hot on its heels.

Dad
Ignore that! My fucking fat fingers!   14:18

MP
I believe you . . .   14:19

Dad
It's these sodding phones. Not the other
thing . . .   14:19

The smile on Paulsen's face slid into something more melancholic. Her fingers hovered over the screen for a moment. She *was* checking up on him – he was spot on with that but she didn't want him to know that. She knew how much that upset him too.

MP
Just wanted to say – found a new Swedish cafe
in Finsbury Park. They do princess cake . . .   14:19

She waited – princess cake was Christer Paulsen's favourite. A traditional Swedish cake consisting of artery-hardening layers of sponge and cream covered in a coating of marzipan. It was a bastard to make and heavy enough to sink ships. Her phone buzzed immediately. It was another unicorn – this time with love hearts for eyes.

Dad
That one was deliberate! Drooling – bring
one next time you come!   14:20

MP
You're on x   14:20

Dad
Come soon ☺ x   14:21

In these moments she could almost pretend nothing was
wrong. Paulsen put her phone back in her bag and got out of
the car. She was banking the red sting of tears in her eyes
would clear by the time she reached the incident room.

31

The woman's name was Joy and she greeted him with genuine pleasure.

'Mr Finn – it's so nice to see you again.'

He returned her welcome with a confected smile of his own.

'I was just in the area – I thought I'd pop in and say hello.'

St Augustus's Hospice in Sutton was the place where his wife died. And he hadn't just been passing, he'd driven there deliberately. Even the journey had brought back some jarringly vivid memories. Oddly, given the circumstances, they weren't sad ones for the most part. They were the last conversations he'd ever had with Karin, and he cherished them like leather-bound copies of treasured books.

Finn wasn't sure why, but he'd felt drawn to the place after leaving Nathan Roach in Ealing. He'd called Ojo and told her not to expect him back at Cedar House for the remainder of the day. He didn't tell her why; she hadn't liked it and he hadn't cared.

'So how are you getting on?' said Joy. 'It must be over two years since . . .'

She tailed off and he nodded.

'I'm good, actually. You were all so kind during that period and I've never forgotten that.'

That much was true. Joy was one of the nurses who'd cared for Karin and he knew his wife had taken to her.

'She was so worried about you – how you'd cope after she was gone. But I must say you're looking very well.'

'Thank you,' said Finn, privately wondering what that said about her professional skill set.

'Is there someone else in your life now?' she inquired tentatively.

'Yes,' he lied. 'It's very new though.'

Her face immediately brightened with warmth. Funny how that normalised you for some people, he thought.

'I was wondering . . .' he said. 'As I'm here – it's a funny thing, but could I see Karin's old room?'

There was an awkward pause and he could see the cogs turning in her head. 'Don't worry if it's occupied.' He produced another big fake smile. 'I just thought, you know – for old time's sake . . .'

She softened, smiled conspiratorially at him. He guessed when you dealt with the bereaved every day, odd and unusual requests like this weren't that strange.

'You're in luck – it's empty at the moment,' she said.

'Thank you. I remember the way.'

'Of course you do,' she replied.

And it was there, a few minutes later, standing by the empty bed where he'd last seen Karin alive, he finally arrived at a conclusion.

When he got back home, he booted up his laptop and opened a folder marked 'K'.

It was a strange quirk but he hadn't watched any videos of Karin since her death. He'd found the idea simply too painful. He carried her voice so vividly in his head – or at least he had – and the memories of her were so strong, that he'd never felt the need to open this folder. Just having it there was enough. But now, today – in this rather strange moment – he finally felt ready. He looked at the thumbnails in front of him, knew exactly which one he wanted and double-clicked on it. An image of Karin appeared wearing a Christmas party hat, sitting on a sofa in their old flat in Balham. She was holding a glass of red wine and staring glassily at the camera.

'I tell you I don't like being filmed – so what do you do? You pick up your phone and turn the fucking camera on. You're such an asshole, Alex.' She looked at the camera and giggled drunkenly. 'But such a *sexy* asshole, I'll give you that . . .' She shrugged helplessly. 'What do you want me to say? Is this supposed to be my version of the Queen's speech?' She sat up straight and put on a posh voice. 'In this annus mirabilis, annus horribilis . . . oh, fuck it.' She took a slurp of wine, grinned, searched him out with her eyes, and her face became serious. 'Tell me how you're feeling?' she said. 'Right now – what's going on in that head of yours?' He didn't reply and she arched an eyebrow expectantly.

'That you're the most bright and beautiful person I have ever known,' he heard his younger self stiffly say. A bashful look of genuine flattery crossed Karin's face, and watching on the screen, Finn felt his heart break all over again.

'That's a description, detective. I asked you to tell me how you *feel?*' she said. There was another silence.

'Happy,' he heard himself say. 'Happier than I've ever been.'

'Really?'

'Really.'

She put the wine glass down and moved closer.

'Put that fucking thing down and kiss me then.'

The image shuddered and went black.

For a second Finn stared at the blank screen as if he were expecting Karin to step out from inside it.

'Say something,' he said to the empty flat, and waited. But there was no reply. The only sound was the quiet hum of his fridge. Slowly he rose to his feet, walked over to the window and looked at the world outside going about its business.

There were two things to consider, he thought. First, that he believed – rationally and calmly – that he was genuinely at a point where he could not and did not want to go on any more. The feeling had seeded itself during the conversation with Nathan Roach, then solidified as he'd stood by the empty bed at the hospice. And secondly, given that's how he felt – what exactly did he propose to do about it? There was no panic, no fear, just a strange calm. A peace, at finally acknowledging a truth.

He walked into the bathroom and turned on the taps of a large free-standing bathtub. The water powered out satisfyingly hot, and he returned to the living room and poured himself a glass of Johnny Walker Blue while it filled. If ever there was a time for the expensive stuff, he reckoned, this was it. The drink fortified him and he considered his options. It would be a civilised way to do it, he thought. Put on some music, pour another glass of scotch, open a vein and simply relax away his life in the embrace of a hot bath.

He tried to imagine what would happen afterwards when he didn't arrive for work tomorrow. Jackie would probably be the first person to raise the alarm, be the one to insist that this was indeed serious. He imagined Skegman waving her away until his absence became impossible to ignore. And when he didn't respond to their calls, they'd eventually break in here and find his lifeless body submerged in a casket of crimson water. Then quite wrongly, they'd all start blaming themselves.

He went back to the bathroom and turned the taps off. A whisper of steam rose above the water and as he watched it evaporate began to interrogate himself. It's what he did with just about every other issue in his life, so it made sense to approach this in the same methodical way. Was he really serious? Did he genuinely want to end things right now, today? Or was this just a cry for help from a man who famously never sought it?

'*For fuck's sake – call someone!*' said Sadie, interrupting his train of thought.

'I'm sorry. I've let you down, haven't I?' he murmured.

Randomly he thought again of the woman with the little girl at the motorway service station. The image wouldn't leave him. She was Karin and the child they'd never had; she was Sadie with Liam, the mother and son he'd failed.

'*It's like living your life in a permanent, silent scream.*'

That's what Roach had said and he couldn't have put it better himself.

In the kitchen he opened a drawer and took out a paring knife. He sat down at the table and placed it in front of him and put his phone down next to it. A simple choice. Karin would hate this. Hate what he was doing, despise him for even thinking of it. She'd foreseen this descent – called him out on it while she was dying. All to no avail. And now here he was, alone and face to face with himself.

He stared down at the two objects, fighting the temptation to stop overthinking this and to just go straight into the bathroom – and the desire was very much there. He picked up the knife, and tried to imagine taking it to his wrist, feeling his skin slice open, watching the blood leak out. Slowly he put it back down on the table and waited for Karin to offer an opinion, but still she wouldn't come. This decision would have to be his. He sat in silence, his mind gloriously empty of every other consideration.

His hand snaked out almost independently and this time picked up the phone. He held it up and regarded it like an alien object. His fingers moved and speed-dialled Murray's number. He watched as the phone began to execute the command. Unlike before in the motorway service station, this time he made no effort to stop the call connecting.

'It's the middle of the afternoon. Shouldn't you be out catching villains?' came a familiar Scottish drawl.

'Sorry to disturb you . . . but I think I might be in a spot of bother,' said Finn.

He explained baldly and succinctly where he was and what he was contemplating. Murray reacted with a surprising calm, and Finn got the sense it wasn't the first time he'd fielded a call like this.

'I can do one of two things,' he said. 'I can call 999 or I can come straight round and we can sit and talk about this.'

Within half an hour he was occupying the seat opposite Finn at the kitchen table. The bath had been emptied and the paring knife returned to its drawer, but the crisis wasn't over yet by a long way and both men knew it.

'I can't save your life – you know that, don't you?' said Murray. 'But I know a thing or two about reaching rock bottom, and that's where you are.'

Slowly Finn nodded.

'I know.'

'Aye, well . . . that's a start,' said Murray. 'It's a good thing – even if it doesn't feel that way. It means you can't go any lower.'

'I didn't think this could ever happen to me,' murmured Finn. And he meant it too – the one thing he'd always prided himself on was his mental strength. He'd never seen himself as a man who gave up.

'Yeah – you're human like the rest of us. Who knew? I told you before, you're an addict, and that's how you have to start seeing yourself. A dirty, filthy, lying little addict.'

'You with your technical terms,' said Finn. 'So what do I do about it?'

Murray took a thoughtful sip from the cup of coffee Finn had made for him when he'd arrived. He pulled a face.

'What the fuck is this muck?'

Finn looked mildly offended despite the circumstances.

'Ethiopian Yirgacheffe – it's actually quite expensive.'

'It's poncey, is what it is. Haven't you got any instant?'

Finn sighed.

'That's what Karin always used to say.'

There was an awkward silence.

'And that's the problem, Alex,' said Murray. 'All roads lead back there with you, don't they?'

Finn didn't answer. He didn't know what the future held on a minute-by-minute basis, never mind beyond that. It was twenty to five in the afternoon and he had no idea what even 6 p.m. would look or feel like.

'So anyway . . . have you ever heard of the American poet Robert Frost?' said Murray. 'A smart man – let me enlighten you about him. He said everything he'd ever learnt about life can be summed up in three words.'

He left a deliberate pause, but made sure to look Finn in the eye.

'It goes on.'

Finn was irritated. He didn't need simplistic platitudes right now. But Murray held up a hand.

'His point was – no matter what happens, the sun's always going to come up tomorrow. The question is, how do you feel about that?'

Finn tried to focus his muddled mind.

'I don't care – and that's really the heart of it; I only want to do these things *with* Karin.'

'I'll ask again. Do you *want* to see the sun rise tomorrow? Yes, or no?'

Finn thought about a woman wearing a Christmas hat laughing helplessly, the same face in a hospice bed too weak to even lift a glass of water. He put his head into his hands and massaged his scalp. When he emerged, Murray's eyes were still locked on him, laser-like.

'Yes . . .' he said finally. 'The answer's yes.'

'Right. Good – because that, in my line of work, is what we call a contract. If you want something – and you've just told me that you do – then you have to give something back in return . . . that's how this works.'

Finn breathed out.

'Okay . . .' he said. 'What do I have to do?'

'Easy,' said Murray. He picked up his phone and began stabbing at it. 'I'm forwarding you a contact card. It's for the best bereavement counsellor in the UK. She's based in Marylebone – I doubt you can afford her but I don't give a toss about that, you're going to go and see her.'

Finn opened his mouth to protest, but Murray held up a finger.

'You won't get through this without therapy. Simple as that. It's up to you. I can only tell you so many times. You can ignore me if you want, but now you've seen where that goes . . .'

He was deadly serious now, and Finn understood the stakes. It was now or never – either recognise he had a problem and accept help, or be consumed by it. He'd finally run out of road.

'Do you know how hard it is for me to get close to people?' he said. 'Karin was the only one I've ever allowed in.'

'I know,' said Murray quietly. 'And now it's time to let go.'

32

Murray slept in the spare room. Finn had tried to insist it wasn't necessary, but the Scotsman made it clear he wasn't leaving him alone overnight. They'd talked into the small hours. The banter had continued, but it had also been raw and frequently intense. When he woke the next morning, Finn was already dressed, shaved and busy cooking. A large jar of Nescafé was on the kitchen table.

'I hope you're not being so titanically stupid as to think you're going into work today?' said Murray.

Finn turned, a spatula dangling from one hand.

'Afraid so – we can argue about it over breakfast if you like, just before I leave.'

He turned back to the cooker, ignoring Murray's glare of disapproval.

'And what exactly are you making there?' his guest said, suspiciously eyeing the contents of the pan Finn was prodding.

'Halloumi cheese with scrambled eggs and baby plum tomatoes.'

'Oh, for fuck's sake . . .'

'It's fried – you're Scottish, you'll be fine with it.'

'Poncey . . .' muttered Murray under his breath. He picked up the instant coffee, went over to the counter and switched the kettle on. 'So how are you feeling today?'

He threw the question out lightly, but for a moment the only sound in the room was the crackle from the pan.

'I Googled that counsellor in Marylebone. Two hundred and twenty-five quid a session – you weren't exaggerating about the cost, were you?' said Finn. Before Murray could respond, he held up the spatula again. 'I've got an appointment next week – it's the earliest date she could manage. So don't bother going all Braveheart on me . . .'

'Racist,' muttered Murray. The kettle finished boiling and he tipped some water into a mug lined with coffee powder. 'That's good. But you should give your mind some time to rationalise what happened yesterday. Are you sure you're okay?'

The truth was, Finn did feel different. He'd slept well, largely because the emotion of the previous day had left him exhausted. But on waking, he'd felt fresh and rested. He was a long way from being over his problems and he knew that, but it did feel like something fundamental had shifted, that he'd reached an accommodation within himself. A ship stranded in the middle of the ocean that was now at least pointing in the right direction.

'Why do you think I'm up? I wanted to catch the sunrise,' he said.

The two carried on swapping barbs over breakfast and afterwards Finn had a brief wobble as he remembered the bath, the blade and the choice. Now, just hours later, it felt bizarre and dreamlike, but he was also aware it had been all too real. He'd been absolutely ready to go through with it; of that he was sure.

'I can't stop you going in,' said Murray. 'But I'm on the end of a phone if you need me. Don't be a hero – if you feel yourself struggling, call me.'

Previously Finn might have agreed with little intention of doing so. This time he nodded and meant it.

When he arrived at Cedar House, he got precisely the reception he'd been expecting. Ojo was frosty, Paulsen tight-lipped, Dattani and McElligott both awkward. The rest of the room was subdued and pretended not to notice anything was wrong. He couldn't blame them. There was some bridge-building to be done – but that would have to wait. For now, he needed to get back on the horse again and his first priority was to find Sadie and Liam Nicholls' killer.

'So where the hell were you yesterday?' said John Skegman in his office, as Finn finally responded to the multiple requests he'd received for a conversation.

'Is this where we're at now?' he replied. 'I have to report my precise movements to you?'

Skegman slumped back into his seat.

'No, of course not. But no one in your team had a clue where you were. There's two unsolved murders and I honestly don't know where you are with any of it. Don't you think we all deserve a bit better than that?'

'Yes,' said Finn.

'So?' said Skegman.

'I was following my nose on something, but it didn't lead anywhere. Just one of those things.'

Karin had always said Finn was a bad liar. He liked to think in the years since her death it was a skill he'd developed rather well. Skegman's face suggested otherwise.

'I don't know what's going on with you, Alex . . .' He stopped abruptly, wearily running his hand through his hair. 'Actually that's not true – I *do* know. And as one human being to another – I *get* it, I really do. But there comes a time when I have to question how long I can put up with this for?'

Finn felt a flush of guilt. One thing he was already sure of was that there needed to be less lying going forwards.

'That's fair enough – so what do you want to do?'

'I'm sorely tempted to send you home on extended sick

leave, and make Jackie acting SIO. Do you want to give me a good reason why I shouldn't?'

The problem, thought Finn, was that he couldn't think of one. He recalled all the discussions they'd had like this over the last two years. A good working relationship he'd soured with lies – the dishonesty of an addict. It was time to change that dynamic.

'If I told you yesterday was important, you probably wouldn't believe me, and I wouldn't blame you,' he said. 'But it *was* important.' He let the words hang for a moment. 'Let me work the Nicholls murders through to some sort of conclusion. Then you can do whatever you want with me. How does that sound?'

Skegman considered it.

'Alright, Alex. I'll give you that – but I will take you at your word. This is last chance saloon now, no ifs, no buts. And if I see anything that concerns me before then . . . you're done.'

Done meant desk-bound, Finn knew. His professional reputation severely dented, his career – the sole thing that had propped him up since Karin's death – in tatters. Around the Met, he would forever be the detective who 'wasn't the same' or who'd 'lost it'. He could almost see the usual suspects tapping heads and rolling eyes. Labels like that were hard to shake off and he couldn't allow it to happen.

'It won't come to that,' he said, and hoped he was right.

'There's nothing in Sadie's life that suggests the killer was someone from outside the local area,' he said a short time later, addressing a generally rather sullen-looking team in the incident room. They needed the leadership he hadn't been providing, and Skegman had joined them to see for himself what the group dynamic was. Work had continued the previous day in Finn's absence. They were now certain there were no significant people in Sadie's life they'd overlooked. They'd pored over every aspect of her world and found no obvious suspects.

'For me, that means we're looking at someone local,' continued Finn. 'Especially if we think there's a potential connection to the Stratford murders in '93.'

'And where are we with that connection?' said Skegman.

Finn shrugged.

'It's in the mix – I've sent some of the evidence that was collected at the time to be DNA-tested – the lab's still working on that.'

'So who was around then – and how credible are they as suspects now?' said Skegman. He addressed the question to the rest of the room; projecting a sense he'd had enough of the muted atmosphere and wanted to see some life from them.

'We've been through this. There's a few – but I don't know how credible they are,' said Ojo. 'Personally, I think Tom Daws is worth a deeper look . . .'

'Why?' said Paulsen, roused now too. 'The man's got Alzheimer's. From what I've seen, I doubt he could have killed two people and then cleaned up after himself. And he doesn't have a car either – I think it's almost impossible for him to have done it.'

'His daughter told you he'd gone walkabout a few times recently – how do we know what state of mind he's in right now?' said Ojo. 'Wasn't he saying some pretty weird stuff to you as well?'

Paulsen nodded.

'It's true – there was something a bit odd. He's said it a few times now – about having seen a butterfly recently. It seemed to really shake him up. I'm not sure what it means. But . . .'

She shook her head.

'What?' said Finn.

'I know it sounds crazy – but when he said it yesterday, I had a sense of déjà vu. As if I kind of half knew what he was referring to – but couldn't place it.'

'Don't ignore that feeling, Mattie, it might be important,' said Finn. 'He may not be the killer, but it's possible he saw something – something significant which stayed with him.'

'Such as?' said Dattani.

'Only thing I could think of was maybe a tattoo or some jewellery?' said Paulsen.

'Or maybe a logo of some sort?' chipped in McElligott.

Finn frowned.

'Maybe. But perhaps you're all being a bit too literal. Try and see it through his eyes – how his mind is working now. Given his condition, it might something a bit more oblique. An image that's triggered something.'

After a few seconds of silence, there was another collective shrug.

'I thought Daws told uniform he was in the pub the night Sadie died?' said Ojo.

'Maybe – but let's clarify exactly when he left. Presumably, Ronnie Fordyce would know. It's worth checking,' said Finn.

'He couldn't be faking the Alzheimer's, could he?' said McElligott.

Paulsen waved the idea away.

'No chance – I've seen the hospital letters on Abi's table. It's real, alright.'

'Okay, that's Daws. Who else is there?' said Skegman.

'Fordyce – he was rumoured to have been having a relationship of some sort with Vicki Stratford and has previous convictions for GBH. There's something a bit disingenuous about him too that I don't like – enjoys projecting the "good neighbour" thing a bit too much,' said Paulsen.

Ojo shook her head.

'We've looked into him quite deeply. He's kept his nose clean for years, and there is nothing tying him to Sadie or Liam.'

That was certainly true, thought Finn – he couldn't recall a single reference to Fordyce anywhere in Sadie's hard drive.

'I don't buy him as a child killer either,' continued Ojo.

'What about this guy Sadie slept with – Hermitage?' said Skegman.

Finn looked across at Dattani.

'Did you find out any more, Sami?'

'Not really – he doesn't seem to have any criminal connections. His life looks pretty vanilla – if anything, he comes across as quite a decent bloke. He's spent his whole career working for different charities,' said Dattani. 'It doesn't look to me that whatever that missing hour at the Royal Grand was about, it was connected to Sadie. But if you're really keen, we can pull him in and push him on it?'

Finn weighed it up.

'Call him – let him know we'd like an explanation, see what he says.'

Dattani nodded.

'What about Patrick Clarke and this other guy he claims to have been with?'

'I'm comfortable ruling both of them out,' said Finn.

'Based on?' said Skegman.

He ran through his conversation with Roach the previous day.

'I believe him – and there's nothing to link them forensically with either crime scene. Neither man has a motive either.'

'They don't necessarily need one.'

'We still don't know exactly why Clarke attacked an unarmed woman in the street,' said Ojo.

Finn nodded.

'We don't, but he's served his time and I haven't seen anything that suggests he represents a threat to anyone now.'

'So where does all this leave us?' said Skegman.

'I still like Alan Baxter for this,' said Paulsen immediately.

'Any particular reason?' said Finn.

'There's three as it goes. One, he's a piece of shit. Two, he lent Sadie money. I've been going through some of the door-to-doors uniform did and there's others in that street who borrowed from him as well. I made some calls and it turns out one kid ended up in casualty when he didn't pay him back on time. A broken collarbone. There are other stories knocking about like that too.'

Skegman was listening with interest.

'It's feasible – he might have gone round to collect his money and things got out of hand,' he said.

'We've discussed that. But he was in the pub all evening too,' said McElligott. 'He's the one who corroborated Daws and Fordyce were there all night.'

'I've been in that shithole – Baxter's got a son who fills in for him,' said Paulsen. 'He's like a mini-me. They're virtually interchangeable. I can easily buy he slipped out unnoticed for a bit. There's motive and precedent there and he's old enough to have been around thirty years ago too.'

'But why would he have killed Vicki Stratford and her son back then?' said Ojo.

Paulsen shrugged.

'That's point three, isn't it?'

They all looked at her.

'Because he's a piece of shit,' she said.

McElligott and Dattani both laughed, Ojo looked down, unable to stifle a grin of her own, and even Skegman allowed himself a rare smile. Finn watched them, pleased to see the earlier tension in the room dissipating.

He walked across to a water cooler at the back of the room and poured himself a cup which he downed in one. It was as he looked up that he felt the hairs on the back of his neck rise. Slowly he took his glasses *off* and looked again. And that's when he saw it properly – realised it had been staring them in the face the whole time.

The butterfly.

33

David Hermitage walked into the coffee shop, made a beeline for the stairs at the back and descended. The room was deserted and for a moment he thought he'd made a mistake, gone to the wrong place.

'Over here,' said a voice. He turned and saw Lucy sitting by herself at an alcove in the corner. He joined her and took the seat opposite.

'I didn't think you'd come,' she said.

'I just want to get this over with. How do you want to do it?'

'I want the money in cash.'

He looked at her sourly.

'Thirty thousand pounds in cash . . . that's ridiculous.'

She smiled coldly at him.

'What's ridiculous is giving you my bank details – or any means by which you could trace me later. You're the deputy CEO of one of the country's biggest charities – don't tell me you can't get the bank to play ball.'

Enough, thought David. He'd come in good faith, but now she was taking the piss. He'd deceived his wife for this woman, was now scamming his mother-in-law out of her savings. And now another demand. He was getting the horrible sense that this might never end. It was time to do what he should have done from the start.

'No, I don't think so,' he said.

'I've already told you what will happen if you don't—'

She stopped mid-sentence because under the table his hand had dropped on to her knee. He began to squeeze it, hard.

'I'm not paying you a penny. You're right – I am the deputy CEO of a major business. And you're right to be wary. You *should* be scared of what I can do.'

One of the coffee shop's staff came down the stairs. Humming quietly to himself, he began replenishing the supply of sugar, stirrers and napkins. David held Lucy's gaze, his hand still in place as if daring her to call for help. He saw the idea forming in her eyes but saw it fade just as quickly. He allowed the barest hint of a smirk to show – just so she knew he knew. The man behind them picked up a few discarded cups and trays from the tables and went back upstairs.

'At least you're being honest now about who you are,' she said. 'So much for all that "I was just trying to help a friend" bollocks.'

'And you're so much better, are you? Your friend has just died and this is how you respond? You try and profit from it?' The hand on her knee tightened even further and she let out a small involuntary whimper. He enjoyed the sound – the boot was on the other foot now.

'You're going to forget you ever met me, and if you do go to the media, the police or anyone else – then something very nasty can and *will* happen to you.'

He stood up feeling like he was finally in control of this. Best of all, he could now see the fear in her eyes.

Paulsen was standing at the back of the incident room. They all were now. Finn was pointing at the board where the crime scene photograph of Vicki Stratford's dead body was pinned up.

'I honestly haven't got a clue what you're talking about,'

said Skegman, staring at the pictures with bemusement. In fairness, the rest of the team looked equally unconvinced.

'That's because you're all taking it too literally,' said Finn. Using his glasses, he gestured at the picture again. 'It's in the silhouette – look again, tell me what you see?'

Paulsen tried once more. In many ways it all looked pretty straightforward: Vicki lying prone, face down on the ground, arms by her sides. Her long platted black hair running down the length of her back, bisecting it in half. Blood had soaked into the carpet around her in two large patches. Paulsen took Finn's advice, pulling back this time and taking in the general *impression* of the scene. Bloodstains had smudged and smeared into inky whorls and patterns on the back of the dead woman's cotton top. She felt that sense of a Rorschach blot again. And then suddenly – there it was – the image behind the image. The feather-white body with its black spine down the centre, the wing-like pools of crimson on either side. The splash of colours combining together into something terrible and beautiful at once. It was like a Salvador Dalí painting – a surreal, nightmarish outline of a giant insect. And now that she could see it, she couldn't see anything else. She looked instinctively over at Finn, who gave her an approving smile of recognition.

Skegman was still staring so hard his brow had almost furrowed into an arrowhead. 'I'm seeing two separate crime scenes but definitely no butterflies.' He shrugged helplessly again. Finn pursed his lips with frustration.

'You won't find it in the detail, John,' he said.

'I can see that they're both wearing white tops, that the blood makes it look a bit like the wings you get with a snow angel maybe, but apart from that . . .'

He shrugged.

'What about the rest of you?' said Finn, looking around for support.

'I *can* see what you're getting at – it's quite abstract, but you're right – there's definitely something about the shape of it,' said Paulsen.

Ojo and Dattani looked less certain. The detective sergeant was carrying the slight look of contempt she always wore when she wasn't sure about something, while Dattani simply looked baffled. Ojo shook her head.

'I don't know . . .'

'Hold on,' said Finn, striding over to his desk. 'There's something else I want to show you.' He emptied some A4-sized photographs from a brown envelope and held one up. It was a picture of some tagged evidence.

'Sadie wore a hairpiece the night she died – long platted black hair, just like Vicki. If you put her in that hairpiece against the white top she wore at the gala dinner . . . then they're dressed almost identically.'

Skegman still looked unsure.

'Maybe. But even if you're right, it's still an incredibly tenuous link to something Daws randomly mumbled a few times,' he said.

'I accept that,' replied Finn. 'And I'm not saying this is conclusive by any means, but you've got to try and see it through Tom's eyes – or to be more specific, his fractured mind. If he did kill Vicki Stratford all those years ago – *that's* the image that's lodged into his subconscious ever since. Or rather, how he's interpreted the memory. It's not from a photograph either, that's the key – these pictures haven't ever been in the public domain. He could only remember it that way if he'd actually *been* in the room with Vicki – *seen* it with his own eyes. This butterfly's been haunting him for literally longer than he can remember.' He looked around the room, aware he was still struggling to convince most of them. 'Just roll me with me for a moment, because if there's even the smallest chance I'm right about this, then we surely can't ignore it.'

Skegman looked at him dubiously and yielded to the logic.

'What exactly are you suggesting happened then, Alex?'

Finn pursed his lips and thought.

'What if Tom killed Sadie because he forgot that he'd already done it once before, thirty years ago? Even shifted the body to match what was in his mind's eye.'

Ojo looked like she had a headache.

'Hold on, guv – there's a whole boatload of questions that raises,' she said. 'Not least of which – why would he have killed the Stratfords back then?'

Finn held up a hand acknowledging the point.

'I agree. The idea needs a *lot* of standing up. But I've got some thoughts about that too,' he said.

'Good, because so far there's nothing here you could put in front of the CPS,' said Skegman. 'You'd need something a lot stronger than a crime scene that might look like an insect if you happen to be standing on your head.'

Finn ignored the jibe.

'I know – but I think I know where we can get that from,' he said, already reaching for his phone.

Tom Daws was sitting in his armchair working on the *Times* crossword when Abi entered the living room, slipping her coat on.

'I just need to nip into the office for a short while – something's come up. Will you promise me you'll stay here?' she said.

He frowned.

'Five across. Seven letters – "to secrete".' He looked at her and smiled. 'It's bugging me . . .'

She leant down next to him.

'Are you listening to me, Dad? It's important. Luke's gone for a run – he'll be back shortly. Promise me you won't go out? I can't deal with another disappearing act.'

'Of course I won't, and there's no need to talk to me like I'm five years old.' He turned to look at her suddenly even as the words came out, the minor flash of irritation melting away as quickly as it had come. 'I can remember when *you* were five years old. You couldn't go to sleep unless your bedroom light was on. We always had to creep in later and turn it off. You were scared of the monsters in the dark.'

She smiled.

'I can just about remember that.'

He reached across and put his hand on her cheek.

'I've done right by you, Abigail, haven't I?'

'Of course you have. Where's this coming from?'

'I've always tried to do the right thing.' He pointed at a framed photograph on the wall. It was a black-and-white image of a crowd carrying banners and flags on a march of some sort. A younger, more vital version of the man in the armchair was holding up a large home-made banner with the words 'Support the Railway Workers' scrawled on it. 'It's important to me . . .' he continued, 'while I've still got my marbles – some of them anyway – that you know that.'

'I've always been proud of you. You're my hero, that's what I tell everyone.'

The words didn't seem to soothe him.

'You're everything to me. Your mother and I – we had to make some tough choices once. And I know it's been hard for you, but whatever happens, I love you – don't ever forget that.'

He began to cough, a small tickle turning into a minor fit. Abi grabbed a cushion, placed it carefully behind his head.

'Shush now, you're agitating yourself. Just stay put until Luke gets home, okay?'

He slowly relaxed into the chair and got his breath back.

'Conceal,' she said. 'That's your answer – seven letters – "to secrete".'

She leant across and kissed his forehead.

In the incident room, Finn had finished his phone call and was still trying to sell his theory about Tom.

'There's a lot we don't know – especially about the relationships between these people thirty years ago. And the man I spoke to doesn't come across as someone capable of killing children either. But that means nothing – as everyone in this room knows.'

Skegman nodded silently. Finn was right – they'd all been in the job long enough to know killers came in all shapes and sizes, from all sorts of backgrounds, with any number of motivations, sane or otherwise.

'One other problem with this – Sadie wasn't wearing her hairpiece when she died. She'd taken it off by then,' said Ojo.

'I know – but I think he might have seen it earlier when she was heading off to the gala dinner. If he killed Vicki and Ben Stratford, I'm banking it was enough of a traumatic event to profoundly affect him, Alzheimer's or not. Again, see it from *his* point of view. I think the sight of Sadie in that outfit with that long, dark swinging plait triggered something. "I saw the butterfly again" – that's what he said, wasn't it, Mattie? I think it was enough to put him in some sort of fugue state.'

Finn's desk phone began to ring. He apologised and went over to answer it. The conversation was brief and he returned with a renewed urgency.

'When Tom went missing yesterday, Catford Police took his fingerprints as a matter of routine. I called earlier and asked to have them sent over to the lab who are looking at the historical evidence from the Stratford crime scene. They've got a match . . . partial prints on the lamp that was used to beat Vicki Stratford to death.' He was already reaching for his coat. 'I think we've found our man.'

The drive across south London was a sober one. Finn took Ojo and Paulsen with him, aware of the need to do this sensitively. None of them had any idea how Daws might react. Any kind of interview would also require careful consideration in conjunction with a medical assessment first.

'Do you think Abi knew?' said Paulsen. The question had been weighing on her mind since they'd left Cedar House.

'Someone must have helped him – there's no other explanation,' said Ojo.

Paulsen thought about all the conversations she'd had with Abi since they'd met only a few days earlier. She remembered her frantic concern in the park as they'd searched for Tom. Was she a woman genuinely in the dark about his past? Or had her behaviour been that of someone desperate to keep a secret? Paulsen hoped it was the former. But as they sped across south London, most of her thoughts were reserved for her own father. The long goodbye had already begun and this investigation was only doubling down on her sense of powerlessness. In part, that's why she hoped Finn was wrong about Tom, that he wasn't the man they were looking for. Because it would represent a small victory of sorts against the disease, a middle finger to the damned thing. She stared bleakly out of the window, her hands slowly balling into fists.

They pulled up in Pennington Road and walked up to the Daws' front door. Finn rang the bell but there was no response. He tried a second time, waited, then turned to the other two.

'Jacks, do you want to try the pub? Mattie, maybe give Abi a call – see if she can tell us where her dad might be?'

'Guv . . .' said Ojo and pointed at the door – it was easy to miss, but it hadn't been closed properly. It wasn't ajar, but neither had it been pulled shut.

'Someone in a rush to get in, or leaving in a hurry?' said Finn.

He pushed tentatively and it swung open.

'Hello?' he called, but there was no reply. He exchanged a look with the other two and they stepped inside. They moved through into the living room and immediately stopped in their tracks.

'Oh no . . .' said Paulsen under her breath.

Ojo immediately reached for her radio, calmly calling for back-up and an ambulance. Finn simply remained still, his eyes sweeping across the room to take in the full picture.

Tom Daws' lifeless body was suspended from the ceiling, a long electrical cable wrapped around his neck. The top of it was tied to a light fitting that had partially come through the plaster. His eyes were bulging beneath heavy lids, giving his face a strange, distorted look. A small veneer of foam had formed around his mouth, soaking into his beard. Finn looked across at Paulsen and Ojo.

'I know there's a time and place to say "I told you so" – but I can think of some fairly compelling reasons why he might have done this,' he said.

'Guilt over Sadie and Liam?' said Paulsen.

Finn nodded.

'And Vicki and Ben too.'

'Over there . . .' said Ojo. She was pointing at a side table by an armchair. It had been tipped over, the contents of a cold cup of tea staining the carpet. As they moved into the room properly, they could now see newspapers and books strewn on the floor.

'Looks like some sort of struggle,' said Paulsen. Finn walked up to the suspended body and got as close as he dared without touching anything. He peered up, pulled his phone out and turned the torch on, angling it at the dead man's neck.

'Look at this . . .' he said. There were visible red marks all around the throat. 'The cable didn't do that, that's someone's hands around his throat. He didn't commit suicide – he was murdered.'

34

For the second time that week, the world descended on Pennington Road. The cordons cutting off both ends of the street were back in place, manned by uniformed PCs on either side. At the Daws' house, the forensic team who'd only just completed their work at Sadie Nicholls' flat were beginning the hunt for trace evidence all over again. Finn had requested that a forensic pathologist take a look to confirm his initial assessment of the scene. Watching as the man went about his work made him feel increasingly uncomfortable though. Daws' distended eyes and the haunted terror of his bloated expression were a sharp reminder of what might have been.

It was only twenty-four hours since Finn had been sitting at his kitchen table staring hard at a paring knife. By a hairline, the cordon could be outside his flat today, the pathologist studying his body instead. Finn knew Murray had been right – he should have taken time off and allowed his mind to properly process what had nearly happened. There was no chance of that now – once again, events had got in the way and that would have to wait.

The forensic suit he was now wearing – complete with nitrile gloves, overshoes and face mask – wasn't helping his growing claustrophobia. After a conversation with the pathologist and a brief chat with the crime scene manager, he went outside to get some air. As he emerged on to the street, he lifted up the hood of the suit and pulled the mask away. Just like his first visit here, many of the street's residents were out on their doorsteps to see for themselves what was going on. Whereas before there'd been excited interest in what was happening, this time he could detect both sadness and fear permeating the onlookers. The PCs manning the cordons were fielding questions from some of them. Finn tried to blot everything out and focus only on his thoughts. They'd only just identified their prime suspect, and now he was dead before they'd had the opportunity to question him.

Jackie Ojo was on the other side of the road, speaking to one of the residents. Skegman had arrived on the scene too and was talking earnestly with the uniformed inspector marshalling the door-to-doors. Ojo caught the DCI's attention, pointed at Finn, and the pair crossed over to join him.

'So what are we looking at? Did he kill himself?' said Skegman.

Finn shook his head.

'I don't think so. The pathologist agrees with me – looks like someone strangled him then strung him up.'

Skegman's beady eyes narrowed, like a little boy who'd been refused a chocolate biscuit.

'To make it look like a suicide – or to make some sort of point?'

Finn shrugged.

'Your guess is as good as mine. We've put another forensic team inside Sadie's flat and they've already found a fingerprint match for Daws. I'm confident that, now that we've got a DNA sample to work with too, we can improve on that. Same goes with the historical evidence. I'm as certain as I can be that he's our killer.'

He felt no satisfaction in the words. There was little justice in this for Jill and Lily Nicholls and if anything, the death raised a multitude of new questions.

'What about the skip in New Cross?' said Skegman.

'We're cross-checking and re-examining everything in light of what we now know,' said Finn.

'And what *do* we now know? Are we saying that Daws committed all four murders – the Stratfords and the Nichollses?' said Ojo.

Finn stared down the street. His head felt full, like he needed a long walk to see the shape of this properly.

'I'm as certain as I can be that he killed Vicki. His fingerprints were on the murder weapon. Dean Rawton's prints were only ever found on some of the items recovered from her flat. I think someone planted them there to frame Rawton.'

'Were they planted by Daws, or someone protecting him?' said Skegman.

'Jackie and I had this conversation earlier. Given that we believe Daws couldn't have moved Liam's body on his own – it's highly likely someone helped him. My guess is it's the same person who helped him thirty years ago.'

'And what about the witnesses who say they saw Rawton running from Vicki's flat back then?'

'All came in a flurry well after the event, according to Peter Tolson. I think they were put up to it to help sell the lie.'

Skegman ran his tongue around his lips as he considered it.

'Ronnie Fordyce then?' he said.

Finn nodded.

'He's the obvious candidate – he and Daws were pretty much inseparable.'

Even as he said the words, Finn felt uncomfortable, and it was an instinct he'd learnt not to ignore. The pieces were falling into place, but historically he knew this was the moment when he needed to be at his most cautious. There remained a nagging doubt in his mind about Daws too. He wasn't jumping to firm conclusions just yet about any of it – past or present.

'We've got people out looking for Fordyce. He's not at home and isn't answering his phone either,' said Ojo.

Skegman and Finn exchanged a look.

'What about their alibis – weren't Daws and Fordyce both supposed to be in the pub on the night Sadie died?' said Skegman.

Finn smiled ruefully.

'I'm sure they were. But it was Alan Baxter who corroborated that, and I'm far from convinced he's a reliable witness.'

'He was also working behind the bar,' said Ojo. 'I doubt he could have had eyes on them all night. There's plenty of wiggle room there.'

Skegman looked over at the pub and scowled as if it had personally insulted him.

'Would Fordyce kill Daws though? If you're right about him, he's gone to a lot of effort to protect him for an awfully long time – why would he hurt him?'

'That's the one bit that does make sense to me, actually,' said Finn. 'If Daws killed Sadie and Liam because in his confused state he thought they were Vicki and Ben Stratford, then he was clearly a man whose mind was starting to *leak*. Now if you're Fordyce and you're relying on him to keep some pretty big secrets – that's not a good situation. So when Daws went missing again yesterday . . .'

'. . . it might have panicked him into acting,' said Ojo, completing the thought.

'Exactly. He'd been lucky up until that point – all that stuff about a butterfly was pretty oblique. It could easily have become something a lot more incriminating.'

'Always assuming that Fordyce *is* the other person we're looking for,' said Skegman. 'Is there anyone else who could be in the frame?'

'There's Abi . . .' said Ojo. 'She's very protective of her father. Who knows what she knew?'

'And where is she right now?' said Skegman.

'In the pub with Paulsen – we needed to get her away from the house for obvious reasons.'

'And her brother?'

'Went out on a run earlier and hasn't returned yet. He didn't take his phone so we haven't been able to get hold of him. Uniform are keeping an eye out.'

'Alright – let me know when you find Fordyce. And tell me how it goes with Abi. What kind of state is she in?' said Skegman.

'What do you think?' said Finn.

'I just don't understand it – why would anyone want to hurt my dad?' said Abi Daws in a hoarse whisper. She and Paulsen were sitting at her father's favourite table in the middle of a deserted Lamb's Head. Once she'd been informed about what had happened, Abi had come straight home. Paulsen managed to intercept her before she could reach the front door. Scenes of crime hadn't arrived at that point and the site needed protecting. She hadn't been able to stop her looking through the bay window though. Abi had seen her father's legs suspended above the ground, saw enough through the glass to make out the appalling expression on his face too. And at that point, she'd completely broken down. Paulsen had used the moment to shepherd her gently away to the pub.

Once he realised what was going on, Alan Baxter immediately closed the place to give them some privacy. The lounge was as dark, smelly and cold as it had been on Paulsen's previous visit and Abi couldn't stop shaking. Baxter, who'd initially been hovering behind the bar, unsure of what to do, was now striding towards them with a brandy glass in his hand.

'Drink this, Abs, it'll help,' he said, but she waved him away.

'I think I'd throw up . . .' she rasped.

Paulsen glared at Baxter and he retreated to the bar again. He took a swig of it himself, then began pouring the remainder of the drink back into the bottle. Paulsen flashed him a second look and he got the message.

'I'll be upstairs – just shout if you need anything,' he said. Abi nodded and he left them alone.

'Why are you so sure he was murdered?' she said after waiting for the door to close behind him.

'I didn't say that – and we're not sure yet,' replied Paulsen. 'It's far too early to know exactly what's happened. How was your dad the last time you saw him?'

Paulsen was acutely aware that Abi was a potential suspect. As she'd comforted her on the short walk to the pub, the thought had crossed her mind that this might have been a mercy killing. Tom's death certainly simplified things. If Finn was right, and Daws had killed two women and two children, then a very difficult future might just have been averted. His death was certainly convenient, and it was easy to see why it might have been a tempting solution to a horrific problem. But could she really have been so cold-blooded? It looked like quite a struggle had occurred and it would have taken quite an effort to string the body up like that.

Abi was now sitting with her arms wrapped tightly around herself while her teeth were gently chattering as well. The colour had completely drained from her face. Again, Paulsen was trying to keep a dispassionate view – you would be in a considerable state of shock if you'd just killed your own father.

'He was quite emotional, and it makes sense now, if that's what he was planning to do. It's like he was saying goodbye, you know?'

She was looking at Paulsen like they were old friends, and it made the detective feel guilty. The one thing she knew was that it was always foolish to form premature theories. Anything could have happened in that living room. Daws could have kicked over the side table himself in frustration or had a violent argument with a visitor and then killed himself. And even as she thought these things, she realised she was still desperately hoping that the old man wasn't the killer they suspected him to be.

'Do you mind me asking you some questions?' she said.

Despite the circumstances, it wasn't the worst moment for this. Given Abi's emotional state, if she was lying, there was every chance she might slip up and give something away.

'Will it help?' said Abi.

'The more information we have, the more chance we have of piecing together what's just happened. But only if you feel up to it?'

Abi looked anything but up to it but nodded anyway.

'Did he ever explain to you what the butterfly meant?' said Paulsen.

Abi looked at her helplessly.

'No – I haven't got a clue what that was all about. It came up a lot, but in the last year or two, he's said a lot of strange things. You know how it is?' Paulsen nodded, her face masking the stab to the heart the question felt like. 'Why do you ask – do you think it's important?' continued Abi.

Paulsen took a deep breath.

'We think it's possible it might be connected to the Nicholls murders.'

Abi looked confused, almost as if her brain couldn't take the idea on board.

'In what way?'

'That he might have seen something important that night which distressed him,' she said, improvising quickly.

'I don't see how he could have. Ron was with him all evening. He was certainly a bit upset that day though – he'd gone on one of his walkabouts earlier.'

Paulsen remembered Abi telling her in the park that he'd gone missing previously. It felt significant, and she was about to follow up on it when Abi put her head in her hands and closed her eyes.

'I'm sorry,' she murmured.

'It's alright, take your time,' said Paulsen.

After a few seconds, Abi looked up again. If anything, she looked even paler than she had before.

'Do you remember what time he went missing that day? It might be important,' said Paulsen.

Abi looked almost defeated by the question.

'About three, four o'clock maybe? He was only gone a few minutes. He didn't even get as far as the end of the road. Patrick met him in the street and brought him back – I didn't even notice he'd gone until the doorbell rang.'

She looked at the end of her tether now and Paulsen felt the resonance of it, even a little envy. Abi would never see her father disintegrate completely, forget who she even was. There had to be some relief in there surely, she speculated.

'One last question, if that's alright? What time did your dad get home from the pub that night – do you remember?'

The look on her face suggested it was one question too many. There was a pause while she cast her mind back.

'I was already in bed but I heard them come in. Ron brought him back around eleven, I suppose?'

She suddenly put her hand to her mouth.

'Oh God – I never thought . . .'

'It's okay, I shouldn't be asking you all this now,' Paulsen lied.

Abi's face contorted in silent agony. Her whole body was shaking violently now and for all her experience, Paulsen suddenly felt wholly inadequate.

'Do you want some water?' she asked, but Abi didn't seem to hear her; she was somewhere unreachable now. Paulsen looked around, saw a metal paper-napkin dispenser on a table by the door. She went over and pulled a sheaf out from its jaws. She brought them over and passed some across.

'Where's my brother? He needs to know . . .' said Abi.

'We're still looking for him. Do you know where he might have gone?'

She shook her head, but before Paulsen could ask any more, she heard the pub door creak open behind her. She turned around to see Finn stepping in. When he saw what state Abi was in, he held back and motioned at Paulsen to join him. Abi had now clamped a napkin around her mouth as if trying to keep her grief bottled in. Paulsen made her excuses and gently slipped away to join Finn at the door.

'She's just told me Daws went walkabout in the afternoon before the night Sadie died,' she whispered, checking she was out of earshot. 'Mid to late afternoon – probably around the time Sadie would have been heading for the station to catch her train to the gala dinner.'

Finn seized upon it immediately.

'So maybe that's when Tom saw her? Dressed in that top, wearing the hairpiece – the spitting image of a dead woman. And that image plants itself in his mind, growing as the evening goes on,' he said.

'She also said Fordyce brought him home at around eleven . . .'

'The timing fits. We really need to talk to Fordyce – but he still hasn't shown up,' said Finn. 'What do you make of her?' he said, motioning discreetly at Abi. Paulsen exhaled.

'Genuinely in shock – if she's faking it, it's a pretty good act.' She looked around again, briefly caught Abi's eye and smiled reassuringly at her. 'There's one thing we still don't have any idea about – *why* Tom would have killed Vicki and Ben Stratford in the first place. What the hell happened back then?'

'I don't know,' said Finn thoughtfully. 'But I think I know someone who might.'

35

Ronnie Fordyce stared with pride at the long strip of cabbages that lined the right-hand side of his allotment. It was funny how your priorities changed as you got older, he thought. He'd worn plenty of different faces throughout his life – soldier, businessman, builder – one or two other things too that he wasn't so proud of. But always fiercely loyal to his friends because that's what mattered. He believed passionately that he was a good man, his moral compass set in the right direction – whatever bumps in the road there might have been along the way.

A decent life wasn't built on being perfect, because no one can lay claim to that. These days it seemed all the millennials wanted to do was knock each other down for this, that and the other. Cancel culture, whatever that was. They didn't seem to understand that you don't go through life untarnished – the trick was to *strive* to be the best person you could be and accept that sometimes it wasn't always possible. Now, happiness was a simple row of cabbages, a pint in the Lamb, and the odd afternoon out on the golf course. His whole life had been a dog fight to get to this point and just as he'd achieved it, it felt like it could all be lost in a heartbeat.

The sun was beginning to peek through the clouds, and he felt an unexpected glow of warmth on his face. Closing his eyes, he allowed himself to bask in it for a few seconds. This was why he loved coming here; it was a place where time could stand still if you allowed it to. He'd turn his mobile off, put his worries to one side and lose himself in the sheer pleasure of tending to some vegetables. Simple moments, simple choices, simple pleasures.

But when he opened his eyes again, all the thoughts he'd been trying so hard to suppress washed back over him with a vengeance. There'd been moments on his journey when he'd proclaimed to anyone who'd listen that he didn't regret a thing he'd ever done. That he was a man who always looked forwards, never back. But right now, when he thought about all that was at stake – he felt sick to his stomach. You can try and ignore the past, but it won't forget you. Like an arm reaching out, with a hand slowly unfurling, it will pull you back eventually.

'Nice little spot you've got yourself . . .' said a voice with a sharp Australian twang.

He jolted with surprise and turned to see Luke Daws standing at the far end of the allotment. From this distance, caught in shadow, he was almost the spitting image of the way his father had once looked on a sunny morning in Port Stanley.

'Mind where you tread – it may not look like much to you, but a lot of work's gone into this,' he said.

'Sure, mate,' said Luke with an easy smile.

He made a slightly exaggerated effort of tip-toeing up the side of the cabbage patch until they were face to face.

'Dad told me I'd find you here – I thought we could have a little chat. We haven't had much chance to talk since I got back.'

Above, the clouds were floating slowly across the sky again, the brief warm interlude already over.

'I wanted to speak to you in the pub the other night, but if I didn't know better, I'd say you were trying to avoid me,' continued Luke.

Fordyce sighed.

'It's good that you've come back – Abi needs you here.'

A slight tautness crept into the younger man's otherwise friendly demeanour.

'No. We wouldn't want her to have things too hard, would we?' he said.

The two men locked eyes.

'How's your mother? She used to email me every now and then, but I haven't heard from her in a while,' said Fordyce.

'She's just fine, don't you worry about her. I'll give her a nudge though if you like – remind her who you are. Or were . . .'

In younger, more impetuous days, Fordyce might have risen to that. But this was Tom's son, and he could remember him as a child. It was interesting to see the man he'd grown into.

'What is it you want, Luke?'

'Like I said . . . just a chat. About you, me, and my dad.'

He smiled again.

At the pub, Alan Baxter had allowed some of the street's residents inside to help console Abi. Word had got around that she was there and a delegation had knocked on the door to check that she was alright. Baxter's son was busy laying on trays of teas and coffees, as everyone did their best to rally round. The official unofficial line was that Tom had committed suicide, and Paulsen saw no reason to confirm or deny what was being said. She'd flat-batted away their questions with the truthful response that it was all too early to say. In amongst their murmuring concern, she'd caught a few comments to the effect that 'it was probably for the best'. She couldn't believe Abi hadn't heard them either.

Paulsen's mood wasn't good anyway. Tom's death had hit her surprisingly hard, despite their suspicions about him. She liked Abi, felt a connection to the family, and wasn't comfortable with the current ambiguity of things. She desperately hoped that this wasn't going to end with the pair of them in an interview room together. Out of the corner of her eye, she could see Alan Baxter acting the genial host, coordinating, sympathising, hugging . . . and that irritated her even further. She waited until he was alone and went over to join him.

'Shouldn't you be down the road doing your job?' he said, opening fire first.

'You don't seem too concerned by what's happened,' said Paulsen. 'I thought you and Tom were old friends.'

'That's out of order,' said Baxter immediately. One or two heads turned on the other side of the lounge. He turned his back on them and lowered his voice. 'Me and Tommy Daws went back years. Don't you dare come in here and say something like that to me, police or not.'

Paulsen kept her face neutral. In truth, she'd deliberately gone looking for a reaction and was pleased to have got one. His emotion seemed genuine – the brief flash of anger betrayed real pain and she almost felt sorry for him.

'Fair enough,' she said. 'I have one or two more questions I'd like to ask you, if that's okay.'

His nostrils flared again.

'Now? Seriously?'

'What time did Tom and Ronnie leave this place, the night Sadie Nicholls and her son were murdered?' said Paulsen, ignoring him.

His face screwed up in angry confusion. He looked not unlike his own dog, Paulsen thought, who was currently sitting watching the kerfuffle around Abi in a similar state of bemusement.

'Are you taking the piss or something? The man's just died – have a little respect.'

'We could do this at the station if you prefer – obstructing a murder investigation's a pretty serious offence.'

He was about to lay into her again when he saw the look on her face and realised she wasn't joking. He rolled his eyes.

'I don't know – near enough eleven, I suppose.'

'And were they in the pub all night?'

'I think so – what's this got to do with what's just happened?'

'They didn't leave at any point and come back? You're quite sure about that?' she said.

Now Baxter was silent.

'If you know more than you're saying – it would be a serious mistake to keep it from us,' Paulsen continued, indecently enjoying the threat more than she should. Baxter sniffed loudly, snot rattling somewhere in his nasal cavity.

'I was working, not keeping my eyes trained on two regulars who were sitting having a quiet drink. And if it comes to it, you can't prove I'm lying about that and neither could any smart-arse lawyer.'

'What do you think happened to Tom Daws this morning?' she said.

It took a few moments for the implication of the question to settle. It was quite clear the idea that Daws might *not* have killed himself and had potentially died by other means hadn't crossed his mind. The realisation seemed to sweep across his features in slow motion.

'It's obvious, isn't it? He killed himself because of his condition.' Baxter tapped the side of his head. 'He didn't want it to get any worse and didn't want his family to suffer either.'

He nodded over at the group in the corner and Paulsen followed his gaze. Abi looked boxed in and uncomfortable, and briefly, they caught each other's eye. Paulsen gave her a small nod, acknowledging that she needed rescuing.

'The more I think about it . . .' continued Baxter, 'the more it feels exactly the sort of thing Tom *would* do. He always put other people first, that's just who he was. You didn't know him – he was a lion of a man. There was nothing he wouldn't do for you. You don't get people like that these days.'

And this time as he spoke, Paulsen was left in no doubt that he believed with absolute conviction every word he was saying.

By the time David Hermitage got home, he was already regretting what he'd done. Bravado was one thing, reality something else entirely. The threat he'd made to Lucy in the coffee shop was essentially an empty one. If she did choose to talk to the media, she could destroy him and there was nothing he could do about it. The simple fact of that hadn't changed. He'd gambled – using intimidation to try and ensure her silence – but was now far from convinced it had been the right play.

'Stupid, stupid, stupid,' he said out loud to himself, his foot tapping nervously under the table. He wondered what Emily might say when he told her that he hadn't paid Lucy off after all. She would just want this put to bed and not be hanging over them any more. He grabbed his phone on an impulse and quickly tapped out a text.

Sorry about earlier – didn't mean for things to get so unpleasant. How about I give you 10,000 in cash and we call it evens?

He pressed send, then stared at the screen and waited.

'So why don't you tell me what happened to Sadie Nicholls?' said Luke. He and Fordyce were walking and talking together through the stretch of deserted allotments.

'Why would you ask me that?' said Fordyce, staring straight ahead.

'Because it's got your stink all over it, *Uncle Ron*. Come on . . . a woman and child are battered to death. In that house, in *that* room?' Luke stopped. 'How stupid do you think I am?'

Fordyce stopped too.

'Let me ask you a question, Luke. Do you really want to know? Will your life be better for knowing?' he said. 'Get on a plane, son. Go back to your mum and get on with your life.'

Luke shook his head.

'It's all a bit late for that. And it's not as if I can't guess the shape of things, is it? Why do you think I'm here?'

Their eyes locked again and Fordyce sighed. He put a hand up to shield his eyes as the sun came out from behind a cloud. He took a second to enjoy the warmth again, a sense this might be the last moment of tranquillity for a while.

'The day Sadie died, your dad went out on one of his walk-abouts. Looking back, my guess is he must have come across her while he was out. For whatever reason, that addled head of his confused her with Vicki Stratford. I don't know why – it had never happened before.'

Luke smiled.

'That must have been awkward,' he said. Fordyce ignored him.

'Abi rang and asked me to take him to the pub because she had stuff to do. I thought it would help – it's usually some-where he relaxes.'

'I remember. Warm beer, frozen chips, boring chats about football . . .'

Again, the tone struck Fordyce the wrong way, and again, he chose not to rise to it.

'It seemed to work – he settled down for a bit – but later, Sadie walked past. She must have been on her way home from somewhere, and Tom saw her through the bar window and got agitated again. Someone from the golf club called me on my mobile and I got distracted. Your dad went off to the toilet while I was on the phone. When he didn't come back, I went to look for him, but he wasn't there.'

Luke was listening intently now, his face giving nothing away.

'So what did you do?'

'Went to find him, of course – I knew he couldn't have gone far. And he hadn't – he was out in the street, looking dazed. It was when I got closer that I saw the blood on his hands.'

'Well now ... that must have rolled back the years,' said Luke.

'Fuck's sake. You wanted to know what happened and I'm telling you.' Luke gave a laconic smile and motioned at him to continue. 'I saw the door to number eighteen open and the light on inside. Tom wasn't making much sense – just rambling really.'

'So you went to take a look?'

Fordyce nodded.

'It was horrific. Sadie was dead; he'd smashed her head completely open. The little boy was next to her. I thought he was dead too, but ...' he faltered, finding it difficult to speak, 'then he made this gurgling noise. When I went over to check, half his brain came out in my hands ...' Fordyce stopped again. He looked up – part horrified by the memory, part ashamed.

'Oh Ron – you didn't, did you?' said Luke with mock horror. 'You put the little fella out of his misery? Like twitching roadkill?'

Fordyce nodded slowly.

'I had no choice, Luke; I did him a favour.'

Luke smiled grimly.

'What a hero. And let me guess – you cleaned up after-wards, didn't you? Just like before.'

'I had to. My DNA was all over that kid, and unlike your dad, I've got a criminal record. It wouldn't have taken the police long to find me. I took Tom back to my place and cleaned him up as best I could and gave him some sleeping pills. I took him home, made a point of popping back into the Lamb to say goodnight to Al, and then I moved the boy's body.'

Luke blew through his cheeks.

'Wow. That's cold, Ron – even for you. What about Abi – didn't she notice something was up?'

Fordyce shook his head.

'She was already in bed. When I saw him the next day, he didn't even seem to remember what had happened. I thought it was probably a blessing.'

Luke clapped slowly, the sound echoing across the allotments.

'So how does it feel to be a child killer?'

'Luke . . .' whispered Fordyce.

'It's quite an exclusive club. The things you've done for my old man, eh?'

Fordyce looked at him sharply.

'And you. Don't forget that.'

Luke stopped again.

'What kind of life do you think I've had?' he said.

'I know what happened back then was difficult, but it was for the best. I'm aware you've had your problems in the past too, but the important thing is you've clearly made something of yourself.'

'Have I? What do you know about me? About my life and who I am? You know nothing – you're just bluffing, you old bullshitter.'

Fordyce held his ground, tried to find his old authority.

'That's enough now, son,' he said.

'I'm not your son – I think we can both be fairly sure about that,' said Luke with an unexpectedly high-pitched giggle. This time Fordyce stepped forwards and grabbed him by the shoulders.

'Listen, you ungrateful little bastard – if I wanted to, I could put you on the fucking floor. We did it *all* for you.'

But even as he said the words, he could see everything about Luke was wrong. He didn't seem thrown by the sudden aggression, or even bothered by it. That amused grin was still infuriatingly in place. If anything, there was a strange sense that he'd been waiting for the moment.

'You're forgetting something, Uncle Ron,' he said, baring his teeth. 'You're getting old . . .'

36

Finn was sitting in his car, parked outside of the cordon. His phone was propped up on the dashboard, and a pair of wireless buds were plugged into each ear. After a few seconds, the FaceTime call he was trying to make connected and a portrait-sized image of Peter Tolson displayed on the screen. He'd texted him the news regarding Daws, together with his suspicions over the man's connection to all four murders. The retired detective inspector had promptly accepted his request for a follow-up conversation. If Finn was curious as to how he'd received the information, he soon found out.

'How sure are you about this?' said Tolson immediately, not bothering with any pleasantries.

'I'm not sure about anything,' replied Finn. 'Other than the fact that Tom Daws is dead.'

He talked through the chain of logic they'd been following. Tolson hadn't initially been convinced by the butterfly theory but the fingerprints taken from the historical evidence were more persuasive.

'Jesus – so you think someone set Dean Rawton up back then?'

'Like I say, nothing's concrete yet, but in my opinion – yes, it's pointing that way,' said Finn.

Tolson's tension melted into something else, a shot look forming behind his eyes now. Finn suspected the defensiveness he'd seen from him in Winchester had come from a sense of unease, an instinct that something important *had* been missed back then. And there was a price too – if Daws was the killer, then Rawton had served thirty years for something he hadn't done. It was time that couldn't be clawed back and there was no amount of compensation that would make amends for it.

'This is why I wanted to talk to you, to see if you could help me join the remaining dots,' said Finn.

'Whatever I can do to help,' said Tolson.

No one liked finding out they might have fucked up fairly profoundly, but the way you responded was the main thing. Finn had met with – worked alongside – plenty who'd be wriggling at this point, laying the blame at other people's doors. It was clear that despite the immense implications, all Tolson wanted now was the correct outcome.

'As far as I can remember, Tom Daws was a pretty straight-up guy. My main memory was that he was quite political – he was interested in how rank-and-file coppers were being treated by management, and how the Police Federation looked after them. We had a couple of quite long chats about that.'

Finn tried to think it through logically.

'Showing an interest in that sort of thing, making conversation with you ... it would have been a good diversionary tactic, especially given that he had no previous. He was giving you very little reason to consider him suspicious.'

'He also told me he'd been working on the railways the day of the murders – I remember that much.'

'Was that ever confirmed?'

Tolson nodded, but with the discomfort of a man who could feel the sands starting to shift under his feet.

'I think so, but this was thirty years ago and he was never seriously in the frame. There were others we were looking at harder.'

Finn felt like he could see the threads of something, but not the full picture yet. A fragment of another conversation came back to him.

'There *was* a connection between the Daws family and the Stratfords – Luke was friends with Ben Stratford.'

'Maybe so . . .' said Tolson. 'But they were only children back then.'

Finn strained to try and remember exactly what Luke had said. In years gone by, he'd have recalled it instantly – he'd built his reputation on that kind of attention to detail. He realised guiltily just how fogged his mind had become recently. He'd almost missed perhaps the most important clue of them all.

'Luke told us he'd been playing with Ben on the day the Stratfords were killed,' he said slowly. From Tolson's expression, Finn could see he was beginning to see the significance too.

'I believe so, earlier that afternoon . . .'

'So who picked Luke up? His mother?'

'That would have been my assumption at the time.'

'Unless Tom lied to you about being at work – which would explain how he got inside Vicki's flat . . .'

The words hung between them as Finn stared down the street at the chipped black door of the flat where two women and two children had been slaughtered.

'I thought you'd want to do this somewhere private,' said Lucy Ahmed, as she opened the hotel room door. 'I've given reception your name and work address – told them I was expecting you as a guest. But they know who you are – just in case something happens to me.'

David looked at her sheepishly. She'd picked a Holiday Inn in central London for their meet, and he hadn't argued the point. He was carrying ten thousand pounds, as promised, in a rucksack and hadn't been in a hurry to hand it over somewhere too public.

'Thanks for giving me another chance,' he said.

He put the sports bag containing the money on the bed and looked at it awkwardly. In the films, people always seemed to make a thing of counting the cash at this point. Lucy walked over, unzipped the bag and peered inside.

While he watched her, David remembered the girl with the Geordie accent, the one who seemed so vulnerable as she lay in bed next to him. He remembered too the little boy with the toothy smile and the passion with which Sadie cared for him. Absently he rubbed at the now scabbed cuts on his wrist.

'This is fine,' said Lucy, her voice giving away no emotion.

'And I trust this is an end to it all?' he said as lightly as he could manage.

Lucy picked up the bag and walked to the door. For a moment he thought she was going to leave him hanging but then she stopped.

'I know where you went . . . after Sadie left the hotel.'

He met her gaze levelly.

'I have no idea what you mean.'

'And I've been ringing around some of the other girls who were there that night. I've got a fair idea about what happened. What you did.'

'But no proof,' he said. 'You should take your money and go, while you're still ahead.'

She nodded but didn't move.

'Sadie was kind. She had to fight every single day just to keep her head above water, but it never made her mean or bitter. You . . .' She stared at him for a moment and it felt like she was staring right through him. 'You have everything and yet you're just an empty vessel.'

She turned and left.

The words were still ringing in his head when he got home. Silly little bitch, he thought. Who was she anyway? Just an out-of-work barmaid who'd got lucky and managed to get one over on him. Good luck to her – see how far that ten grand gets her. He still had a career, his wife and family. She was right, he did have everything – she was the one with nothing. He smiled at Emily as he took his jacket off.

'Are we okay now?' she asked.

'I think so, and saved ourselves twenty grand in the bargain. All in all, things could have been a lot worse.'

Perhaps he said the words with just a little too much smugness because immediately her expression clouded over. Before she could speak, the doorbell rang and David was mildly grateful for the intervention. He went to open it and froze when he saw who was standing there.

'DS Ojo and DC Dattani, MIT,' said the stern-faced woman with the warrant card. 'Can we have a word, please?'

A few moments later they were all sitting in the living room together. The mood was uncomfortable and David was acutely aware that Emily was avoiding his gaze.

'What's this about then?' he said to the two police officers.

Ojo leant forwards.

'An escort who was working as a hostess at the Knights Association dinner has come forward, claiming she was assaulted by a man in one of the hotel rooms that night.'

David shook his head immediately but he noticed the blood draining from his wife's face.

'I don't know why you'd be asking me about that. As I told your colleagues before – I went for a walk around the block after Sadie left. To clear my head—'

Dattani cut in.

'And as they told you – we'd check the CCTV. We did

301

– there's no sign of you. You're lying. What were you really doing after Sadie left?'

Emily turned her head finally. It felt like a wall-mounted machine gun training its barrel on him. He licked his lip nervously.

'I didn't stay very long. I caught the train home. You can ask Ronnie Fordyce what time I got back.'

Dattani glanced over at Ojo. She was staring hard at David now.

'What do you mean?' she said.

'He was parking his car as I walked back from the station – I said good evening to him, but he completely ignored me. He must have heard me though.'

'What time was this?'

'I don't know – about half past eleven? Maybe later. The point is, I couldn't have been with some girl at the hotel, I was back in south London.'

'It didn't occur to you to tell us about Fordyce earlier?' said Ojo.

It took a moment for Hermitage to register the point she was making.

'He was just parking his car, that's all.' Hermitage shrugged. 'I'm telling you now though – that's got to work in my favour, surely?'

Ojo shook her head.

'The timing of it doesn't help you out in the slightest. There's still a full ninety minutes between Sadie leaving the gala dinner and your own departure.'

He crossed his arms.

'And a misunderstanding about timings doesn't make me some sort of rapist.'

'Who said anything about rape?' said Dattani. 'We haven't specified the offence.'

David said nothing.

'David . . .' said Emily.

'I haven't done anything, Em,' he said.

Ojo and Dattani glanced at each other briefly and David felt his world teetering in that look between them.

'You should know something,' said Ojo. 'In the last hour, we had a tip-off from another hostess who says she saw you going upstairs with the alleged victim. She identified you by name.' Hermitage paled. It wasn't hard to guess who that might have been. Bitch, he thought. 'The victim's also now been shown a photograph and confirmed you as her attacker.'

David shook his head.

'No, no, no . . . you've got this all wrong.'

Ojo produced a pair of handcuffs and began to read him his rights. He ignored her, focusing everything on his wife.

'These are lies. From someone *malicious*. Don't believe any of it. We'll talk later and then . . .'

He broke off because she was already on her feet and heading for the door.

'I don't know what to do, where to go,' said Abi, as she and Paulsen walked back up Pennington Road. They'd left the temporary retreat of the pub, and almost by instinct Abi had begun to head for home. She stopped when she saw the scale of the police operation outside.

'It's okay – we can book you into a hotel for the night, get you away from the area,' said Paulsen, but Abi didn't seem to hear, her eyes now transfixed on the gowned scene-of-crime officers going about their work.

'Where's my brother? I need to talk to Luke,' she said.

'I'll try and find out for you,' said Paulsen. 'Are you okay to wait here for a moment?'

Abi nodded and perched on a small brick wall in front of one of the houses. Paulsen was reluctant to leave her alone but could see Finn further up the road talking to one of the crime scene investigators. 'I'll be right back,' she promised. Finn turned to greet her as she joined him.

'Any sign of Luke Daws, guv? Abi's desperate to see him.'

'Not yet.'

'Should we be worried?' said Paulsen.

Finn nodded.

'Yes – I think everything's relevant right now. We haven't found Ronnie Fordyce either, although his car is still outside his home. His phone appears to be switched off, which is concerning me, and he hasn't used any of his bank accounts this morning either. Luke's phone is still in the house so our options have been pretty restricted.'

'CCTV?' said Paulsen.

'We're going through the camera footage from the high street but if they've been using the backstreets . . .'

'Could they be together?' said Paulsen.

'It's more than odd they've both gone missing at the same time.'

He talked her through the conversation he'd had with Tolson, also the information Ojo and Dattani had just relayed regarding Fordyce's movements on the night of the murders. Finn had caught up with them as they'd been leading a hand-cuffed Hermitage to their car.

'So it's as we thought – Daws killed Sadie and Liam then Fordyce cleaned up the scene afterwards,' said Paulsen.

'I'm ninety-nine per cent sure now that's the sequence of events. It's harder to prove Fordyce set up Dean Rawton thirty years ago, but if I were a betting man . . .' said Finn.

Paulsen processed the picture that was now forming.

'If you and Tolson are right – then Luke might well have been present when the Stratfords were killed . . .' she said slowly.

'That thought's occurred to me too,' said Finn. 'But he would only have been about five years old then.'

'Young enough to have been pretty fucked up by it . . .'

Finn nodded.

'And the two people who might just have some answers to all this happen to have gone AWOL,' he said. 'My concern is if Tom was killed to silence him . . .'

'. . . then Luke might be in danger too?' said Paulsen, completing the thought.

'We need to find both of them – now,' said Finn.

Paulsen looked over again at Abi – she was still perched on the wall, looking lost.

'I ought to get back to her,' she said. 'She shouldn't be left alone.'

She broke off. The uniformed inspector who'd been talking to Skegman earlier was now sprinting down the pavement towards them.

'You two need to come up to the allotments – we've found a body there.'

37

A tooth lay embedded in the soil. There were one or two more close by, like sweets fumbled by a toddler. The body of Ronnie Fordyce had been dumped in a small brown shed behind where they'd scattered. His face was barely recognisable, beaten to a fleshy pulp. He'd been left crumpled in a heap over some sacks of topsoil. There was a puddle of blood on the rotting wooden floor, dripping slowly into a smaller viscous pool on the ground outside.

Finn was kneeling as close as he dared without contaminating the scene. The nature of the injuries suggested a sustained and frenzied attack. It was hard to associate the broken thing in the shed with the proud, well-groomed man he'd seen patrolling around Pennington Road.

'I don't understand – I can buy Fordyce killed Tom to silence him. But why would someone then kill him?' said Paulsen who was standing a few yards behind with the uniformed inspector still in tow. Finn stood back up, snapping off the nitrile gloves he was wearing and pocketing them.

'We don't know yet that Fordyce *did* kill Tom. Maybe someone else killed both of them. But the fact that Luke's been gone so long now is beginning to look pretty incriminating.'

It took a moment for the implication to sink in for Paulsen.

'You think Luke might have killed his own father?' she said. 'Why? As far as I can see, they barely had anything to do with each other.'

Finn shrugged.

'Until we can sit him down and talk to him, I can't answer that. But he's the only man left standing who was in that flat with the Stratfords in 1993.' He turned to the inspector. 'Did anybody see anything?' he said, gesturing at the rest of the now sealed-off allotments. The inspector shook his head.

'No – but we've got people down at the entrance checking for witnesses just in case.'

'Finding Luke Daws is now the priority,' he told him. 'Forget the house-to-house work in Pennington Road for the moment – that can wait until later. Get every available man you've got on to it.'

The inspector nodded and skirted away, reaching for his radio. Finn pulled out his phone and rang the incident room. He gave an immediate instruction to ensure that every UK port and airport was put on full alert for anyone matching Luke's description. Throughout, Paulsen had stayed focused on the pulverised pink mass that used to be Ronnie Fordyce's face.

'Assuming it is Luke . . .' she said. 'He hung Tom up like an animal on display and then did *this*.' She pointed at the body. 'Look at him – there wasn't just anger behind that, there was fury. Why would he hate them that much?'

Finn rubbed the back of his neck thoughtfully. He'd been rolling the same question around his own mind since they'd got there.

'The only thing that makes any kind of sense is that it's rooted in what happened thirty years ago.'

'So what the hell did take place back then?' said Paulsen.

Finn stared out across the rows of neatly tended vegetables. There was a strange calm about the whole scene, despite what had just unfolded there.

'We've heard it since the investigation began: Tom Daws was a decent, ethical man. I think whatever occurred in '93 wasn't premeditated – that it just happened out of nothing, for whatever reason.'

Paulsen was concentrating intently on what he was saying, Fordyce almost an afterthought now.

'Say you're right and the murders were spontaneous,' she said. 'Tom tells his mate Ronnie, who then uses his contacts to plant evidence at the crime scene and produce some helpful witnesses. Dean Rawton gets arrested and sent down for it. The only loose end would be Luke – a small child who could open his mouth and give them away at any point.'

Finn nodded in agreement.

'When exactly did Tom and his wife split up?' he said.

'I don't know, but Luke was pretty young at the time, I know that much. Abi said their mother met some guy from Melbourne.'

'Forget what we've been told,' said Finn. 'My guess is that guy was a total fabrication. I think she took Luke to Australia to protect their secret while Tom raised Abi here on his own. Thanks to Fordyce, everything was neatly tidied up behind them.'

'And stayed that way until Tom got ill and the memories started leaking through,' completed Paulsen. 'So why didn't the whole family go?'

Finn shrugged.

'Good question. It's all just a theory at this point; we've got no evidence. Shame the only people who can tell us anything are dropping like flies,' he said.

'You sound like you're enjoying this,' said Paulsen suspiciously.

Finn's jaw tightened, as did his demeanour.

'I wouldn't go that far,' he said, nodding over at the corpse in the shed. He wasn't going to admit it to her, but he *could* feel a difference in himself. Enjoyment would be pushing it as a description, but there was a sharpness to his thinking that he hadn't experienced for a while and it felt good.

'What about Abi?' she said. 'How much do you think she knows about any of this?'

In the rush to get to the allotments, they'd left her with a constable in Pennington Road, while a family liaison officer was hurried down to take care of her.

'Possibly everything, possibly nothing at all. But until we can get Luke into an interview room, other than their mother she's the only link to the past.'

Paulsen looked idly down at the ground. Fordyce's scattered teeth were catching the light of the sun, gleaming in its rays.

'We know more or less who did what, both now and then – so why does it feel like we still know next to nothing at all?' she said.

Abi Daws was sitting on her own in the back of a police car, her eyes still transfixed on the small house further up the road. It had been the strangest hour of her life – her father was dead, her brother was gone, and no one seemed to know what to do with her. There almost wasn't the room in her head to compute what was going on with Luke. The longer he was missing, the longer it unsettled her. She was just about holding herself together, but if something had happened to him too, she wasn't sure she'd be able to cope.

She wanted to believe her father had killed himself rather than the possible alternative. When she remembered the discussion she'd had with him earlier that morning, it felt like that's what he was trying to communicate to her – that he was ready to go. If that was the final conversation, it wasn't the worst one to take away, she thought. She'd looked him in the eye and he'd been there – present – in the look he'd given her back. She would remember and be grateful for that, for the rest of her days.

There was a tap at the window and she looked up, expecting to see the police constable who'd been looking after her. Instead, she saw Luke peering down and opened the door with instant relief.

'Where have you been?' she said. 'I've been so worried about you.'

'We need to talk. Do you trust me?' he replied.

'Of course . . .'

He looked around furtively.

'Come on – let's get away from this circus.'

It was as she got out of the car that she noticed he wasn't wearing his running gear; she wondered how he'd been able to get changed.

'Shouldn't we wait for the police? They've been looking for you,' she said.

'Abs – I really need to talk to you. It's important. Please . . .'

She looked around uncertainly, then nodded and followed her brother.

'It's awful. That poor man,' said Lynda Clarke, peering through her curtains. It seemed to Patrick that there'd finally occurred a crisis for which a cup of tea and some cake would not be enough to soothe his mother. The injuries he'd sustained had meant he'd had to cancel all his ongoing work and the day was already feeling like lockdown all over again.

'What do you think happened?' said Lynda turning back to him. 'It's got to be connected with that young woman and her son, don't you think?'

'Fella killed himself because he was losing his marbles, more like,' said Patrick.

Lynda was still peeking through the curtains.

'Then why's there so much police over there . . .' she said. 'Something bad happened to that man, mark my words . . .'

'Come and sit down, Mum, you're only going to wind yourself up.'

She turned, a look of fear crossing her features now.

'I don't feel safe. Who'd have thought it, after all these years living here? I don't feel safe in my own home.'

With a wince of pain, Patrick rose to his feet and went over to her.

'Nothing will happen to you here. I promise – I won't *let* anything happen to you.' He looked her in the eyes and she calmed down.

'You're a good son. You know I've never doubted that, don't you?'

He smiled back at her.

'It's what keeps me going, Ma,' he said. He glanced over her shoulder and out the window and saw a familiar silhouette walking past, his dog trotting alongside him as usual.

'Put on another pot of tea, will you – and slice up some of that carrot cake of yours. I just need to nip out for a minute.' She began to look concerned again. 'I won't be long – something I've got to do.'

The smile on his face retained its warmth, but his eyes were focused on the balding figure receding into the distance.

He followed Alan Baxter for a few streets. His whole body felt sore and he wasn't quite sure what he was going to do, but he'd reached a decision of sorts back in the living room. The beating he'd taken was the final straw in a long and complicated saga. It was time to end the strange dance going on between the two of them. Baxter turned and walked down a small alleyway. He stopped and waited as his dog ran around in a small circle and then began to squat. It gave Patrick enough time to make up the ground between them.

'Baxter . . .' he shouted.

The older man turned, but the usual leer of intimidation wasn't there.

'What do you want? Whatever it is, I'm not interested. In case you ain't heard, I've just lost a good friend.'

Patrick fixed him with a long, hard look, saw enough discomfort in the other man's expression to know it had unsettled him.

'I think it's way past time you and I had a conversation. I mean . . . it's been *years* in the coming, hasn't it?'

Now there was a glint of something else in Baxter's eye. He tied the dog lead around the lamp post his pet was busy defecating against.

'If that's what you want, then that's what we can do.'

He stood facing him and crossed his arms.

Jackie Ojo was standing at the far end of Pennington Road talking to a white-gowned forensics officer. Following David Hermitage's revelation that he'd seen Ronnie Fordyce parking up on the night of Sadie's murder, she'd immediately ordered a forensics examination of the vehicle. The boot of a black Audi A3 Saloon was open behind her and the area around it had been cordoned off. A cordon behind a cordon. It hadn't taken long to apply some luminol and establish traces of blood inside the car. It was also clear an attempt had been made to thoroughly clean the interior recently. She was quite certain, as she watched her colleagues carefully collecting fibres, that they would soon find definitive DNA proof that the body of Liam Nicholls had been stowed here. Now that they knew the make and colour of the vehicle too, they could also retrace the route to the skip in New Cross via CCTV. She pulled her phone from her pocket and called Finn to tell him the news.

'It's another piece of the jigsaw falling into place, and confirms at least one part of our theory,' he said.

He shared his and Paulsen's current thinking regarding Luke and Ojo nodded along to their logic. As she listened, she found herself just as interested in Finn as she was in the investigation. There'd been a small subtle change to him which was hard to pinpoint. He sounded *engaged* in a way she hadn't heard for a while.

'Do me a favour, Jackie. Go and sit with Abi Daws until her FLO arrives. See if you can get any more out of her about her brother. He's the key to all of this.'

It took less than thirty seconds for her to call him back and tell him Abi, too, was now gone.

38

The River Quaggy stretches nearly four miles under and through south-east London. Close to Pennington Road, it thins out into no more than a muddy stream – the dividing line between two rows of suburban back gardens in neighbouring streets. Closed away from the world, it's where Abi and Luke Daws used to play as children. Abi recognised immediately where they were going as Luke led her down a small thoroughfare by one of the end-of-terrace houses.

The last time she'd used it she'd been a foot or two shorter and several decades younger. The path led to a wooden fence overlooking a steep bank down to the water. Back in the day, there'd been a wire fence there, riddled with holes which they used to slip through. There was no need for that now; the new barrier ended a few feet further up the path than the old one, leaving a clear route down.

'Why have we come here?' she said.

'Don't you remember doing this as kids, Abs – when we wanted to get away from Mum and Dad?'

'Of course I do, so why are we doing this now? The police want to know where we are . . .'

She held up her phone which was already displaying a missed call.

'Please – it's like I said, I just need to talk to you. The police can wait. After what's just happened to Dad, I want some privacy with my sister and there's too much noise going on out there.'

She softened as she saw his face. Nothing good was waiting for them. Just cold hotel rooms and the whole weight of their grief about to press down. She could understand the impulse to find somewhere more personal. She liked how that felt too; it had been a long time since they'd been a proper brother and sister to one another. She wasn't flush with money, so visits to Australia had become more and more difficult in recent times. She FaceTimed Luke and her mother a fair bit but it wasn't the same thing. The distance between them wasn't just geographical. She knew too that he'd had his problems over the years and felt guilty she hadn't been able to do more to help. If ever there was a moment to reconnect, this was it.

'Alright,' she said, pocketing her phone.

A narrow concrete bank lined either side of the running water and the pair began to slowly wander down the length of it.

'I'd forgotten how calm it is here,' she said, taking in the surroundings more fully now. That was about its only merit; the water looked dirty and the occasional chocolate wrapper or empty beer can floated past as they walked. Several of the back gardens looked familiar, exactly how Abi remembered them from her youth. It almost felt like when they emerged, their parents would be waiting at home with dinner on the table. The memory produced a jolt of pain.

'You really cared about him, didn't you?' said her brother, watching her face closely.

'Of course I did. I'm just sorry that you didn't get the chance to form a stronger bond with him.'

He gave her a sideways look, the water running alongside them the only sound for a moment.

'Did Dad ever talk to you properly about it? Open up about what really happened back then?'

She looked at him quizzically.

'The divorce? No, not particularly. But then he always kept his feelings close to his chest.'

'So what did he talk about then?'

There was an uncharacteristic harshness to his tone, but given the raw grief they were both experiencing it was perhaps understandable.

'His job was everything to him – but you know that. He always felt the responsibility of it – his *duty* – making sure people were looked after properly.'

Luke snorted with derision.

'And how much did I come up in conversation over the years?'

She looked at him, concerned. He'd never asked her questions like these so directly before.

'He was always pleased to hear from you, Lukey. If something good happened in your life, it put a smile on his face for the rest of the day.'

'Is that right,' he muttered.

Abi didn't know what to say. The gardens on either side had given way to crumbling brick walls and above them she could hear the sound of traffic passing on the adjacent road. The bank they were walking on was narrowing too, tapering into the water. Soon, they wouldn't be able to go much further, and she stopped.

'What are we doing down here, Luke?' she said. 'This is silly. We should get back up the road. Face up to this.'

He halted and turned to look at her.

'You really are fucking stupid, aren't you?' he said.

'So are they in it together?' said Ojo.

She and Finn were standing by his car, regrouping while the search for Luke and now Abi was intensified. Paulsen was sitting inside the vehicle, her phone clamped against her ear as she scribbled on a pad propped up on her lap.

'I can't tell you that, Jacks – I don't know if Abi's gone off to meet her brother or whether she just needed some time on her own, but she's not answering her phone and that worries me,' said Finn.

'Maybe she's protecting Luke then?' said Ojo. 'How close are they, anyway? That whole relationship's got to be a bit weird, hasn't it? They seem to have lived separate lives for the most part.'

Before she could say any more, the passenger-side door of Finn's car opened and Paulsen emerged to join them.

'Sami hasn't been able to get hold of the mother in Australia, but he says Alice Daws reverted to her maiden name of Alice Bellamy not long after she moved there.'

'That's interesting,' said Finn. 'She didn't waste any time shedding her old life then.'

'She lives in . . .' Paulsen glanced down at her pad, 'some place called Cootamundra and works at an Amcal in the centre of town.' She looked at their blank expressions. 'It's a chemist's chain – she's a pharmacist by trade.'

'What about Luke – did Sami find anything useful on him?'

'Yes, this is where it gets interesting – sounds like he was basically a drifter with a history of drug abuse. Local law enforcement are emailing over what they've got – it's quite late over there, but the guy Sami spoke to had a quick look on their system and said he'd been inside on a number of occasions.'

'For what?' said Ojo.

Paulsen referred down to her pad again.

'Mainly drug-related offences – robbery, dealing, that kind of thing – but also some assaults as well. The worst was a stabbing for which he did seven years. Sounds like he nearly killed someone . . .'

'I don't understand,' said Abi, holding her ground. 'Why are you so angry with me? What is it you think I've done?'

She'd put his reaction down to grief, but as she looked at his face, she was now beginning to wonder if there wasn't something more to it.

'I wanted to give you a chance, to be honest,' said Luke. 'Did you *know*?'

A dark suspicion was beginning to form in her mind; one she didn't like at all. Had he ever even changed into his running gear that morning – ever left the house, when she went off to work earlier?

'Know what?' she said.

Luke shook his head, with something half between contempt and pity.

'What have you actually done with your life? You could have been anything you wanted, with the start you were given. You were handed it all on a plate. But there's no relationship, no children . . .'

'Stop it—' she said sharply. That particular jibe cut deep.

'. . . no career to speak of,' he continued. 'You just funnelled backwards. An old spinster living in the house you grew up in. You could have had it all but you did nothing with it.'

'And what you done with yours exactly?'

Abi felt lost. She just wanted to put an arm around him, wanted him to put an arm around her.

'I can't do this, Luke. I don't have the energy. If you want to hate me right now and that makes you feel better, then hate me.'

He was looking into the water now, his face inscrutable.

'I want to ask you a question – the same one I asked Dad and Fordyce.'

He turned his gaze back to her.

'Do you think I'm a good man?'

'So the whole laid-back Aussie thing was just an act,' said Finn. 'That makes a lot of sense to me – if he was traumatised as a child, then suddenly ripped away from his father and sister, it could well have had a profound effect on him.'

He was interrupted by a loud blast of blues and twos from what sounded like one of the nearby streets.

'What's that about?' said Paulsen.

As if on cue, Finn's phone began to ring. He answered it and the conversation was brief.

'Uniform have got a possible sighting of Abi and Luke together,' he said. 'Two people matching their descriptions walking along a stretch of the river near Westmore Grove.'

'That's literally the street behind here,' said Ojo. 'What the hell are they doing down there?'

Paulsen squinted over her shoulder.

'The river runs from the park – it must come through the gardens along here,' she said. Finn processed the information.

'Jacks – you go with uniform. Tell them to go easy – we don't know what the relationship is yet between Luke and Abi, and I don't want them spooked,' he said.

Ojo nodded and hurried away.

'So where are we going?' said Paulsen.

'I think we can shortcut it from here . . .' he replied.

They accessed the river from the back garden of one of the nearby houses. A shallow fence bordered the water there and it was a simple matter to climb down to the slimy, moss-encrusted bank. The pair were now standing by the same muddy stream Luke and Abi had followed earlier. They peered in both directions trying to get some bearings. The water was murky and dank and carried the faint whiff of rotten eggs.

'Guv,' said Paulsen urgently, pointing at something downstream. He looked over and saw at first what he thought was an old refuse sack lying by the side of the water in the middle distance. He soon realised it was something bigger and more substantial.

They ran down the bank until the stream narrowed again into something more like a small canal and splashed across the water. The fallen body of Abigail Daws was face down in the mud on the other side and when Finn turned her over he saw a nasty gash on her forehead leaking blood. He immediately grabbed her wrist and felt for a pulse.

'She's alive,' he said.

'Thank fuck,' said Paulsen, with genuine relief. She leant down to help the stricken woman. Abi wheezed weakly, then began to cough up dirty brown water.

'Why didn't he finish her off?' said Finn, remembering the frenzied assault on Fordyce at the allotment. He looked around again but everything was calm; up above them he saw the top of a lorry passing by on the street.

'Because he heard the sirens,' he said, answering his own question. 'Stay with her,' he shouted at Paulsen, who was already calling for an ambulance. He began to wade through the water. There was no sign of Luke the way they'd come, and there was no obvious route back up to the street. The only direction he could have gone was further down the river.

Finn turned a sharp bend and was confronted with a wide tunnel a short distance ahead. The sour-smelling water was now almost waist-high. He waded through into the opening of the underpass and found himself in darkness. There was an immediate splashing sound close by, and something clubbed into the side of his head. It felt like a brick and he fell forwards.

Hands tightened around his throat and forced his ringing head down into the ice-cold water. Suddenly there was just muffled silence and nothing but blackness. The water rushed into his lungs and he realised with genuine fear that he might only have seconds now. He tried to push back, but the hands around him felt like steel manacles. For an instant, he remembered the barrel of the gun he'd put his forehead to almost a year before, saw a paring knife on his kitchen table.

Heard a voice.

'*Live,*' said Karin.

And then there was clarity. He'd return to that moment in the years to come.

With a burst of strength, he pushed his face and body further *down* into the water. The action took his attacker by surprise and momentarily wrong-footed him. Finn took his opportunity and wriggled free of the loosened grip, twisting his body sideways. Spitting out filthy water, he hauled himself back on to his feet. The dark shape of a man was standing in front of him in the gloom and instinctively Finn swung a fist. It connected hard with what felt like a bony cheek and he heard Luke stagger back with a cry of surprise. He could hear shouting now too, but couldn't tell where it was coming from. Luke threw a punch of his own which caught Finn just below his throat. The water was slowing them both down, like a pair of exhausted boxers in the final round of a heavyweight bout. This time as Luke came again, Finn ducked away, avoiding the blow. He snatched a much-needed mouthful of air and prepared for the next assault, but it didn't come.

The splashing and shouting had increased, and the dark shapes around them were multiplying too.

'*Easy ...*' screamed a voice and he realised there were uniformed police entering at the far end. They converged on

Luke and Finn staggered out of their way. He watched as they subdued him, heard a primal howl of despair echo around the tunnel.

'Are you alright?' said a voice.

'I will be,' said Finn. And meant it.

39

Finn had required some minor stitching to a head wound and had then been held up at the hospital while he was checked – then cleared – for concussion. There'd also been some concern for how much water both he and Luke had swallowed. A young doctor gave him a sober lecture about the amount of raw sewage, animal waste and pollution it probably contained. He'd been given a course of antibiotics and wondered if the gods weren't actually trying to kill him off this week, after all.

After borrowing some ill-fitting clothes at the hospital, he'd made a quick stop at home to change and then returned to the station to catch up with Skegman. The media team had informed the press a man had been taken into custody by the detectives investigating the Nicholls killings. The press release revealed he'd been arrested on suspicion of two *other* murders and two counts of attempted murder. It also stated the police weren't now looking for anyone else in relation to Sadie and Liam's deaths.

'They can't make head nor tail of it,' said Skegman with undisguised glee. 'I've been inundated with calls from reporters wanting an off-the-record briefing. I told them all they can piss off and wait.'

'They'll have to – we still only know the shape of things. Not any of the actual detail of it. What's Luke been like since you brought him in?' said Finn.

'Hasn't said a word. To be honest, his psychiatric state is more of a worry than his medical condition.'

'Patricide will do that for you . . .'

'I'll be happier once he's been interviewed,' said Skegman.

It was going to be an interesting conversation, thought Finn. He was in no doubt the forensic evidence from both crime scenes would overwhelmingly prove Luke murdered both his father and Fordyce. He may not even try to deny it. The real challenge was whether they could get him to answer the outstanding questions. They owed it to Dean Rawton for one, and Finn still felt a very personal debt to Sadie and her son. He was mindful too that another mother and child deserved some long overdue justice. He could feel a much-missed old feeling beginning to form: anticipation.

A search of Fordyce's allotment had taken place and the bloodied ashtray used to beat Sadie and Liam Nicholls to death had been recovered from it. The remains of a small bonfire, too, had been discovered, with what appeared to be the burnt remnants of Liam's clothing inside. With some answers starting to fall into place, the mood in the incident room was much lighter than it had been for a while. Finn still felt under scrutiny from his team, but it was more bemused curiosity than suspicion. None of them knew exactly what journey he'd been on over the past few days, but it was as if they could sense there'd been an important shift of some sort. There'd also been a brief text exchange with Murray.

How are you getting on, big fella?

Nearly drowned, may have E.coli. Nicked a killer. Tip-top then – thanks for asking.

It was Paulsen who seemed most affected by the day's events. Abi was now recovering in hospital. Her injuries had turned out to be relatively minor but rather like her brother, it wasn't her physical condition that was the prime concern.

'She just doesn't understand why Luke would do any of this. And she's got no one now. We're still trying to contact the mother, but it's the middle of the night in New South Wales,' she said.

Finn thought briefly about Jill and Lily Nicholls and the long emotional journey awaiting them as well. He was going to have to learn how to live side by side with other people's grief going forwards, he realised.

'Let's try and find her some answers, Mattie,' he said in reply.

40

Even before a word was exchanged in the interview room, Luke Daws' whole demeanour was different. The light, friendly Aussie who Finn and Paulsen had met in Abi's house was long gone. Finn was fairly sure he'd never existed in the first place – more an artificially contrived character to match a few expected stereotypes. In his place, a silent figure, whose brooding stillness exuded menace. A duty solicitor was with them, and Finn was guessing he'd not got much change out of his client when they'd talked earlier. As they went through the formalities, he wondered what was going through Daws' mind. If he was right, Luke's whole life had led him to this room – to this conversation.

'Let's be quite clear – we've matched your fingerprints to those found on the flex wrapped around your father's neck. We have a DNA sample from you too, so we can now compare that with anything we find at either crime scene—'

Finn stopped as an amused grin spread across Luke's features. 'Is something funny?'

'You sound like you want a gold star, mate. I nearly drowned you back there – there's probably a clue in that, don't you think?'

'Is that a confession, Luke?' said Paulsen.

'If you'd like it to be,' he replied.

The solicitor whispered into his ear, but he barely seemed to notice.

'For the record – did you kill both Tom Daws and Ronald Fordyce?' said Paulsen, seizing the opportunity. Luke leant back in his seat as if reclining in a deckchair.

'Shall we come back to that one? I've got a feeling it'll come up in conversation again . . .'

He poured himself some water from a jug on the table and took a couple of noisy gulps. The solicitor tried to talk to him again but he turned his head away as if bothered by an unpleasant smell.

'Why did you come back to the UK this week?' said Finn.

'Just for a visit. I haven't been for a while – and with Dad starting to get ill, Abi wanted me to come over a bit more. I think she was hoping I'd help her with him as things got worse. Careful what you wish for, eh?' He smiled broadly.

'But you flew back early,' said Paulsen. 'You brought the flights forwards by a few weeks – why?'

'Does it matter?' said Luke.

'I think it's everything,' said Finn.

Luke looked surprised, motioned at him to continue like a teacher encouraging a promising pupil.

'I think you decided to come back early the moment Abi told you about the murders. Or more specifically, *where* they happened.'

This time there was no reaction. His face was neutral as he listened. Finn looked across at the PC standing at the back of the room. There was something too contained about Daws for his liking, a sense that things could easily escalate. He'd seen what this man was capable of, could still feel his hands around his neck.

'You seem to have it all worked out,' said Luke. 'But you're guessing, aren't you?'

'We just want to establish what happened this morning – and why it happened,' said Paulsen. But Daws hadn't taken his eyes off Finn.

'Maybe you do – but this one . . .' He nodded at Finn. 'You *need* to know how all this fits together, don't you? I know a case of OCD when I see it.' He grinned again.

'I think you came over because you knew what had happened,' said Finn. He leant in. 'You suspected it was your father straight away. You returned because you thought his crumbling memory was on the brink of giving up a very old and incriminating secret . . .'

Luke shook his head.

'You're still guessing.'

'Maybe – but you're right about one thing – I *do* want to know what happened thirty years ago.'

'Why ask me?'

'Because we've found your father's fingerprints on the lamp which was used to beat Vicki Stratford to death,' said Paulsen. She let that hang before adding, 'And we'll be re-opening the investigation into those two murders in due course.'

The smile disappeared from Luke's face, something harder replacing it.

'Now here's another guess – I think you were a witness to what happened back then,' said Finn. 'Or quite possibly something *more* than that . . .'

Luke didn't react for a moment, simply stared at Finn.

'I was just a kid.'

'Five, weren't you? Here's the thing – Ben Stratford was stabbed with a pair of scissors, and his mother beaten to death with a lamp. The forensics from the crime scene suggested Ben died first. So why didn't the killer use the same weapon?'

Luke shrugged.

'Just before we came down here we checked with the lab – there's no prints at all on those scissors,' said Paulsen. 'So how come there's a fragment of your dad's prints on the lamp, but nothing on the scissors?'

'How the hell would I know?' said Luke, his voice sounding dry and reedy. 'It was thirty years ago.'

'I think someone wiped them both clean and missed a bit.' Finn let that sink in for a second, then added, 'And because I think you stabbed Ben.'

The idea hadn't just come to him. He'd been working through the possible scenarios ever since he'd waded out of the tunnel in Lewisham earlier. He and Paulsen had thrown the theory around in the incident room, and as he looked across the table, he couldn't help but think of the old Kate Bush track 'The Man with the Child in His Eyes'. Somewhere in that hard, angry face opposite was a trace of the five-year-old boy he'd once been.

'You don't understand,' said Luke.

'So you were there, then?' said Finn.

The solicitor had heard enough and whispered in his client's ear.

'No comment,' said Luke.

'What don't we understand?' said Paulsen.

'No comment.'

Finn looked across at Paulsen.

'I mean – you hear about children who've committed murders. And you wonder – without help, what becomes of them? Keeping something like that buried would be enough to turn anyone into a monster . . .'

'I'm not a monster,' said Luke, coming off-script, his voice cracking.

'Says the man who murdered his father this morning . . .' said Finn.

Luke brought his fist down on the table in a burst of fury. *'He's the monster.'*

The PC behind him stepped forwards immediately, but Finn waved him back. The solicitor looked like he wanted to say something to Luke too, but then, seeing the look on his face, decided against it.

'So tell us what happened,' said Finn.

'You're desperate to know, aren't you?' snarled Luke, trying, failing to calm himself.

'We just want the truth,' said Paulsen.

There was a long pause.

'Why was your dad a monster? Everything we know about him says that was the last thing he was . . .' said Finn.

'Stop . . . speaking,' said Luke slowly, putting his hands against his head. 'Just be quiet for a second.' His voice was quivering with emotion. Paulsen looked at Finn for a lead; the solicitor and the PC were doing much the same. Luke was rubbing his eyes, massaging his forehead with his fingertips now. Finn gently raised the palm of his hand.

'Take all the time you need, there's no rush,' he said.

Finally, Luke looked back up at them.

'I'll tell you how I remember it – but then I get to ask you a question. Okay?'

Finn nodded in agreement.

'Me and Ben were playing in the bedroom. We'd been cutting up cardboard with his mum earlier – making soldiers or something. Then Dad arrived to pick me up and they started chatting in the living room. We got bored and began chasing each other around the room . . . cops and robbers, I think. I picked up the scissors and pointed them at him – it was just a game. But Ben was in his socks and he skidded on the carpet. Next thing I know, there's blood spurting out from his neck like water from a hose.'

He faltered, looked down at the table.

'It was an accident?' said Finn.

'That's what I've always *believed*,' he said, the words sounding carefully chosen.

333

'But they thought you did it deliberately?' said Paulsen. 'Tom and Vicki?'

Luke nodded.

'She screamed like you've never heard when she saw the blood, said I'd stabbed her son, and ran into the living room to call an ambulance. Dad . . .' he shook his head, 'panicked. He picked up a lamp and hit her over the head before she could get to the phone.'

'To protect you?' said Finn.

'I don't think he thought about it, he just did it. He was trying to save me, or at least save my future. Which is funny when you think about how things have turned out.'

'What happened next?' said Paulsen.

'I remember her moaning on the floor. Dad was standing over her with the lamp, looking horrified. Just for a second, we caught each other's eye – I've never forgotten that. Then he hit her again, and again, until she stopped making any noise. Like putting a half-dead animal out of its misery.'

'And then what?' said Finn.

'He went straight to his mate, didn't he? Good old Uncle Ron . . . and you know the rest. They tried to make it look like a break-in. They gave me some sedatives and knocked me out for the night, then Dad, Ron and my mum decided what they were going to do about it.'

'And Abi?' said Paulsen.

'Was kept out of it. They wanted to keep at least one of us clean. And you've no idea how much I've resented her for that over the years.'

'But how did they keep you quiet? You were five. Surely they didn't keep you drugged up until you emigrated?'

'No – they made up some cock and bull story for Abi about me being ill and needing to recover, told her I was staying

334

with a friend of the family in Scotland. Which was sort of true. It was Ron's sister.'

His eyes were red now, the emotion of it beginning to over-take him.

'They kept telling me to keep it a secret. To be honest, I was so traumatised I couldn't talk about it anyway. There wasn't really much danger of me telling anyone anything. I couldn't speak, couldn't eat, couldn't sleep. Just a lot of screaming and bed-wetting, as I remember.'

Luke wiped his nose with the length of his hand. Again, Finn got a sense of the child, not the man. 'Not much has changed over the years, to be fair.'

'So what happened today?' said Paulsen.

Luke looked up at them both.

'Here's where I want to ask you a question . . .' He didn't wait for their permission. 'Do you believe me – when I say it was an accident?'

Finn regarded him carefully, weighed it up . . . taking just a little too long in the process. Luke laughed.

'And there we have it . . .' he said, pointing at Finn's face. 'You want to know if I killed my father and Uncle Ron – yes, I did. You want to know why? Because of *that* expression right there.'

'I don't understand,' said Paulsen.

'I've seen it all my life. Mum never believed it was an acci-dent. You could see it behind her eyes every time she looked at me – she thought I was something evil. And when my life started bending out of shape . . . she never said it, but I knew that's what she thought. The drip, drip of it every day. That I was lying about Ben, had *always* lied. It was there in her eyes – the judgement . . . the *disgust*.'

'And your dad?' said Finn.

'I asked him about it again this morning when we were alone. I wanted to know – before he completely lost his mind

– what he really thought. And you know what he said? That he *forgave* me.'

Luke laughed again. Loud and from deep inside.

'*He's* the fucking killer. The man who panicked and smashed a woman's head in. The guy who killed a mother and her son. I was just a kid playing cops and robbers with my friend. But *he* forgives *me*?'

'And you lost your temper when he said that to you?' said Paulsen.

Luke nodded.

'Tell me I'm a monster long enough – and it becomes a self-fulfilling prophecy.'

'And Fordyce? Abi at the river?' said Finn.

'Ron never believed me right from the beginning. All those chats he and Dad used to have – I think he convinced him of it over the years. As for Abi, she had the life I should have had. Perfect fucking Abi.'

'Is that why the family was split up?' said Paulsen. 'To protect her?'

'Yeah. Sainted fucking Abigail was protected from it. While I was buried on the other side of the planet.'

'But you didn't kill her by the river . . .' said Finn.

'Or tell her the truth today,' said Paulsen. 'You could have – why didn't you?'

A single tear rolled down Luke's cheek, splashed on to the table. He touched it gently with the tip of his finger.

'Because I didn't want *her* to look at me like that.'

41

'I thought it was a hate crime. Someone who loathed women,' said Paulsen afterwards.

She and Finn were in YoYo's having a much-needed post-interview coffee. Luke had been charged but there'd been a strange emptiness as they'd left the room. They'd got their answers but there was little satisfaction, just a sense of need-less tragedy. Lives wasted, with only pain and further heart-ache remaining for those still standing.

'It was rage, alright,' said Finn, remembering his first impressions of the crime scene. 'But the fury of a father trying to protect his son all over again.'

'I can't stop thinking about Vicki Stratford . . . Can you understand why Tom did what he did?'

'Would I have killed an innocent woman to protect my son, do you mean?' Finn pursed his lips as he thought about it. 'How often do you hear someone say they'd do *anything* to protect their child? I don't have any, so I guess I'll never know. But I can understand the impulse in the moment – however wrong it was. You know what they say about the road to hell being paved with good intentions . . .'

Paulsen prodded at her coffee with a stirrer as she consid-ered it.

'And do you think Luke was telling us the truth about Ben Stratford – that his stabbing *was* accidental?'

Finn leant back in his chair.

337

'His whole life was shaped by that moment. Never mind all the guilt his father kept buried – how much has *he* been carrying over the years? Mix it up with a good dose of resentment and self-doubt and you've got quite the cocktail.'

'You haven't answered my question,' said Paulsen.

'I know,' he replied. Behind them, a coffee machine hissed and gurgled. 'Yes, I believe him when he says it was accidental. Why? Don't you?'

Paulsen shook her head.

'No. Look what he did to those two men today, and God knows what else in Australia. Some people write their own truths – I think he *did* do it deliberately and he knows it deep down. Everything since then has been denial. Including what he just told us.'

Before Finn could respond, they were interrupted by Jackie Ojo, who was striding across the cafe towards them.

'Thought I'd find you two in here,' she said. She saw the look on their faces. 'Christ, you both look shattered . . .'

'It's been a day, Jacks,' said Finn.

'I'm afraid it's not over yet either,' said Ojo. 'You might want to come back over the road . . .'

A fight had been broken up just five minutes from Pennington Road. Patrick Clarke and Alan Baxter's simmering animosity had finally bubbled over in the alleyway where they'd met. Extraordinarily, given the battered state he was already in, it was Clarke who'd come out on top. No one had needed to call the police. Word had soon reached the nearby crime scene at the Daws house and some officers had gone to investigate. They'd found Baxter flat out on the ground, howling in pain, while Clarke was slumped, exhausted and bleeding, up against a fence. Baxter's dog was still tied to a nearby lamp post, barking furiously. Paramedics were called and shortly afterwards both men were taken to Lewisham Hospital.

'You didn't need to come,' Paulsen told Finn as they drove back across south London. The route from Cedar House to Lewisham was becoming burnt on their brains.

'Neither did you,' he replied. 'Could have let uniform mop this up.'

'You nearly drowned earlier,' she said, ignoring him. 'You should be at home, resting.'

'Yeah. Probably,' he said. 'But let's face it, we're both a bit fascinated by Patrick Clarke. When we get there – you check in on Baxter, I'll talk to Clarke.'

'Really?' she said, unimpressed.

'Yes. He's in a lot of pain apparently – you'll enjoy that. Besides, there's a theory I want to test out.'

Finn had put in some calls before they'd left, and he shared with her what he'd learnt. Paulsen's eyes widened.

'Interesting,' she said.

'Isn't it?' he replied, with a conspiratorial grin.

A nurse led Finn through a ward where Clarke was lying in a bed in the far corner. It was hard to tell which cuts and bruises were new and which were merely additions to the old ones. His eyes were bloodshot and he looked absolutely wasted.

'Hello again . . .' said Clarke casually, as if greeting an old acquaintance. Finn closed the curtains around the bed and sank into a chair next to him.

'They tell me you gave Alan Baxter quite a beating. Apparently he's got a broken collarbone. I don't know whether to be impressed or appalled, given the state of you,' he said. 'I suppose if I ask you what happened, you won't tell me?'

'We had an exchange of words. He said a few things, I said a few things. It escalated. He's an old man. Even with me in this condition, it wasn't his smartest move,' said Clarke.

Finn thought that was rather understating matters. Given the obvious pain Clarke was still in, to inflict the damage on Baxter that he evidently had must have taken a superhuman effort. The fight, by all accounts, had been loud and unpleasant. It had also been foolish, given the number of police close by.

'Want to tell me why you did it? I mean, you've got plenty of reasons to have an issue with Baxter. He's an open racist, who may well have been responsible for the attack on you earlier this week.'

Clarke shrugged.

'As I say – things escalated.'

'He got lucky,' said Baxter, with as much fury as the painkillers coursing through his system would allow. His right eye was puffed up and purple, while his cheek was scraped red raw. It looked to Paulsen like his head had been jammed on the ground and dragged hard across it. His arm was in a sling and his pallor was a nauseous green. He looked a mess, and she was just about professional enough to keep her own small satisfaction at that from showing.

'Where's Samson?' he said. 'The doctors won't fucking tell me.'

'Your dog's at the pub with your son. One of our officers took him back. I'll relay your thanks to him.'

He glared up at her with his good eye and she smiled pleasantly back.

'Do you want to tell me what happened?' she said.

'That black cu—' He corrected himself. 'Clarke followed me. I was just walking my dog, that's all. He was looking for a fight – the man can't control himself. You know that. You know his history, and yet you do nothing about it – and this is what happens.'

'There does seem to be some bad blood between you. Don't you think now's the time to tell us how it started?'

Baxter looked away.

'Alan?' said Paulsen.

'I've got this theory about you, Patrick,' said Finn. 'And you're welcome to correct me if I'm wrong.'

Clarke laid his head back on his pillow with a sigh.

'Go on then – I like a story.'

'Before I came down here, I looked over the details of your previous conviction – the assault on the woman in the street. The victim, Cassie Wilcox, didn't live far away from you, did she?'

Patrick continued to stare up at the ceiling.

'So I asked some of our uniformed officers in the area to mention her name to a few people, see what they could remember about her. And do you know what they told me? That she used to be Alan Baxter's girlfriend once upon a time ...'

Clarke didn't take the bait.

'... which puts an interesting spin on things, don't you think?'

'I barely knew Cassie,' said Baxter.

'We've been told you were in a relationship with her. In fact, a number of your neighbours have confirmed that.'

'Relationship's too strong a word for it.'

Paulsen let her distaste show without commenting.

'Doesn't it get boring walking round with a face like a slapped arse all the time?' said Baxter.

'How would you define your ... whatever it was ... with Cassie, then?' said Paulsen.

'We hung around for a bit. She was a good girl. But then Clarke attacked her and she wasn't the same afterwards. It messed with her head. She left – I don't know where she went off to – but wherever she is these days, I hope she's doing okay.'

'That's very decent of you, Alan. But perhaps not the whole story, eh?'

'Is there something you're waiting for me to say?' said Clarke.

'No,' said Finn. 'You lie there, and I'll do the talking for the both of us. So, what do we know about Cassie Wilcox? She was assaulted badly one night and pointed the finger at you. You never denied it. Investigating police could never establish a motive, and neither you nor Cassie ever explained it. We also know a year before, you blamed yourself heavily for the death of the boy in the Lake District . . .'

'Is this going to take long?' said Clarke.

'We looked into Baxter as a possible suspect in the Nicholls killings. One little titbit of information that emerged was that he has form for knocking his girlfriends around.'

Finn paused. Clarke looked almost like he was napping, but he wasn't. He'd closed his eyes now, but there were frown lines on his forehead as he listened.

'Let's imagine one night he lost his temper with Cassie. *Really* lost it, and hurt her badly. He leaves her bleeding in the street and then you come along and find her. You do the right thing – you call an ambulance and you call the police. You comfort her until they arrive, and then she turns on you – terrified of Baxter – and accuses you of the attack.'

Clarke still hadn't opened his eyes.

'I think you made a decision in that moment,' continued Finn. 'I've got a horrible feeling the officers investigating back then saw a black man and an injured white woman and judged it a bit too fast.'

Clarke's eyes snapped open.

342

'And I think you decided to use that. Far from denying it, I think you decided to accept the guilt. Because you thought you deserved it. In your mind, a prison term was the *least* you warranted for the death of that boy. How am I doing?'

Clarke didn't reply.

'I can understand why you spooked Baxter out now. He knows he did it, you know he did it – and yet *you* served the time for it. No wonder you got in his head.'

Clarke turned to look at Finn properly for the first time since he'd arrived.

'Aren't you going to charge me? I just put a man in hospital.'

'Actually, we'll be looking to talk to Cassie Wilcox again – just in case her view of things has changed over the years.' Clarke nodded, though it was hard to tell whether it was with approval or resignation. 'You don't have to do this again, Patrick,' said Finn softly.

When he finally got home that evening, one thing hadn't changed for Finn. His flat remained empty, and when the adrenaline rush of the day's events began to subside, he felt himself sinking back into a familiar dark mood. The journey to whatever normality was supposed to look and feel like wouldn't be overnight. Earlier in the week, he would have retreated into a glass of his favourite single malt, but this time he made a conscious effort to resist its call. Instead, he took a shower, embraced the hot water and began to plan. The following day was going to be busy; there were a number of things he already knew he wanted to do. As he collapsed into bed, he wondered how Luke and Abi Daws were feeling right now, thought too about Jill and Lily Nicholls.

'*Sleep, you idiot,*' said a voice and he fell into a deep and welcome slumber.

42

Morning

'I want tinned mushy peas,' said Nancy Deen as Mattie Paulsen sat down at their kitchen table in her dressing gown, clutching a box of granola. As usual on a Saturday morning, Nancy had let her partner enjoy a lie-in.

'What?' said Paulsen, shuffling the contents of the box into a bowl.

'I thought I'd make us fish and chips tonight. And I like those tinned mushy peas from the supermarket, so . . .'

'Can't we just *buy* some fish and chips – you know, from the chippy?' interrupted Paulsen, as she splashed some milk on to her cereal. 'It's a lot less work.' She gave the mixture an unenthusiastic stir. Nancy watched, less than impressed.

'Mat – what is it?'

'Nothing,' said Paulsen.

'Nothing, my arse. You've been weird since you woke up.'

Paulsen sighed, looked at her sheepishly.

'It's Dad. I rang Mum after you went to bed last night, had a chat with her.'

Nancy's expression was already switching from irritated to concerned.

'Has something happened?'

'No. But that's kind of the point. He's a lot worse than he was a few months ago – you just don't really notice it's changing. And there's stuff been going on she hasn't been telling me about.'

'What sort of stuff?'

'She found him in the garden the other day in his underwear. He hadn't a clue what he was doing out there. For about three minutes she thought he'd properly disappeared. She was just about to raise the alarm when she saw him out there in his boxers.' There was a catch in her voice. 'It's all a bit Tom Daws . . .'

'No, it isn't. It's not the same thing at all.'

As usual, Mattie had shared the details of the whole Nicholls investigation with her partner. She'd always found it helpful unloading on someone who wasn't a police officer, while Nancy genuinely enjoyed following what she did. Paulsen had now given up completely on her breakfast.

'When I spoke to Abi at the hospital yesterday, she said she was actually pleased her father was dead because she wouldn't have to see the worst of it now. It was the one consolation she'd managed to find in all of this.'

'Her situation is completely different to yours,' said Nancy automatically. Paulsen knew she meant well, knew too that the statement didn't possess an ounce of logic; Alzheimer's was Alzheimer's, whoever it afflicted.

'I woke up in the night, Nance, and just for a moment wished he was gone too. How bad is that?'

Nancy was already scrambling to find something positive to counter with. Paulsen bit her tongue and let her.

'He's still got a strong sense of self. That's not gone yet – he knows exactly who he is and who you are. We should go and visit them again this weekend.'

Paulsen nodded guiltily.

'It all feels a bit five to midnight. And I don't quite know how to deal with that.'

And this time, all Nancy could manage was a small, sympathetic smile in return.

The sun was shining down on Winchester, and Finn was taking some time to have a proper look around the city. He wanted to use the day constructively, to relax a little. Flashbacks to the paring knife, the hands around his neck and the ice-cold waters closing over his head were still all too frequent and he could feel his body pleading for a breather. He visited the cathedral and wandered its grounds, took in the City Mill as well – only briefly shuddering as he watched the flow of the neighbouring River Itchen. It was a useful reminder that the entire world didn't centre on one small corner of south London.

'Don't see why you needed to come down here again,' growled Peter Tolson as Finn stepped through into his living room.

'Partly, so I could give you this in person . . .' he replied, handing over a bottle swathed in tissue paper. Tolson unwrapped it, raised an eyebrow.

'A Speyside? You like them sweet then?'

Finn began to goldfish and Tolson chuckled.

'It's very thoughtful – and you didn't need to, Alex. A reward's the last thing I deserve.'

'That's also why I came; I was worried you might be feeling like that.'

The pair sat down and Tolson put the bottle on the floor by his feet and frowned.

'I'm afraid I do. It's hard not to in the circumstances.'

'In your shoes, I'd have probably come to exactly the same conclusion about Rawton. DNA testing back then was nothing compared to what it is today, neither was forensic science, CCTV—'

'It wasn't the dark ages either,' said Tolson, interrupting him. 'My gut told me something was wrong and I ignored it. I let the victims down – worse still, put the wrong man away and let the real killer escape. And four people died this week because of that mistake.' He shook his head. 'I could come out with all sorts of self-justifying crap – but I fucked up and that's the truth of it.'

His gruff Yorkshire accent made the confession sound even blunter. Finn's eye caught randomly on an ornate Thai tapestry hanging on the wall. Tolson was a decent man who didn't deserve to have his retirement tainted like this. Without his input, Finn doubted he would have got to the truth of what had happened in Pennington Road. They were all of them, every single day, walking the tightrope of a critical mistake.

'Whatever I say to you probably won't change how you feel. But if I've learnt one thing this week – it's the importance of letting go.'

Even as he spoke, Finn could see the advice wasn't really being received, despite a polite nod. This would haunt Tolson for some time to come. There was still a new investigation to follow into the Stratfords' deaths, in which his decisions would come under renewed scrutiny. And as he drove back to London, Finn had a feeling that bottle of whisky wasn't going to last long.

Afternoon

Drakeford House was only a five-minute walk away from the sparse industrial estate where Cedar House was located. An anonymous red-brick building, it was where Murray hosted his regular Alcoholics Anonymous sessions. The small bland room he used for the purpose was where Finn had first stumbled in and met him nearly a year before. This time he waited on the street outside, as his friend wrapped up a meeting with a small handful of attendees. Glancing through the window, Finn couldn't help but smile as he watched Murray address the room. He recognised the body language, the look on his face. Some sage advice was undoubtedly being dispensed, but all wrapped up in that bone-dry Glaswegian humour of his.

'What the fuck is this?' said Murray a short time later, eyeing the box Finn was carrying under his arm as he entered. 'I hope that's not a puppy in there – I'm honestly not good with cute animals.'

Finn sighed and put the box down on a nearby table.

'It's a coffee machine. Don't worry, not a poncey one – just a cheap effort from Argos.'

He dug into his backpack and pulled out a small brown paper bag. 'And these are beans – they *are* quite poncey. It's by way of a thank you.' He put them on the table too. 'You're very welcome.'

Murray surveyed the scene.

'Pure caffeine. You really want to send my clientele a message, don't you?'

Finn looked alarmed.

'I'm kidding, you great jelly,' said Murray with a wry smile. 'That's actually a very nice gesture – thank you.'

The two grabbed some chairs and sat down, and Murray asked him how he'd been. Finn described the mood he'd felt the previous night, the way a familiar gloom had crept up on him just before bed. Also, his meeting with Tolson in the morning which had left him with decidedly mixed feelings.

'Aye, well, you didn't think it was going to be an easy ride, did you? You're still intending to see that counsellor next week, I hope?'

'Yes,' said Finn honestly. 'But there is one thing I wanted to ask you . . . it's a bit embarrassing.'

349

'Oh Jesus – there are limits,' said Murray.

Finn rolled his eyes. He explained about the voices he'd been hearing. Firstly, Karin, literally from the day she'd been cremated, and more recently Sadie. Told him too of Karin's silence and sudden re-emergence while his head was being held under the waters of the River Quaggy.

'I don't understand – what exactly is your question?' said Murray.

Finn looked at him hesitantly.

'However odd it might sound – I do take a genuine comfort from it. I know it's not really her, but it feels like she's with me. Is that healthy or just part of the addiction, something I should try and lose?'

Murray weighed it up then shook his head.

'See what the counsellor says, but I don't mind it – you don't want to banish her completely. That's not part of the healing process,' he said.

'*See,*' said Karin.

Evening

Finn had saved the most difficult conversation for last. It was the one he'd been thinking about for most of the day.

'I'm sorry, Jacks – I'm really sorry,' he said.

She looked at him quizzically.

'For what exactly? Getting pissed the other night and lying about it? Bit weird, but ultimately not the end of the world.'

They were at a wine bar in Clapham, the same one they'd adopted as their regular meeting place for their irregular blowouts. It was a tradition between them, which usually coincided with the end of a major investigation. An unspoken agreement existed that rank meant nothing on these occasions and what happened in Clapham, stayed in Clapham.

'I've been lying to you for a lot longer than just this week,' he said. 'Sometimes in big ways, sometimes small … but pretty consistently.'

She took a thoughtful sip of her wine.

'This is about Karin, isn't it?' she said.

He nodded.

'Then you shouldn't be apologising to me, I should be apologising to you – for not noticing that you were struggling so much,' she said.

He shook his head dismissively.

'It all reached a bit of a head this week – I won't bore you with the details . . .'

He glanced away awkwardly. She was looking at him hard now, with cop's eyes.

'I thought I noticed something different about you over the last couple of days,' she said. 'I'm still not entirely sure how I'd describe it . . . but you seemed a bit more switched on than you've been for a while.'

Finn stared down at his Diet Coke. He certainly hadn't gone teetotal but was still feeling no great desire to have anything stronger.

'I'm not over Karin. I never will be. But I finally reached a point where I can't pretend there isn't a problem. An acceptance of that, if you like.'

'So what are you doing about it?'

He finally turned his head to meet her gaze.

'I spoke to Skegman earlier – I'm going to take a sabbatical. Not sure how long yet – but it's so I can give myself some proper time away from the job. I rushed back too quickly after Karin's death, which was my choice and it was stupid. I haven't taken a real break since. There'll be a process obviously, but off the record, I'd be very surprised if you weren't asked to deputise for me. I recommended you earlier but I

351

was pushing at an open door – you're the DCI's first choice anyway.'

Ojo looked surprised.

'Don't give me that – you'll have me saying nice things about the shifty sod if you tell me stuff like that.'

Finn shrugged.

'We live in strange and miraculous times,' he replied.

'Seriously – I'm pleased for you,' she said. 'And I think it's the right thing to do. Assuming I get the job, I'll just be keeping the seat warm for you – kicking Paulsen when she needs a kick, kicking Dave whether he wants one or not . . .'

They both laughed.

'So what are you going to do with your time off?' she said.

He frowned.

'I've never understood that phrase people use – the one about 'finding yourself' – I always thought it was rather twee. Just meaningless waffle, really. But since Karin died, bit by bit I seemed to have lost myself a little. So *that*, I suppose. Working out who I am all over again.'

'A clue . . .' said Ojo. 'He's inflexible, anally retentive and usually found somewhere halfway up his own arse.' She lifted her glass and smiled. 'It'll be good to have him back.'

43

Sergeant Ray Hansell brought his car to a halt behind a rusting pickup truck and turned off the engine. He grabbed his jacket from the front seat and pulled it on. Cootamundra never got too cold even in the winter, but he could feel a draught to go with the uneasy feeling in the pit of his stomach. It didn't help that they'd come to this late either. The woman's workmates had taken a couple of days to inform them, and his own colleagues hadn't exactly prioritised it. It was only when the cop from London had called that someone had belatedly made the connection with their misper. He looked at the building in front of him and felt his unease grow.

Prison cells were the same the world over, Luke Daws mused. This one, in Wandsworth, was colder than any he'd ever experienced before though. It was fitting he was back in England. Growing up, every time he looked in the mirror he was aware it was an English face that stared back at him. Born and bred in south London, he'd never felt like he belonged to Australia. Not that he felt particularly English now – he was a man who belonged to no place and no one. That didn't particularly bother him either. He'd always felt disenfranchised, always would. Now at least there was no one left to judge him – he doubted very much Abi would ever come to visit. Families just fuck you up, he thought.

★   ★   ★

Hansell walked up to the house. Like all the residential buildings in the area, it was detached with a low, peaked roof. At the front was a patch of unruly grass, while clay pots with dead bougainvillaea plants were by the door. It was hard to tell how long the front garden had been left neglected. He rang the bell, not expecting an answer – and didn't get one. There was no need for drama though – it was standard practice to call a police-approved locksmith to gain access in these situations. He was about to reach for his phone, but something about the stillness of the place continued to bother him. He opened the garage door and saw a small hatchback inside. Wherever the former Alice Daws was, she hadn't driven there. He really ought to call that locksmith, he thought, could grab a sandwich and eat it in his car while he waited. Two minutes later, after curiosity had got the better of him, he'd banished all thoughts of locksmiths and food.

'*Shit* . . .' he said under his breath, as he peered through the kitchen window.

Luke wondered if the nightmares would stop now. He didn't have them so much these days, certainly not as many as when he'd been in his teens. But when he did, that feeling of the scissors puncturing Ben Stratford's neck was as clear as it had ever been, the warmth of the blood as it sprayed across his face – equally vivid. He'd carried those memories all his life but absolutely none of it haunted him as much as the look in his mother's eyes. The *suspicion*. But that was something he didn't have to worry about any more. From here on, people would always know exactly who he was and what he'd done. And in a funny sort of way, it brought him a sense of closure. The ambiguity was gone. He was a monster – and that's how the world would always view him. He stretched out on the cell's narrow bed. At least now he might finally be able to get some rest.

In the end, Hansell used his baton to smash one of the windows and climb through. The sickly-sweet smell hit him instantly, like an old acquaintance. He slipped on a mask as he entered the kitchen. Alice Bellamy was sitting slumped back in a chair at the table. Treacle-thick – almost black – dried blood was everywhere. The way she was positioned, with her head hanging back over the chair, made it easy to see how she'd died – a large slit, visible across the width of her throat. And as he got nearer, a cluster of flies dispersed like a cloud above her body. It was only when he could see her face that he saw where they'd been congregating – around the two dark empty sockets where her eyeballs had once been.

The End

ACKNOWLEDGEMENTS

I cannot lie – writing this book rather helped keep me sane during the various lockdowns of 2020 and 2021 (if you're reading this a few years on – I *really* hope these words have dated!). Fingers crossed, the continued adventures of Detectives Finn and Paulsen have helped divert and distract you too.

Writing during a pandemic has been a strange experience – the first words of this novel were written right at the start of the coronavirus crisis and by the time I typed the final full stop I'd actually received my first covid vaccination. Trying to stay ahead and anticipate what kind of world we'd all be in when this book was published has been an interesting exercise – as the year went on I took the view that I'd try to envisage a society just beginning to emerge back into some sort of normality.

As ever there's some important thank yous – to my agent Hayley Steed and the Madeleine Milburn Literary Agency for keeping me on the straight and narrow throughout. To my brilliant editor Eve Hall and the equally brilliant Sorcha Rose at Hodder for making sense of another complicated plot full of tangled timelines. And a big thank you too to former Met detective Stuart Gibbon for his absolutely priceless knowledge of police procedure.

So what next for Alex Finn? Well, we wouldn't want him to get too comfortable would we . . .?

THRILLINGLY GOOD BOOKS FROM CRIMINALLY GOOD WRITERS

CRIME FILES BRINGS YOU THE LATEST RELEASES FROM TOP CRIME AND THRILLER AUTHORS.

SIGN UP ONLINE FOR OUR MONTHLY NEWSLETTER AND BE THE FIRST TO KNOW ABOUT OUR COMPETITIONS, NEW BOOKS AND MORE.

STRIPES PUBLISHING LIMITED
An imprint of the Little Tiger Group
1 Coda Studios, 189 Munster Road,
London SW6 6AW

Imported into the EEA by Penguin Random House Ireland,
Morrison Chambers, 32 Nassau Street, Dublin D02 YH68

www.littletiger.co.uk

A paperback original
First published in Great Britain in 2022
Text copyright © Darren Charlton, 2022
Illustration copyright © Karl James Mountford, 2022
Eagle illustration p.336 copyright © Maks TRV/Shutterstock.com

ISBN: 978-1-78895-306-1
ISBN: 978-1-78895-590-4 (exclusive edition)

The right of Darren Charlton and Karl James Mountford to be identified as
the author and illustrator of this work respectively has been asserted by them
in accordance with the Copyright, Designs and Patents Act, 1988.

A CIP catalogue record for this book is available from the British Library.

Printed and bound in the UK.

10 9 8 7 6 5 4 3 2 1